THE
OPERATIVE

OTHER BOOKS AND AUDIO BOOKS
BY WILLARD BOYD GARDNER:

Race Against Time

Pursuit of Justice

THE
OPERATIVE

A NOVEL

WILLARD BOYD
GARDNER

Covenant Communications, Inc.

Covenant

Cover image by Ingo Jezierski, Photodisc Green © Gettyimages

Cover design copyrighted 2007 by Covenant Communications, Inc.

Published by Covenant Communications, Inc.
American Fork, Utah

Printed in Canada
First Printing: January 2007

11 10 09 08 07   10 9 8 7 6 5 4 3 2 1

ISBN 978-1-59811-231-3

To Brent Hall, rock solid

CHAPTER 1

In the port city of Aden, Yemen, on the Arabian Sea

Rhiana Daniels still felt nervous jitters during an act of espionage.

The meet was supposed to be simple: a face-to-face with one of the United States' most valuable civilian assets in the Middle East. He would be wearing a traditional Arab dishdasha robe draped over his body and a red-and-white checkered Shumaq wrapped neatly around his head. If he adjusted the loose tail of the headdress with his right hand, a brief verbal exchange would follow. If not, both agents would pass each other on the sidewalk like strangers. Simple.

Rhiana watched as he approached her along the shoulder of a single-lane road between two of Aden's cultural landmarks, the Gold Mohur Club, a defunct Western nightclub in serious need of renovation, and the all-but-forgotten Pearl Hotel perched on a high rock outcropping above a cerulean sea. Willing her contact to follow through with the signal, she found herself nervously fingering the Titian silk scarf that covered her shoulder-length ebony hair.

She knew his ruggedly bronzed face and kind golden-brown eyes well, but since he had yet to touch the tail of his headdress and initiate the meet, she walked steadily forward, eyes straight ahead. As they neared one another, she recognized a sort of tentativeness in his expression that set a lump in her throat. Something was wrong.

The front doors of the Pearl Hotel stood ajar, but she saw only a shadowed glimpse of the vacant front lobby against the backdrop of the glaring sun. At the Gold Mohur Club on the other side of the lane, even less activity was visible. Nothing seemed quite right. She felt the familiar warning tingle on the back of her neck.

Rhiana's contact slowed his pace and crossed the street toward the Gold Mohur Club. From the back of the Pearl Hotel, a lone Arab emerged and jogged across the street toward him. The tingle intensified into a burning sensation along her spine, and her fingers trembled as two more Arabs turned the corner of the building and stalked toward the agent. Rhiana kept her eyes to the front, looking at the ground. Heartsick, she knew there would be no signal.

As the first Arab shouts began to echo between the buildings, Rhiana quickened her pace, but she couldn't suppress the urge to look back at her contact. She turned her head slightly and watched as three Middle Eastern men seized him by his robe and flung him around. One produced a pistol and jammed it into his side, forcing him toward the street. In an act of selflessness, he didn't struggle, but turned his body away from Rhiana, forcing the three men to turn their backs on her. Rhiana shuddered and turned away as a single tear formed at the corner of her eye. She wiped it away, determined to manage her emotions and control her thoughts—it wasn't supposed to be this way.

Afraid that staring would raise suspicions, Rhiana forced herself to look forward and kept walking as the leader of the assault, now a block behind her, issued wild commands. She recognized the European sounds and sporadic Portuguese words of the rare southern Suqutri dialect of Arabic. Few mainland Arabs understood the strange language, spoken exclusively on the southern coast island of Socotra, and even fewer could speak it. This wasn't a state-sponsored kidnapping.

Rhiana strode forward on weak knees, nausea making her face feel flush. Her contact had little chance to escape, and even less if she was captured with him. Rhiana well understood not only what happened to Western women in the hands of Arab criminals, but also the kind of coercion that could be brought to bear on the men captured with them.

A pale yellow Saab sedan, its four-cylinder motor racing, climbed the bluff and pulled to the curb in front of Rhiana. Keeping her face turned slightly away, she fought to maintain a steady, unhurried gait as she searched ahead for a side street in case she had to run. A single male occupant exited the Saab and stood by his open door, but his attention was fixed on the kidnapping.

"Bon. Très bon," Rhiana heard him utter under his breath. French wasn't an unusual language for the streets of Aden, but it wasn't the language of ordinary street thugs. She risked exposing herself to glance at the man's face, but he turned his back and bent into the driver's seat of the Saab. All she saw was the back of his well-worn leather jacket and his houndstooth driving hat. As she passed, she looked down at the bumper of the car where the license plate had been removed. She wasn't surprised. She'd have precious little to report to her CIA chief of station in Yemen's capital city of Sana'a, but even so, she had to get word to the embassy as quickly as possible.

As Rhiana turned the corner and entered a side street serving the back of the Pearl Hotel, the shouting subsided with the thumps of car doors slamming, and the whine of hastily driven vehicles faded over the crest of the bluff. Her breath came in short gasps. For the first time in over a year, Rhiana Daniels allowed herself to weep openly. The hostage wasn't just a highly protected U.S. intelligence asset. He was also her father.

She hadn't even cried when her husband left her—maybe she should have. She'd managed to put her life back together since then. The CIA had taken her back, and she'd tried to convince herself that she could handle anything, with or without Kamir Daniels. But she was wrong. Their love had been the real thing, and she couldn't go through this without him. She hadn't allowed herself to admit that before. She needed him. But she wasn't even sure where he was . . .

CHAPTER 2

In the city of Dili, Timor Leste, on an island in the Indonesian archipelago north of Australia

They say you can never go home again, but I had no place else to run. Other than my pursuers, only one person stood poised between me and safety, his brown skin made darker by a wide smear of jungle mud along the edge of his cheek. His straight black hair held at least a week's accumulation of grease, and his eyes shifted from me to the chasing hordes as I prepared to take the last few punishing strides to safety.

Driving the edges of my shoes into the sticky, wet sod, I carved a sharp turn to the left. The lateral, shearing pressure on my knees threatened to buckle my legs, but letting up now was not an option. I had to make it home. I'd spent too much of my life running. First it had been an impulse, then a coping mechanism, and finally a way of life—and it had always led to complete and utter disaster. It would be different this time.

The dirty figure in front of me shifted his weight forward to brace for impact, but I wasn't going to make it easy for him. Just as he lunged forward, I dipped my head and dove to the ground, driving my hands forward between his ankles and knocking his feet out from under him with my shoulders.

As I slid, a lopsided ball of wadded-up sweat socks wrapped in packing tape slapped across my face and wobbled to a stop amidst a tangle of lush green jungle.

"Safe!" I yelled through a chorus of screaming boys who were now in the process of dog-piling me, which happened after any close play at home. In this case, my light blue beret acted as our makeshift plate. I might have tried to prevent the melee at the plate, but how do you tell that many laughing kids not to pile on?

I barely understood these boys, Timor-Leste natives who spoke Portuguese, the official state language, and peppered it with a jumbled mess of Austronesian phrases from their native Papuan, Tatum, and Bahasi dialects. It didn't matter, though. Fun was understandable in any language—and these boys loved to play baseball with a taped-up sock.

It wasn't really baseball, but rather a field-expedient derivative I'd invented because I was a long way from home and missed my Seattle Mariners. I was determined that the next American League all-star would be a homeless boy from the Indonesian archipelago island of Timor-Leste.

Over the clamor of excited boys I heard a distressed voice calling my name. "Kam-Dan, Kam-Dan." My name isn't Kam-Dan, but it sufficed for the neighborhood boys. For some reason Kamir Daniels, more properly Abdul-kamir Daniels, was far too difficult for small Indonesian mouths to pronounce. Abdul-kamir was literally translated as "servant of perfection," but judging by the way I was treated growing up with two older sisters, it meant "perfect servant." My name bespoke a proud heritage of Western and Eastern bloodlines, but like any red-blooded American boy, I had decided long ago to lose the *Abdul,* and for as long as I could remember, I had been called Kam.

"Kam-Dan, look, man in road," yelled one of the boys.

"Officer Daniels," announced the smug voice of Hans Bafus, who was standing next to the dirt turnaround that passed as our baseball diamond. Hans Bafus was my boss, a persnickety, sallow-skinned Frenchman in charge of my unit in the International Police Monitor Corps. His Dutch-boy haircut did nothing to enhance what little respect his men had for him.

I stood up and did my level best to rub the soil off my navy blue trousers and dashing French-blue polyester blouse. And yes, when it's part of a uniform, it's manly to call it a blouse—one of those strange puzzles of life. The disconcerting part was that my ensemble screamed "gas station attendant," not "police officer."

Hans cleared his throat into his fist and raised his eyebrows. Out of sheer habit, and without due respect to Hans, I tucked in the tails of my shirt and pulled the seam in line with my trousers.

Hans shook his head again and rolled his eyes, a mannerism he'd perfected as my supervisor for the last ten months. "Your cover," he said.

I looked around at our frond-strewn baseball diamond but didn't see it.

Hans shook his head. "You are out of uniform."

I pointed to my head, hoping one of the kids would help me out. The crowd of children parted, and one of the smaller kids came forward with the hat, cowering in Hans's presence as he handed it to me.

Hans's lip quivered, and through clenched teeth he said, "I suggest you do your best to hide the filth all over your blouse and trousers. You are to meet with the cultural attaché of the American embassy as soon as possible. I hope your little game was in its last set of quarters."

The temptation was just too much for me. "Innings," I said, slapping the detestable blue hat against my leg to get the dirt off. "And a set of quarters only makes a half. Besides, I went off duty over an hour ago."

His face pursed up like that of a fat man trying to hit high C on a French horn. Then his mouth relaxed into a sardonic smile. He leaned forward for an instant. "My apologies," he said, "I hadn't smelled the alcohol emanating from your pores."

I looked around at the faces of my little pack of hooligans, but none seemed to understand what Hans had said. I asked, "What does the cultural attaché want with me?"

Hans's narrow eyes didn't move from mine. "Maybe," he said, "he wants to give you a medal." He spun on his heel and tramped off to take out his anger on some other innocent subordinate.

"Hey, when am I supposed to meet this guy, Hans?"

Without even so much as a backward glance, Hans pointed toward the dirt road leading into our empty lot and said, "Right now, and right here."

A black Chevy Suburban with tinted windows and a variety of black powder–coated antennae crept slowly down the road. My mind raced through all the small indiscretions that marked my employment history with the state department in Timor-Leste, but nothing came to mind that deserved an unexpected visit from a man in a black Suburban. Well, there was my indolent attitude.

I wasn't the most beloved employee ever hired by DynCorp, the private defense contractor that employed police monitors in destabilized countries on behalf of the United States Department of State, but I also hadn't done anything wrong. I'd applied and been accepted as an international police monitor, a job that invited experienced cops to spend a year helping developing countries establish quality police departments. Although the program was administrated through a private corporation, I suspected it had close ties to several prominent three-letter acronyms in the U.S. government. It wasn't a bad experience if you believed in purgatory. I didn't believe in that religious stuff—didn't really even know what most of it meant.

The tax-free salary and finishing bonus almost made up for having to live with three other men in a forty-foot-square cinder-block hut in the jungle outskirts of the capital city of Dili. The only running water was the water that ran out of the two-liter bottle that constituted our individual daily ration. Two liters satisfied our nutritional needs as well as any hygiene requirements we might confront living in Indonesia. I won't even mention the bugs because it makes me itch. Life as police consultant in Dili was tolerable—like I said, if you believed in purgatory.

As the Suburban came to a stop, the rear window lowered with a hum to reveal a dim interior. I was hesitant to approach—maybe because I knew that anything involving smugness from Hans meant bad things for me. I managed to scatter my clan of orphans and latchkey kids—most were lucky if they had a door on their home, let alone a latch to put a key in. On the positive side, however, they'd been exposed to Western sports—even if it was sockball.

Poverty was the norm in this neighborhood, and despite Hans's feelings about it, playing ball with the locals was good police work. Not only did a few innings on our makeshift diamond occupy time that might otherwise have been spent in unwholesome pursuits, but there was also very little about my assigned area of the city that I didn't learn through my young friends. Hans did not agree with me, of course, but he was obliged to allow me my off-duty time for fraternizing.

One of my little ones was slow to leave the diamond. "Don't worry, my little friend," I said to Megawati. "Mega" was a wiry boy of about eleven years who'd been reluctant to join our daily games until he discovered an aptitude for blocking plays at the plate. He liked that I could never really stop him from giving every player who crossed the plate a mind-jarring forearm shiver, even though he often got the worst of it. Heaven help him if he ever made it to the States to play real baseball. He was a good boy, one of my favorites, and was nearly always the last kid to leave my side after our games.

"Beat feet, Mega," I said, moving my fingers in a walking motion.

He didn't really understand much English, but we eventually worked things out with a minimum of big words and a fair number of nods and gestures. Megawati shrugged and wandered off well behind the other boys, who were waving and throwing their sock ball back and forth.

I yelled at the backs of the retreating boys, "Oh yeah, I was safe." They broke into a discordant chorus of "Yeeer out, Kam-Dan!"

As I watched their backs and thought about the impending uncertainty of what awaited me in the Suburban, I couldn't help but wonder what would happen to these kids—no one here was going to help them, and they couldn't help themselves. Maybe baseball with a dirty sock would have to be enough.

I placed the grimy French-blue beret on my head at a jaunty Parisian angle and presented myself at the open window of the sinister Suburban. What was the worst they could do—make me work nights and weekends?

CHAPTER 3

A broad-framed, well-conditioned man in his late fifties with a tan face and stylishly unkempt graying hair leaned up from the backseat of the Suburban and greeted me with an indifferent gaze.

"I'm Pat English." He said it as if I should know who he was. "Is it too late to welcome you to Dili?" He examined my face. "You speak Arabic?" It was a statement, not a question, so I didn't say anything. Resting in his lap was a stack of light-gray file folders, each crammed with dog-eared papers. I got the feeling that fluency in Arabic wasn't the only thing Mr. English knew about me. My mouth dried up, and I pulled my collar away from my throat.

Mr. English took a series of slow, deliberate breaths and delivered his opening salvo. "We'll give you your full year's salary and finishing benefit for the police monitor bit. I'm offering you an additional assignment, outside of Timor-Leste." His manner was flat, his delivery equally level and smooth, as if I were but one of any number of contacts he'd meet today with an ambiguous offer and a super-cool demeanor.

It was clear I wasn't in trouble, but I didn't relax all at once. The heat under my shirt collar dissipated slowly as I considered how to reply.

"But before I get ahead of myself," he pulled one of the gray folders from his pile, "you do speak Arabic?" This time it was a question.

"Yes, I . . ."

"Some weird southern Arabic dialect? Squirty?"

I hesitated. "*Suqutri.* Yes."

"Languages aren't my thing," he said.

"You're the cultural attaché in a foreign country."

"Yeah, oh well." To add to the sarcasm, Mr. English rolled his eyes. "You are fluent in this Squirty language?"

I nodded.

Mr. English leaned forward in the bench seat and looked me over, paying particular attention to my face. I have wavy black hair and golden brown eyes—an old girlfriend once called them smoldering—and my olive skin allows me to pass for a sultry Mediterranean beach bum. No one had ever asked me if I was from the Middle East, but no one ever mistook me for the prince of Denmark either.

He nodded and his demeanor changed, the scrutiny over. "Can you fool a native?"

I didn't say anything for a moment because I'd never tried to fool a native Arab. I might look the part and sound the part, but the Middle East wasn't in Ohio, and you had to know how to act. I gave Mr. English an equivocal, "Probably, in some places. But the government must be crawling with people who speak Arabic. Why me? Besides, I can't imagine Hans Bafus has painted a very charming portrait of me."

"Do you put that much stock in Hans Bafus's opinion?" He paused, maybe to see how I would react, then shook his head. "Hans Bafus is a Frenchman with a German given name. He has his own problems."

I looked to where Hans was waiting, pretending to be far enough away that he couldn't hear what was being said. When he noticed us looking at him, Hans seemed to get the point and turned on his heel and stalked off toward the street.

"You've been requested," Mr. English said. "Specifically—by name. And Squir . . . uh, Suqutri isn't that common, especially since fluency and . . . skin tone—uh, authenticity—seem to be important." He stuffed his gray folder back in the pile without ever having looked at it. "You'll be doing a little translating and low-level diplomacy. Maybe some advice on protocol. The shoe fits."

"And what exactly is low-level diplomacy?"

"Sorry. Not unless you accept the assignment. Then you'll be briefed."

"And if I'd rather decline and finish my obligation here?"

Mr. English let loose with a long, slow sigh and placed his left hand on his pile of folders. As the fingers of his right hand flipped over each tab, he called out a title. "FBI background check. Seattle Police Department employment history. CIA investigative report. Personal references. Surveillance reports. Psychological report. Coworker evaluations. Ah, here." Mr. English withdrew a worn file from his collection. "Here it is, the thick one. November the twenty-first, two thousand and four. Washington State Patrol Case Number 04-WSP50304. Revised Code of Washington section 46.61.502. Driving under the influence. The accident happened on Interstate 5 . . ."

"Enough. I'm familiar with the case," I said. I clenched my jaw and felt the sting of guilt rise like a lump in my throat. "What's that got to do with anything?"

"Nothing. And everything. That's up to you."

"You brought it up." I wasn't sure I had the patience for Mr. Pat English.

"The interesting thing is that no one at your department brought it up when we checked your background. Not the supervisory staff. None of your coworkers."

"So, it's forgotten. What's so interesting about that?"

"Because the only one who has trouble getting past it is you. We both know you came to Timor-Leste because you couldn't completely exonerate yourself."

I stared at the bent pages poking out from the edges of the folder, dozens of them, and wondered what it all added up to. The words themselves were harmless, maybe even in some places impressive. I'd been a good cop—once.

Mr. English said, "Your contract with DynCorp runs out in just over a month. What then?" He let a moment pass. "You have what we need. Maybe we have what you need."

"Is that what you think?"

Mr. English, for the first time, really looked at me —into my eyes. "Someone with a great deal of influence thinks that." Mr. English peered down into his lap at the heavy stack of folders. "And no one blames you." Mr. English hid behind a mask of professional nonchalance, but his stony eyes revealed an undercurrent of deeper, hotter emotions. "You're not the first cop to second-guess your decisions, Mr. Daniels." His words were delivered frankly and with detachment. It beat pity. "Every cop has one— the memory of a call that never should have happened."

It had been nearly two years, and I still didn't know how to talk about it, much less how to feel about it. Then this complete stranger dove right in.

Mr. English placed the file back in his lap. "You can't run forever, Kam. I've watched people try. The inside of an amber bottle is a deep, dark place. You need this assignment."

"What I really need," I said, turning away from the open window, "is not to generate any more of those lousy gray folders." I spun back toward him. "You sit there, smug and superior in your armor-plated government war wagon. You don't know me. You don't know anything about me. What makes you the expert?"

"Kam . . ."

My voice was louder now. "So, you've read my files. You've read the report. And now you think you really know me?"

"I believe I know the man you were," said English. "Maybe you're not that man anymore. Maybe you never were. Or just maybe you still are." Mr. English nodded into the rearview mirror at his driver. The Suburban's brake lights flickered as the vehicle crept forward.

I slammed my fists on the sill of the open window, causing English to jerk back in his seat. "You don't know anything about me. You don't know how I felt then—how I feel now." The wheels crunched gravel as they started to turn and the Suburban pulled away. "What makes you the expert?" I yelled at the rear window. "You know so much? You don't know me. You don't know what I need." The vehicle turned a corner and disappeared into the Timor-Leste jungle. "You think you know what I need?" I screamed. "You think you know what I want? You have no idea." My protests were swallowed up in the thick jungle canopy surrounding our open lot.

The government war wagon was gone. Where the emotion had come from, I didn't know, but my display left me angry and embarrassed. I turned on my heel, fists clenched and jaw set. That's when I noticed Megawati standing at the edge of the jungle foliage near our first base line, watching me.

"*Ita ba nebee,* Kam-Dan?" he asked in a shaken Tetum dialect.

I had no idea what he said, but I waved him over and put my arm around his shoulder.

"You going?" he asked. "With white man?"

"No, I'm not going. Kam-Dan stays right here." I wasn't going to let Mr. Pat English, or Hans Bafus, or any of these people push me around. I wasn't going anywhere. Timor-Leste was what I needed. I had it good here. I looked down at Megawati and thought about the other boys. They needed me, needed my stability. "Right here," I repeated, roughing up Mega's hair.

"Good, Kam-Dan get drunk and play ball." Megawati smiled and tugged on my hand.

I looked down into Mega's searching eyes and didn't like what they reflected. He was a product of generations of neglect and alcoholism—he'd been raised with those expectations. And I was fulfilling all of them.

* * *

The next morning, I walked the cracked and uneven streets of Dili not wanting to admit where I was going, but determined to arrive at the embassy soon after it opened to the public. I'd had a chance to clear my head and make a few decisions. It had been a long, fitful night, and I didn't want to endure an equally long, frustrating day. Maybe Pat English was right. Maybe he had something I needed.

A Marine who looked for the entire world like a seventeen-year-old boy told me to wait in the lobby of the embassy. My uniform and U.N. identification got me inside with an escort—another young but tough and proficient Marine.

I was taken to the office of the Ministry of the Interior, where I was told I could see Mr. Pat English, cultural attaché. I wondered if all cultural attachés around the globe were CIA plants. I ran my tongue around the pasty inside of my mouth before turning the doorknob to go inside, not sure how I would be received after yesterday's drama. I was greeted by an exceptionally attractive, twenty-something woman sitting behind a mismatched set of outdated office furniture. An oscillating fan swept back and forth on the corner of her desk, making her streaked blonde ringlets bounce around her ears.

"Good morning," I said. "I'm Kam Daniels, to see Mr. English."

"Hi, I'm Miss Davidson, Mr. English's assistant," she said. "Pat told me you might be coming in." Miss Davidson stood, revealing her height of nearly six feet, and leaned over her desk to offer me her hand. Miss Davidson was . . . remarkable.

"Is Mr. English in?" I asked, wondering if she were taller than me.

"No, he went out."

I wasn't expecting to be disappointed, but I was.

She said, "Pat told me if you showed up, I should give you this." She lifted a large white envelope out of an in-basket and clicked around her desk toward me in high-heeled pumps, the essence of green-tea perfume wafting before her. "Or did you need to talk to him first?"

Did I? It was probably the last thing I needed. Maybe Pat knew me better than I thought. "No," I said.

"Great." Miss Davidson relaxed and sat on the front edge of her desk, crossed her long legs, and opened the envelope. "You'll be traveling undercover in Yemen with a group of religious scholars on a research trip," she said. "Nothing cloak-and-dagger—just a way to allow you to travel freely in Yemen without raising questions. You'll want to appear confident and intelligent, but not flashy."

"A religious scholar? It's a stretch. Mr. English said I was just doing some interpreting. He didn't tell me . . ."

"Your complete legend isn't fully worked out yet." She slipped several sheets of paper out of the envelope and scanned them as she talked. "You'll get a complete briefing once you get to Paris, I'm sure. We only got a partial fax from Washington, so I don't know all the details myself. Our phones are about as reliable as the weather. We're sort of at the end of the world down here."

And Yemen is right on the world information nexus.

"You won't be working under deep cover, but you will be posing as a member of the religious research team while you're in Yemen. You'll be using your own name, at least unless someone tells you differently."

While Miss Davidson tickled my file with her French-manicured nails, I wondered at the perfunctory manner in which she laid out my future, like a travel agent giving me my cruise agenda. She tucked a coil of her frosted, corn-silk hair behind her ear and handed me a full sheet of paper. "This is part of your itinerary, anyway. You take the next available Timor Aviation Services flight out of Dili Airport, make a few connecting flights, and arrive in Paris in the morning. Find your way to the Bastille Speria—that's a hotel," she added. "You'll stay there until someone contacts you. Expect a full briefing then."

"No dead drops or brush passes," I said.

Miss Davidson turned her stunning cobalt eyes toward mine. "Not for this assignment."

"I watch a lot of Michael Caine movies."

Miss Davidson didn't even blink. Either she was too young to appreciate Michael Caine as British spy Harry Palmer or she was a communist. "No super-spy stuff," she said. Miss Davidson held out the white envelope. When I took it, she placed her hand on mine as if to suggest that the contents were very important. "These are your plane tickets and enough money to get you everything you'll need. It's enough to buy you a new wardrobe and keep you comfortable for a while—a long while—should something go wrong. Which it won't," she hastened to add.

I accepted the envelope without counting the money inside. "So, all I have to do is show up in Paris at this hotel?"

"Pretty much."

I didn't like the way she qualified that statement. "What do I tell people about my leaving?" I asked.

"You won't have a chance."

"Clever," I said. The magnitude of what I was doing was slowly hitting me. "So, as far as anyone here goes, I finally got tired of doing the Great Australian Salute at the bugs and hit the road?"

"That's funny. I've never heard it called that." She swatted at an imaginary fly circling her face and laughed. "Reassigned, as far as anyone here knows. We'll take care of explaining your disappearance. As far as the rest of your cover, keep it as true as you can," she said.

"My disappearance, huh?"

"Try not to lie, because it gives you too many things to remember if anyone calls you on something. You will need to lie about your profession, however. Don't tell anyone you were a cop, um, police officer . . ."

"Cop is okay with me," I said. "And I thought I wasn't under deep cover."

"Depends on your definition. But let's not raise any eyebrows with the Yemeni Interior Ministry. In any case, it is easier to remember a cover story when it's at least partially true."

"I suppose. How do you know so much about this kind of stuff? You seem to know how to tell a good lie," I said.

"I prefer 'fashioning a ruse,'" she said. Miss Davidson's blue eyes darted toward the office door bearing the name "Pat English" on the frosted glass window, and she couldn't hide a conspiratorial grin. "You can't work in the embassy very long without picking up on a few tricks."

"You could tell me, but then . . ."

"Yep, I'd have to kill you." Miss Davidson made scary eyes and slashed her fingers across her throat.

"So tell me, Miss Davidson, are all cultural attachés CIA operatives, or are all CIA operatives cultural attachés?" Maybe I was flirting—a little. But, even if I'd had a chance with the likes of Miss Davidson—which was as likely as my Timor-Leste boys winning the World Series—I knew in my heart that things weren't right for that. It could never happen.

"Cute," she said, smiling. "I don't want to have to kill you." Miss Davidson held out a smaller envelope, initialed on the sealed flap. "And Pat left you this."

I accepted the envelope and nodded. "What is it?"

Miss Davidson shrugged her remarkable shoulders. "He didn't say. But it seemed to be important to him that you get it."

"Thanks."

"My pleasure, Mr. Daniels." She held out her hand again, and that was that. I'd been drafted into the United States intelligence services.

I left the office of the Ministry of the Interior at the embassy, my feelings vacillating between excitement and doom.

I slid my finger under the flap of the envelope initialed by Pat English and tore it open. It contained only a small piece of paper bearing a handwritten message. I read what it said and crumpled the note in my hands. The queasy feeling subsided and was replaced by an emotion somewhere between shame and hope.

Kam,
I hope this is what you need.
Respectfully,
Pat English, a brother in arms

CHAPTER 4

I arrived in Paris, as instructed, early in the morning and had nothing to do but wait for my contact at the Hotel Bastille Speria. The interior decor made me feel at home in a 1960s spy movie sort of way. Everything from the red-and-black patterned carpet to the narrow stairwells and wooden doors with glass knobs gave me a retro vibe. It was an eighteenth-century building masquerading as a Beatles-era hotel. The small and not overly cozy lobby was vacant but for a lone tourist sitting cross-legged on an uninviting vinyl divan. He looked like a typical tourist, recently retired, graying at the temples, and wearing a leather jacket and houndstooth driving hat. He scratched on a PDA, while the noise of a gated elevator clanged in the background.

I checked in with the clerk, who thankfully spoke English. She gave me a real key, not a flimsy card, and sent me off to the third floor with a well-costumed bellboy who politely carried my one small duffel bag.

The 1960s ambiance didn't stop in the lobby. In my room, two retro red-and-white vinyl-covered chairs, a square, crome-legged table, and a bed draped in pink stripes completed the décor. Martha Stewart would have had a "Cordially Yours" heart attack.

I had no idea how spies met each other at hotels and had been given next to no information about what I was supposed to do, so I checked for messages every so often at the small front desk and spent the rest of my time loose on the streets of Paris. The city seemed clean by Timor-Leste standards. At least you could drink as much bottled water as you wanted, and there were comparatively few flying insects to deal with.

My first morning in Paris turned into a sightseeing vacation. I'd always wanted to see the Eiffel Tower, and there were some sites around the city that were *très neat-o* like the Bastille, where aristocrats were incarcerated and slaughtered in the 1700s largely on the basis of their unfortunate birthright. The view from my hotel window looked directly upon the Bastille, and I couldn't shake the feeling that it wasn't a good omen. But then again, so what?

I started my self-guided tour with a visit to a tourist gift shop. There I filled my shirt pocket with postcards. I couldn't send any, since I'd been instructed not to communicate my travel plans to family or friends, but the cards would help me set a tourist itinerary for the day. I chose cards that interested me and then plotted their locations on a street map.

A couple of city blocks away, on an island on the Seine River, I stopped to admire the gothic grandeur of Notre Dame, which had spent nearly two hundred years under construction. I was awed mostly by the thought of the blood and sweat that went into its creation. Religious devotion such as that was foreign to me, and browsing my tourist booklet about the history of the structure only served to intensify that feeling.

I suppose it could have been guilt surrounding my own lackluster religious experience, but for some reason I felt an emptiness at having spent so little energy in considering my own relationship with God. The men and women who crafted the massive ornate structure before me had given everything, their very souls, to the establishment of this monument. Were they simply deluded? A pinprick to the soul followed that thought, but I dismissed it immediately when a passing East Indian tourist dressed in an off-white, knee-length cotton kurta shirt asked in precisely enunciated British English where he could find a tourist booklet like the one I was holding. He was accompanied by his wife, who wore a brilliant burgundy silk sari with matching bangles on both arms and had a bindi, the symbolic dot of divine sight, painted in crimson sindur between her thin, dark eyebrows. The excited looks on both their faces told me that they were enjoying their Parisian experience. I returned their smiles and handed the husband the pamphlet. He nodded and said a proper thank you.

I moved on from the Palace of Notre Dame to the nearby Hotel DeVille, where I was impressed by the legacy of sacrifice that hung over the spot where so many innocents were executed. Thoughts about my own apathy accompanied me on my way along the Seine toward the Louvre, which I pronounced "Loov-ray" in a vain attempt to bring the problem of pitiable phonics to the attention of the French conscious-ness. The Louvre looked like the big palace from the movie *Chitty Chitty Bang Bang,* a story I liked particularly because it was written by the same man who wrote the James Bond books. To me, that's culture.

In the back of my mind was the thought that someone would soon make contact with me and give me a briefing on my assignment, whatever it was. When I'd left Dili, I was simply glad to be leaving Hans Bafus and the rest of the bugs of Timor-Leste and hadn't really considered the adventure I was about to embark upon. Wandering the streets of Paris like a character in a James Bond novel did a lot to set the stage for my current circumstance, but I had no jazzed-up Aston Martin, and the neatest thing my watch did was tell time in two different time zones, if I could figure out how to set it.

Despite my lack of spy savvy, it was exhilarating to be on to a new diversion. I tried to ignore the inevitable fact that I'd probably do very little exciting work on my sojourn and that working undercover for the government, as exotic as it sounded, was probably like working undercover as a cop—mind-numbing boredom, for the most part. Still, under the circumstances, I held out hope for a few moments of adrenaline-pumping excitement to make the whole thing worthwhile as I sauntered along the right bank of the Seine and thought about the next few weeks of my life. Kam Daniels—secret agent man. Under my breath, I sang the old familiar Johnny Rivers tune—*There's a man who leads a life of danger*—blissfully indifferent about the damage British television had done me—*To everyone he meets he stays a stranger*—and the torpor-inducing era of mindless spy movies—*With every move he makes, another chance he takes*—until I heard myself singing the chorus—*Odds are he won't live to see tomorrow.* It would be overly dramatic to suggest that it gave me a chill—*Secret agent man, secret agent man. They've given you a number, and taken away your name*—but then again . . .

Nothing much happened on the rest of my tour, except that I made the tourist purchase of a lifetime at the Arc de Triomphe. What a treat. A young boy with flair as an entrepreneurial street vendor sold me a length of wooden dowel topped with several palm fronds made from pipe cleaners. Hugging the dowel was a small pipe-cleaner monkey attached to the top of the stick with a rubber band. The boy demonstrated his wares by pulling the monkey to the bottom of the stick and then shrieking as he let go. The monkey slammed to the top of the tree as if Simba and all his lion friends were chasing it. I was one of many tourists who couldn't resist.

I'd made my purchase and started back toward my hotel, wondering how I could exploit the idea in the U.S. and bring the invisible dog-on-a-leash industry to its knees, when the boy who'd sold me the monkey ran up behind me.

"Monsieur, monsieur," he yelled, out of breath, "your change." He said it in English, but I wasn't sure he knew what he was saying.

"Non, non," I said, glad to take advantage of my vast knowledge of the French language with the two words I knew.

"Your change," he said loudly, looking furtively around and holding out a piece of paper currency that could have been any denomination for all I knew. "You take it." He shoved the bill into my hand and took off as fast as he had come, leaving me little choice but to accept the money. It was more than I'd paid for the monkey and probably more than the cost of ten monkeys. Suddenly, the vacation was over. Every instinct I'd developed over nearly a decade of police work kicked in at once, and I became aware of everything and everyone around me.

The bill was wrapped around another piece of paper, but I didn't take the time to see what the message said. The surreptitious way it was delivered told me someone was trying to be very careful, which made me sure that I was being watched. Otherwise, why the "Secret Squirrel" stuff?

I was just getting comfortable with the right bank area of the Seine and felt I knew how to get around that part of Paris. The sudden shift in emotional climate changed all that. My surroundings were relatively open, making it easy for an unseen malevolent force to tail me. I needed to find the right kind of narrow area where I could watch for a tail and be sure I was alone before I looked at the note I'd been given. I reached into my pocket and withdrew the stack of post-cards I'd purchased earlier. Holding them up as if trying to identify landmarks, I turned three hundred and sixty degrees and took a good look around. I didn't see anyone in a dark fedora and black trench coat smoking a cigarette. I was way out of my league, and I knew it. Everything I knew about the secret agent business I'd learned from bad movies. I wisely decided against lurking in back streets searching for a tail and decided that my safety depended on getting back to the Hotel Bastille Speria where I could wait for help.

I walked briskly up the street, keeping the Seine to my right so I wouldn't get lost. I noticed everyone I passed—single men hurrying to meet someone along the river, couples strolling hand in hand and gazing up at the architecture, locals on their daily errands—any of them could be watching me. It was impossible to tell.

Engrossed in the people passing by, I nearly knocked over a young girl distributing handbills on the sidewalk. I stopped abruptly as she held out a small square of orange paper and nodded to me. Still wary, I absently took the paper. It was an advertisement for a new exhibit in a local art gallery.

"Thank you," I said.

The girl stared into my eyes and then looked to the side at a man just turning into the front doors of a neighborhood bakery. I saw him from the back—a tall man with long, dark, straggly hair. When the girl's gaze returned to mine, she had a worried look on her face.

"Thank you," I said again, dropping the handbill and hurrying down the sidewalk, my attention still on the front door of the bakery.

Now completely paranoid, even approaching the hotel, I entered the lobby wary and alert. Behind the registration desk stood a bored young man in a dark blue suit, thumbing registration cards as if no one else in the world existed. A thirty-something couple waited near the front entrance as if for a taxi, their attention clearly on the road outside. Otherwise, the lobby was quiet and appeared safe. I took several steps toward the stairs to my room and then turned around, getting the attention of the clerk.

"Messages?" I asked, hoping for some word from my contact. "For Daniels?"

"Kamir Daniels?" asked the clerk a little too loudly.

"Kam," I said. I rarely used my full name unless passports and visas were involved.

"No, sir," he said in only slightly accented English, turning to look at the key boxes to make sure.

I looked again at the couple by the door and then walked up the stairs to my third-story room. No one was in the narrow hallway, so I walked past my door once to make sure it was closed. At the far end of the hallway, I turned and walked slowly back, wondering what I'd gained by looking at the closed door. I should have left a toothpick wedged in the door when I left. If the toothpick had been gone on my return, I'd have known someone had been in my room. My BBC-inspired secret agent training was failing me, but my police instincts were in high gear.

Standing beside my door, I slowly turned the small glass knob and found the door locked, just as I'd left it. I knew I wasn't going to be able to get inside without making a noise, so I slid the key into the lock and turned it once. I swung the door open and then stepped back. Nothing happened. Leaving the door open, I rode the elevator back to the very public lobby, where I picked up a French newspaper and stared at the unfamiliar words for fifteen minutes of nervous curiosity, long enough for an intruder in my room to wonder where I'd gone, get bored, and leave. I didn't want to blithely enter my room and get shanghaied, or whatever bad guys did to secret agents in the new millennium.

I had used the same bit of subterfuge once on a high-risk search warrant. I'd kicked the door in and then waited two hours before sneaking into the house. It probably wasn't a strictly legal rendering of the completely uninspired Knock-and-Announce rule that applied to police search warrants, but I'd hoped in that situation to lull the bad guys into a false sense of security before I exposed myself to danger. As it turned out in that case, no one was there. As I found out on my second visit to my hotel room, the same was true today. No one was there.

Resisting the urge to look at the note I'd been given, I did a more comprehensive search of my room. I found nothing unusual, and my belongings were still there. Everything else in the room appeared to be just as I'd left it. In the now relatively secured room, I sat on the bed and examined the note in my pocket.

It consisted of one innocuous line: "Job interview, 1800 hours, Le Pied Rare." It was signed simply with the letter *R* and folded once. There was no reference to *The French Connection* and no warning of certain doom. It was merely a note. I was at the same time relieved and infuriated. It was a message from my contact, but the manner of delivery gave me the feeling that all this spy stuff wasn't as innocent as it appeared. Whoever *R* was, he was going to hear about it.

I placed the note back in my pocket, resisting the urge to burn it like a real spy would—or eat it. I'd had enough secret agent man for one afternoon. I relaxed for a few minutes while the adrenaline rush subsided, and wondered what Le Pied Rare was, or more specifically, where it was. Deciphering the mystery location would be as easy as asking one of the hotel staff, but I tried to work it out myself as long as I wasn't doing anything else. Besides, discretion, I decided, was an asset for any international spy on a secret undercover mission.

Le was easy, and I knew what the Pied Piper was, although I had to admit I had no idea what *pied* really meant. *Rare* was a tricky word since I couldn't quite separate it contextually from its English meaning. Who was I kidding? After about five minutes of looking at a map for clues, I locked up my room and asked a passing maid who, through a combination of crude English and French hand gestures, gave me directions.

I left the hotel and easily found the restaurant, a hole-in-the-wall café that featured lots of toy pigs and a framed drawing of the Pied Piper—which was a pig with a flute. For me, it was a short intellectual leap from Le Pied Rare to the Raw Pig, and thus the quaint little French restaurant was renamed in my head. It was only a short distance from the hotel, and I was sure I could find the Raw Pig again for my meeting tonight.

Until then, I had a few errands to run. I would eventually need new clothes and a few odds and ends for my shaving kit to get me through a tour of Yemen. Yemen doesn't do Wal-mart. Neither, apparently, does Paris—at least not within walking distance of the eleventh arrondissement, a section of town that looked like it was a mixture of housing, hotels, and history. The most rugged pants I could find to buy within walking distance were pleated khakis that went well with the outdoor shirts I bought—at least, that is, if I wanted to look like a summer camp counselor. I didn't care much, never having been a slave to fashion. I knew what size I was in fatigues and Levi's, and in the real world I could get by with bulk purchases of pocket T-shirts. It's not shopping; it's resupply. Besides, I knew enough about travel in Yemen to know that I could pick up some very functional items of authentic clothing when we arrived. Not only would they be more useful given the climate and terrain, but they would also cost a fraction of what I'd had to fork out for the khakis.

I found a place where Parisians could buy outdoor gear that would do for a walk through the vineyards, but the store lacked the kind of inventory that qualified it as a real outfitter store. Not finding anything useful, I fiddled with a nifty P38 military-issue can opener about the size of a zipper pull that I found in a plastic container at the checkout counter—an impulse item. I threw a piece of paper money in front of the clerk and pocketed the P38 and a roll of duct tape that was a cheap imitation of the black ninety-mile-an-hour tape I was familiar with. But it would do. I got change back, but I didn't recognize the coins. Outside the shop I wrapped the P38 in tape and tied the small lanyard hole to my bootlace, then tucked it under the tongue.

Just before I was due at the Raw Pig, I made a quick stop at the Hotel Bastille Speria to drop off my wares. Still a little uneasy about my new job as an international spy, I took a deep breath and flung the hotel room door open, only to be embarrassed in front of my neighbor across the way who inadvertently witnessed the dissonant mixture of flourish and fear with which I thrust myself into the room. *Kato? I know you're in there, Kato.*

After that minor humiliation, I left the hotel in a timely fashion and navigated flawlessly to the restaurant and walked inside. The Raw Pig was an informal place where one might expect to eat a quick lunch or light dinner. I was greeted by a host who spoke English, and he directed me to a matched pair of tables that had been pushed together to accommodate the large dinner party already seated there.

Immediately I was confronted by one of those I-should-have-known moments where everything comes together in an instant. The infamous *R* who'd signed my note was seated across from the only vacant chair at the table. "Shock and Awe" is a military catchphrase referring to the ongoing fight against terror, but *R* had done me one better. I felt stun and horror. The true identities of the religious scholars at the table were a mystery, although it's hard to fake that academic nerd look, even for an experienced spook, but the identity of *R* was no mystery at all. *R* wasn't a master spy—she was my wife, Rhiana Daniels, the sable-haired beauty I'd abandoned just over a year ago.

CHAPTER 5

I would have pulled out a chair and thrust out a hand to greet the strangers who were all staring at me from their table at the Raw Pig, but my arms momentarily stopped taking instructions from my brain. Rhiana's eyes met mine for an instant, but she glanced down at her place setting as if to suggest discretion regarding our relationship. The discomfort showed on her face, as it was undoubtedly apparent on my own.

My stupor was broken by a muscular man—who appeared nothing like a religious scholar—standing in front of me with his hand out. "Kamir, we're glad you could make it. I'm Clyde Holmes and these are my associates. This is Darrin Adams." He pointed to the science nerd sitting against the wall next to him. Darrin was built like a cotton swab, with oily black hair and a cowlick, his height and academic pedigree being the only things that differentiated him from Alfalfa of *The Little Rascals*—oh, and the nine-inch-thick glasses. "Darrin is a graduate student in the Religion Department at Brigham Young University," said Clyde. "Actually, it's an interdisciplinary PhD under the departments of history, sociology, philosophy, and religion. He's here with me."

Darrin came to his feet and offered his hand.

"Tell Mr. Daniels about your research," Clyde said.

Darrin gazed around the table. "My dissertation . . ." he stammered, "concerns postmodernist trends in . . . religious hegemonies."

No one said anything.

"It's actually very interesting." And with that, Darrin took his first opportunity to fall back into his seat and functionally disappear.

"It really is fascinating, Kamir," said Clyde. "You should get him to tell you about it."

Post-homogenized-religious-hedge-money-hedgehogs. "Oh, I will," I said. "And it's Kam."

"Kam, this is Father Andrew Marcy, of Notre Dame." Clyde pointed to another man at the table. "Not the one in Paris," he said. Everyone laughed as if they'd heard that gag one too many times. "I'm sure you've heard of the place."

"Father Marcy," I said, shaking his hand as he stood.

"Just Drew or Father Drew if you must," said the slight man with messy orangey-brown hair and wire-rimmed glasses. "When people call me Father Marcy, it sounds like an Irishman saying, 'Father Mercy'—a little presumptuous, even for a priest." He laughed and fumbled with his chair before sitting again. I don't know much about Catholic fathers, but this one didn't bother with a white collar. Maybe it's not a popular look while traveling to the Middle East.

"And this is Doctor Madeline Black, associate professor of religious sociology and history at Boston College." Doctor Black was as large as her title. She stood up to reveal some hefty legs in a set of knee-length shorts that I knew were going to be popular in Yemen. I offered my hand, and when she caught it, she used it to throw my arm back and forth, nearly dislocating my shoulder. And I thought *I* was manly. "Mr. Daniels, I'm pleased to meet you." Her voice was low and raspy, and her mousy brown hair looked like it had been pruned at the chin with a pair of rusty garden shears. I got the feeling she didn't put up with a lot of nonsense.

Clyde turned to his last table partner—I couldn't wait to hear the introduction. He said, "This is Rhiana Monroe, professor of religious sociology from the University of Washington . . . State. I think you two have spoken on the phone."

Professor of what? And she's using Monroe? *Her maiden name.* It was like having a croquet ball shoved down my throat. As a pejorative signal to a former husband, the change was understandable, but we weren't even divorced.

"Yes, we have," I said, just keeping it close to the truth, as directed.

"Nice to meet you, Mr. Daniels. We're excited to get to know you." Rhiana reached over the table and shook my hand as if for the first time, but the awkwardness of a year's absence made her swallow hard. Rhiana wasn't a rookie CIA case officer, but under the circumstances her discomfort was understandable.

"We've already been served," said Clyde, "so if it's okay, we can get started while you wait to order."

I felt like I was watching a bad movie in slow motion. Rhiana seemed to expect me to know a lot more than I did, and I didn't get a warm feeling that she'd be an understanding master spy if I messed things up during this impromptu job interview. A little advance warning would have been nice.

Darrin picked at a hard roll while we spoke, no doubt contemplating the depths of his anthrophobia. Doctor Black just stared off into space and took random bites of food, chewing like a horse in need of a good teeth floating. I couldn't look at Rhiana. Father Andrew looked at me with practiced interest, so I focused on him when I wasn't looking at Clyde, who was cordial throughout dinner and did most of the talking. But I couldn't get my mind off of Rhiana.

She had always been an exceptionally beautiful woman with luminous hazel eyes, silky dark hair, and flawless ivory skin protected from the sun by the gray northwestern skies. There was no quantifying the mental anguish we'd both suffered over the last year, but it hadn't dulled her exotic good looks.

I'd first seen her on the job at an intelligence conference in Bellingham, Washington, not far from the Canadian border. She was presenting information on Middle Eastern terrorism, and I was ignoring the details of her talk in favor of just staring at her—like Rod Stewart says, the attraction was purely physical. After I actually met her, it didn't take long to realize that Rhiana had other charms beyond the physical, including a willingness to give up her career with the CIA to be my wife. The romance was whirlwind, and the marriage was fairy tale.

"Mr. Daniels?" Rhiana repeated, snapping me out of an emotional haze.

"You *could* call me Kam . . . Oh yes, I had a great trip," I said quickly, hoping I was answering the right question. "I got in last night and spent today on the town. I've never been to Paris, so . . ."

"But would you like to order something?"

"Oh, what? Yes. I'll have . . . whatever you're having, Clyde. Thanks." I didn't want to be the dork who couldn't decide what to have, especially during a job interview—even a contrived one. A waiter, who I hadn't seen approach the table, nodded and scuttled off to the kitchen with my order. I hoped it wasn't something disgusting like a raw pig.

"I'm glad you had a good trip," Clyde said. "Where did you fly in from last night?"

"Dili," I said without thinking.

Rhiana, who had been sipping water, choked. She started to cough and had to stand up to clear her esophagus. We all waited for Rhiana to begin breathing normally again before Clyde went right back to what was turning into an inquisition.

"Dili? That's odd. We were told you had a family emergency back in the States, and that's why you were late getting to Paris. Is everything okay?"

Not even a little bit. "Oh that, yes. You know it turns out that it wasn't as critical as we first thought. Everything is fine now." I felt like a first-year law student who hadn't done his homework. I looked around the table at the expectant faces. Rhiana looked terrified.

"Where's Dili?" asked Darrin. *Now* he had to get interested.

"Well, Philadelphia, actually," I lied. "We call it Dili back in the neighborhood." I could have said Dili was a neighborhood in Seattle, but I didn't think that fast. Dili just kind of inspired Philly.

"I thought that was Philly," said Doctor Black.

Rhiana was past terrified and looked sick now.

"Well . . . in some neighborhoods," I continued. "I'm from . . . the neighborhood where . . . we . . . call it Dili."

I couldn't believe any of them bought my story, but they were polite enough not to press me on it. Rhiana, on the other hand, looked angry enough to drive her fork through my hand.

"Anyway, everything turned out fine back at home . . . in Dili." *Change the subject.* "I wondered if you could tell me a little about the research you're doing in Yemen."

"Of course," Clyde said. "We're doing some preparation and establishing the itinerary for next year's sociological study of the Book of Mormon, the Yemen portion of the book of First Nephi. A few years ago, some of our associates did a geographical study of the area, and we're following up with a study of the area from the anthropologic viewpoint. Next year we plan to bring an interdenominational group of scholars from a number of related fields to expand the study. For next year's trip we're going to need camp hands and support people as well as a cook."

There was a pause, a pregnant one. Clyde stared at me, and everyone else seemed to want me to say something. It started to look more and more like I'd missed my cue. A cook? "Well," I said, trying to work out the logic of Rhiana's thinking on this, "I'm your man." I wasn't really. I couldn't cook a lick. Suddenly I was assaulted by an image of me at Boy Scout camp almost two decades ago sitting over a fire eating some kind of charred thing that tasted like the tongue of my shoe. Rhiana's eyes were the size of two moons at harvest. "I've cooked a lot at . . . camps." There was that vision again—of me with the tongue of my shoe on a sharpened stick over a blazing fire. I could almost smell the athlete's foot and mildew rising in the vapors. "I'm a very good cook."

"Oh," said Clyde, looking at Rhiana. "I thought . . . So, you're a cook. That's great."

"Actually . . ." Rhiana started but couldn't finish.

Slowly, ever so slowly, I realized my monumental mistake, but I was determined to make this thing work, if only because Rhiana was involved. And maybe the free world depended on me. Who knew?

"Actually," I finished for Rhiana, "I'm a great cook. I've been involved in feeding as many as three hundred people." I was thinking back to when I was on the kitchen crew in second grade. "I've also been involved in feeding smaller groups of anywhere from ten to twenty people." I didn't think this was what Miss Davidson had in mind when she told me to keep my lies close to the truth, but this was as close as I could come—because I was great at bringing chips to parties.

"Interesting," said Clyde. He looked at Rhiana, who now had her head down. "If only you spoke the language. Right now we could use a guide and translator." He said the last two words so slowly and with such emphasis that I inferred three things: one, that I was supposed to be the translator—you didn't have to be a rocket scientist; two, that Clyde was in on it; and three, that I was now considered a dork.

Clyde said, "With a name like Kamir, we just assumed . . ."

Doctor Black and Father Andrew nodded. Rhiana's head was kind of traveling in an elliptical pattern that could have been interpreted as a nod—if you squinted your eyes really hard. Either way, she was still quite attractive, even when she was thunder-mad. I had just one chance to turn this interview around.

I said, "You should taste my specialty."

"Oh, what's that?" asked Clyde. Rhiana stopped rolling her head. "Desserts."

"Desserts?" said Clyde. Everyone but Rhiana and Clyde were looking at each other in utter confusion. Clyde seemed simply frustrated, and Rhiana held a monopoly on rage.

"Yep. Desert desserts. Yemen cheesecake and Yemen meringue pie." I got a delayed reaction chuckle from Father Andrew and a nervous cough from Doctor Black. Rhiana's eyes lit up like hot embers. "But all cooking jokes aside, I do speak the language. My mother is Yemeni. I'm very much at home in Yemen. I'm your man. Your guide and interpreter, I mean."

Clyde said, "Oh, you had us going, Kam. The cook. What a sense of humor. Rhiana can fill you in on the details, and she'll help with your travel arrangements. She's taking care of all that. And . . . we're all looking forward to some of that . . . Yemen meringue pie." Obviously, my sense of humor wasn't fully appreciated among smart people, and Clyde just wanted to tie up this little meeting and get me out of there before I really messed things up. Apparently, the plan wasn't for me to be a cook from Dili.

"Thanks," I said as my food arrived.

I still wasn't sure what I'd ordered. Pork, I assumed. It wasn't raw. Eating was uncomfortable, not because of the French cuisine, but because I hardly knew how to answer a question. I'd been a cop all my professional life, and I'd done all kinds of undercover and plain-clothes police work, but this was somehow different. It wasn't every day I dined with my estranged wife of over a year in the company of religious scholars while posing as a Yemeni guide and future camp cook on a secret mission for the CIA. I made up a whole bunch of lies about what it was like growing up in Pennsylvania and was fortunate that Darrin didn't ask me to spell it. Doctor Black talked for a while about the Amish but didn't ask questions. It's a good thing, because I didn't know the difference between the Amish and the Mormons sitting at the table with me. Each new topic of conversation brought new forms of stress and tension to Rhiana's face. Eventually, it was too much for her, and she had to do something before I really made a mistake.

"I'm sorry, Kam," said Rhiana, looking at her watch. "I have so much to do to get you ready to travel. If you don't mind . . ." She stood and placed her napkin on the table, her eyes telling me to do the same. "I need you to sign a few things back at the hotel."

"It was nice to have met you. I'm sure we'll get to know each other better on our trip," I said, putting into words Rhiana's greatest fear. I dropped my napkin on the table and left the restaurant with Rhiana. I felt uneasy, especially under the strange circumstances, but I was glad to be alone with her. There was so much I wanted to say, and so much I was sorry about. Even though it was unexpected, the reunion was overdue. So was my explanation for leaving her in Seattle. I had a lot to own up to. I wanted to look at her and beg her to take me back.

"What was that?" Rhiana said just outside the doors of the restaurant.

"Rhiana, I'm sorry. Not just for today. I have a lot . . ."

"The cook? The COOK? What were you thinking? As a translator, you'd make a great cook?" Rhiana put her face in her hands and shook her head. After a long moment, she looked up. "I wasn't sure how this was going to turn out, Kam. When I saw you come into the restaurant, I felt . . . I thought maybe . . . A year hasn't changed anything, has it?"

If I had let my mouth follow my feelings, I would have said things I didn't really mean. I let a moment pass, but the right thing to say didn't really come to mind. I started to reach for her and stopped. "They didn't tell me it was you," was all I could say.

CHAPTER 6

It seemed like there was nothing to say and everything to say. Turning down the street in front of Le Pied Rare, Rhiana and I walked side by side in silence. At least we were walking together. I had imagined this day differently. I thought someday I would return to Rhiana, fall at her feet, and beg forgiveness. She'd weep for a while and then welcome me back in a long embrace and an even longer kiss. Then we'd spend a few days talking and . . . But it hadn't happened that way. I glanced in Rhiana's direction but saw the smoldering anger still present in the crease of her brow and the downward turn of her lip—anger that went far deeper than my pathetic performance at the restaurant.

"Rhi?" I finally said.

She looked away and didn't answer.

"Rhi?"

This time she turned to look at me, the crease between her eyes deepening.

"What?" I said, suddenly irritated. "You're mad at me? Why are you mad at me? Do you have any idea what it was like walking into the pig palace and seeing you sitting there?" I wasn't sure how to characterize my own anger.

Neither of us was prepared for this. Rhiana stopped and turned toward me as if she was ready to say something. She shook her head and started walking again. I followed like a desperate jilted lover.

"Rhiana, don't."

She stopped and turned, bringing me to a halt right in front of her. "You have some nerve bringing that tone."

"What tone? You want tone?" I said.

"It beats having nothing, which is what I had after you left."

"I know. I . . ." What was I supposed to say?

The muscles in Rhiana's jaw quivered. "Do you have any idea what it feels like to find out that your spouse has left you, and you don't even know why or where? It was bad enough when you left home, but Kam, you went halfway around the world, and we never even had a chance to talk about it."

"Rhiana, I know I hurt you . . ."

"You don't know. That's just it, Kam. You don't know, and you don't seem to care."

"That's not true." We were drawing looks from passersby so I nodded down the street, and we started walking again.

"You're going to have a hard time convincing me that your actions were those of a caring, loving husband."

"I don't remember getting a phone call from my loving wife." I turned my face away in self-righteous indignation, an emotion I didn't feel, but I was grasping at ammunition for a fight I knew I would never, never win.

"I tried," she said. "I called everyone I knew. I didn't know where you'd gone or if you were okay. Do you know how worried I was? I was your wife, Kam. We were still married. Do you know how I found out that you ran away to East Timor?"

"It's Timor-Leste," I whispered.

"Oh whatever, Kam. I had to pull some serious strings to locate you."

"Let me guess. You called in a few favors from your buddies at the CIA?" I was beginning to get a glimpse of what Custer might have felt like at Little Big Horn. "You didn't have to worry. Until yesterday, I was just fine."

"Well, that just shows how selfish you are, Kam. I wasn't just fine."

Somewhere in the conversation, we'd stopped walking again to face each other. We were both getting a little too loud and had been the subject of more than one uncomfortable glance.

My side of the argument was really pathetic and was getting more so each time I opened my mouth. I said, "You sure seem fine. Back to work, I see. And it didn't take you long to lose my name, did it, Ms. Monroe? Now you're dragging me into something, and I don't even know what it is. Do you know what a shock it was seeing you in the restaurant just now?"

"Everything you needed to know about this operation was in the materials I sent to the embassy in Dili—which is not in Philadelphia by the way—including the fact that I was the case officer in charge."

Somehow, a whiny "Uh-uh" wasn't quite the right thing for me to say. "I didn't know . . ."

"You didn't know?" Rhiana screamed in a whisper. She was the only person I knew who could do that.

"No, I did not."

"So, you're saying that this trip to Yemen is just about seeing how much farther away from me you could get? After you were done in Yemen, where were you going to run, Kam? What is wrong with you?"

The look on her face told me she hadn't intended that last little barb the way it sounded—but the question was valid. I wished at that moment that I'd had an answer. I wished I'd had a solution. I was angry, but I was also the victim of my own stupidity. I shook my head, and we both started to walk slowly side by side, neither of us speaking.

Rhiana was a smart girl—a CIA case officer assigned to a volatile area of the Middle East. She knew when she hit a hot button, and she knew when to pull back. The silence gave me a chance to get some perspective on our situation. But the question had to be answered.

"I didn't think it would be this way," I said after a few minutes.

"The job?" She'd calmed down.

"Our reunion." I wanted to reach out and hold her. I wanted to reassure her. I wanted to be near her. But I couldn't. Was it because of the pride, the guilt, the embarrassment? I couldn't tell the difference anymore.

"I didn't know if there would ever be a reunion," she said.

We walked on, letting a few more moments pass in silence. She said, "Were you hoping I'd divorce you?"

"No. I never wanted that," I said.

"What then? I've had offers, you know." A smirk flickered across her face.

I wasn't sure what that meant, but I knew what she was fishing for. I shook my head. "That's not what this was about." But it occurred to me that there had been someone else in my life all along. Me. I'd put my own problems and my own needs above Rhiana's, and it had led to an impossible situation.

"What was it about, Kam? The whole thing. You left me without any explanation."

Our hands touched in passing, and I wondered if she had done it on purpose. It would have been nice if she had. I'd never stopped loving Rhiana. When I left Seattle bound for Timor-Leste, I'd convinced myself that I was doing it for her—that she'd be better off without me. Now I realized who I was doing it for. We had a lot to work out, and we weren't going to do it walking on the streets of Paris. Maybe if we could come together on this mission, we could come together on a few other things, too.

"Why the note this morning?" I asked. "Why not just meet me and we could have talked?"

"I couldn't get away from our group. Clyde is in charge of the trip. He's the only one who knows who I really am. The others will be with us until we get to Yemen and get our travel passes. Madeline has forged a gender bond with me, and she's deathly afraid to travel— don't tell her I told you that. It was just easier to send you a message than break from the group. Clyde set it up and watched the delivery for me."

"I didn't know who *R* was."

"I've been signing things with the letter *R* since before we met," she said.

"But, in my own defense, I've been an idiot since long before that."

Rhiana half smiled. "Didn't they tell you anything in Dili?"

"Yeah, they told me to get on an airplane and James Bond would meet me at a hotel in Paris."

"That's it?"

"Yup. So now what?" I asked.

"'Now what' the mission, or 'Now what' us?"

"Both, I suppose. I know we can't put our lives back together before Madeline wonders where you've gone, but . . ." We'd walked a good distance from the Raw Pig, so we picked out a stone bench at a street-side park and sat down.

"A lot has happened in the last year. I've gone back to work. A lot of things have changed," Rhiana said.

I wanted to know what kind of things, besides her last name, and I wanted the specifics, but I couldn't bring myself to ask about us, not yet. "And this mission?"

"There's not a lot I can say right now. Operational security."

"At least give me the briefing I was promised in Dili. You can lie if you want. Go ahead, shine me on."

"You're too smart for that," she said. She put her head down and thought for a moment. I don't know if she was deciding what kind of lie to tell me or how much of the truth to divulge.

"Telling me I'm too smart to be shined on is just a clever way to shine me on. I may not be in your league, but I've been shined on by the best of 'em. Do you want me to name names?"

Once she'd made her decision, she looked up and said, "We need the research team until we secure our travel documents in Sana'a. The research team is expected by the Yemeni office of tourism, and we'll have more freedom to travel outside of the cities as part of their team than on our own."

"I guess that means you're not going to be traveling on a diplomatic passport."

"No, we're visiting professors, at least I am. You're our interpreter," she said.

"I'm not the cook?"

"Once we're in Yemen, we'll separate from the group. I'll be able to tell you more then."

"So now I just tag along?"

"You and I can't spend much time together," Rhiana said. "We don't know each other, and you're supposed to be beneath us all. We're professors and you're . . ."

"How come you get to be the professor?" I was hurt by the prospect of having to keep Rhiana at a distance, but I could see she was right.

"You're lucky I don't turn you back into the cook." Rhiana fidgeted with her ring finger, which was glaringly bare. "Kam?" she said.

"Yeah?"

"Before we go ahead with this, I need to know . . . Do you really want to be here? I mean, now that you know this involves me?"

As I hesitated, the hopeful light in Rhiana's eyes dimmed. I don't know why it took me so long to formulate an answer. It was an easy one. How about "I love you and I never want to be away from you again"? But instead, all I could say was, "I have no place else to be."

* * *

After enough time had passed to convince the others that we'd been signing my travel documents at the hotel, Rhiana and I made the long walk back to the Raw Pig. I stayed outside and reluctantly watched Rhiana walk away to join her colleagues, who were still seated inside the restaurant talking. I'd been the source of a lot of pain over the last year, and my guilt was made that much worse by the fact that Rhiana shared very little of the blame. Seeing her walk away, back into her old life as a CIA operative, wasn't easy.

I turned my back on Le Pied Rare and started back toward my hotel. The thought of spending the evening brooding in my room made me stop. I retrieved a postcard from my pocket and looked at it under the bluish haze of twilight. It was a picture of a jazz trio that read *Caveau de la Huchette.* I considered taking the Saint-Michel metro but figured a taxi would get me there with less chance of a major geographical catastrophe. I didn't want to be lost in Paris's underbelly; I was fluent in Arabic, but French was just plain Greek to me. I hailed a passing Citroen taxi and showed the driver my postcard. He knew the place and sped off. It occurred to me that I was running away from my problems again, but the smooth, rolling motion of the taxi lulled me into a comfortable stupor of denial.

The Caveau de la Huchette was advertised as one of the most popular jazz joints in Paris. The street front was deceptively small, decorated with a dissonant mix of wrought iron, neon, and heavy stone masonry (authentic or not I couldn't tell). It looked like something you'd find in New Orleans; of course a Parisian would argue that New Orleans was simply an inferior copy of Paris—*yeah, sure, whatever.* Jazz music and dancing took place on two floors all night long in the Caveau, which I decided to pronounce "cave-o" like a hipster. It cost me 60 francs to get in and 40 more for my first drink. I couldn't begin to tell you if that was a steal-of-a-deal or a rip-off—the relative value of a franc was completely lost on me, and besides, I was using euros and had no idea of the exchange. I slipped into a seat at a corner table in the shadows of the stone grotto and listened to the music.

I measured four comforting fingers of the amber liquid in the thick glass on the table in front of me, then leaned back and stared at it. I moved the glass around on its coaster but didn't drink. Megawati, Hans Bafus, Pat English—what did they know?

The jazz joint was really my first chance to relax and contemplate what had happened today. I swirled my drink as I considered whether this was a chance to rekindle things with Rhiana, or the death knoll of my marriage. We'd talk later. Ironic. It was the not talking that had torn us asunder before.

I looked back at my glass and noticed that it was empty. I quickly ordered another, losing a fight that I knew I'd have to face sometime. I just couldn't do it now. I spent the next two hours somewhere between panic and shame, ordering drinks and nursing them through each set the jazz trio played.

They were good, and I recognized a few of the riffs, although I couldn't put a name to very many of the songs. Each time they took five, a friendly looking young man wandered out on the small stage and played soft background music on the piano. I learned from a handbill on the table that he was a music prodigy from Tel Aviv who would be sitting in with the trio later that night. Apparently he loved to play, so he took the opportunity between sets to loosen up. I enjoyed his soft, straight style as much as I enjoyed the headliners. I watched his fingers dance across the keyboard and wondered that it had come so easily for him—a simple pleasure and a simple life. Why couldn't it be that way for me?

As evening turned to late night, the dance floor filled up and crowd noise took away from the music. I decided it was time for me to leave. I liked the music, but the atmosphere was getting to be a little too young for me, and I was suffering from jet lag and second-hand smoke inhalation. I set a few more euros on my table and stood up. Two booths away I saw the piano player hunched over his table, holding a mechanical pencil poised over a leaf of handwritten sheet music. Maybe even prodigies had to work at it.

I changed my mind and ordered another in a series of "last" drinks, drank it quickly, and made it out the door just as a rowdy group of college bar-hoppers came in. It was great timing.

The September night air wasn't bitter cold, but it was fall in the northern hemisphere and my body clock was set for Timor-Leste in spring. I shivered once and pulled my light jacket collar close around my neck.

"Excuse me, sir." The feminine voice was quiet, almost timid. I turned and saw an alluring set of olive eyes framed within the rectangular opening of a heavy black burqa. The Arab head covering caught me off guard outside the jazz club, but it wasn't unfamiliar to me. "Excuse me, Mr. Daniels?" the woman said.

"Kam," I said, my eyes locked on hers. I didn't know her, but her eyes reminded me of the haunting, searching eyes of the Afghan Girl staring at me from the cover of *National Geographic*.

"Don't leave yet," she said in English with only a very slight accent. "Let's go back inside."

"Inside?" I said, looking around at the people milling in front of the Cave-o. *Another CIA contact? A come-on?*

She nodded her head slightly and repeated what she'd said before. "Quickly. Inside. There is danger here." She glanced down the street.

"Wait. Who are you?" I tried to grab her shoulder.

"I have to go. When you find them, tell them *he is*." She shrugged away from me and disappeared wraithlike into the darkness of the Paris streets.

"But wait. Who?" I called after her. *Find who? Tell them he is what?*

CHAPTER 7

A small crowd of friends exchanging good-byes lingered near the door of the jazz joint. I looked for the mysterious Arab girl who'd just told me that I was in danger, but she was gone. It didn't matter. I ran my palm over my stinging eyes.

The crowd disappeared into the Caveau de la Huchette, and I took a few tentative steps away from the front door to the Cave-o, looking back over my shoulder for the girl. All too late I felt the familiar hot prickling of adrenaline on my spine as an Arab, larger than me and with a face that looked like a cross between Mick Jagger and Gonzo the Muppet, started toward me from across the street. I turned and thought about asking the man what he wanted, but the faraway look in his coal-black eyes left me no doubt about what it was he wanted.

Another group of students, laughing and paying no attention to me, passed on their way into the jazz joint. Against the pressure of the Arab's burning stare, I turned behind the kids and followed them back to the safety of the Caveau crowds. But I was one step too late.

Just inside the wide entryway of the club, I felt the powerful force of the Arab's hand on my shoulder and turned to look into his hateful black eyes. I was a skilled fighter, having been in my share of bar brawls as a police officer, but I didn't overestimate my odds. Unlike a drunken husband who will back down when the odds aren't in his favor, I knew this man would fight—and this time, I was the drunken husband. It didn't feel very good.

I took a polite step sideways hoping to slide by him, but his tall, lanky body blocked the doorway. The Arab put his lips to my ear and said in perfectly enunciated Arabic, "Shut your mouth or you will meet Satan without the top of your head." Not your typical French mugger.

The Arab produced a nickel-plated semiautomatic pistol from his pocket and made sure I caught a glimpse of it in his hand before he brought it up and rested it along my throat at the base of my cheek.

During my career as a police officer, hundreds of people, mostly women attending safety workshops, had heard me warn of the dangers of letting a bad guy take you to a secondary crime scene—the place you're taken to be killed. "Might as well be killed in front of everybody," I'd say. "Scream for all you're worth," I'd tell them. "The chance of being shot by a mugger is pretty low. If they do shoot, the chance that they'll hit you is even lower. If the bullet does strike you, what's the chance of it being a fatal hit? The odds, according to the FBI's unerring database of information about such things, are single digit." It sounded so good coming from the FBI. Not so good now. The barrel felt roughly the size of a lightbulb socket pressing into the underside of my chin. Where was that FBI statistics guy now, when I needed him to reassure me of those single-digit chances that this guy was only going to wing me?

Most Arabs, myself included, were pretty nice people and would condemn armed robbery, but I was pretty sure this wasn't about the money in my wallet. I was also pretty sure this guy had planned for this to take place away from the club and not in the threshold of its front doors.

A twenty-something woman was standing near the host's station being helped into a knee-length leather overcoat by an overly tan man trying to look half his age in an open-front disco shirt with gold chains draped against his hairy chest. The woman saw us in the doorway and recoiled, drawing the attention of the Arab. While his attention was split between me and the woman, I threw myself out the door and grazed my face on the sidewalk as I fell into the gutter outside the club.

"*Shaytan,*" the Arab said through his clenched teeth as he came after me.

Stumbling to my feet, I took off as fast as my legs could take me. *FBI statistics, don't fail me now.*

Which of us would prove to be the fastest I couldn't know, but I was determined to make the man work to catch me. Had the Arab stopped and taken aim with his pistol, my history on the planet would have come to an abrupt and ignominious end. But fortunately for me, he pursued instead. Trying to shoot a gun on the run is a lot like trying to thread a needle on a roller coaster. But if I hadn't run away, I'd be as good as dead. I guess what I told thousands of Seattle soccer moms was pretty good stuff. Snaps to the FBI.

I hadn't paid enough attention to where I was during my taxi ride to the Cave-o, and I had no idea where I was running. Ideally, it would serve my purposes best to run toward a populated area and either disappear into a crowd or at least use witnesses to dissuade my pursuer from ripping me limb from limb and disposing of the leftover parts in the Seine River.

My most immediate problem was that, like most normal humans—and non-Olympian athletes —I possessed a finite capacity to exert myself at maximal intensity. And the alcohol wasn't helping. Put more succinctly, I was running out of steam and my pursuer was still back there, running after me and yelling caustic comments in Arabic, most of which were drowned out by the deafening pounding of my heart.

Ahead of me, a hundred yards away, I could see a string of head-lights that promised to be a main road. I didn't dare look back, but I feared I was losing my lead as my thighs burned for lack of oxygen. Another hundred yards at a dead sprint, which had slowed noticeably for both of us, was a long, long way. The only thing keeping me going was my fear of a painful death. I was so tired I might have conceded if I had thought he'd kill me mercifully and without a great deal of discomfort. From what I knew about the Middle East, I doubted he'd give me the benefit of the doubt, even if he was after the wrong man. Somehow I doubted that too, and I had yet another issue to take up with *R*—if I ever saw her again.

By now I felt like I was running through waist-deep green silly-slime, and despite my lead, the voice of the angry Arab was getting closer. I pushed forward, moving ever so slowly closer to the thoroughfare that, as it turned out, had been more than a hundred yards away. *That's France for you,* I thought. Meters didn't make any sense to me anyway.

I turned back to check my lead, and when I turned my head forward again a brilliant explosion erupted before my eyes, and my body lost contact with the ground until the pavement of the Paris street clawed at my jacket as I rolled helplessly over a curb and struck the side of a building.

"Shaytan." The words hissed in my ear as the darkness closed in on me and the footsteps of the pursuing Arab faded into the night.

Lights flashed before my eyes, and a short chorus line of denim-clad legs surrounded me. I heard a familiar sound that took a few moments for me to recognize—gravel crunching on pavement beneath the tires of a vehicle gearing down to stop. There was a flurry of excited French, and then I felt a hand on my chest.

"Up," I said, trying to get my arms under me to push.

"English," the man touching my chest told his friend. He helped me to my feet and steadied me until I pushed his hands away and tried to stay upright on my own power. I wavered for a few moments before the pavement reached up and slapped me again, despite the several pairs of hands that tried to break the fall.

"You ran into the street," I heard in accented English from a young man kneeling over me. "I couldn't stop. It was too sudden."

"I was being chased." I looked into the young man's face. A small crowd had gathered, and faces looked down on me from all directions. "A mugger."

"I couldn't stop," repeated the young man.

It wasn't until then that I realized I'd been struck by a car and that the young man was the driver. There was a buzzing going on in my head, and the muscles in my face wouldn't allow my mouth to function correctly.

"Hospital?" the young man said to some of the bystanders. Several of them shrugged and there was more discussion in French.

"Hotel," I said. "Bastille?" I couldn't get the rest of the hotel's name to come to mind. Apparently it was enough. I drifted in and out until a taxi summoned by a bystander with a cell phone arrived and I was helped inside. The Frenchman negotiated with the taxi driver and paid him enough to get me where I wanted to go.

My hotel wasn't far away, and as we pulled up at the lobby doors, I fumbled for more money and gave the driver far more than he was owed. He thanked me with a grateful smile and left me to stumble across the sidewalk and through the doors.

It was early morning, and the lobby was unoccupied but for the lone clerk who looked up at me with wide eyes. I didn't know what my face looked like, but from the intensity of the sting, I could imagine. I put my head down and stepped directly to the elevator.

By the time I was in my room, I had no desire to lick my wounds or check the mirror. I crept gingerly onto the bed and propped my jaw on the pillow. There I stayed until the first light of the morning glowed through the 1960s drapes.

CHAPTER 8

The morning after being attacked at the jazz joint and run over in the street, I met my traveling partners on an airport bus in front of the hotel. By then I'd had a chance to see myself. The facial bruising, worse on my jawline, was thankfully slightly camouflaged by a day's growth of beard, but there was no way I could explain the multidirectional abrasions. I looked as though I'd been beat up by a disc sander.

When Rhiana saw me at the curb holding my duffel bag and sporting road rash all over my face, she came directly to my side.

"Kam, what happened?" she asked.

"You tell me," I said.

More discreetly, and looking over her shoulder for Madeline, her conjoined twin, she asked, "Who and where?"

I turned toward her to explain, but at that moment two inconvenient things happened. First, Darrin wandered out of the hotel doors carrying two suitcases and a carry-on. He made it right up to us before he noticed my face and recoiled slightly at the sight. "What happened to you?"

"I fell down the stairs."

I could see his pre-PhD brain trying to reconstruct the accident and account for the various angles at which the stairs, the walls, and the handrails must have accosted me. "Flip," he said.

I wasn't sure if that was an epitaph or a description of what he thought happened to me, but I didn't want to get into the details with anyone else until I'd had a chance to talk to Rhiana.

The second inconvenience occurred as Rhiana reached for my chin to get a better look at the damage. She smelled what I would have called in a police report "the stale odor of intoxicants" on my breath.

Her eyes asked the next obvious question, and I shook my head. "A couple . . . last night. That's all," I said under my breath to her.

Rhiana's eyes closed slowly as she shook her head.

Darrin had gone to the side of the arriving bus and was loading bags onto a sheet-metal shelf inside.

Rhiana looked at me and wrinkled her nose. "Forget to pack your toothbrush? Don't point your breath at anyone, and see if you can get the window down." She no longer seemed concerned—just angry.

We all made it to Charles de Gaulle International Airport without another Kam-related incident, and it was a good three hours later before we boarded the plane. I had a chance to brush my teeth several times, and I chewed a half a tin of cinnamon Altoids that I picked up at the airport gift shop. At that point, my mouth was in worse pain than my face. Aspirin didn't do a thing.

No one in our group bought my story of falling down the stairs, but they were too polite to call me on it. I might have come up with something more original. Rhiana ignored me as promised, and even though I understood the procedural reasons, it hurt.

Taking spy secretary Miss Davidson's advice, I put my best effort into being unnoticed by the small group of intellectuals, who weren't very socially oriented anyway. Except, of course, Darrin, who, using lots of big words that you only hear in college, told me about the subtle changes in the way Arabs in the U.S. observed their religions and . . . blah, blah, blah. By the time he used the word *hegemony* twice I was no longer following his thesis—and at *penultimate* I tuned out completely. *Thank you, Darrin. The world no longer needs Nytol.* But, in fairness to Darrin, his mind-numbing recitation did take the edge off my pain.

Although no one said anything about it, I could tell by what they didn't say about Yemen or the Middle East that the members of our group had a few jitters. Terrorism was always a concern when Westerners, especially Americans, traveled in the Middle East. Precautions were just part of the game. During a moment of silence in the bus, I mentioned that the cities of Sana'a, Ti'azz, and Aden were fairly safe, but I guess they weren't fans of the word *fairly.* No one talked to me after that.

Having been to Yemen many times, I knew what to expect and didn't worry too much about the dangers. I had my own issues to contend with as the six of us waited in various lines and eventually boarded the direct flight to Sana'a on Yemenia Airways. It wasn't as scary as it sounded.

After a prolonged wait at the gate, I shuffled onto the plane and took a seat across the aisle from Darrin and between Clyde and Father Andrew in the emergency exit row. I tried several different sitting positions to deal with the discomfort I owed to my night on the town until I found a way to sit that didn't make me want to scream. Then I looked around.

A woman alone with an infant fought a valiant battle with her jacket, her carry-on, a diaper bag, and a wiggling baby and looked as if she were about to lose it when a seasoned Arab-looking business traveler, who'd probably spent more time on a plane than the pilots, shored up her flank by taking the carry-on and stuffing it into the overhead. There were a fair number of Arabs on the plane, none of whom seemed bent on killing me. Still, I was wary.

I tried to avoid looking directly at Rhiana, who had chosen an aisle seat next to Madeline, just ahead of me across the aisle. I had to admit, she looked pretty good considering she was haggard by the day's work—and it was only 0900 local. I'd noticed a long time ago that Rhiana was one of those women who got prettier as the day wore on. I wondered what she'd look like by 1200 hours, or better yet by 1730. I still loved her—I'd never stopped.

The passengers were settling in, several fidgeting in their seats in an attempt to control their anxiety, and others ready to endure the boredom of the flight. Darrin was sitting directly across the isle from me and was untangling the headphone cords to an MP3 player.

As the attendants prepared to secure the cabin door, a late passenger was allowed to board. It was the same man I'd seen writing on his PDA when I checked into the Hotel Bastille Speria. He still wore his fashionably conservative leather Ike jacket, but not the houndstooth driving hat. He scanned the passengers with quick, intelligent eyes under thick, graying brows. No carry-on, I noticed as he passed the steward station. When his eyes met mine, he quickly looked away, then passed me without another glance and sat to the rear of the cabin. We were already twenty minutes behind schedule. Thanks, Tardy Man.

The Yemenia Airways 737 took off with a rush and pointed itself southeast for the nine-hour direct flight to Yemen's capital city, Sana'a. Rhiana had insisted on a nonstop since it best ensured that our luggage would meet us at our destination instead of going off to Jakarta or Kuala Lumpur.

Once we leveled off and the captain reassured us over the intercom that we were flying at the correct altitude and bearing, Darrin leaned over to eavesdrop on a riveting conversation between Clyde and Father Andrew.

Father Andrew said, "Yes, but I think the new Pope will keep that kind of thing in check. He's been pretty conservative so far."

What they were actually talking about, I didn't know.

Clyde said, "Do you think significant policies will be affected?"

Father Andrew gave the question a shrug. "What do you think, Darrin?"

"Oh, uh," said Darrin from across the aisle, where he sat beside a clean-cut Arab twenty-something young man in Western clothes. "Well, every religion has a group of, uh . . ." He looked around, conscious of anyone within earshot. I squirmed a little at Darrin's shyness; it was brutal. ". . . self-proclaimed progressives who have convinced themselves of their superiority over the organization's representatives. They often make the unsubstantiated claim that the rank and file are less acquainted with, uh, the real world." Darrin looked like he thought he might have offended someone. "They don't, uh, usually know what they're talking about. The less vocal and more numerous stabilizing members of the organization generally have a, uh, a clue. And, they are the ones living in the real world."

Intellectual discourse with a Generation X vibe.

Clyde, sitting closest to Darrin, said, "I can buy that."

Father Andrew nodded. "Works for me."

Indubitably, I thought. *And you are strange ducks.*

Darrin sank back to his seat and retreated to the comfort of whatever was on his MP3 player.

Clyde glanced over to see that Darrin was cocooned away in his headphones, then shrugged. "He's got a way with words . . . a way to go," he said, more to Father Andrew than to me. "I hoped bringing him along would loosen him up a little. He's very bright."

Father Andrew was smiling. "I can tell. I wish more of our young priests were as astute. They get out of the seminary thinking that the rest of the world is living in some kind of never-never land. Especially in smaller communities."

"You don't have a monopoly on that problem. I've heard the you're-not-living-in-the-real-world argument more than a few times," said Clyde.

Father Andrew said, "It usually takes them a month or two of hearing confessions to wise up. Once the choir director tells you her real problems, you tend to wish the whole world were a little more naïve." Father Andrew leaned over me to get closer to Clyde. "Any chance he could give next month's sermon?"

Clyde returned a conspiratorial nod. "Pretty good chance in our church."

The two sages laughed politely, both well-mannered enough to respect the other's ways. I liked these guys—Mormon, Catholic, or not.

"You've been to Yemen before?" I asked.

"Second trip," said Clyde. "Five years ago we mapped the travels of Lehi through the wilderness. We mapped from Jerusalem south through Saudi, then we started to map Yemen. September Eleventh cut things short, and then we lost our grant. There's still a lot to do. This time, though, we want to look closer at the cultures along Lehi's proposed route and not so much the geography."

"Lee-who?" I asked.

"Lehi. A prophet written about in the Book of Mormon. He and his son Nephi took their families to the Americas just before Jerusalem was taken into captivity."

"I didn't think there was an America back then."

Father Andrew wasn't talking, but he was listening.

"There wasn't," Clyde said, "but the land mass was here. It's referred to in the Book of Mormon as the promised land. We call it the Americas from hindsight."

"So, Lehi was a Yemeni?"

"Well, it wasn't Yemen back then. And he was from Jerusalem, but we believe he spent some time in Yemen on his journey into the wilderness. We think Lehi's family probably traveled along the incense trail, where they could take advantage of established wells and the existing social and economic infrastructure. By looking at the relative distances and by comparing them to Book of Mormon records of Nephi's children's births, we've learned that the family of Lehi probably made it well into Yemen and turned east on the incense trail within a year of leaving Jerusalem. The Book of Mormon indicates a place name in the Yemen area called Nahom. And an ancient stone marker bearing the name Nahom was discovered in Yemen relatively recently—by archeologists of another faith." Clyde waited, eyes gaping open, for me to have a religious epiphany. I didn't—but maybe I should have.

"Is that important to you?" I asked.

"Well, certainly. The discovery of the Nahom marker is . . ."

"No, not that. Didn't you believe in your religion before this marker thing? Is it that important to you that someone else discovered something about your religion?"

"Well, it certainly lends credence to . . ." Clyde said, then stopped mid-sentence.

A bell went off, and the captain gave us all permission to roam about the cabin as long as we had someplace to go and as long as we didn't hang out near the forward cabin. Rhiana sidestepped out of her seat and made her way to the back of the cabin, inviting me to join her with a firm nod of her head.

Clyde was deep in thought, so I excused myself and followed Rhiana to the rear.

"I need to tell you about last night," I said as we reached the rear restroom door.

Rhiana slowly placed her tensed fingers on the bridge of her nose. "What?" She didn't sound very receptive.

I gave her a moment, then said, "An Arab guy tried to kill me last night. I ran away and got hit by a car."

"Part of some drunken brawl?" Rhiana said a little too loudly. The passengers in the rear seats didn't seem to notice us, although I knew eavesdropping was an international pastime on airplanes.

I spoke more softly. "He called me *Satan.*"

Rhiana's eyes closed slowly on that revelation. She took a deep breath, held it, and then let it out. "You weren't hurt?"

"Is that a rhetorical question? Have you seen my face?" So much for wifely pity.

"I need to think for a minute," she said.

"Obviously you know something I don't. What about the woman who warned me?" I asked.

"What woman?" That revelation seemed to take Rhiana off guard.

"Outfitted in Muslim garb. Nice touch. Is she with you?"

If Rhiana had articulated what her eyes were expressing, she might have said something indelicate. But, in classic Rhiana stoic style, she repressed everything and drew a veil of cold professionalism over her face. "Did you tell anyone else about this?"

I almost said no, because that was the truth. "Uh, I told Darrin."

"What?"

"I told the taxi driver who dragged me home last night," I said.

"Kam." Rhiana had never been one for teasing. I felt it broke the tension. I was wrong. "Stop it," she said.

"I told Father Andrew. In confession. He said I had to go back and apologize for getting my blood all over the Parisian streets and for pointing my feet toward Mecca as I careened over the hood of the car. Very wrong of me."

"Do you think you're funny?"

"What? You haven't told me anything, Rhiana. I'm completely in the dark." I hadn't set out to be angry, but I suddenly found myself spoiling for an argument.

"I will tell you when we get to Yemen. This isn't the place." She looked around again, and although I doubted anyone could hear us, I think our body language was completely understandable to the other passengers. Agitation has a way of being transparent.

I pressed my advantage and said, "What kind of operation begins under a cloud of secrecy between operatives? I'll tell you: a bad one. One that gets swept under a thick government carpet, or worse, one that gets a whole bunch of good people fired . . . or killed."

"Kam, I . . ."

"And you haven't told me anything about why *I'm* here. And don't bother telling me it's for my Arabic. The CIA must have hundreds of fluent agents licking their chops for an assignment like this."

Rhiana had gone quiet and calm, despite her usual private but fiery demeanor with me. "You're making a scene."

I wasn't, or maybe I was. I bit my lip.

"We have a few things to work through," she said. "No one knows about the Arab last night?"

"Work through?" I whispered to her. "How long do you think these MENSA candidates are going to buy this? How long do you think these people are going to buy that you're a college professor?"

"Clyde is aware of who I am and will run interference. Besides, unlike some other people here, I did my homework."

"Oh, right. Like I said, all they told me was . . ."

"You don't have to be a part of this, Kam. You can be on the next flight out of Yemen. But don't you dare blow this." Rhiana was generally a very serious person, but this wasn't just her putting on a stern face and making an idle threat. She was reacting from a place very deep inside her soul.

I decided to lighten up a little. "I didn't tell anyone," I said. "But I won't be a pawn in your little game of checkers."

Rhiana's face didn't change. "If the game is checkers, you wouldn't be a pawn."

"Well good, because I won't . . . What? Why are you so smug?"

"I'll let you figure it out, Einstein."

I did. "I'm about ready to tell everyone on this plane I've been shanghaied by the Milton Bradley metaphor police. How about that?"

Rhiana nearly laughed. "I'm surprised you knew it was a metaphor, and at this point, telling anyone anything would be treason."

"Oh, sure. Arrest me for treason against board games and the English language. I'd like to be at that trial."

"You would be," she said. "You'd be the defendant." Rhiana didn't laugh when she torpedoed a person with sarcasm. "We can't talk here. You've got to play along, at least until we get into Yemen. These people expect you to be a minor player. Please don't be a drama queen and get everyone wound up. And your face is bleeding."

"Yeah, and my teeth won't be biting into an apple for a month," I said, rubbing my jaw. I glanced up the aisle at Darrin starting to drift off to the quiet sounds of whatever was playing on his newfangled device. Probably a sociology lecture. It was sad, in a pathetic sort of way.

Rhiana said, "The cover I've designed for you is that although inexplicably bright with Arabic, you're otherwise slow, dull-witted, and don't talk much to people."

"You just made that up," I said.

"Yes, but we're going with it."

"I'm dull-witted? Do you really think I can pull that off? Sir Laurence Olivier, I'm not. I've never had any formal theater training."

"Then quit acting like a goober."

"A goober?" I said. "You're a Central Intelligence Agency operative, and you just called me a goober."

Rhiana whispered, "CIA case officer, and I called you a goober because you are one. If anything else comes up, just keep it consistent and as real as you can. And, by the way . . ."

"What?"

Rhiana leaned over, touched me graciously on the shoulder, and spoke into my ear. "I didn't have to invite you on this trip. And I don't tolerate men who pout." Then, loud enough to be heard, she straightened up and said, "I'm so sorry, Kam. When I made the arrangements, I had no idea you were this terrified of flying."

"I wasn't . . ." There were a lot of eyes on me, and I realized that even though no one could have heard our earlier conversation, Rhiana and I were the center of attention. "I'm not a drama queen," I whispered. Then I gave up and sauntered back toward my seat. The women looked at me sympathetically, and the men were suppressing laughter. Over my shoulder, loud enough for all the passengers to hear, I said, "Yemen—can't live with 'em, can't live without 'em." Pretty funny on a plane bound nonstop to Yemen. Some of the men broke their silence and laughed out loud, but the women probably didn't appreciate cheesy chauvinist humor at the expense of their gender.

I startled Clyde when I returned to my narrow seat next to him. He seemed a little preoccupied, but he was a long, long way from Utah—in a number of important ways.

Clyde slid his legs to the side to let me into my seat and then leaned over me to look out the window at the vast expanse of water below us. "The Med?"

I took a look. "The world's biggest bathtub."

"I've been thinking about what you said."

"What did I say?"

"It isn't very important—or it shouldn't be. I guess I got my faith and my knowledge mixed a little. Point taken," he said.

I said a lot of things, probably too much, but I rarely made a good point. I was intrigued but at a loss.

Clyde said, "About who discovered the Nahom marker."

"Yeah, well, just a thought." I was still completely lost.

"Have you ever been there?" Clyde asked pointing out the window.

"On the Mediterranean? Yeah, once. I remember my dad took us to Turkey in '86. We stopped by Greece for a dip."

"You've always been a world traveler, then?"

"My mother is Yemeni. We went back and forth once in a while. Yourself?"

"Yemen, five years ago on the trip I told you about. I always wanted to travel. You know, on kind of an academic adventure."

"Indiana Jones?" I believed it; he had the right attitude. "I've been to Utah. Skiing," I said after a short silence.

"Greatest snow on earth," said Clyde.

"Especially if you grow up skiing on rain. On my first trip to Utah, I didn't know there was such a thing as *feet* of snow. I wiped out, lost a ski in three feet of powder, and had to rent for the next week."

"Bummer," said Clyde.

"It was the best ski week of my life."

"Utah has its charms."

"Can I ask you something about that?" I said.

"Utah's charm?" he asked.

"No, not really that. But nothing heavy," I said.

"Nothing heavy?"

I was pretty certain that Clyde really was a BYU religion professor. That would be hard to fake, even for the CIA. But he also knew something about why Rhiana and I were traveling with his group. I considered asking him what he knew outright but decided against it. Honesty might be a good policy, as I'd learned from years of police work, but it's a terrible interrogation technique.

"I'm interested in your church and wanted to talk with you about it," I told Clyde, thoroughly lying.

"I thought you said nothing heavy." Clyde laughed. "What do you consider light conversation?"

"I don't mean to pry; I just thought that as long as I was going to be . . ."

"No, no, I love to talk about the Church. It's just not every day someone walks up and asks like that."

"I gather you guys don't drink alcohol." That about summed up my knowledge of Mormons.

"That's a dull place to start. There are a lot of people who don't drink. And the reasons are so obvious. Tell me, what else do you know about Mormonism?"

I'd plumbed the depths of my religious knowledge in my first statement, but I didn't want to appear too ignorant. What exactly did I know about Mormons? "Tell me about that Mormon book."

Clyde had a wonderfully disarming smile, one that told me I was terribly ignorant and that it was okay. "That's a great place to start," he said. "The real name of our church is The Church of Jesus Christ . . ."

Rhiana chose that moment to interrupt. Leaning around in her seat, she said, "Clyde, when you have a minute, we need to go over tomorrow's itinerary." She looked at me. I couldn't tell if she'd heard what we were talking about or not, or if her play for Clyde's attention was meant to prevent me from making another conversational spy faux pas. "Whenever," she said. "It's a long flight." She whipped back around, flinging her shiny black hair. If she knew I was going to pump Clyde for information, she didn't show it. But I knew she knew. I just did.

"So it's not really the Mormon Church," I said.

What followed from Clyde was a lecture, not completely uninteresting, about the origins of the Mormon religion. I found out quickly that the Mormons, despite what might be believed in mainstream society, did not worship a golden book.

I hadn't done a lot of wondering about concepts like truth and religion, having been caught up in just trying to make my life work. Most of what Clyde said could be filed under, "If I'd wanted to know I'd have asked," but a few things intrigued me.

"So," I said, "what about all the other religions and beliefs out there? Doesn't it seem mathematically unlikely that there are no other true religions out there?"

"Hmm, mathematically speaking?" Clyde leaned back in his chair. "Does it make a thing any less true when it's surrounded by conflicting ideas?"

I thought for a minute. "But there are so many good ideas in so many different religions," I said. Not that I was any kind of expert.

"That, I won't argue with. There's a lot of truth out there."

"I suppose," I said, not sure I agreed entirely, but not sure why I shouldn't. "But does anyone really know what's true?"

"That argument has been leveled at just about every organized religion throughout history. Unimaginative, if you ask me."

I suppose I had asked, and I was probably pretty near the bottom of the imagination scale. I shrugged and nodded at the same time—complete ambiguity of response. If in doubt, bail out.

"A lot of people struggle with that. I look for answers—some I get and some I don't. But," he said, "just because I don't get an answer for every question doesn't mean there isn't one."

I gave up another shrug and nod.

Clyde said, "You have to start somewhere. Do you believe in God or a deity of any kind? That's a place to start."

"Yes." I said the word, but it felt a little funny. I felt a little disingenuous because I'd never given religion, or my belief in God, much place in my life.

"Good, now let me tell you what I believe about God and where we came from and how we came to be in the state we're in." The things Clyde went on to tell me about the origin and destiny of mankind were ideas that had never entered my mind before. I had no idea that Mormonism laid claim to such a broad concept of the purpose of life, including the purpose of a savior. It sounded so clear when he explained it but so far removed from my experience with life. I didn't have much of a response, and I was pretty uncomfortable anyway. When Clyde wound down, I decided to change the direction of the conversation and make my play for a little information about my current circumstance.

"Rhiana hasn't told you much about me, has she?"

"No, not really. Only that you possess a special language skill. She worried that you wouldn't volunteer. I don't really know how things work in your . . ." he leaned closer and glanced at Father Andrew, who was working his way through a thick book that looked unbeliev-ably boring, ". . . line of business."

"This isn't my line of business," I said. I was probably saying too much. Having an intimate conversation with someone was probably the fastest way to blow a cover. I needed to get him talking before I said something stupid. "Did she say anything else about me or my role here?"

Clyde didn't respond for a moment. He was fidgeting with an airline magazine written in squiggly Arabic. I wasn't fooling anyone, except maybe myself.

"The only thing Rhiana told me was that she felt very strongly about having you with us." Clyde laughed and then looked over at Darrin, who was asleep. My guess is that he wasn't faking the mouth-wide-open-slobbery-chin look. Clyde went on. "Guides who speak English are all over in Sana'a. You don't get far without one. We delayed our trip for three days waiting for you—and you specifically. I'm assuming you are a key player. Anything else you want to know, you'll have to ask her yourself."

I shrugged it off as if I knew everything anyway.

Clyde shoved the magazine into the seat pocket and said, "For what it's worth, I think your being here has very little to do with your language skills," Clyde turned his head toward me and said under his breath, "and a lot to do with whatever is . . . or was . . . between you and Rhiana."

Score one for naïve Mormons everywhere. Clyde didn't miss much.

CHAPTER 9

Our plane landed at Sana'a International Airport in Yemen not quite eight hours after takeoff; the place was the quintessential study in inefficiency. The building, about the size of a modest grade school, was not as large and accommodating as some of the world travelers on the flight had expected. I visited the men's room as a first order of business and was hesitant to use the plumbing to wash my face. I need not have worried, because no water came out of the spigot when I turned it on. Having been to this very airport several times, I wasn't surprised.

The queue to get passports stamped was not long but was moving at a pace that rivaled the curing of paint. Each time the line moved an infinitesimal distance toward the immigration counter, I would moan, "Yemeni, Yemeni, Yemeni, what is going on here?" to the complete distraction of Rhiana.

Once we made it to the desk, the officer seemed very interested in knowing who Rhiana was married to and the whereabouts of her marriage license. The Middle East was like that. She kept telling the man that her marriage was immaterial, but he didn't seem to understand, seeming to be completely illiterate in English except in his ability to ask official immigration questions. Finally she took Clyde's hand and smiled sarcastically. The officer seemed to get the point and let them through. I passed inspection without a second look, but I very dearly wanted to have been the one Rhiana had turned to.

Near the baggage claim area, an army of filthy-looking but entrepreneurial young men stood guard lest anyone pass without paying them for a baggage trolley. I waltzed by without a care and picked up my one bag to add to my small carry-on for a very manageable load. The rest of the group wasn't so lucky. They had loads of equipment to pick up, and they paid nearly eighty Yemeni rials for their trolleys. I helped the other sociologists with their bags but stayed clear of Rhiana in accordance with her edict that I not make my relationship with her conspicuous.

Customs was a breeze for me and a hassle for the rest of the group. Their equipment, mostly cameras, computers, and digital voice recorders, was pawed over by half a dozen overly enthusiastic customs agents who wanted to make sure that the equipment wasn't somehow related to weapons of mass destruction. After nearly forty-five minutes of requesting supervisors and repeating their story, the scholars got their bags cleared and made it out of the airport.

The stench of a thousand port-a-potties wafted past us. The smell originated from the infamous open sewer, over which floated a flock of empty white trash bags, levitating on the warm air. *Welcome to Sana'a.*

Just outside the main doors, our group was assaulted by a host of would-be skycaps demanding to carry bags for money. They didn't need to bother, because our group had barely approached the taxi lane when another crowd, this time of competing drivers, started pulling at our bags.

Realizing that I'd been hired for just such an occasion, I spat out a few sentences in Arabic, telling the taxi drivers that we had private cars arranged and that we appreciated their concern for our transportation needs. Or something to that effect, but a bit more caustic.

The assault stopped, and Rhiana tromped off in the direction of two early-model Toyota Land Cruisers parked against a yellow curb on the far side of a planting strip that divided the drop-off area in front of the airport. Each Toyota appeared to have come equipped with a driver. Our rides, I presumed. The rest of our group followed and made a pile of bags next to the lead Land Cruiser while Rhiana spoke with the driver.

I could tell just from his look that the man talking to Rhiana from the driver's seat of the lead vehicle was a hard character. His sun-charred head was shaved to a sheen, and two coal-black eyes probed the parking lot from behind his leathered face. He spoke in soft tones with Rhiana until she nodded and turned to our small crowd to tell us to load up. The driver of the second vehicle was an exceptionally handsome young black man who might have passed for a Somalian refugee, of which there were many in Yemen, except he looked too well fed. Muscles like that didn't grow from eating rationed rice. Great. We'd drawn Vin Diesel and Denzel Washington for drivers.

It was a cramped fit, but everybody got a seat in one of the cruisers on or around the luggage. With me in one vehicle and Rhiana in another, the convoy took off on the fifteen-mile trip to the Sana'a Sheraton, where we would spend our first night. The drivers made the drop-off at the hotel and disappeared, leaving me to wonder who they were and where they went for the night.

It was two per room, and I drew Darrin as a roommate—not that I expected a room with Rhiana, but I was disappointed anyway. Darrin and I hadn't been speaking much beyond pleasantries, aside from his earlier academic discourse, because, well, Darrin didn't seem to require any unnecessary social interaction. It was so obvious, in fact, that I could sense Darrin's discomfort.

"Not thrilled with the arrangements?" I asked.

"No, it's not that." Darrin avoided eye contact.

"I'm safe," I said.

"No, really . . ." Darrin wasn't just being shy and timid; it was more than that. I caught him looking at me, and he jerked his head away.

"All right. What is it, Darrin?" I asked.

He demurred, or rather, he shrank. He set his bags on the bed and prowled into the bathroom, where he started the shower and reached for the sink faucet. "In case of listening devices," he said as he opened the valve. "You," he said in a harried whisper, "are involved in some kind of mission."

I wasn't immediately able to respond, not knowing whether to laugh or worry. After a couple of false starts, I forced a serious expression as I looked conspiratorially over each shoulder and said in a bad Russian accent, "The woods are lovely, dark, and deep . . ."

"What?" asked Darrin, scrunching up his face.

"The woods are lovely, dark, and . . ." I saw nothing but confusion on Darrin's face. "You know, like two spies exchanging bona fides on a park bench." Still nothing. "Forget it. What did Clyde tell you . . . just so I don't assume you know something that you really don't."

Darrin hesitated. He knew something. "I told Clyde I wouldn't . . ."

"It's okay. Just hit the highlights so I know where we stand."

"Let's just assume Clyde didn't say anything to me." Darrin wasn't as dumb as he looked. Actually, he didn't look dumb either and probably outscored me in IQ points by a ratio of two to one.

"Fine. We knew you were going to figure this out sooner or later," I said.

Darrin spent a few minutes sitting on the bedside lowering his blood pressure. I sat on the bed beside him. I told him a few things about myself, mostly about my Yemeni family background, and we laughed over my job interview for the cook's position. He confided in me, summoning a hidden confidence I never would have known was there, that my introduction to the group hadn't been very impressive. By the end of our conversation, I felt certain he wasn't going to reveal my true identity. Actually, I didn't care if he did or didn't as long as Rhiana didn't get one more thing to hang over my head.

Now if only I knew as much about this little trip as Darrin did, we'd be even. But I could fix that.

"Darrin, buddy. Let's go get something to eat. Maybe we can talk about your dissertation. I'm very interested." One more in a series of lies.

* * *

From the front, the Sheraton Hotel in Sana'a looked a little bit like a small version of the Rose Bowl in Pasadena. The rounded exterior and the series of small arches over the front doors made it look like a small football stadium might be hidden inside. On top sat twin signs in neon, one saying *Sheraton* in big block letters and the other saying the same thing in Arabic script. Although a Western enterprise, the interior was decorated in Turkish rugs and brass antiques, giving it a Byzantine feel. Stale tobacco odor permeated everything, but that was just the way it was in Yemen. They hadn't heard of the Clean Air Act. I wasn't a fan of the ambiance and never had been.

Seated at a table for two in the hotel restaurant with Darrin enjoying a hot bowl of Yemeni saltah, chicken soup that makes your face sweat, I took a bullet for the cause. "Tell me about your PhD," I asked.

Darrin hadn't seemed overly comfortable with me, especially since my cheesed-up face drew so much attention and was probably pretty unappetizing, but I'd said the magic words and Darrin lit up, a different incarnation of the man I'd met in Paris. "Simple really. Religions practiced close to their place of origin, or where there are a sizeable number of practitioners, are observed differently than in places further from the place of origin . . ." So far I was following him, but the clouds of boredom were on the horizon and sweeping forward.

My mind wandered. I looked at the spoon that had been placed beside my plate to make Westerners comfortable. Utensils were some-what optional in Yemen, and saltah was almost always eaten with bread—sopped up and slathered down the gullet. My grandmother claimed saltah was the most filling soup on the planet—it's the bread, Grandma. I looked around for a roll.

"Anyway," Darrin went on (and on), "when you examine the way a belief system operates in isolation, or in various degrees and mani-festations of isolation, issues like tolerance and flexibility in the reli-gious dogma become apparent and can be studied using a religious rigidity matrix that I've developed . . ." He was losing me. Not that I didn't understand, but I didn't think his studies were going to change the world. If he were on the verge of developing a better way to strain tuna, *that* would be something.

Actually, what he was droning on about was something I'd seen firsthand. My mother, a native Yemeni and thus a Muslim, came to the United States with my father with a number of ideas that she later abandoned—distrust of the West being one of them. But she'd fallen in love with an American, and by the time I knew her, she was an exotic, dark-skinned American whose religious beliefs and obser-vances had become very private. We still traveled to Yemen often, because although my mother gave up much of her ethnicity, she never gave up her family. For that I was glad, because I had great memories of family in Yemen. Even though I'd lost track of the cousins.

"And," said Darrin, draining the life from me, "as we study these trends, we get a better understanding of how globalization affects religious observance and we can project what kinds of religious controversies will plague us in decades to come." Darrin took a breath, perhaps his first during his explanation.

I'd been staring at the next table, where a middle-aged couple had dined quietly and then left a good two inches of blush wine in the bottom of a bottle that now stood as the centerpiece to their table. I wasn't a wine person, but I hadn't had a drink for a while. Darrin watched me and followed my gaze to the other table, then his eyes came in line with mine. I didn't like what I saw reflected in them.

"I don't . . ." I said without thinking.

"I'm sorry," said Darrin.

"I didn't realize you knew."

"You smelled of it in Paris and on the plane. I'm not judging you," said Darrin. It's what people say when they are judging you. He had a right to judge.

"Do you ever get tired of fighting it?" he asked.

Leave it to Darrin to ask the question of the year. "No," I said, "but I think I'm tired of losing the fight."

I think we were both embarrassed but for different reasons. Darrin retreated back to his one-man conversation about his revolutionary discoveries, and I thought about the person I'd become. Eventually, I realized that Darrin had stopped talking.

"Oh," I said, then realizing that *oh* wasn't enough, I said, "Hmm." I was almost done with my saltah, and Darrin's was getting less hot (I'm not sure the stuff ever actually gets cold).

"At BYU does your church sponsor these studies?" I asked. I thought it was a fantastic question, a question beyond my ordinary intellectual capacity.

"Sponsor?" He thought about it. "No. I mean, my major professor approves the project, and, well, they let me come on this trip. They support the research; they know I've got a very important project going. You see, the implications are . . ."

"Darrin," I interrupted, "I can see why you're here. Obviously, very important stuff. But, what about the others? Clyde, Father Andrew, Madeline . . . Rhiana?"

"Dr. Holmes," Darrin said as if I, as hired help, should maintain a subservient decorum, "is planning next year's research trip. Father Andrew and Dr. Black are along because they're academic associates of Dr. Holmes's, and they've both done some research on Yemen before. Next year's trip is going to be one of the first interdisciplinary and interfaith research projects of its kind."

"And Dr. Monroe?"

Silence—the kind that follows acute anxiety.

"What college does she come from?" I asked.

"University of Washington." Although it was clearly supposed to come out as a statement, Darrin's inflection couldn't hide the questions lurking in his mind.

If he was suspicious, then I was suspicious. That's how the manipulative mind works. "Don't you know?" I asked.

"She's a sociologist from U-Dub." Darrin looked into his bowl of saltah.

"But you've never heard of her before?"

"She studies Yemen," Darrin peeped, a couple of do-re-mis higher than normal.

"Have you studied her research?" I asked.

"Well, no."

"But you've seen her name on articles?"

"No." Darrin was getting quieter. One more negative affirmation, as we called them, should do it.

"And before Paris, you never heard her name?"

Darrin's shoulders dropped. "No. She's with you, isn't she?"

I didn't give him an answer.

The trick to twisting someone for information was to know how to dangle the bait and when to set the hook. The bait had been taken with a series of nos, and I was about to set the hook. I leaned ever so slightly closer to him. "Darrin, you didn't have any choice in this, did you?" The silence wasn't very long, but it was punctuated by one attempt to say something that came out only as a sigh.

Now to land him. "You figured it out." I didn't give him a chance to say anything. "Then you just had to follow along, didn't you?" The answer was in his eyes, but I wanted it on his lips. I put into words the way he was feeling. "It wasn't fair. They could have asked. But they didn't, did they? Clyde just added her to the group. Then he added me to the list. He never thought to tell you what he was up to. Isn't that right? And you're too polite to make an issue out of it?"

Darrin looked furtively around, but it was just the early dinner crowd. "I just had to go along with it," he said. "We were supposed to leave days ago," he said. "Clyde told me we were waiting on another scholar, a last-minute thing. I knew right away something wasn't right. We'd planned this thing for nearly a year. No one else was supposed to come. I've never even heard of her. I knew she wasn't a sociologist as soon as I met her."

The next step in this process was to cut the head off and gut the fish, a poor metaphor for what I would actually do. The bottom line was that, after taking Darrin apart, I had to rebuild him. Give him back his confidence in what was going on around him. The last thing I could afford to do was create a liability, someone who got so angry that he blew the whole operation. I had to get Darrin comfortable again, stop him from thinking too much, and reduce his anxiety. Cut off his head and take away his guts.

"I can tell you that you were supposed to be informed up front." I could be a fat liar at times.

"I was?" Darrin looked up from his bowl.

"Yeah, we need you in on this. We need a smooth player who can make the other researchers comfortable," I told him. Smooth player? I am a crackup: part ex-cop, part slick Willy used car salesman.

Darrin nodded. After all, what can you say after someone calls you a smooth player?

I'd struck pay dirt; now it was his turn to tell me something. "Actually," I said, "this isn't that big of a deal. We just need to make a few contacts and do a little diplomacy."

The quizzical look he gave me was classic textbook stuff. Darrin seemed genuinely confused, which meant that what I'd just said didn't agree with something he knew. It might take a little finesse and some time, but I was sure I could eventually weasel out of him what I wanted to know. Darrin got impatient while I was planning my next subtle chess move, adroitly calculated to reveal the purpose of this impromptu visit to Yemen.

"To locate the mass graves in Djibouti?" Darrin asked.

"Yes, to locate the mass graves in Djibouti. Precisely." It wasn't exactly what I was expecting, but pay dirt was pay dirt.

"I will do whatever you ask," he said, "I promise." Somehow, from one professional to another, "I promise" seemed a little naïve, but coming from Darrin, it was wholly convincing. "Can I tell you something?" he said.

"Sure."

"I went along with this because I'm a patriot," he said.

"I think we're all patriots, Darrin."

"No, not like that. All my life, I wanted to be a Marine," he said.

I looked at him through his fat little glasses. "A soldier?"

"Not a soldier. A Marine." Apparently Darrin was serious.

"Really?"

Darrin took off his glasses and held them up. Even from a distance I could see the light bending in the lenses. Thick.

I said, "Eyes, huh?"

He nodded. "Nothing I can do about it. I'm one of those rare Laser-Assisted In Situ Keratomileusis rejects."

"I was with you until you started speaking Eskimo."

"Eskimo isn't technically a language. Maybe *Inuit* is the word you're looking for? Inuit is the most well-known Eskimo language, followed by Yup'ik and . . ."

My body language and the blasé look on my face must have been screaming boredom.

"Oh," said Darrin. "Uh, that means LASIK surgery. I didn't qualify for the procedure."

"It's a big military. I'm sure you could have found something," I said.

"I didn't want something. I wanted the Marines. Ooh-rah."

"What does that mean, anyway?" I'd heard the familiar vocalization a hundred times and never wondered what it really meant.

Darrin shrugged. "Nobody really knows. Just a Marine thing, I guess. Maybe like *amen* or something—to put it in my vernacular."

"Semper Fi," I said, for lack of anything better to say. "Why the Marines?"

"Ever since I was little, I liked the Marines." Darrin slid his glasses back on and looked at me carefully. "This is going to sound stupid," he said.

"Try me."

"I've never really been part of a group. I never really fit in anywhere. I was sort of forgotten. I guess I kind of romanticized the Marines. They don't forget each other. They never leave a man behind."

I couldn't deny that Darrin seemed genuine about his Marine fantasy, but as I looked at him, I thought he made a better PhD candidate.

"I know what you're thinking," he said. "You're right. I would never make it as a Marine."

"You never know, Darrin. But I know a patriot when I see one. I guess I don't have to worry about you spilling the beans."

Darrin shook his head. Coming from him, it was as good as a blood oath.

I now had the Djibouti card to play on Rhiana; she'd be utterly shocked at my ability to ferret out information—but now wasn't the time to impress her. We were scheduled to meet one of Rhiana's people at the embassy, where I was sure I'd learn even more.

CHAPTER 10

The U.S. embassy in Sana'a was a building that sat alone, surrounded by what the Yemeni people might have considered gardens. It was hard to tell if the structure was a small palace or a massive home. Built in the same architectural style as the other historic buildings in Sana'a, it was a fortress of tan stone and ornate filigree colored with white gypsum powder. If you were into gingerbread houses, you'd feel at home except for the updated security doors and windows. It was five stories, each decorated with a flourish of what I had always thought of as decorative icing. In fact, the whole place reminded me of a square Victorian cake made by a very bored chef with both too much icing and too much time on his hands.

The embassy was a place Rhiana knew well, and she'd been surprisingly accommodating when I'd told her I wanted to accompany her to her meeting here. I'd seen very little of the insides of the embassy during my travels, having only had occasion to brave the stony-faced Marine guards when I needed help with a passport issue. I'd never been invited to find out what waited behind those guards. Rhiana, on the other hand, seemed to have the run of the place, because we passed the Marines at the front gate without even a sideways glance. No passport, no picture identification, no problem. Just past the guards, in a lavish anteroom decorated in hanging rugs and local art, I met Roger.

"Kam, this is Roger Jones, the cultural attaché here at the embassy," said Rhiana.

Roger wasn't fooling anyone. His hair was a nondescript color between brown and blond and was conservatively parted on the side.

He wore a dark polyester suit, white cotton shirt, cheap tie, and thin-soled shoes that probably never walked very far.

"Cultural attaché?" I asked, knowing that all CIA agents were "cultural attachés" as the need arose.

Roger smiled and shrugged. "I'm whatever they tell me."

"Roger, this is Kamir Daniels." Rhiana threw my name out as if it explained everything.

"Right." He looked at my marred face, didn't ask the obvious question, and said to Rhiana, "Do you both want to come into my office?"

Rhiana's eyes swept from Roger to me and back to Roger. The real question was, was I invited to be a confidant in the local CIA inner sanctum? If Rhiana said yes to the invitation, she was implying that she trusted me; if she said no, then . . . Judging from the look on her face, neither option suited her.

Roger came to the rescue seconds after the moment became awkward. "We can talk here. No secrets." That was spy double-talk for, "I have a lot of secrets, but I'm not telling you any of them." Implied was the idea that he was smarter than me and could provide Rhiana with a complete briefing right in front of me, and I would be none the wiser.

A dumb smile from me made him all the more confident.

Roger invited us into a reception room where I could stare up at stained-glass Roman arches and fretwork spandrels while I reclined on a twentieth-century armchair. Even within the quiet halls of the embassy, Yemen's battle between ancient and modern continued.

A short distance away, Roger and Rhiana sat facing each other on a couch that matched my chair and cunningly excluded me from their conversation.

"I think we have all the equipment you'll need," said Roger. "An encrypted satellite phone."

"And who answers that?" asked Rhiana, taking mental notes.

"Well, of course you can call here. Our numbers are programmed into the phones. There's a number for the operations center. Someone there will be monitoring your operation . . . at least by phone."

"What do you mean, at least by phone? In Washington?"

"Another center. They'll be monitoring," Roger said.

"Where? What center?" Rhiana was getting a little apprehensive.

"It's an operations center in Western Europe. It's just a little closer to the op. We thought it would be better." Roger wasn't actually perspiring, but I could sense his pores beginning to open. "Your operators will have access to their own central command center."

I was loving it; nothing better than making your boss sweat.

Rhiana pursed her lips, and she took a breath . . . more of an exasperated sigh. "Roger? Why isn't our command center in the United States or on one of her ships?"

"Well . . ."

"Our Delta Force escort isn't going to settle for anything less than absolute, ironclad protocol. We don't run operations out of foreign command centers."

"Rhiana . . ." Roger was flailing. The sun had shifted, and the stained glass painted his cheeks with a sick yellow. In a few more minutes, he'd be a pale green. ". . . You know there are always changes in these kinds of operations."

Rhiana didn't look mollified. "What changes? I want to know everything right now. We're well into this op. Assets are in place, Roger."

"Well, actually, this is an improvement," said Roger. "It's just going to take a little time to get used to the idea."

It sounded like a fabulous improvement—all government improvements should take a long time to get used to and, in the end, they shouldn't work. I leaned back in my overstuffed chair and crossed my legs, palm under my chin. I didn't even have to pay a price for admission.

"Spill it, Roger." Rhiana, the noncompromiser, was in full gear.

I was going to tell Roger that I recognized Rhiana's mood and that he should do what she asked, but he seemed to sense the same thing. Rhiana wasn't the most subtle coworker . . . or wife.

"Our situation," Roger glanced at me, trying to read my eyes, "has garnered some international attention."

I recognized that as government lingo: the cat's out of the bag, and we've lost complete control. I could have translated that to Rhiana, as her official interpreter, but she spoke government-ese better than I did.

"No, Roger," said Rhiana.

"And, we've been able to drum up additional support for the operation. That's always a good thing, wouldn't you say?" Roger was looking at me, rather than at Rhiana.

I couldn't very well agree with Roger without risking my already tenuous matrimonial situation, so I stared at him. *No love from this camp, buddy, but I do feel for you.*

"No. Roger?" Rhiana put an accusing finger up and shook her head. "Don't."

"Wait, Rhiana. Hear me out. We all want . . ." His eyes darted my way again, and he decided to rephrase. "This is a delicate situation, and certain international entities have taken notice. They seem to believe they have a stake in the outcome of this operation. They are insisting that they have assets assigned to the team, and our government isn't in a political position to say no. The more support the better."

Translation: other countries are meddling in our business. Again, I relied on Rhiana's fluency in the language of government.

When she responded, she showed a great deal of poise. "Roger. Do I look like I'm new at this?" Rhiana stood up. "Give it to me straight, or I'll do this by myself." She turned toward the exit arches. I didn't know if I was supposed to storm out behind her and thumb my nose at Roger or sit there until he kicked me out.

"Rhiana, stop," said Roger.

She did, but she didn't turn toward him.

"Rhiana, the international community wants in on this one, from the top down. You and I have no choice. I gave you everything you asked for, but you have to come partway, too. You're going to have some international company on this."

That got Rhiana turned around in a hurry. "Who?"

It was only a hunch, but I didn't think Rhiana liked international company. I leaned forward and put my elbows on my knees. I didn't want to miss a thing.

"They're Special Forces," said Roger.

"Who?" She took a step toward Roger, closing in on his personal space.

"They're elite troops."

"Who are they?" Another step and Roger was literally back-pedaling. If I was smiling now, it wasn't intentionally.

"They're French, and you met them yesterday. They're your drivers," said Roger.

I wasn't savvy enough to know what emotion I was supposed to have until I looked at Rhiana's narrowing eyes. Outrage, definitely outrage.

After a wicked moment of silence, Rhiana recovered enough composure to say, "I've worked with Delta Force before, and they won't go along with this. No way, no how. Especially not with the French."

"I know," Roger muttered. "That won't be a problem."

"I'm not going to juggle two different teams of . . . What are you saying? You told me a week ago we'd get Delta Force escorts, real soldiers from the United States. You promised me certain assets on this operation, Roger."

"Well, I got you two French soldiers. They are special forces from the *Groupe d'Intervention de la Gendarmerie Nationale* . . ." Roger paused and looked at me, this time long enough to draw Rhiana's gaze toward me looking up from my comfy chair. ". . . And I got you him."

* * *

We left the embassy in a huff, with Rhiana walking so fast that I felt like a child who couldn't keep up with his mother. Rhiana had been given about all she was going to get from Roger.

He'd issued her an encrypted iridium satellite phone equipped with a GPS transponder and a separate solar panel recharger about the size of a small notebook. Roger explained the function of both devices to a frigidly aloof Rhiana. I tried the self-possessed, laid-back look myself, but I got a little excited with the James-Bondish portable solar panel recharger.

Roger gave us more information about the security role the French GIGN soldiers would play and outlined their chain of command through the United Nations command center in Vienna. I would have bet that he was about to tell Rhiana that she would fall into the same U.N. chain of command, but then he hesitated and told her to phone her status reports directly to him. I don't know who he was kidding. I knew he'd forward those reports to the U.N. center and take his orders from them—whatever it took to mollify his high-maintenance operative.

Then, of course, there was me. Roger made a big deal of how he'd moved heaven and earth to locate me in a remote part of the world and have me recruited and brought onboard. If I was his trump card with Rhiana, he didn't have a very good hand. A dismissive look from Rhiana showed that she felt the same way.

Roger's last instructions were to play nice with the GIGN soldiers, make morning and evening status calls to him at the embassy, and avoid doing anything that would lead to a major polit-ical embarrassment or a war. I knew Rhiana, and I knew what she was capable of—the last bit of advice wasn't a polite joke.

But Roger wasn't all bad. Upon learning that the U.N. would be taking operational control of the mission, he pulled in a very private favor. He'd arranged for a parallel command center located on an aircraft carrier in the Gulf of Aden to monitor her position through the GPS function of her phone. Emergency helicopter extraction would be available for American government personnel if she made connection to a number programmed into her phone, but only under the direst circumstances, and he said *dire* about five times. I called it the "phone-a-friend" option, and they both just looked at me. They didn't watch enough TV.

As we passed the gardens outside the embassy, I asked, "Not so thrilled to be leading a multinational United Nations team of high-speed, low-drag special operators into combat?"

I got a scary look in return. "Remember, you're slow and dull-witted."

For a moment, I empathized with Roger.

Our cab arrived, and we sat in the backseat in relative silence, except for my inane questions.

"You're not still mad at them, are you?"

"Mad at whom, my government?"

"No, the French."

Rhiana shook her head, not in the mood for banter. "I'm not mad at the French."

"I've never worked with the French special forces," I said. "I've had special French salad dressing a couple of times. I've had special French fries. But never . . ."

"Stop it, Kam."

"I'm not the one who got all sour over it. Hey, did you know the French have designed a new flag . . . a white cross on a white background?"

"You're not funny," said Rhiana. "One of these days you're going to mouth off at the wrong time. There's nothing wrong with the French."

The taxi driver, who probably only understood that we were having an argument involving the French, kept peering at us in his rearview mirror.

"I didn't say there was," I said. "In fact, I think the French are great . . . chefs. You would have to be to host so many conquering armies."

Rhiana didn't even give up an irritated raise of the eyebrows. I let a few more minutes pass before I tried her again.

"How come Roger doesn't want me to know what 'the situation' is?"

That drove Rhiana out of her morose stupor. "Who said he doesn't?"

"Come on, I'm not brain-dead. The only thing he didn't do was wink twice every time he said 'situation.'"

"It's not important. That's just how Roger is."

"Then tell me what it is. Or more to the point, tell me why I'm here."

"You know why you're here. A little translating and advising on . . ."

"Rhi," I put my hand on her knee. It was comforting. I missed her. I'd been a fool. "I'm a lot of things, but maybe the only thing I'm not is naïve. And don't try to tell me that I was someone else's idea, like this French U.N. thing."

"I won't." Rhiana let out a small sigh and dropped her shoulders.

I said, "I've bitten off and chewed everything I've been told so far. One more lie isn't going to choke me. You asked for me. I just want to know why."

There followed a long silence while we both let things sink in. Hot and dusty, the city passed outside our windows as our taxi driver took our lives in his hands around every corner and along every straightaway. We pulled into the parking lot of the Sheraton Hotel, and the driver stopped at the front doors.

"Kam?"

"Yeah." I recognized the forlorn look in her eye.

"*I* asked for you. I begged. That's going to have to be enough for now."

"Well then," I said, taking her hand and squeezing it gently, *"Vive la France."*

CHAPTER 11

"The Yemeni government is not going to let us go north up the coast," I said to Rhiana as she threw open the rear doors of the hotel and searched the Sheraton gardens, twenty acres of local foliage going from spring's green to autumn's olive drab surrounding a poolside restaurant called Waves, where we were scheduled to have a clandestine meeting with our new allies.

"I told Pierre to meet us by the tennis courts." Rhiana peered through the foliage along a walking path.

I said, "Even if you miraculously get travel permits from the Yemeni office of tourism to go north—which you won't—once we get outside of Sana'a into the Yemeni countryside, it will be a different story. You know what kind of border issues the Yemeni military have with the Saudis. They probably won't even honor the permits."

"They're late."

"Do you realize what kind of people are in northern Yemen?"

"Where are they?" Rhiana checked her watch, ignored me, and forged deeper into the gardens along the path.

"The Palestine Liberation Organization for starters. They've been training there for decades. Are you listening? The Yemeni military keeps everyone out of that area. These are not the same guys who hang around Sana'a and intimidate tourists. Those are the nice ones." I found myself walking behind Rhiana, trying to keep up and wondering why I even bothered. We'd passed the tennis courts long ago. "Do you care?"

She continued to ignore me, which wasn't to say that she didn't care.

"And you're dragging real people into this. Nerds, Mormons, weird Boston College ladies, and one is even a Pope."

"He's not the Pope. He's a priest." Rhiana increased speed. I took little jogging steps along the garden path to keep up, casting away overhanging branches from in front of my face as I went.

"Same thing. At least I know you're listening."

"Not the same thing."

We'd circled the courts several times when Rhiana saw Denzel leaning against the fence by the corner of the courts. I couldn't tell where he'd come from.

"Dandré?" said Rhiana.

"Madam." With a nod of his head he indicated a narrow path behind us. Rhiana spun around. The Vin Diesel clone was standing several feet away.

"Pierre, I didn't know you were out here."

"Pardon, madam," said Pierre. "We've checked the area. It is secure. Dandré will keep watch."

I had to begrudgingly give Pierre his due for taking the safety measure.

"This way," he said, leading us to the outer edge of the court along a row of high-arching trees.

Rhiana said, "Pierre, this is Kamir. He's our guide and translator. He knows who we are but not why we're here." That was Rhiana's way of sending a not-so-subtle message to Pierre to keep the discussion in general terms. Apparently this meeting was for the in-crowd only. I got a stern look from Rhiana that told me to play along. I was growing accustomed to it.

"Very well." Pierre's English was good.

"You were fully briefed?" asked Rhiana.

"Fully, madam."

"Me too," I said. "Oh wait, no, I wasn't."

Rhiana turned away from Pierre and gave me the slitty-eyes and off-with-your-head look. Apparently, children and estranged ex-cop husbands on secret missions were to be seen and not heard. "We need a native Yemeni to travel with us," she told Pierre. "Our travel permits will require it. He speaks several dialects." Rhiana was pretty amazing. She could speak to Pierre and give me dirty looks at the same time. She was a master communicator when she wanted to be.

"*Fantastique,*" said Pierre.

Rhiana said, "My information will take us to Midi, a fishing village in the north."

Pierre, the model of French gallantry, furrowed his brow. He looked at me, as if trying to decide how much to say in front of me, then spoke. "Mademoiselle, pardon. Our sources suggest a major city in the south."

"Your sources are out of date. Our military raided an apartment in . . . that city just after the incident, and the results were negative," said Rhiana.

"But madam, recently our sources . . ."

"It's old information," she said. "Don't worry about it. We have a good lead in Midi."

Now it was Pierre's turn to be ignored and mistreated. It was, apparently, my break.

"We can secure travel permits to Al-Hudaydah, on the west coast, then work our way to the north. If we get stopped, our very charming and resourceful translator will feign ignorance. That shouldn't be difficult for him."

Break over.

"Any other plans of a specific nature," said Rhiana, "will wait until we speak to my contact in Midi."

Pierre didn't look very happy about this arrangement, but he was a gentleman about it and seemed to know who was boss. He was her muscle, and he knew his place.

"I will report this arrangement to my superiors at the United Nations command center in Vienna. Is there anything else?"

"I don't know how long it will take to arrange the permits. I'll be in touch. Thank you, Pierre," said Rhiana.

Dandré was still lurking in the shrubs, making sure we were safe from curious ears. He met Pierre on their way toward the parking lot, where they disappeared together.

"That was cloaked in mystery," I said. "Especially the . . ." I winked, "major city in the south. What? You don't think I know where Aden is?"

"Op Sec," she said.

Short for Operational Security, Op Sec was the excuse many government agencies used to limit the flow of information. "I'm a great believer in security," I said.

"Good." Rhiana was probably a little more abrupt than she'd wanted to be, so she invested two sentences in damage control. "I'm sorry. Thanks for understanding."

"I said I believe in security, not that I want to be shut out." I skirted a row of prickly shrubs and turned toward the hotel, turning my back on Rhiana and walking away.

Rhiana followed. "Kam, wait."

". . . Again." Throwing that in her face was a dirty trick—but it beat the truth, which still eluded me anyway.

"Kam, please. I'm not turning my back on you."

I stopped, still a good distance from the hotel doors.

Rhiana came closer. "Kam . . . I know I didn't understand what you needed after what happened in Seattle. But I'm not shutting you out. You shut me out."

"Only because you couldn't talk to me about it. How did you ever expect to understand?" I said.

"Kam, I wish I could change things. But right now it isn't about you."

"You're telling me I'm being kept in the dark for my own good?"

I was pretty sure Rhiana realized how absurd it was to lie to me any longer. She stared into the distance for a long while, giving us both a chance to think.

Rhiana had always been good at whatever she put her mind to. She had been a rising star in the intelligence business, a woman in what had been a man's world just a decade earlier. She'd spent a good part of her life in the Middle East with her father, never really knew her mother that well, and had filled the various voids in her life with government service. When we'd met, I'd taken her away from all that and for a short time had given her a stable, happy life.

Rhiana turned her gaze on me. "You're right. I've been keeping secrets for so long, I forget who to trust."

"Trust me," I said.

"The truth is . . ." She didn't finish, and I knew at that moment she wasn't going to.

"Is it Op Sec or is it me?"

"Is that what you think? That I don't trust you?"

I shrugged.

"That's not true," she said. "You know better. You never told me what kinds of things you did at work. When you went on SWAT call-outs, it was practically a state secret." She paused to let a few things sink in. "You know what kind of work this is."

"I know how to keep secrets," I said.

"I know. But you're the guy who always said there's no such thing as a secret—there are things you know, and things you tell someone, but there are no secrets. Do I have the right guy? You taught me that."

I had said that—numerous times. There is no such thing as a secret. I nodded.

"Kam, I do trust you," Rhiana said.

"Then why does a twenty-something-year-old graduate student from Utah know more about this mission than me?" I probably shouldn't have said it, but her reluctance to tell me the details of this mission still stung, and my wounded pride won out. I'm not sure what I expected, but I couldn't read Rhiana's reaction. Was she hurt, angry? Or was she about to *laugh*? "Darrin?" She snorted.

"Yes, Darrin," I said.

"Darrin?" Definitely laughing.

"You can't blame Darrin for spilling his guts," I said, wondering if she was angry to the point of delirium. "I twisted him pretty good." I hadn't really considered Darrin's fate when I made him talk to me.

"I'll bet you did." Still laughing, maybe more of a giggle. Definitely not angry. "Let me guess, mass graves in Africa? Djibouti, if I remember right."

It was my turn to be stunned, but I wasn't laughing.

She said, "Do you really think I'd risk an operation like this by telling Darrin what it was about?"

"No mass graves? No Djibouti?" I hate it when I should have known better.

"No mass graves." Rhiana was in better spirits.

I shook my head. "How do you keep it all straight?"

The laughing suddenly over, Rhiana said, "I lie, you lie. I trick people, you trick people. I withhold information, you withhold information. What kind of business do you think we're in?"

"I didn't realize those things applied to our life together." It was a cheap shot, but again, my wounded pride was in control.

"You didn't, huh? You were the expert at withholding information," she said. And that was it. She'd summed up our entire marital conflict in one statement, succinctly and accurately.

"After what happened in Seattle, if you'd been a little more . . ." I wasn't sure what more she needed to be.

"More what, Kam? More caring, more loving? More what? After the accident you never said one word to me. You never even tried to talk to me. I didn't even realize how much it hurt you until it was too late."

"It's not that simple, Rhi. I just . . ." I'm not a crier, but I felt it coming on—a flood or a wave burning in my chest and threatening to spill out. Deep breaths. "After the accident, I . . ." What could I possibly say?

"Don't," she said, putting her hand on my shoulder. "I wanted to talk to you. If we'd have had more time in Paris . . . for us. Maybe I'm mixing up our personal problems with this mission, I don't know. When I asked the state department to send you here, I didn't really know how hard it would be to see you. I thought you'd see that the request came from me, and then if you showed up I'd at least know that you wanted to be here . . . with me. It didn't work out that way." Rhiana's hand had moved from my shoulder to my hand, and she gently squeezed. My face was hot, and there were already tears there.

"I don't know what I want." That wasn't true. I wiped away what I could and continued with the deep breaths. "We have a few minutes now. Trust me, Rhi."

Rhiana collected herself, let go of my hand, and took a cleansing breath. She looked around the gardens and said very quietly, "We're here to locate a hostage before the captors realize who they really have."

When Rhiana released the cleansing breath, I thought maybe this talk was going to be about us. It wasn't, but just hearing the truth felt good. "I haven't heard anything in the news about a hostage," I said.

"You wouldn't. He's not famous; he's just important. Clyde knows about it. Langley approached him about letting us use his trip as a front to get travel permits so we could move freely around Yemen. Darrin started to realize something wasn't right, so we sidetracked him with the mass graves story. The others have no idea I'm with the CIA, unless Darrin has blabbed about the graves."

"I don't think so. I had to work Darrin pretty hard." That wasn't terribly accurate, but I didn't want Darrin to be the focus of Rhiana's wrath.

"We only need the researchers until we secure clean travel permits. As soon as we get into the dirty work, they'll be flown out of the country on the guise of an embassy travel warning. The four of us will stay behind and continue the mission."

"The four of us meaning you, me, and our two French soldiers?"

"Exactly," she said. "It was supposed to be two Delta Force operators."

"And Roger thought differently?"

"No. Roger doesn't allocate, he requisitions. The U.N. stepped in. I don't know why. Now do you understand why I was angry at the embassy?"

"Let me see if I understand your feelings about this," I said. "The U.N. isn't competent enough to bake a cake, and now they are in charge of your hostage rescue. I think I can see why you'd be upset. So who's the hostage?"

Rhiana hesitated and said, "Nobody knows. I mean, not his real identity. Even the people at Langley only know him by his code name. He's been a civilian informant for nearly three decades. We think his captors don't realize who they've got. We'd like to get him back before they realize who they have."

"So, why all the secrecy about his identity? Somebody in very deep?"

"He's an informant. Not just a floater that we use once in a while, but someone who has been providing the CIA with high-end source intelligence for a long time. He knows everything about this part of the world. And, more importantly, he knows everyone." She shook her head. "If his cover is blown, countless lives will be at risk. Not to mention his own."

It was time for me to have an attitude adjustment; actually, it was long overdue. I didn't know who this guy was, but I knew how I'd feel if a fellow cop were in that situation. "Maybe your strange behavior makes some kind of weird 'super spook' sense."

"It does," said Rhiana.

"So we're going to Midi?"

Rhiana gladly accepted the change of subject. "That's the plan."

"Based on what?" I asked.

"Based on intelligence sources."

I sneered. "Intelligence sources? That's a fancy way of saying that a bunch of clowns made up some stuff."

"That's not true."

"It is true," I said. "I never had a good reason to trust someone else's intelligence, and neither have you. I'll bet your French friends feel the same way."

"But you're talking about cops. I'm talking about reliable information. Real source intel."

"Yeah, I'm talking about cops. Real cops who risk their lives on what they learn wearing out their own shoe leather. We develop our own information and draw our own conclusions. I'm not running off into PLO-infested territory in northern Yemen just because some unknown voice from Langley tells me to. I'll get my own intel, thank you."

Rhiana was actually smiling.

"What?" I asked.

"You."

"What me?"

"Just you," she said. "It's good to see you acting like you again— like a real cop," she said. "I wasn't sure which one of you was going to show up. The you of the last twelve months, or the real you."

Rhiana touched my cheek, and I stepped closer to her, not knowing if I'd been complimented or slammed and not caring because I hadn't been this close to her for over a year and she smelled so darn good.

"I've missed you, Kam. Now do you understand why I needed you here?"

CHAPTER 12

Rhiana used her spook phone to call a taxi to meet us a few blocks from the embassy. I spent most of the taxi ride back to the hotel convincing Rhiana that we should at least try to verify some of Langley's precious "reliable source intelligence." She relented and said she had a few old contacts in the city that we could check. At the hotel we freshened up, and then Rhiana gave another taxi driver the address to the American Institute just southwest of the city in the Al Qa, the Jewish Quarter of Sana'a.

Despite the agonizingly unsophisticated opinions of anchors, pundits, policy makers, and politicians, Arabs and Jews have been living in uneasy harmony for centuries in Yemen. Here Jews and Arabs coexist with healthy doses of grudging respect tinged with cultural bias, and they have done so since before the Queen of Sheba. The fringe elements of society still went about castigating their fellow men with unmerited and undeserved ridicule, or with car bombs—violent at either extreme—but as is usually the case, the overwhelming majority of the locals, regardless of their religion, found better things to worry about than hatred.

Mary Catherine was just such a local. Somalian by birth, Arab by culture, Jewish by tradition, and Christian by given name, Mary Catherine had no choice but to rise above petty partisanship. She was the plump cleaning woman at the American Institute in Al Qa. As such, she had access, probably through eavesdropping, to the conversations of informed Westerners and Arabs alike who frequented the Institute to trade secrets.

The purpose for the Institute was somewhat vague in my mind.

Mary Catherine had worked there ever since she had been discovered by the American government during the Cold War, when Yemen was under the surreptitious control of the Soviet Union. During Yemen's Russian period, Mary was a star in the Yemeni spook system. During the last decade, with the USSR gone, Mary had disappeared into semi-retirement. Our mission today, we decided, was to seek her out and pump some conspiratorial life into the jolly behemoth. Her loyalties, Rhiana told me before we arrived at the Institute, lay with whoever was in the right.

"Bonjour, Madame Mary Catherine," said Rhiana. Because you never knew what language would pop up in a Yemeni conversation, one had to be somewhat intercontinental.

"Good morning, my dove," said Mary in passable English, enveloping Rhiana in a massive hug that promised to squish the air right out of her. Mary's shoulders were draped in bed linens, freshly perfumed over a bakhour brazier on the balcony just outside the doors of the breakfast room where we'd found her at her duties. The smoky, musky fragrance—Yemen's answer to dryer softener—drifted into the breakfast area on the hot breeze and made my nose itch.

"*SabaaH al-khair.*" Good morning, I said, keeping a healthy distance from Mary's deadly embrace and using Arabic to reinforce my cover du jour.

"Who's your friend?" she asked Rhiana, ignoring me.

"He's with me. On the project," said Rhiana. That was spook-talk for "it's okay to talk in front of him."

It's not uncommon for a Westerner to be out and about solo in Sana'a, Aden, or Ti'azz, but it was more common for out-of-towners, especially women, to be accompanied by a guide. As Rhiana's guide, I'd simply wanted to throw a full-length thobe over my Western clothes, but Rhiana felt it would be unauthentic since the local men in Yemen typically wore a jacket and futa, or knee-length sarong. A compromise was reached. I found myself agreeing to a dark wool futa wrapped around my waist, a disco-era polyester shirt, and a coarsely woven black suit jacket, but I wore wool socks and my combat boots in defiance of local custom and Rhiana's wishes. I was stylin'. My boots were a great conversation starter; I became popular with the taxi driver since many men wore thin leather oxfords without socks. Boots say "cool couture" in any culture. Of course, no Yemeni man of any bearing would go out without his jambiya, a curved dagger that was tucked into the belt of his futa, in front, and worn with the handle pointing straight out. Every man had one, and the penalty for drawing it without legal provocation was codified in the law. You'd probably get in less trouble for pointing your AK-47 assault rifle at someone than for pulling your jambiya. Every once in a while I pointed to it and gave Rhiana my most devilish look; she wasn't intimidated, and I don't think she liked my sense of humor. Her taste for my comic sensibilities was on-again, off-again—mostly off-again.

Mary looked me over as if she saw right through the charade, then addressed Rhiana. "It's been a quiet week."

"How so?"

"Not very many people are talking about this missing man you're wondering about." Mary unfurled another sheet and walked through a set of double doors to the balcony. With practiced flair, she waved the linen over the coals glowing hot in the brazier until the odor had sufficiently embedded itself in the fibers of the sheet. "How much one hears in Yemen is not so remarkable as how much one does not hear." With a practiced hand, Mary folded the sheet and slung it over her shoulder and then waved another linen over the brazier.

At times I thought the Yemeni people invented the art of vague statements. But Mary was right. The Yemeni government kept close track of everything, especially the secret police, who everyone knew about; so much for secrecy. If the significant kidnapping was not the topic of every dinner conversation, something was very wrong—or at least out of the ordinary.

"Nothing?" said Rhiana.

"Two men of the Hashid tribe lunched here," Mary said. "They suspect Saudis in the north. They always do. The Englishmen who visit the library here blame the Eritrean gunrunners on the west coast. They fear them and so cast suspicion on them for every mishap in Yemen."

"You don't think it's either?" Rhiana asked.

Mary made an ear-to-ear smile, forcing her wide cheeks up under her eyes. "It is what has not been said that intrigues me."

"And what is that?" asked Rhiana.

"Kidnapping is a game of politics. And politics is a game of posturing." She smoothed another bedsheet over her shoulder and delivered the last line of her riddle. "No posturing, no politics."

"You don't think the captors have political motives?" Rhiana asked.

Staying in character, I said in Arabic, "What other motivations are there?"

Rhiana didn't look pleased with my intrusion, but she let the question stand.

Mary slid her gaze toward me. "If you have to ask," she said, "you are either very naïve or extremely idealistic."

Our conversation ended when a Scotsman in a dirty kilt stepped out onto the balcony. The Institute was a good place to collect information but not to talk for very long. Mary belly-laughed and lumbered away with her linens to make the morning beds. Rhiana stood in stony, pale silence.

* * *

After we were well away from the American Institute building, I asked, "What was that all about?" Our taxi was still waiting at the street, its meter ticking away.

"Believe it or not," said Rhiana, "that was Mary Catherine's way of saying it like it is."

"What does she sound like when she beats around the bush?"

"I don't know. She's always like that. But maybe you're right."

"Say that again."

"Maybe the usual suspects aren't to blame."

"I don't remember saying that, but if it makes you feel better, I'd like to take credit. What's the going theory?" I opened the door for Rhiana, and she slid into the back of the taxi.

Rhiana didn't answer.

I said, "Every time I ask a question, you go into major shutdown mode." Yet another Sana'a cab driver was going to listen to us argue.

"It's not shutdown mode. It's need-to-know mode," she said.

"You've taken need-to-know office politics and raised it to an art form. Secrecy I understand, but just plain holding out will get someone killed. Believe it or not, while all this goes on around me, my brain is still awake and functioning. I'm drawing conclusions just like you are. We can either both come to completely different conclusions, which will ultimately dictate our wildly different reactions to situations and quite possibly get us killed, or you can loosen your grip and tell me what's going on here."

"The agent who was kidnapped was feeding us information about . . ." She didn't finish.

I shook my head and rolled my eyes. "Even if I wanted to tell someone, Rhiana, I don't know anyone to tell."

"He was generating intelligence about the political leanings of various factions in Yemen."

"Like the PLO, the PLF, ANO, HAMAS, and al-Qa'ida?"

"Somebody's been watching CNN. Actually, he didn't concern himself with the major players. He kept an eye on Yemeni tribal issues."

I ignored the barb. This was more like it. Information I could sink my teeth into. I agreed with Mary Catherine already, and I didn't even need to listen at keyholes. I said, "Let's give him a name. John Doe? Or, maybe he's Slavic. Petar Petrovic? How about just Our Man, or The Man from U.N.C.L.E., Uncle Bob, anything?"

"Our hostage acted like he had something really big. He was abducted just before he could pass it on. But so far, none of our normal channels are picking anything up."

"Then it's simple," I said.

"Oh, really? Enlighten me."

"It's not political."

"I've thought about that. But if that's the case, we've got nothing."

"On the contrary, my friend. We've got everything."

"I'm waiting, O Great One."

"Money," I said.

"This isn't Seattle, or anywhere in the West for that matter. Nobody has asked for money. Besides, these are Arabs, and money isn't their religion."

"Someone tried to get to me in Paris. They'll try again, and when they do, they'll lead us to the money."

Rhiana shook her head. "It's not that simple, Kam."

"It is to me. Follow the money."

* * *

It wasn't easy to convince Rhiana that moneygrubbing was a global, nondenominational pursuit. I had to engage her in a friendly dispute as we left the American Institute en route to the Sheraton Hotel. Each time she offered up some PhD-derived argument about the nature of Arabs, I countered with my own special brand of argument—rolling eyes. I'd been a cop too long to ignore money as a motivation.

The first rule of criminal investigation is that all people always lie, and the second rule is follow the money—both apply as much to international espionage as they do to the street. Actually, the second rule of criminal investigation is that you can't enter a crime scene without leaving something behind. That rule didn't seem to have much relevance, so I made an off-the-cuff amendment to the rules of investigation and replaced it with follow the money. I hadn't watched *The French Connection* seven times for nothing.

"But Kam, they haven't asked for money," Rhiana complained for about the fortieth time.

I tilted my head and got ready for another big roll of the eyes.

"If you do that again, you'll get the back of my hand on the side of your head."

"You would physically abuse your own husband?" I was acting more myself than I had in months, and I could tell it pleased Rhiana.

She said, "Maybe I'm not hearing you. Where's the money in kidnapping an informant?"

"The money is in shutting him up."

"If that were the case, why not just . . ."

"Exactly, Rhiana, our hostage is probably D-E-D dead by now."

Rhiana's eyes reddened. "Kam, don't."

I can be a little slow on the uptake, so I said, "Don't what? It happens in this business. Our job is to find out who did it and administer justice."

"Please." Rhiana opened her purse and withdrew a wad of rials. She peered over the seat and counted out a sufficient number of bills to pay for the ride and give the driver a generous tip. She put the remaining money back in her purse and wiped tear streaks from her neck.

"Rhiana, you didn't have something to do with the kidnapping, did you? You're not feeling responsible?"

She didn't say anything.

"Do you know him pretty well, this hostage?" I asked.

"I'm one of the few people who know his real identity. I'm his control officer. I run him without a bridge agent—no cutout. I can't reveal his identity."

"You sound like a bad movie. It's freakin' me out. Bridge agent? Cutout? Spy lingo translation please."

"I ran him," she said. "But there was more to it than that. He worked in denied areas"—she looked at me to see if I understood—"places we, the government, aren't supposed to be, and I collected his intelligence in person without the use of an intermediary, or cutout, to insulate the CIA from the information source. No bridge agent. And now I've said too much." We both took a few minutes to look out our windows at the passing city, not saying anything to each other. Rhiana collected herself and forced herself to smile at me. "I just have to get used to the idea that it's you, me, and a couple of French fries here to find him."

"Ouch. They are *French Special Forces*, Rhiana. *Special.*" That was me, mocking again.

"I just wanted American soldiers. I'd have taken Radar O'Reilly and Corporal Klinger if they'd offered."

I reached out for Rhiana and cupped her chin in my hands. "I am in a dress," I said.

"Yes. Yes, you are. Actually it's closer to a skirt, not a dress. And you're going to have to learn to sit politely in your dress."

I put my knees together and tucked the excess of the futa under my thigh. "Pardon me, ma'am," I said.

Rhiana laughed. "Okay, detective, let's follow the money."

Our taxi dropped us at the Sheraton, where we hoped to get a few minutes alone in the hotel room to go over Rhiana's other source intelligence. Then, we'd make a solid investigative plan, get travel permits accordingly, and find the money trail. I was confident.

Madeline, the shining star of Boston College's Department of Sociology and Histrionics, met us in the Sheraton lobby.

"Rhiana, Rhiana, where have you been? Clyde needs you. He's frantic. We've been looking all over for you. Come on." She took

Rhiana by the sleeve and dragged her away, casting a malevolent glance in my direction. "He's trouble," she said loud enough for me and all the other patrons in the lobby to hear. And then more softly, to Rhiana, she said, "I mean it. I think he's wanted or something."

Clyde stood waiting, appearing much more at ease than we were led to believe. "Rhiana. Kam." He nodded to each of us. "The concierge called and told me there was a problem with our visas. The hotel staff is working on it. You two seeing the sights?"

"We've been to the embassy. No one said anything about it on that end."

"I'm sure it's not a problem. Maybe just a mixup," Clyde said.

"We're getting kicked out of the country," said Madeline, having given up on us and now appealing to the lobby crowd. Drama queen.

Actually, the incident raised my eyebrows, and I considered it more than a coincidence. After all, the third rule of investigations, or is it the fourth—I'd lost track—is that there are no such things as coincidences. My raised eyebrows didn't go unnoticed by Rhiana, who gave me a look as if she thought the same thing.

Rhiana and I stepped a few paces away from the others.

"What do you think?" she asked.

It had been my experience that the Yemenis knew just about everything that went on in their country. It was uncanny and unnerving. Rhiana wasn't what you would call a deep-cover operative in Yemen, more of an embassy employee who most people figured as a CIA plant. That's just the way things worked in the spy business. But we were all suspect now.

"Yemen is yanking our chain," I told her.

"The Yemeni government is cooperating with us on this."

"Well then, the highly cooperative Yemeni government is yanking our chain."

"Unlikely," she said.

I let that go, even though I knew that it was not only likely but was a certainty. I also knew what went along with that kind of chain yank, and I looked in the lobby for questionable persons watching us. I didn't see anyone, but that didn't mean we weren't under surveillance.

Rhiana and I walked back in the direction of the front desk, where Clyde waited patiently for the clerk to get off the phone. Rhiana leaned close to my ear. "I guess the game is on."

"Yes it is. And we're up to bat."

* * *

"Anyone could know we're here at this point." Rhiana plopped on the bed in her hotel room and kicked off her shoes. The familiarity was comforting, and we were finally alone.

Having sensed our need to work this thing out, Clyde had convinced the rest of the crew that a relaxing walk in the famous Sheraton gardens was just the thing for them. Rhiana had countered that she thought our visa problems had to do with my late addition to the group and that she and I needed to talk. Leaving us in the lobby, Father Andrew, Darrin, and the overly theatrical Madeline followed Clyde to the back of the hotel to the garden doors. Clyde and Father Andrew led the way while Darrin talked with Madeline. Maybe Darrin's introversion and Madeline's flair for the dramatic would blend to create the beginnings of a lifelong bond. Or not.

As soon as the foursome had disappeared, Rhiana and I had retreated to her room. There were so many things we could have talked about, but we weren't in Yemen to put our marriage back together.

"Who, exactly, knows about our real purpose here?" I asked.

"It looks like everyone knows we're here," said Rhiana.

"Who was supposed to know? We'll work it from there," I said.

"Okay," she said, "Roger at the embassy, probably his secretary. Above him, maybe anywhere from twenty to a hundred people at Langley would know bits and pieces about our work here. The CIA brass would know most of what's happening here in Yemen, at least theoretically. They don't always keep close tabs at those levels."

I considered sitting on the bed with Rhiana, then decided on the short round-back chair that sat in the corner. Pretending to be coworkers was driving me insane. "You know those people better than I do. Is it safe to rule out a leak?"

"Probably." Rhiana nodded.

"Okay then, of the people in Yemen, who, besides the six of us, knows we're here and why?"

"Not many people. Pierre and Dandré." Rhiana swung her feet off the edge of the bed like a little girl and sat on her hands. That image, juxtaposed against the stoic CIA case officer that I knew she was, made for an interesting snapshot.

"And you said the Yemeni government was greasing the wheels for us?" I asked.

"That leaves the door wide open, doesn't it?"

I started to think like a detective. "We need Roger to find out who cancels things like visas."

"I'll call him."

"I think our best ploy is to have you work on the problem as if you're just trying to straighten things out for our research trip. You know, business as usual as far as the Yemeni government knows."

Rhiana nodded. "I'll call Roger and find out what he knows."

"Good, and I'll sit here and admire your beauty." That was me, flirting.

The hint of a smile I got back from Rhiana was hard to decipher, but things were definitely getting more comfortable between us. As promised, I did admire Rhiana as she spoke to Roger on the phone.

When she got off the phone, Rhiana said, "Yemenia Airways would not verify that we had return tickets out of Yemen. That is grounds to cancel our visas, as stated clearly on our visa applications."

"But you have the tickets? Right?" I asked.

"The office manager at Yemenia Airways, a guy named Abdulaziz al-Sakkaf, called the travel office last night and told them we hadn't booked a return flight."

"How helpful of him."

"You can bet he didn't wake up in the night with a sudden case of heartburn about the recent arrival of American scholars and happen to look us up to ensure we had a return ticket to Paris. I'd like to know who put him up to this," said Rhiana, the little girl now replaced by the professional agent.

"It's time to wear out a little shoe leather," I said. "Rhi, wait a half an hour and call Yemenia Airways. See what you can do to light a fire under our friend, Mr. al-Sakkaf. Scare him good."

"What am I supposed to tell him?"

"I don't know. Have Roger do it from the embassy. Tell him anything. Play to what he already suspects. Have Roger tell him that the Yemeni Secret Police suspect him of manipulating flight records at the direction of known terrorists and that they've tapped his phone. Emphasize the phone tap. I can use that." An idea was forming in my mind.

Rhiana nodded. "Where will you be?"

"At his office. I just want to gauge his reaction. See what he does. If he knows he can't use his phone, who knows what he'll do."

I lifted the envelope given to me by Miss Davidson in Timor-Leste from the inside breast pocket of my jacket to reassure myself that I had everything I might need—cash. It felt thick, but I still didn't know how much money was in it. I let it drop back into my pocket.

"He probably won't do anything," said Rhiana.

I shrugged and turned to leave. "It's my shoe leather, remember."

"You remember what Roger said about embarrassing the U.S. government or starting a war, right?"

"What?" I batted my eyes. "Little ol' me?"

"Kam," she said.

I turned around. Rhiana pointed a delicate finger to her eye, then to her heart, and then she pointed to me. It was a gesture we'd given each other every day when I left for work. I always returned it: my eye, my nose, my eye, my heart, point to her, and then hold up two fingers. I know I love you too. It had been a long time. On weak knees, I turned for the door before she could see the single tear run the length of my face.

About forty minutes later, unbeknownst to him, I followed a perturbed Mr. Abdulaziz al-Sakkaf from his office door at the airport to a waiting taxi. My taxi followed his to the Sana'a public bathhouse. But Mr. al-Sakkaf wasn't there for the bath.

My own sense of modesty and male decorum had prevented me from visiting such a place before, but I knew that the bathhouse was Yemen's answer to the men's club. This was a logical place for Mr. al-Sakkaf to meet someone on the sly. I waited until he disappeared behind the double wooden doors of the establishment and then got out of my taxi, throwing who knows how much money through the window at the driver.

Upon entering the bathhouse, I was invited into a small, private dressing room. You didn't get inside unless you were going to bathe, so I played along. Standing on a freshly laundered reed mat, I removed my clothes and donned a clean white bath sarong, which I tied around my waist. Then, in stages, as I made my way through the rocky underground passage, I was assisted in cleaning my feet in fresh hot water and then my body, followed by my hair. Cleanliness and modesty were paramount concerns in the baths, which were heated by fires in tunnels under the caverns. The fires were fueled by loads of garbage, including such things as rubber tires that burned black outside the bathhouse, plastics that had recently been introduced to Yemen through European imported goods, and even excrement from the public toilets—it had been done that way for centuries with very little waste. Gross—but efficient.

Inside, the vaguely familiar odor of fragrant herbs and oils hung in the thick steam. I was led yet further into the labyrinth until I found myself in a room where I could sense, rather than see, the presence of other men lounging against the walls behind a curtain of steam.

"Is everything all right, friend?" asked the attendant in Arabic as he spread out a towel on the warm rock surface of the floor.

I assured him it was and took my place prostrate on my towel.

As the steam cleared occasionally, in between visits from the Johnny-on-the-spot attendant who bathed the hot rocks in cool water to thicken the mist, I could see the vague shapes of men in various poses of recline, and I could hear bits of clipped Arabic echoing in the chamber. I didn't see Mr. al-Sakkaf.

Part of the culture of the public baths was an unwritten custom of prudish personal modesty and a delicate concern for individual hygiene, and it included a tradition of seclusion that extended beyond the tunnels of the bathhouse. Who was present and what was said in the bathhouse, under the cloak of steam, stayed in the bathhouse. Often, delicate topics not quite fit for the boardroom were decided in the steam room, probably not unlike sauna talk in the United States, although the standards for hygiene in Yemen were far superior. In the West, a sweaty naked man could sit down right by you in a sauna and try to sell you a used car. At least in Yemen, that same man would have been cleansed on the way in, would be wearing a sarong, and wouldn't elicit unwanted chitchat.

Through the hissing steam, I picked out muffled discussions about jobs, women, and politics. Typical stuff. One conversation revolved around the westernization of Yemen—the good, the bad. Generally, the two men conversing seemed tolerant of change. A third voice expressed some regret. Okay, he cursed the West and made a few impassioned remarks about days gone by and lamented about Arab traditions lost. I thought the conversation probably represented the general sentiment all over Arabia. No one was plotting the demise of New York City—not that those plans weren't being made somewhere, but not by the average Arab folks. Yemen's geography, along the Red Sea and very close to the continent of Africa, lent itself to a special concern for events there. Someone in the darkness mentioned Somalia, and someone else commented on the plight of Eritrean refugees along Yemen's west coast. But nobody tapped me on the shoulder and told me there was a hostage being held in such and such a place and that so-and-so was responsible for his capture.

I wanted to call out into the mist for Mr. al-Sakkaf and see what kind of reaction I got. I didn't even know if he was in the room. I should have waited outside.

I don't know how long I'd been inside the steam room, but a couple of shadows had come and gone. I checked the drawstring on my sarong and prepared to get up when I sensed a presence enter the room and come toward me.

You were followed. It was the voice of a woman, sensed but not heard. But there were no women allowed in the bath on the same days as men. Never.

The shadowed presence came closer; close enough that I could see a vague form through the steam, hovering over me, searching the vapors.

Get out. The voice again, perhaps a girl's voice. It was impossible.

I slowly rose to a sitting position, then got to a knee, ready to lunge away if necessary.

With the rush of adrenaline in my system, the voices of the bath-house faded, and I could hear my heart beating in my ears. I didn't have to be told more than twice. Staying close to the ground, I gathered my towel and crawled slowly toward the entrance so as not to disturb the steam. As soon as I could make out the dark shape of the tunnel leading back toward the dressing rooms, where the steam dissipated, I stood and walked out. Just as I passed the threshold, the steam room erupted in a din of shouts and cries. There were curses in Arabic, and bodies were running for the exit passage. I ran up the tunnel toward the main entrance, dodging the attendants responding to the shouts in the steam room. I stopped long enough at my dressing room to snag my suit jacket and boots. Leaving the rest behind, I charged for the outer door and slammed through it at a dead run. The hold I had on my boots prevented me from getting into the jacket, but the half-naked bodies that poured out the door screeching like banshees behind me created enough of a diversion that I wasn't noticed.

I ducked into a recessed doorway adjacent to the bathhouse entrance and donned the jacket, buttoned it up to cover my bare chest, and stepped into my boots. The white terrycloth sarong didn't exactly go with my coat, but luckily fashion wasn't a great concern on the streets of Sana'a, and I wasn't its slave. I still had the envelope of U.S. currency in my jacket—thank heavens for skirts, or I would have put it in my front pants pocket—and I felt good about the prospect of getting back to the Sheraton by taxi.

I stepped out of the doorway alcove and then ducked back in when I saw the late-boarding passenger from the Yemenia Airways flight to Yemen, Tardy Man, standing outside the bathhouse with Mr. al-Sakkaf. He was still wearing his leather jacket and coordinated driving cap. Very English-professor chic. People on the street stopped what they were doing to join in the confusion of half-naked men in matching sarongs. I heard the word for knife used by some of the men from the bathhouse. Hidden in the shady alcove, I watched and listened.

The ancient wooden doors to the bathhouse opened, and the Arab who had chased me through the dark streets of Paris walked out of the darkness—I recognized him immediately. He was a bad man. I couldn't think of a better name for him than Faasid—literally "rotten" in Arabic. Faasid moved toward Tardy Man and they held eye contact for just a moment before Faasid shook his head slightly. He'd lost me, and Tardy Man didn't look very happy about it.

CHAPTER 13

Mr. al-Sakkaf of Yemenia Airways made quick work of leaving the bathhouse neighborhood, and neither Tardy Man nor his Arab thug, both still lingering in front of the bathhouse doors, knew where I'd gone. Their next task, I was sure, would be to find me. One of them would probably go to the Sheraton and watch for me there; I had no idea where the other would go—perhaps to the embassy, hoping I'd panic and run for safety. There was no telling. The only thing in my favor at the moment was that there was a good possibility they'd split up. One on one I could handle them. I wanted the head of the snake first—Tardy Man. So I decided to follow him.

The most well-known urban foot surveillance tactic used by cops to tail bad guys was known as the "A-B-C" method or the "parallel pursuit" pattern. Good Guy A followed the Bad Guy and was trailed at a safe distance by Good Guy B. Good Guy C paralleled the Bad Guy on the other side of the street. The beauty of the pattern was that B kept a watchful eye on A and C, providing cover from a distance, and C was able to watch the Bad Guy trying to take quick corners or evasive maneuvers. A good A-B-C team could gracefully switch positions often enough to prevent the Bad Guy from getting too familiar with a single person behind him. Theoretically infallible.

But for me, the A-B-C surveillance plan had some glaring shortcomings. First, there was only one of me, call me Good Guy S—for Solo. This shortcoming presented obvious logistical problems. Second, these men had been tailing me ever since Paris. They knew what I looked like and where I was staying. The third problem had to do with my wardrobe. I was shirtless and wrapped in a glorified towel. I had a jacket and my boots, but I was still going to attract some unwanted attention—not advisable under the current circumstance.

As the excitement abated, the interrupted bathers milled back toward the bathhouse to return to their baths. Faasid loitered at the front door for a few moments, scanning the bathers, and then stalked down the sidewalk and disappeared. Tardy Man stood alone, scanning back and forth along the road wondering where his American prey went. Eventually, he ambled across the street in the middle of the block, forcing a wizened old Arab on an oxidized Vespa scooter to swerve around him.

I threw the A-B-C surveillance method to the wind in favor of my own method, the B-V-C or Be-Very-Careful method, and I tailed Tardy Man for two blocks from the opposite side of the street. I stayed well back, knowing that if he saw my telltale white sarong, he'd peg me immediately. I also knew it would take Tardy Man only one or two simple evasive maneuvers to lose me. Luckily, he didn't walk very far.

Tardy Man took a direct route to a hole-in-the-wall café and went inside. The windows of the café were covered in strips of butcher paper advertising cheap Internet access. I held my position and watched the café a half a block back at a small open-air music shop built into a narrow alcove. I picked up a CD by Nawal Zoughbi, Arabia's answer to bleached-blonde bubblegum pop music, and turned the disk over in my hand as I kept an eye on the café.

Tardy Man didn't stay long in the café, perhaps long enough to speak with someone or make a phone call, but not long enough to eat. He pushed the glass doors of the Internet café open and walked straight to the curb, peering down the street at the passing cars. He'd called for a ride.

I took three giant steps toward the sidewalk before I realized I was still holding the CD. The shopkeeper was only a step behind me. I asked him if he had a phone. He snarled at me, snagged the CD away, and marched back to his shop.

"I need a taxi," I told the shopkeeper.

He shrugged his shoulders and shook his head, still glaring.

I left the music shop and went to the next business on the sidewalk. This one sold cheap clocks of all sizes that hung on splintered wooden planks tacked to the walls of an alley between two buildings. The shopkeeper gave my bath sarong a once-over and then told me he had no phone. Even if I could find a phone, I was going to be too late. Unless a taxi materialized in the street, I wasn't going to get what I wanted.

I left the clock shop and ventured closer to Tardy Man, who was still waiting by the curb. I was still a block away, but the closer I got, the more I realized that this was going to be my only chance at him.

I looked around for an alley I could pull Tardy Man into. They were all blocked by makeshift shops built of scrap lumber and musty blue tarps held together with twine. In any other neighborhood in Yemen, I'd have found dozens of blind alleys and alcoves tailor-made for a mugging, but not this neighborhood. It was crime prevention by virtue of rickety shops.

I moved another block farther away from Tardy Man, crossed the street at the intersection, and fell in behind a group of three burka-robed women, covered head to toe in thick black cotton, walking down the sidewalk carrying the day's shopping in canvas tote bags. The traffic surged in rhythm with the streetlights, and Tardy Man periodically searched down the road for his ride and didn't seem to notice me closing on him.

I started to panic as I got closer to him, having no idea what I was going to do. I slowed down and tried to get a grip; I couldn't accost the man in the open street. I thought about it. I might never get another chance.

I stood within fifty feet of Tardy Man when a white, American-made van bearing the name of the Taj Sheba Hotel painted in gold script along the side and back panels pulled to the curb in front of the café. The door swung open, and Tardy Man stepped into the van before I could even consider the possibility of confronting him. It was over . . . until I spotted the old man on the Vespa threading his way through traffic back toward me.

I bolted into the street waving my arms and yelling at the old man, "Sell it? Sell it?" I didn't know the word for scooter so I made motorcycle driving gestures with my arms. Some Arabic specialist I was.

The old Arab shook his head. "For work," he said. "No sale." He looked me over. I probably appeared as desperate as I felt, even dressed in bath clothes. His face bore the lines of decades of Yemeni living and all the tumult that must have gone with it. "I'll lend it." He rolled the worn out Vespa to the curb and got off.

The Taj van was pulling away from the curb. "U.S. currency," I said as I pulled a rough third of my wad of cash from the envelope and thrust it at him.

He took the money and fanned the bills with an ever-widening grin. "Sold." He nodded, smiled, and turned his back on his trusted scooter. Capitalism at work in the ancient city.

I slid onto the seat and ungracefully wobbled the machine into traffic and made a U-turn, wondering how much money I now owed the U.S. government. The van was well ahead of me, so I coursed the little scooter through traffic until the back of the van and its gold lettering came into view waiting at a traffic light.

If it wasn't bad enough that I was a man about town in a terry-cloth sarong, now I was a man about town on a motor scooter, terrycloth sarong waving in the breeze, and white hairy legs luminous above my combat boots. Very chic.

As discreetly as I could, given the circumstances, I followed Tardy Man and the van along several main streets until they pulled up under the massive portico of the Taj Sheba Hotel. Tardy Man was the only passenger, and after he stepped out of the van, he walked straight into the front entrance. I slid the Vespa between two parked cars and took off for the front doors of the Taj as they closed behind him.

The Taj was an upscale place with restaurants and shops, much like the Sheraton. The only difference was that the people who stayed in the Taj could travel back home with a more exotic-sounding hotel to tell their friends about. Tardy Man's choice of hotels told me that he wasn't keeping a low profile.

The opulent splendor of the marble-floored lobby and gilded, velvet furniture didn't really go with my fashion ensemble, especially the unlaced boots flopping around on my feet, but I went inside anyway. I passed a reception counter where an army of clerks stood looking busy, but there wasn't a patron in sight—it was late afternoon, perhaps before the evening rush. A couple of Arab teens were laughing behind the bellhop counter, and they stopped to watch me scuttle by and then resumed their snickering.

I found Tardy Man in an alcove facing a bank of elevators, staring up at the floor indicator. He apparently wasn't very concerned about someone following him, because he'd made a straight shot to the hotel and wasn't even looking over his shoulder.

I backed out of view around the corner of the elevator alcove and waited for the bell to tell me when his ride arrived. After I heard his doors slide shut, I stepped into the alcove and watched the yellow numbers above the doors light up in sequence.

It was a short ride to the third floor, where the number indicator paused; either Tardy Man got off or someone else got on. The light went out, and I was pretty sure the elevator was no longer in service. To be sure, I rang for it and watched the number three light up, and then the car descended. The door opened on an empty car.

I was about to be caught flat-footed in the elevator if Tardy Man decided to come back down, so I charged up the stairs next to the elevator shaft and caught myself before blasting through the fire doors to the third floor. After a deep breath, I eased the door open and peered back and forth down the hallways running out in each direction. Everything was silent. Tardy Man's room had to be fairly close to the elevator, because I'd been pretty quick running the stairs and he'd obviously made it into his room before I got there.

I went back to the lobby to look for a gift shop so I could change my look and make myself presentable—knocking on doors in a hotel was one thing, but doing it in a terrycloth wrap was another. I found a tourist-grade, full-length thobe and slipped it over my head. Maybe it was the Westerner in me, but I also thought it was about time to get something more than a towel around my legs. The best I could come up with from the gift shop was a pair of navy-and-dark-green checkered flannel pajamas. I threw the top away and slid into the trousers. I slipped back into the jacket, even though it didn't go with the thobe very well. In any case, I felt much better. In my new digs, I felt just a little more anonymous. Now I needed a weapon.

I passed the café, where early evening diners were in full swing. I stepped just past the vacant host's station as if I were looking for friends. I sidled up next to an unbussed table near the door and cupped my hand over an unused napkin folded around a set of cheap silverware. I extracted the butter knife, which I slid up the wide sleeve of my thobe. Mission accomplished.

Two Westerners sat at a round table by the door drinking dark European beer. My pulse quickened when I saw it. How long had it been? I took an involuntary step toward the table with the beer on it, then stopped abruptly. I had a problem. I searched my soul, and all I found was the image of Megawati, my little Timor-Leste friend, telling me to get drunk and play ball. It was enough—for today.

I left the café, nervously thumbing the butter knife as I walked—it was then that I discovered that my butter knife was actually a soup spoon. A soup spoon. I cursed my tactile ineptitude. I slid it into my boot, for what reason I didn't know. Maybe in case Bill Cosby assaulted me with jiggly Jell-O.

Now dressed in at least passable clothes, I approached the registration desk and asked for two extra pillows. The clerk asked me my room number and promised to have them delivered. I told him that I would prefer to take them myself. He hesitated, but then made a call to housekeeping. A few moments later, a perturbed-looking maid walked the pillows into the lobby and handed them to me. I said my thanks and walked straight past the bank of elevators to the stairwell.

Back on the third floor, I started knocking on doors, holding the pillows in front of me like a room service steward might do. No one answered until I'd reached the midpoint of the corridor. There I met my first irritated American businessman. He told me he didn't order pillows and waved me on my way. No tip.

The rest of the hallway was hit and miss. I had two more rejections and one lady who wanted the pillows anyway. I gave her one and told her in really bad English that I needed to find the patron who really had ordered the pillows. She seemed a little put-off that I wouldn't just give her the ones I had and go get more for the other guest.

Room number 348, the last door on the right, would finish this wing of the third floor. By now I wasn't holding out any hope. Maybe Tardy Man was smarter than he looked and had raced to another set of stairs to get to a different floor. For that matter, he might have used the Taj Sheba as a ruse and gone to a completely different hotel. I don't know how seriously these bad-guy types take their job, but I knew that real professionals almost always employed some type of subterfuge in their field craft.

I gave the door a good bludgeoning with my fist and heard smothered movement inside. The door opened a crack. It took both of us a moment to recognize each other. Tardy Man tried to jam the door shut, but not before I had a good portion of my arm wedged inside his room. I bent my knees and thrust my hips against the weight of the door, and Tardy Man fell backward as the door swung open.

I stumbled and turned on one foot, kicking the door closed with the other. "Room service," I hissed as I dropped my remaining pillow and got a hand on Tardy Man's throat. I grasped his right arm and pushed him further into his darkened room. His eyes remained cool and focused as I swept his left foot from under him and drove him down. I expected to hit the ground, but we struck the end of his mattress instead. I let go with my hand and ran my forearm over his throat. Then, remembering my failed attempt to procure a weapon, I pulled my leg to within reach and retrieved the soup spoon from the top of my boot. With the basin portion in my hand, I let the silver handle flash before Tardy Man's eyes in the dim light and then held the cold metal against his neck. The calm reserve left his eyes and was replaced by a moment of uncontrolled spastic blinking.

"Who are you?" I asked.

It was dark in the room, which was lit only by the glow of the courtyard lights diffused by sheer blue curtains that danced in the slight breeze coming through the open glass slider. I put more pressure on his neck with the spoon handle.

"Name?"

"Barbier," he said. "René Barbier. Please don't hurt me. I have a family." The tremor in his French accent didn't match the steeled look in his eyes.

"Who do you work for?" I asked.

"Électricité de Normandie." I knew a lie when I heard one and pressed down harder. After we both heard a few things crack in his throat, he decided that wasn't his final answer. "I'm a marketing consultant." He coughed. "I work for an oil company."

"You're no marketing consultant. What are you doing in Yemen?" I demanded.

He used the cold stare method another few seconds, but I wasn't buying it. "I'm a private contractor," he finally said. "Put the knife away. We don't have to do it this way."

I was pretty sure we did, but I eased off with the soup spoon just enough to give René incentive to talk.

"The Bakil." Barbier wheezed and tried to clear his throat.

I knew the Bakil well; they were the most feared Yemeni tribe in the interior, and maybe the whole country. If Barbier was telling the truth, I'd just stumbled on a huge lead. "Let's start with why you want me dead," I said.

"Not dead. Dissuaded. But perhaps now you'll have to be eliminated." The man had confidence—this wasn't his first rodeo.

"Dissuaded from what?"

"If you don't know, then I suppose my work has been in vain." He seemed amused.

"What's an old frog like you doing with the Bakil?"

"Oh, is that it?" he said. "You call me a French frog and I call you an American pig? Mr. Daniels, this isn't the way it's done."

I just about asked how he knew my name, but I didn't want to give away my ignorance. "The way it's going to be done today is that you tell me everything I want to know." I drew the spoon handle across his neck to give him another taste of cold steel—or in this case, pot-metal flatware. It was a good thing it was dark.

"All right, mon ami. We all want to be alive when this is over." He cleared his throat. "I raise funds."

"For the Bakil? Blood money for a bunch of two-bit local terrorist thugs? Figures. Anything for a buck."

"Ignorant American. You're working for the wrong side. The Bakil are without schools, hospitals, medicine. Their government gives them nothing while the wealthy in Sana'a and Aden thrive. You don't understand this because you are a privileged American. You're civilized, and you assume that's the answer to everyone else's problems. Try being civilized in the east of Yemen, Mr. Daniels."

"Fund-raiser? For schools? Sure. This is exactly how the local PTA does it. In fact, Mrs. Spencer just down the street sent an Arab thug after Mr. Jones when he wouldn't buy a cupcake at the bake sale last week. Is that what you want me to believe?" I edged the spoon around Barbier's throat just under his ear.

"Believe whatever you want, you insignificant pig." Barbier put the *p* on *pig* with a pretty good pop.

"If I'm so insignificant, why are you so hot to see me . . . dissuaded?" I asked.

"Do you really expect me to harass Miss Monroe, a CIA case officer, and bring upon myself the wrath of the United States? Stirring up the United States government would be inconvenient for me and my associates. It's just not done. Even in this game there are rules. You, however, are a deniable operative . . . Your death in Yemen will be disavowed by your precious, arrogant government. At best, it will be ignored. Why do you think they brought you in? You're a stooge. You don't even know it."

I hated it when my adversary was smarter than me. I tried to ignore the kind of sense Barbier was making, but it occurred to me that he might be right. Why bring an ex-cop all the way from Indonesia to rescue a hostage in Yemen? Barbier had me so mixed up, I doubted Rhiana. But I knew better.

I drove the spoon harder into his throat. "You're very perceptive, François, but you didn't count on one thing."

"Oh, please tell me," said Barbier.

I drew the soup spoon to the back of his neck and pressed it against his vertebrae. "I'm just a government patsy. So what if I accidentally pith some French frog in a hotel room? Who is going to care?"

For a flickering instant I think Barbier thought I might just do it, but my bluff was short-lived. Pounding on the door and yelling in Arabic interrupted our conversation. It had to be Faasid, Barbier's rotten minion.

It's hard to sound tough holding a spoon, but I made do. "This severs your spine if you make a noise."

I searched around for another door—who was I kidding, this was a hotel room. There was only one exit. Maybe Faasid would go away. Maybe pigs would fly.

The card controlled lock activated with a click, and the door swung open. The lanky silhouette of Faasid filled the brightly lit doorway. It took a moment for him to fully realize what was happening. I bolted for the balcony through the open slider.

Barbier scrambled off the bed after me with Faasid close behind. They caught me at the rail, and I'm not sure if they pushed me over or if I actually jumped, but a pig did fly—at least an ex-cop from Seattle PD.

CHAPTER 14

It was two full stories to the concrete patio in the courtyard outside of René Barbier's hotel room. I knew from my training as a police officer that a typical commercial building averaged stories of about eleven feet. I also knew that thirty-four feet was the magic distance a person might fall and have a statistically comfortable chance of survival. I'd learned that in a tactical class. Why that memory chose to surface at that particular moment of my life seemed obvious. I knew that I had roughly twenty-two feet to fall before I came to an abrupt stop— twelve feet short of statistical death. I wondered if René and Faasid were as savvy about that fact as I was, but my moment of mathematical arrogance was short-lived.

Before I'd enjoyed my guaranteed twenty-two feet of free fall, the fronds of a passing palm tree spun me like an Olympic diver, and I lost track of my proper orientation to the earth. My body rolled, and my arms and legs sprawled through the air, but my brain was preoc- cupied with the approaching ground. Somehow in my rolling flurry, my brain did the math. Only a few more compassionate feet existed between me and instant deceleration. I wondered if I'd feel it. I hit the edge of a red-and-white striped linen cabana, followed by an outdoor lounge chair, and then the concrete surface of the pool deck, and it became a moot point—I felt it.

I made a hollow thud on impact, like a baseball bat hitting a watermelon. The air in my lungs left my body and refused to come back for several moments after the fall.

The sound of a glass slider opening beside me roused me to semi- consciousness. I was aware of a shadow hovering over me, and there was a voice, too, but nothing I could understand. The sounds seemed muted at first, then they ran together, buzzing louder and louder.

I tried to lift my arm, but nothing happened. The shadowy figure turned brighter, and I saw that it was an Arab woman in a nightgown. The voice was her husband berating her for letting a man see her dressed in such a shameful way. I still couldn't move, and as I tried to expand my rib cage to pull air into my lungs, I felt tremendous pain. It was either breathe in pain or suffocate in relative comfort.

I tried again to move my arms, but they weren't having it. There was more pain as my nervous system sent nasty bright hot signals to my brain. I did, however, roll slightly to my left. The man standing over me told his wife to call the front desk and summon an ambulance. When I tried to roll again, he placed his hand gently on my chest and shook his head. At least he wasn't Faasid or René. So far so good.

"Haadhihi aw-wal 'aaSifa ramley-ya lee," I struggled to say. This is my first sandstorm.

He seemed puzzled but nodded and brushed the sweat-laden hair off my forehead. Very fatherly. The woman returned and told him that someone was coming to help.

Rhiana wasn't going to like this.

In an effort to say Rhiana's name, I opened my mouth and expelled all the air I could. What came out probably sounded like a grunt, but it was progress. As we waited, I was able to move my feet, which was a huge relief. Soon after that I moved my arms, against the urging of the husband who kept telling me to be still.

"No moving," he said. Marcus Welby, MD, he was not.

"Pushed," I groaned.

"From how far?" he asked, looking up the side of the building.

"I think I was thrown."

"How many stories?"

"Um," I said, trying to recall René Barbier's room number. It was strange that only moments earlier I could have told him exactly how many feet I'd fallen with all the irrelevant statistical information. "Eleven feet per floor," I told him.

He turned to his wife and shook his head.

"I could have done three stories, easy," I heard myself murmur. The man's face swirled into multicolored fuzz, then faded to black.

* * *

As the world turned pretty much back to normal, I found that I was prostrate on a hospital gurney in the overcrowded triage area of an emergency room. I couldn't have been hurt too badly because I was unattended in a room filled with wailing people. I turned my head, something of a private victory, and saw an endless line of ailing patients seated on circa 1970 vinyl benches. Attending them was a haggard army of nurses and aides going from patient to patient, explaining the admittance procedures and making apologies about the long wait. I wasn't a fan of hospitals, but since I'd just been lofted off a building, I thought a thorough examination might be prudent. But I couldn't stay here that long.

I didn't see a door nearby, but a green exit sign displaying both Arabic and English letters promised a way out. I pulled myself to a sitting position and threw off the thin blanket that had been draped over me. Other than the blanket, it didn't appear I'd been treated at all—no dressings or splints—and I was relatively sure, after a little moving around on the gurney, that I hadn't ruined anything vital.

My thobe was gone, and I was naked from the pajama bottoms up, but they'd left my boots beside the gurney. It's a good thing, too; the hostage rescue would be nothing compared to the nightmare I'd cause for the Yemeni public health community if I had to fight for my boots.

I wrapped a thin, tan blanket around my shoulders and swung my feet over the side of the bed, lowering myself to the floor and enduring a series of painful signals to my brain. From the knees down I felt fine, but my back refused to straighten completely and my thigh throbbed. I stretched out the elastic waistband of my checkered pajama bottoms and saw the reason written in crimson and violet along the outside of my leg. The skin was abraded over a deep and penetrating bruise that ran from the front of my thigh around to the back of my knee. My spine started to move okay, but both shoulders felt tight, and a lightning-like spasm ran the length of my neck from my scalp to my shoulder blades as I took my first step. I let out a gasp and reached out for the gurney, grinding my teeth until the wave of nausea and intense burning passed. I was light-headed and sick to my stomach.

As I slipped my feet into my unlaced boot, I noticed an aide, who looked to be in his early twenties, squatting by a small girl on the other side of the room. The girl, no more than six, wore a sour expression, then smiled reluctantly at whatever the young man said to her.

I made a half-hearted step away from the gurney and paused, not sure I could actually walk unassisted. I took another tentative step, then another.

"Sit," said a voice from behind me.

Pretending I didn't hear, I strode on, trying to hide my unsteady gait.

"Excuse me. You must lie down," insisted the voice.

"I must find my friend," I said, taking another step away from the gurney.

The voice was coming from the nice young man who'd made the girl laugh. His eyes narrowed as he looked back and forth between me and the gurney I'd left empty.

No one would have called what I did running, but I shuffled as fast as I could toward the exit door at the end of the hallway. There were angry voices behind me telling me to stop, but no one pursued me down the hallway. I made it to a set of old wooden doors at the exit and thrust through them into the bright light of morning past a sign that said Al-Thawra Hospital. I disappeared into the maze of narrow, winding streets of Sana'a . . . in my pajama bottoms and boots, still clutching my stolen blanket.

CHAPTER 15

The Al-Thawra Hospital, as I soon found out, was near the old center of town, and it took me no time to lose myself in the labyrinth of streets. The morning traffic was just beginning to swell onto the arterials, and it wasn't hard to find a taxi to take me back to the Sheraton Hotel. I told the driver I'd had a family emergency in the middle of the night, which explained the way I was dressed, and promised him a large tip. He shrugged and nodded at the back door of the taxi, looking critically at my blankie.

At the Sheraton, I took the back stairs to Rhiana's room. I knocked on the door, wary that René Barbier knew I'd eventually come back here.

Madeline answered the door, not just a little perturbed at the hour I came a callin'. "Look at you. You don't get that from falling down the stairs . . . in two different countries." She pointed her chubby finger at me and examined a fresh set of injuries. "I don't know what your problem is, but I'm watching you." I pulled the blanket tighter around my neck as Madeline retreated into the room.

Rhiana appeared at the doorway, smiling at Madeline's diatribe about how strange I was. The smile faded to concern when she saw me. The road scuff on my face was healing, but the frond marks and patio furniture bruises were new.

"Out here," I said, waving her into the hall.

She looked me over top to bottom, taking in the whole blanket-pajama ensemble.

"Rhi?" I gestured again to the hallway. Madeline was talking to herself in the dim light of the hotel room, something about seeing me in irons, no doubt.

Rhiana didn't move, but I heard her frustration escape in a long, forced sigh.

"Rhi," I whined, "hear me out."

The look in her eyes said there would be very little hearing out.

"Kam, Darrin is just about in tears," she said. "He's convinced you've gone to Djibouti without him. I spent two hours last night trying to convince him you were okay."

"I know, but . . ."

"You *don't* know. Where have you been?"

"Big score, Rhi."

"You look awful. What are you wearing?"

"A blanket and pajamas." I couldn't tell if Rhiana's look was of pity or something not as genteel, but I went on. "But I found the guy." I was a little less excited, wondering at Rhiana's coolness. "Tardy Man. The guy who got on the plane in Paris after the rest of us. René . . ."

"Barbier?" she said under her breath.

"He's the guy who sent his goons after me in Paris . . . How did you know?"

"After you left, I was thinking about what happened to you in Paris. I had Roger examine the travel documents of everyone on our flight. Barbier came up using a known alias." She didn't elaborate.

"Frenchman," I said. The information I'd risked life and limb for was hardly getting the animated response I'd been hoping for. Roger was getting all the credit, and he hadn't even done a flying two-and-a-half triple twist off the Taj balcony.

"René Barbier is a well-known French intelligence operative," Rhiana told me. "Or he was. Now he works for anyone with the money to pay him. Turkey, Greece, Pakistan, Belarus . . . whoever has the cash. According to Roger, he went rogue about two years ago and has been working in Yemen and Saudi ever since."

"Roger's just a little wealth of information, isn't he?"

"Kam, we have ways of doing things. Procedures. Policies. Do you remember those?"

"Barbier is working for the Bakil," I said. "Did Roger know that? He told me he's raising funds for schools. He's a regular Bakil philanthropist."

"The Bakil?" said Rhiana. "No. Our sources consistently point to his affiliation with the Palestine Liberation Organization training on the coast in the north."

I had to really suppress an unwholesome remark about Roger's information.

Rhiana studied my tousled hair and my palm frond–marred neck and chest. "Please tell me that you didn't do anything stupid to get that information."

"Exactly what do you mean by *stupid*?" The way the conversation was going, I couldn't very well give Rhiana a blow-by-blow of my evening. I said, "Barbier's thug is Bakil." Not necessarily a lie.

Rhiana said. "And you know a Bakil tribesman by sight?"

"He had . . . the Bakil look." Massive lie; there's no such look.

I told Rhiana a heavily edited version of the "subtle subterfuge" I'd used at the Taj Sheba Hotel to identify René Barbier and his Bakil sidekick. I left out almost everything.

Rhiana looked like she was just about to ask me to elaborate on the "subtle subterfuge" part, but she just stared at me instead. She knew whitewash when she heard it. "It's now past six AM. That took you all night? Do I want to ask?"

"I doubt you do," I said. "Good solid police work is like that. Almost magical, but it does take time."

"So he knows we're on to him?"

I raised a finger like a good college lecturer and said, "You know, I think he's a pretty smart man. We have to assume he knows we're on to him."

"Great. Now what?" asked Rhiana.

The question sounded rhetorical, as questions posed by angry people often are, so I didn't say anything.

"Well?" she said. Her tone still sounded slightly rhetorical. Rhiana paced to the end of the hall and then back.

"We need to get everyone to the embassy this morning," said Rhiana. "They'll have to wait there until we can get them a safe flight out of Yemen."

"Which of us is 'them' and which of us is 'we'?" I asked.

Rhiana looked at me for a moment, then turned away and held onto the door handle. She paused as if she wanted to say more but didn't. Then she gently opened the door and went inside.

"Um, that wasn't a rhetorical question," I said as the door clicked closed in my face. "And I have a taxi driver to pay. Can I borrow a twenty?"

* * *

The rest of the morning brought with it the promise of a hot, sweaty, uncomfortable day. Maybe that was because the only rest I'd had was on the pool deck at the Taj. After borrowing some money from Darrin to pay my taxi, I made a valiant effort at showering, but the water didn't feel all that great on my various injuries, so I settled for a combination sponge bath, spit bath. I gathered up what little I'd brought with me into my small duffel and set it by the door. Darrin was doing much the same thing, with a lot more luggage. I waited for him to throw straps over each shoulder and get a bag in each hand before we made our way to the parking lot together. Buds.

On the steps of the hotel entrance, we waited for our rides and watched the heat vapors blur the mud-brick cityscape. It was a little like staring at an M. C. Escher drawing. When the two Land Cruisers arrived, Darrin went straight to the second one, driven by Dandré, and hoisted his equipment into the back, working toward the best possible fit. When he was done, he fetched his associates' bags and did the same while they sat on the steps and talked quietly.

Rhiana left her bags for Darrin to carry and approached Pierre, who was sitting in the driver's seat of the lead vehicle. They talked for a few minutes until an animated discussion ensued. Neither looked very happy with the other.

I walked casually up behind Rhiana and asked over her shoulder, "What's the hold up, ma'am?"

Rhiana and Pierre stopped arguing, and Rhiana answered after a brief conspiratorial silence. "We're just finalizing a few details about the route to the embassy," she said.

"When you have a moment?" I backed off a few steps for propriety's sake, to let Rhiana and Pierre finish.

They exchanged a few clipped words before she walked over to me.

"I'm nervous about the delay," I said, looking around.

"Pierre is upset that we're ditching the scholars. He thinks their absence will make it impossible to move freely outside the city. He insists on reporting the change in plan to his command center and waiting for instructions."

"Is he being difficult?" I asked.

"No, he has a protocol, and he wants to follow it."

"Hard to blame him," I said, looking out over the parking lot.

Rhiana said, "I have to call the embassy anyway. They want to know when we leave. Roger's been on the phone with the U.N. command center all night. They can get these people out of Yemen today."

"And we're staying?" I asked.

Rhiana looked back and forth between Pierre and me. Pierre offered a glare in Rhiana's direction that must have been a remnant of whatever conversation I'd just interrupted. "*We're* going to the embassy." She raised her eyebrows as if to suggest that if I said another word in front of Pierre, I'd die where I stood.

"We're really exposed out here," I said, walking away from Rhiana and toward our group. "We have to get this crowd moving." I wasn't saying anything that both Rhiana and Pierre didn't already know. Pierre nodded and dialed his cell phone, or what was probably more accurately a satellite phone, heavy on the encryption just like Rhiana's.

Rhiana gave the general order to find a seat in one of the two Land Cruisers, and Father Andrew, Clyde, and Rhiana got in with Pierre, leaving room for Madeline, Darrin, and me with Dandré. Madeline didn't look like she wanted to ride with the likes of me.

Pierre started the engine and said something to Dandré over a small two-way radio, the twenty-dollar kind you buy your kids at Target. I jumped in the backseat behind Dandré and looked at Madeline next to me. Then I winked. I'm sure the disparaging look she returned was simply a result of Yemeni sand in her eyes.

Dandré slipped out of the driver's door and strode to the back of his vehicle. He opened the tailgate and slammed it. "She is not shutting," he said, then cursed as the blood-chilling, ultrasonic whip of a bullet passed overhead. I recognized the unique sound of distant rifle fire immediately, and so did Dandré.

CHAPTER 16

Dandré, with his head down, made a move toward the driver's side door, but three more rounds slapped the back of the Land Cruiser. Dandré's radio was chattering away, and I saw Pierre screaming into his radio as the tires of his Land Cruiser spread sand and gravel in an arc on the pavement.

"Dandré!" I yelled.

He'd moved to the passenger side for cover and still had his head down. Madeline, who was just figuring things out, was screaming, "I knew it, I knew it," and trying to slap me. Pretty brave if you considered her point of view.

Darrin threw the passenger door open for Dandré and jumped across the middle console into the driver's seat. I saw Dandré's head come up in the passenger seat, and the Land Cruiser lurched forward with a shriek.

A high-caliber slug penetrated the headliner of the Land Cruiser and ripped a jagged scar in the dashboard between Darrin and Dandré. Darrin swung the Land Cruiser wide into the oncoming lane, sending a string of Yemeni drivers off the road. Madeline and I were thrown back and forth against the sides of the vehicle as Darrin fought for control.

Struggling against the side-to-side movement of the Land Cruiser and its straining suspension, I worked the manual window crank until I could squeeze my head and arm outside. Nothing about the Land Cruiser offered any real cover against what was obviously a high-caliber rifle, so despite the feeling that I was a sitting duck, I was no worse off flailing out the window, but I had a better view.

The most obvious high ground was somewhere in the hotel. I tried to catch a glimpse of a flash signature from the rifle as Darrin accelerated onto the thoroughfare leading away from the hotel, but I saw nothing as the hotel disappeared.

Dandré was communicating with Pierre in precise, clipped phrases on the cheap sporting-goods-store walkie-talkie; it wasn't the high-tech device I might have expected these strack troops to be using, but it was doing the trick.

The Land Cruisers were separated by a few cars now, but I assumed Pierre had a good idea what had happened, because I saw Father Andrew's white face peering out the back passenger window of the other Land Cruiser as it snaked around a corner and disappeared down an intersecting block, tires chirping on the dry pavement.

I slipped back in the window and took a look around now that we were riding on a two-lane avenue somewhere in Sana'a at the mercy of a religious studies graduate student named Darrin. Darrin was too busy driving to be scared, although I thought he might be a shade or two paler than normal. Madeline was pretty ashen too.

Darrin, not in the mood to slow down, steered sharply around a small native boy pushing a wheelbarrow full of slightly used plastic jugs. The maneuver threw me to the other side of the backseat on top of Madeline. I don't know if Madeline was more upset about being shot at or that I was touching her.

I pulled myself back to my own seat. "Do you see the other Cruiser?" I yelled over the whine of the engine.

Both Darrin and Dandré were looking wildly around for the other Land Cruiser, now lost in traffic. Darrin's glasses kept falling sideways across his nose as the vehicle rocked back and forth.

Madeline was back to repeating, "I knew it. I knew you were trouble." In a feat worthy of clowns in a phone booth, she had squeezed her considerable body onto the floor.

"Darrin, we've got to get . . ." I couldn't finish the sentence because I couldn't think of a safe place to get to.

"I'm working on it." Darrin tugged the wheel again to avoid a pedestrian meandering down our lane.

I was about to tell Darrin to slow down when the back window broke apart with a thunderous crash. Everyone's head went down.

"It's coming from another vehicle," I yelled from below seat level. I suddenly understood how Madeline had made herself fit in the small space on the floor—proper motivation. I risked a peek over the backseat and saw a taxi driver directly behind us brandishing a revolver out the window.

Terrified and angry, Madeline wailed from the floor. A small duffel bag toppled onto her head, and she batted at it as the Land Cruiser picked up speed on a straightaway. Her cries were lost in the noise of the accelerating engine and the weaving, screeching tires.

Darrin tugged at the wheel. "It's loose! The steering wheel is loose!" he yelled, fighting to control the Land Cruiser.

I chanced a peek between the front seats and saw Dandré desperately clawing at a backpack stowed on the floorboard under the driver's seat. From the pack he drew a foreign knockoff of a Colt 1911, a .45-caliber automatic pistol that he gripped in his right hand as he pulled back on the slide to check the chamber. He braced the weapon against the headrest and scanned the street behind us. As the Land Cruiser bounced and swerved all over creation, so did the dangerous end of Dandré's pistol, pointing at my head each time the Land Cruiser bucked or changed direction. I recalled the four cardinal rules of firearms safety posted at the entrance to the Seattle Police Department firearms range: All guns are always loaded; Be sure of your backstop and what's behind it; Never point a weapon at anything you are not willing to destroy; and Finger off the trigger until you are on target and ready to shoot.

I'm pretty sure Dandré knew his weapon was loaded, and he was professional enough to have his finger indexed along the slide of his pistol, but he was in blatant violation of the other two rules and was subject to being tossed off the range at any moment. Of course there were always mitigating circumstances, like the taxi full of Arab hatred chasing us through the Queen of Sheba's capital city.

Another round from the taxi driver's gun made its home in the headliner. Dandré responded in kind, and without warning, a painful ringing assaulted my ears, and I felt like someone had stuffed my head twenty feet deep in Play-Doh. All my senses were affected by the concussion of Dandré's pistol, and I was immediately nauseated. Madeline, similarly affected, yelped and dug even deeper into the floor. Two more rounds from Dandré's pistol went off through what used to be the back window, neither of which produced the similar head-splitting effect on me because I was already deaf. I glanced at Darrin, who seemed to be unaffected and who was still sharply focused on every aspect of his driving. Dandré was scanning back and forth across the traffic behind us. I dared to get my head up over the backseat and saw that the taxi had dropped back several cars. Apparently the driver had been discouraged by Dandré's return fire. I immediately forgave Dandré for his police range faux pas.

Darrin was enigmatically in his element behind the wheel. He used steering, brakes, and accelerator together in a grand symphony of superb driving technique to thread the Land Cruiser through the narrow backstreets of Sana'a. Outpacing the other traffic, and increasing our lead on the taxi, he slowed before each tight corner and used the accelerator to pull the vehicle through the apex. He heaved and leaned on the steering wheel to keep himself upright in the driver's seat while the rest of us were thrown forward and side-to-side with each change of direction.

I looked out the back window, now less a window and more a jagged opening. "The shooting has stopped," I said. "No more shots." I wasn't sure if I was making an observation or expressing my deepest desire, but the taxi was far enough back now that the driver had to concentrate fully on driving just to keep up.

Dandré allowed himself an almost imperceptible sigh of relief but kept a vigilant watch on the road behind us, weapon at the ready just over my head. Darrin passed several more cars in the heavy morning traffic, leaving the taxi farther behind.

Pierre said something on the radio that sounded like French gibberish, but Dandré seemed to understand and instructed Darrin to turn left.

Darrin complied, passing a squatty version of a minibus on the right, and gained more ground on the taxi. Darrin wasn't Sana'a's favorite driver this morning, but he was ours.

"Nice driving," I said, surprised that our innocent little Mormon religionist had such command of our Land Cruiser. "Where'd you learn to handle a car like that?"

"I'm from Utah," he said, still concentrating wholly on the road ahead. "You've never driven in Utah?" Darrin was bearing down on the foreign job in front of him, no less than ten feet from its bumper.

Of all the things in the world to laugh at, Madeline chose that moment to be amused at Darrin's remark. She lifted her head up, wriggled her shoulders from their wedged position against the drive-shaft hump, and said, "It's true. I've driven in Utah."

"Side streets," said Dandré in English. His command of two different languages under this kind of stress was commendable. Following more hasty directions from Dandré, Darrin kept us well ahead of the pursuing taxi. For a moment, I thought Dandré was pretty clever, but then it occurred to me that trying to lose a taxi driver who's trying to kill you was pretty elementary at this point. Our disadvantage was that we didn't know the streets, and presumably the Arab driver did. Darrin made another brilliant maneuver, braking and plowing into an alley on the right and then correcting into a left skid that took us down another narrow street.

"Turn left. To the Old City," said Dandré, still periodically scanning out the back window over the top of his pistol. Every time Madeline saw the pistol raised and pointed past her face, she cringed and sank lower to the floor. I felt the same way, still hearing things as if I were three feet underwater—and still on the verge of losing my breakfast in my lap.

"Directions?" asked Darrin. His tone was flat and academic, as if he did this kind of thing every day before lunch. I don't know what kind of language I might have been using if I were in Darrin's position, but I know what I'm capable of, and it wouldn't have been pretty.

Dandré apparently didn't know the city that well either, and he spent a few quality moments craning his head around and trying to get his bearings.

Darrin was doing his best to outdrive the taxi, and he was succeeding. I couldn't see the taxi behind us.

"Are we safe?" asked Madeline.

"No," said Darrin. "If we can just get into one of these alleys," he said, groaning at the wheel as he put the Land Cruiser into a power slide and managed to miss careening into a thousand-year-old wall by less than a foot.

My head struck the window post of the Land Cruiser, which added to the befuddled feeling I was already experiencing as a result of the gunfire in the confined passenger compartment of the vehicle. I'd thank Darrin later.

"Go south," said Dandré.

"South? I don't know . . ." Dandré pointed, and Darrin, his head craning to see around the bend in the alley, put the car into another hard turn, aiming at an even narrower alley. "The wheel is loose," he complained for the second time.

"That way. That way," said Dandré, flailing his pointed finger in front of Darrin's face. "Keep going."

If the taxi was able to follow, I couldn't tell, but it never paid to assume, so Darrin did some more *Streets-of-San-Francisco* driving and eventually turned onto a main road, one with some pavement visible beneath the sand, and we made better time, still unsure if we'd lost the taxi for good.

As we approached another blind corner, Darrin locked up all four tires and brought the Land Cruiser to a sliding stop, throwing me and everything else in the back of the vehicle forward through the air onto Madeline. Dandré nearly hit his head on the dashboard and whipped back into his seat as the Land Cruiser stopped. With a fierce grimace on his face, he uttered a couple of French barnyard epitaphs. "Keep driving, you fool," he yelled. "Keep driving." Then he looked over at Darrin.

There in the driver's seat sat Darrin, holding aloft a perfectly serviceable steering wheel not presently connected to anything.

He handed it to Dandré, who was still scowling. "Here, you drive."

It took us all a moment to process, and then almost as one, we swung our doors open and bailed out.

We'd run just a few yards from the Land Cruiser when I noticed we were one Boston College sociologist short. Bolting back to the Toyota, I found Madeline cowering on the floor in the backseat still covered in luggage. I pulled on the door handle but was unable to get the latch to release. I ran around the other side where my door was still standing open and leaned inside. She was mumbling terror-induced gibberish, and I took two handfuls of her shirt and bodily pulled her over the seat and out my door. A couple of gear bags and an aluminum equipment case tumbled out with her. Struggling against years of Twinkie abuse, she fought to her feet.

Tripping over bags as we ran, we followed Dandré as he waved us forward.

"Only a few blocks," said Dandré. We walked and jogged more than a few of Dandré's blocks until we were part of a crowd moving toward the Old City, where locals sold their wares in a massive sauq, or outdoor market. It was something like Pike's Place Market in Seattle, but it covered ten times the real estate and the street music was different. The place was packed with people, which made it a great, if somewhat obvious, place to hide.

Despite being well off the beaten trail, Yemen had the potential for a thriving tourist industry. In the last ten years, the country had shaken off some of its third-world crust and taken a few tentative steps into the twenty-first century. It was still a dangerous place, ruled largely by desert tribal chieftains and mountain warlords, but democracy was clawing along in a forward direction, and the Europeans were taking note. It was evident here, in Sana'a's largest tourist area, that Eastern civilization was thriving.

The Old City was walled, and the main gates were fenced like a funnel to squeeze the throngs inside. We joined the melee going in. It would have been impossible to change directions if we'd had to, but at the moment, a crowd seemed our safest bet. Dandré led the way, and I followed with Darrin and Madeline sharing third position, desperate not to get separated from the group. Darrin had a hold of my shirttail, and Madeline was nearly hugging Darrin. Anyone paying attention to us would have thought us a pretty nervous group of tourists.

The crowd became more and more dense as we neared the gate, then suddenly we found ourselves inside the Old City sauq where there was room to spread out.

"Dandré," I said. I realized I had a wad of his sleeve in my fist. I let go, but not before he looked down at the creases I'd left, probably thinking about the seventeen ways he could kill me with his bare hands. "They're here, right?" I asked.

After a moment, he said, "You take care of the mad scientists."

"They're religious scientists," I corrected.

Dandré smiled. "Oh, mon ami, they are mad now." Dandré was a jokester. Who knew?

Darrin and Madeline stood close behind me in a daze, probably not picking up on much of anything going on around them.

Dandré stepped a few paces from us and scanned the crowd but didn't seem to be pursuing any preestablished protocol. He had seemed pretty intent on getting us to the Old City, so I had to assume that he and Pierre had worked something out on their radios, if not just after the shooting started, then before. Either that or he was working solo, flying by the seat of his pants, and hoping that Pierre would come to the same conclusion as he about the safety of the busy marketplace.

"But are they here?" I asked again.

Dandré didn't take his eyes off the crowd, but his silence was answer enough. He wasn't sure.

CHAPTER 17

I looked after our less-tactically-minded religionists as we strolled awkwardly several yards behind Dandré, who alternately checked the entrance gate and peered down the several auxiliary streets leading deeper into the sauq.

I smiled at Darrin; it was my way of keeping a stiff upper lip and lending confidence to the troops. It was false bravado. I felt like I'd been gut-punched and needed to throw up.

Our small group was vulnerable, Dandré being our only real protection. I would never make fun of the French Special Forces again. Who was I kidding; how could I resist?

"Dandré's going to contact the other half of our group," I said, not sure we'd ever see them again. "Tonight we'll eat dinner at the embassy and sleep peacefully under the protection of the United States Marine Corps." More comfort to the troops.

Darrin had a look on his face like he'd just sucked the rotten yolk from an ostrich egg. Madeline didn't look much better—but angrier.

Darrin nodded, and Madeline showed her thanks by nodding and rolling her eyes. Neither of them was naïve enough to believe anything I said.

The Old City marketplace was a little bit like a fruit stand that covered numerous city blocks—a farmer's market on steroids. Rickety displays of spices, trinkets, and woven goods stood in various degrees of disrepair in every available space, sometimes spilling out into the path of tourists and customers. I led my wards through the maze of tiny shops, staying just far enough away from Dandré to let him pick his own route through the throngs. We ventured down the midway once but saw no familiar faces.

"Why isn't he using his radio?" asked Madeline after we returned to the main gate area.

I pulled her and Darrin out of earshot of Dandré. "Look, these guys are professionals. They have a plan for every possible scenario. Trust me—he knows what he's doing. There's a good reason he's not using his radio. Let's just get with the program."

I left Madeline and Darrin at a lean-to of hanging pots and pans for sale and approached Dandré.

"Is this part of the contingency plan?" I asked close to his ear.

Dandré shrugged.

"Pierre knows to come here?" I asked.

"I think so," said Dandré.

"And you raised him on the radio?"

"Lost." Dandré looked at me for the first time since we ran from the Land Cruiser.

"Pierre and the others are lost?"

"No," said Dandré folding his tremendous arms over his chest.

"Okay, I'm pullin' teeth here. Help me out. Pierre is lost, and you can't raise him on the radio?"

"No. I don't know where Pierre and the others are, and the radio is . . . lost." Dandré looked into my eyes, daring me to take a cheap shot.

I looked at his massive arms. "Human beings do human things," I said. "I got that from one of my sergeants."

"I didn't know interpreters had sergeants," Dandré said.

"Oh, they don't. I was talking about my sergeant in the Salvation Army, that's all." I could have added that it was the Dili, Pennsylvania chapter of the Salvation Army, but I'd opened my mouth enough. Besides, Dandré knew better.

"The Old City sauq was the emergency rendezvous for yesterday," said Dandré. "We hadn't discussed one for today. Pierre and Rhiana had a difference of opinion regarding the embassy and . . ." He didn't finish, but I knew how sudden, unexplained changes could destroy well-made plans.

"He'll come here," I said. "Where else would he look for us?"

"Nowhere," Dandré said.

"Can you get Darrin and Madeline to the embassy?" I asked Dandré. Our religionists had tired of looking at cheap cookware and had moved to the next lean-to and were browsing shelf after shelf of identical Kodak disposable cameras. Some Eritrean pirate had hit the mother lode, and smugglers had managed to get the entire shipment into the sauq.

"And you?" asked Dandré.

"I'll wait here for Pierre."

"And for Rhiana?" Dandré smiled.

"For Clyde and Father Andrew," I said. I turned my back on Dandré and took a few steps toward Darrin and Madeline. "And for Rhiana." There's no such thing as a secret.

"For whom?" The light voice sailed over the din and clamor of the sauq. There was only one person I knew with a voice that sweet and grammar that precise. Rhiana approached us from behind, followed by the unscathed forms of Clyde, Father Andrew, and Pierre.

"Rhiana," said Madeline as she lunged toward her. The two women embraced. Clyde and Father Andrew stood back, and we all exchanged nods as if meeting up on the outer concourse of a football stadium before the big game.

"How was your trip?" asked Father Andrew.

I looked around and then realized he was talking to me. "Uh, fantastic. Darrin drove. Utah driver." Only Clyde laughed.

Dandré and Pierre had separated themselves from the pack and were engaged in a French conversation with a lot of guttural growling, a few *oui-oui*s, and a lot of *non-non*s. We all had a lot to talk about, but none of us seemed to know where to start.

After Rhiana escaped Madeline's grasp, she walked toward me and took my hand. She looked into my eyes and squeezed. I'd been worried about her too. Madeline grimaced and Darrin looked at us as if an idea were dawning on him. He started to point at us and took a breath as if to speak, but then it looked like it all clicked together for him. He apparently decided that discretion was called for and said nothing else.

After he concluded his conversation with Dandré, Pierre strode over and presented his plan, such as it was, to our group. Dandré, playing second banana, stood supportively behind him.

"We need new vehicles and a place to sort things out."

"I thought we were going to the embassy," said Madeline. Darrin nodded. I think everyone agreed that the embassy was the safest place for us.

"Yeah, and then how about a plane ticket to anywhere but France," I added.

Pierre didn't like that, and his little pursed French lips showed it. "Perhaps for you, Mr. Daniels." He turned to Rhiana. "The embassy . . ." he was shaking his head.

Rhiana finished for him. "We are going to the embassy, but not until I hear back from them."

Madeline said, "Why can't we go right now? Kam said the Marines would be there."

"Yes," said Rhiana, "But we don't know who might be waiting for us on the way. It's better if we wait for instructions from the embassy."

"But they were shooting at us," Madeline whined.

"Somebody is chasing us," said Father Andrew. He got the award for the most obvious observation of the day. It's always nice to clarify things once in a while.

Clyde didn't seem quite as keyed up. "We need transportation. We can wait here until Pierre and Dandré come up with something," he said.

Pierre nodded. "Dandré and I will be back with vehicles. We can plan an approach to the embassy at that time." It all seemed so cut-and-dried to him.

"What's going on here?" said Madeline. "Who are you people?" She pointed a Vienna sausage finger at me. "You . . . you're getting us in this trouble." Madeline turned to Rhiana and in almost a whisper asked, "It's him, isn't it? He's always getting into trouble. Look at his face. He's a terrorist."

"How long before you get back?" Rhiana asked Pierre, leaving Madeline to stew over her own paranoid imagination.

It was a synchronize-your-watches moment. Rhiana exchanged sentimentality for a soldierly demeanor. It was cute, in a militant sort of way.

I had to get my head in the game. I addressed Pierre directly. "We'll check for you inside the main gates every odd hour until

1700 hours, then every even hour just outside the gates. After 2000 hours, if we haven't found you, we'll plan a tactical approach to the American embassy on our own. That goes for anyone who finds themselves separated from the group." I turned right to Madeline and gave her my most convincing maybe-I'm-a-terrorist-and-maybe-I'm-not look. "Multiple meeting places and multiple timings," I said.

Dandré said to me, "An interpreter, huh?"

"I watch spy movies."

Rhiana shook her head, then turned to Pierre. "Not a bad idea," she said.

Pierre grunted his assent—a French grunt. If someone had told me a week ago that a person could grunt in French, I would have thought they were a little weird. But Pierre did it, and Dandré followed suit, each making a distinctly French guttural noise and nodding. And there you had it—U.S. cooperation with the French.

With little left to discuss, Pierre and Dandré headed for the main gates, and the rest of our happy little group stood around and looked at each other. The Old Sana'a sauq reverberated with the calls of salespeople who needed extra Yemeni rials for the monthly budget. It was a good place to hide for a few hours.

Madeline couldn't take her evil eye off me. She raised an eyebrow and asked Rhiana under her breath, "He is, isn't he?"

"He's what?" Rhiana asked.

"A terrorist." Madeline wasn't going to be convinced otherwise.

Rhiana blew her off with a cold look. "Over by the well house." She nodded toward a small stone shed in the common area of the sauq and started walking.

As the group followed, I leaned toward Rhiana. "You've called the embassy?"

She nodded and kept walking, not looking at me.

"And they know where we are?"

This time she did look at me, but it was the irritated look someone gives when they are being asked dumb questions. I got the point.

We gathered in a rough circle beside the well house and probably looked like a tourist group getting together for daily instructions.

Rhiana said to the group, "I'm an employee of the United States government. I have been traveling as a member of this group under a false pretense." I assumed Rhiana would remain vague in her explanation, both because that's what secret agents do as a matter of habit and because she didn't want to paint Clyde into a corner, but her candor got the attention of the religionists.

Madeline was still more interested in me than Rhiana's disclosure and never really took her eyes off me.

"I used your trip to cloak my own movements to and around Yemen," Rhiana said.

"His too?" asked Madeline, pointing at me.

Rhiana wisely ignored the question. "Although there is always an element of risk under such circumstances, the United States government had no reason to believe that there was any specific risk associated with this particular operation." Rhiana sounded as if she were reading a prepared statement drafted by lawyers for a press conference in the governor's mansion.

So far Rhiana hadn't implicated Clyde, but he wasn't the kind of man who would hide behind her skirts. He said, "Rhiana simply needed to move people into Yemen without attracting the attention of some of Yemen's darker elements."

"Like that one," said Madeline, looking at me.

Again she was ignored. Looking to Rhiana for approval, Clyde went on. "This was done with the full cooperation of the Yemeni government and myself." Clyde did his own implicating but didn't mention Brigham Young University. "What happened this morning was completely unexpected and . . ." he looked at Rhiana again, ". . . unexplainable? At least at this point?" Clyde was like a good press secretary, not really answering questions, but clarifying answers.

"Yes," Rhiana lied—sort of.

Father Andew was a trooper and didn't press for more information. "What do we do now?"

"I want to know exactly what this is about and who you all are," said Madeline.

"Madeline. It's not important," said Clyde. "Let's focus on . . ."

"Yes, it is," Rhiana interrupted. "Father Andrew and Madeline, you two have known each other for a long time. Clyde is also who he says he is, a BYU professor. Darrin is one of his students. I'm a government employee. Kamir is a translator." That earned me another suspicious look from Madeline. "Our drivers are operatives from another government. Obviously, they are French."

"What? Like you're a CIA spy?" asked Madeline. She stopped glaring at me and looked at Rhiana.

"Case officer."

Clyde said, "This is nothing new. We all know that people in our situation have been asked to do favors for their governments before."

"This is going to be just like Vietnam," said Madeline.

"What?" said Father Andrew, and then he shook his head. "Let's worry about right now." He looked to Rhiana.

"We are going to hide in plain sight until our drivers come back for us," she said.

Around us the Arab shoppers began preparation for noon prayer, or Dhuhr. The locals knew the proper orientation of Mecca so they could point themselves the right direction, but Muslim travelers would have to figure it out themselves. No doubt, the average guy would look at the Muslim praying next to him, but there were always those who had to do everything for themselves. Never having been Muslim, but with many Muslim family members, I'd heard just about every conceivable argument for how to properly identify the true direction of Mecca, and it always made me think about my Uncle Ammu.

Great-Uncle Ammu almost always found himself at odds with the family over the proper direction of prayer. He waved a withered hand at his young married nephews, who brazenly used a map to find the declination of Mecca. Maps offended Uncle Ammu's Muslim sensibilities; "The declination is always a bit off," he'd complain. And then, heaven forbid, one of the nephews would use a watch to tell the time to start and end prayers. I always got the feeling that Uncle Ammu knew just how many rays of sun had to be seen over the horizon to qualify as Shurooq, the end of morning worship, or the length of the shadows at Dhuhr, the midday supplication. I really liked my cantankerous Uncle Ammu. I don't remember his given name. *Ammu* is Arabic for "uncle," so technically I called him Uncle Uncle, but he never seemed to mind.

I looked at the shadows cast by the members of our crew. Great-Uncle Ammu was right; when a shadow is twice the length of whatever makes it, it's time for Dhuhr. Muslims all over the sauq knelt on prayer rugs, and Westerners mingled in quiet groups to watch the religious observance.

"I'm with them," Father Andrew said, bowing his head and closing his eyes.

Rhiana looked to Clyde, uncertain about the whole concept.

"That's a fantastic idea," said Clyde.

Darrin bowed his head, and even Madeline clasped her hands and shut her eyes. I peeked at Rhiana, who looked like she was going along with the idea. I spent a few seconds trying out a few awkward hand positions for prayer and then gave up. I spent prayer time keeping watch over the group.

After he opened his eyes, Darrin moved closer to me. "Aren't you Muslim?"

I shrugged, then shook my head. My mother had either adopted a very subtle form of Christianity when my Caucasian-American father moved her to the United States, or she'd given up religion altogether. I wasn't sure. All I really knew was that I realized for the first time in my life that I didn't know how to pray.

Darrin waited for a more comprehensive answer. I didn't have one for him. I felt a little like a Sam Cooke lyric, "Don't know much about history," or in this case, prayer. But I did know about tactics, and it wasn't a good time to prostrate myself and close my eyes. I let my eyes wander from the supplicating Muslims to the sauq tourists waiting for the end of Dhuhr.

The locals were still deeply involved in their prayers when my eyes caught movement at the main gates and I saw René Barbier and his Arab thug slithering into the Old City sauq, accompanied by the mesmerizing chant of the muezzin. I couldn't very well announce Barbier's presence to the group or six wide-eyed faces would all turn toward the gates at once. It was indeed fortunate that our heads were down. If that was an answer to prayer, it was a clever one.

Barbier's head turned back and forth as he looked the crowd over, then he headed hastily toward the main midway. Faasid followed, completely ignoring the call to prayer. Disregard for prayer was an act allowable only when actively engaged in Jihad—holy war against the infidels, or in this case, unholy war against me.

CHAPTER 18

International espionage had an intriguing romantic ring to it, but there was no romance about the six of us standing in the open market, ripe for another attack.

Barbier and his minion had passed us and disappeared into the labyrinth of intersecting alleys that made up the sauq, but they could return at any moment.

We stood just inside the gates of Old Sana'a, the tourist crowds standing shoulder to shoulder around the various booths and other attractions that populated the entrance to the sauq. Many of the people here wore native garb, but enough were in Western clothing that our group didn't stand out as badly as I had feared they might. That didn't ease my own discomfort at being in Western dress.

"Let's walk around and fit in," said Rhiana after most heads were up from prayer. "I'm tempted to split up so we're not in such a big group, but then again . . ."

"Rhiana, we've got a problem," I said. The look on my face, and the fact that I hadn't taken my eyes off the midway since prayers started, must have spoken to Rhiana.

She seemed to understand the looming threat, but she shook her head slightly and went on, not wanting me to scare the civilians. She told the group, "But then again, we don't have any way to communicate, and I'd rather have us within sight of each other."

Heads nodded, mostly because no one had any better ideas. I had seen this pattern a million times; ignorance needed action to feel better about itself. It was a typical panic reaction, but Rhiana seemed pretty coolheaded. The others, however, were drawing attention to themselves by their gloomy dispositions. I knew they were tired. I knew they were upset. I knew they were scared.

"You look like the sorriest bunch of . . . Look at you," I said.

It wasn't so much their clothes that set them apart, but Father Andrew was carrying a duffel bag, and Clyde had brought a full-blown suitcase on wheels. It made the lot of us look like our bus had broken down and left us on foot in the Peruvian Highlands.

"We need to look like tourists, not hitchhikers," I said. "Let's ditch the luggage." It was pretty unsympathetic of me, considering my duffel was somewhere in a broken-down Land Cruiser that I'd never see again.

"He's right." Rhiana tossed her small shoulder bag to me. "We look like the cast of *Gilligan's Island* sitting beside our wrecked ship."

The hundred-year-old door to the well house opened freely—after I splintered the edge with a stiff yank. Inside it was simply a crusty hole with enough room around it for a couple of pint-sized duffels and a Samsonite that was too big to carry on.

The professors seemed to value their bags over the advantages of being without. Clyde looked nervously at his suitcase as he rolled it into the well house and seemed reluctant even to let go of the handle, let alone leave it behind. Father Andrew carefully stashed his duffel against the wall, almost like he was tucking it in for the night. The two bags made a sorry statement on the group's situation, and I couldn't help but sympathize after all; these people were a long way from home, and things weren't going very well for them. I threw Rhiana's bag beside the other two and pulled the door shut.

"Let's stay together, but not in a big group," I said.

Madeline wanted to stay with Father Andrew—sort of a reunification between the Catholic Church and whatever brand of Protestantism was favored in the sociology department at Boston College. You couldn't have separated Darrin from Clyde with a crowbar, but I did it anyway, pointing Rhiana toward Clyde and dragging Darrin to my side. If anything went haywire, I wanted Rhiana in the company of someone steady like Clyde so I could go solo with some assurance that she'd have a fighting chance. Darrin wasn't necessarily a liability, but he wasn't Indiana Jones either. I told him to stay with me.

"Who has money?" I asked.

"I do," said Rhiana.

"Why don't Clyde and you find some tourist shopping bags? If you find a dishdasha and shumaq, I'll go native." I looked at my crew, as ruddy as Scotsmen. "Rhiana, you may even want to go native depending on what you find. The rest of us," I said, "will wait here. No one goes out of sight of either the main city gates or each other, but we don't stay grouped up like a gaggle of sheep."

"Flock," said Father Andrew.

Darrin nodded.

"Geese," said Clyde, looking at Rhiana. He nodded slightly as if to lend support to the plan. The rest of the brainiacs engaged in a riveting conversation about the various names for animal groups. Rhiana took a step toward me and spoke softly. "Can you take care of the rest of these guys?"

"Yeh-man." I smiled. Then looking more serious, I leaned toward her and whispered, "Barbier and his clown walked by during prayer."

Rhiana shook her head. "We can't leave the sauq or we'll really stick out."

"Why'd we come here? If I'd been driving, we'd have crashed the embassy gates."

"Subtle," Rhiana said.

"But we'd be sipping sodas around the embassy pool by now," I said.

"Or we'd be dead."

"Either way." I shrugged.

Rhiana shook her head. "Look at them. I know they're mad, but I'm not sure they realize . . ."

"Realize what?" I asked.

Rhiana lowered her voice even more. "What kind of trouble we're really in."

"Do you have a contingency plan?"

"Other than the embassy?" she asked. "I'm sure Barbier knows that's where we're headed. If we can't get to the embassy . . ." Rhiana seemed reluctant to bring up the aircraft carrier waiting for us in the Arabian Sea.

"So for contingency plans we have a taxi to the embassy or helicopters landing in the smoking remnants of a napalm attack—nothing in between?"

Rhiana's silence was answer enough. "If I have to call for a heli-copter extraction, I'll be very unpopular with my supervisor. Besides, they will only pick up two people. That's all they'll authorize—the French and the civilians are on their own. If it comes to that, the hostage rescue is off. Navy Seals have tried twice. We're the last ditch effort; there won't be another."

"Are you telling me that Navy Seals have tried this rescue? Twice?"

"Yes."

"And they failed?"

"Yes." Rhiana's voice got a little softer.

"So you called *me*?"

Rhiana rolled her eyes.

"What happened with the Seals?" I asked.

"Bad intel. Out-of-date information. It's hard to know. The hostage wasn't where they thought he'd be. It happens."

I put my hand on Rhiana's shoulder. "Somehow this is going to work out, Rhi." I wasn't overly optimistic, but I was being unrealisti-cally supportive—a skill I knew went over well in any marriage.

She pulled away, a little sullen. "My job was to locate the hostage and report back so another Seal team could be tasked for a rescue. I wasn't supposed to stir up the whole Middle East."

"To be fair, it wasn't the whole Middle East. Barbier isn't even Eastern. I was following a lead. We were both in on the plan, Rhiana."

Rhiana's eyes closed slowly on a distressed look. "I don't know what you did to stir up Barbier, but it wasn't my plan. You were supposed to follow one man from his office at Yemenia Air. I don't even want to think about what really happened."

"Well, if I'd known a little more about this ugly little charade from the get-go . . ." I said.

"Ugly charade? And what do you call your little evening out with Barbier? The fourth stooge does *Die Hard*? From now on, you leave the investigation to me."

"I thought you were behind me on this. You knew where I was going. I can feel the bite of your knife in my back all the way to my chest."

"Oh, if I stab you, it'll be in the front—so I can look in your eyes."

"That was brutal, Rhi. Even for you." I lowered my voice again because I thought the animal discussion was waning and I didn't want the others to focus on the year-old battle that was warming up between Rhiana and me.

"You were supposed to watch, not . . . You've compromised this entire operation from top to bottom. Now you want to blame someone else? Typical." I watched her as she tried to keep her composure, fighting for complete control of her emotions. Her stoic facade was crumbling.

"You blame this whole thing on me, don't you? I probably had something to do with the kidnapping, too. Right? Hey, while we're at it, let's pretend that I was the one who spread the seeds of hatred between the Arabs and the Western world." I was getting out of control, at least by Rhiana's standards, so I took a breath and let it out slowly. "There's a lot more to this than you're letting on. This is personal for you, isn't it? Who is he?"

Even as I said the words, Rhiana's intense behavior began to make sense—her willingness to involve innocent people, her inability to hide her emotions. The look she returned to me said volumes about what was driving this mission—and yet she couldn't answer me in words. The sting of infidelity in the center of my chest began to intensify.

"What? You don't have anything to say?" I said. I turned away from her and started toward our group, who were thankfully now lost in a discussion about Aristotelian classification.

"Kam . . ." she tried to answer.

"You won't talk to me. Just like when we were married," I said.

I heard a muffled sob behind me. "I thought we still were."

* * *

Rhiana did a miraculous job of suppressing any sign of emotion as we walked back to the group huddled around each other in the sauq—classic Rhiana—and she and Clyde left us to buy what clothes they could find within the walls of the Old City. Father Andrew, Madeline, and Darrin abandoned their fruitful discussion and looked to me for temporary guidance. I didn't know anything about animals or Aristotle, so I suggested we deep-six the trivia and mill around like tourists, keeping our faces out of sight as best we could.

I escorted Darrin down a narrow row of shops featuring "authentic ancient artifacts" while Father Andrew and Madeline hung back a hundred feet or so. We couldn't wander far because safety lay in staying within eyeball range of each other. There were plenty of vendors with rickety tables and overhead tarps set up near the front gates that allowed us the freedom to wander without really going anywhere. Vendors here sold everything from questionable food to "authentic" trinkets sprinkled with some passable ancient artifacts, some of which had been made a month ago in China. Shopping in Yemen hadn't changed much since the reign of the Queen of Sheba.

"You haven't said much," I said to Darrin as I examined a small, chipped clay figurine being passed off as an artifact.

Darrin took the figure from me and rolled his eyes.

"Not authentic?" I said. "Shocking."

Darrin didn't respond.

I said, "I think the adventure is over. Once we get to the embassy we can all have a good laugh."

Darrin set the figurine on the table, and we ducked under another tarp to examine a collection of grain sacks featuring a kaleidoscope of earthy colors and musty scents.

I looked behind us and saw Father Andrew and Madeline actually laugh at something. Darrin was a terrible date. I had to get him talking.

"Do you go to church every Sunday?" I asked.

If there was a Super Bowl of lame questions, that would have been a winner, but it did draw a response.

"Most of the time."

"I have this theory," I said, thinking fast. I'm such a good liar that I sometimes scare myself.

Darrin didn't take the bait.

"Okay," I said, "you've got all these people going to church every week, right?"

Darrin nodded but continued looking at an assortment of dried fruits for sale.

I went on anyway. "And let's say half of those people are good church-going folks—salt of the earth and all that. They probably don't need to be at church to be in good with God. That would include guys like you, Clyde, and certainly Father Andrew."

"And Madeline . . ." Darrin rolled his head back and forth. "All right. Go on."

"The other half are the people who are only at church because they want to show everyone what good people they are—otherwise they wouldn't be there. People with that attitude probably don't get many 'heaven points' just for dragging their sorry carcasses to church. So they don't really need to be there either."

"Uh-huh. I see."

The academic in Darrin was intrigued, I could tell. But I had to bring this little discussion to a point—and I wasn't sure I had one. "So, the good people don't need it and the bad ones don't get anything from it. So what's the point?"

"What about the other people?" said Clyde, walking up behind us. He and Rhiana had bags in hand and smiles on their faces. "Put this on." He pulled a thobe out of his bag. The vertical green stripes and purple filigree seriously clashed with my chinos. "Mmm. Tacky, but fashionable," I said.

Not amused, Rhiana took the garment. "You asked for traditional clothes." She gathered it up and cast the collar around my head. When she let go, the lose robe dropped to just above the boots of the new me. Stylin'.

Clyde stepped back and looked me over. "So? What about those other people?"

"What other people?" I said.

"The people who go to church just to be able to hang on another week in this crazy world. The struggling people."

"What?"

"Churches aren't monasteries. More respite care for injured souls. The attitudes and behaviors of people at church make a lot more sense when you see the people for who they really are."

"You can all go to church later," said Rhiana. "And we can have this conversation some other time."

Clyde was grinning—the face of a brother who got the last jibe before Mom ended the argument.

"Right now," she continued, "we need to check our rendezvous at the main gates. It's almost one o'clock."

Father Andrew and Madeline strolled up to a table next to us so they could be within earshot.

"You five go. I'll hang back, just in case," I said. Now that Rhiana was with the group, I wanted to separate myself. Not because I was mad at her or felt like she'd torn my heart out and had stomped it into the Yemeni dirt. That wasn't it. If Rhiana asked, it was because I wanted to do a little countersurveillance for René and Rotten, his derelict thug.

"Let's go," said Clyde.

Rhiana looked back and forth between Clyde and me and then walked away with the others.

I turned back toward one of the display tables to let them get ahead of me. I expected to see a gnarled old man minding his wares, but I saw someone else instead—the entrancing young Arab woman from the Paris jazz joint, her dazzling green eyes still framed by the thick, dark burqua head-covering she wore before. She looked to me and asked, "You'll tell them?" She shifted her gaze over my shoulder. Reacting to something visceral, a vibrant warning in my veins, I spun around to see what had her attention.

Rhiana and Clyde, bags in hand, took slow steps down the midway. Directly behind them, René Barbier kept pace. Emerging from a hidden alcove ahead of them waited the gangly form of Faasid, his sparse beard looking as though he could have used a shot of testosterone earlier in life.

Almost as if on cue, Faasid slipped his hand inside his open jacket and took a few cautious steps into the midway, flanking Rhiana and Clyde. They didn't see him.

Father Andrew and Madeline strode well ahead of Rhiana, and Darrin stood on the other side of the midway, drawing his fingers down a length of cord for sale by a cart vendor. Things were about to go sideways.

CHAPTER 19

"Behind you," I screamed, lunging toward Rhiana and inelegantly evading bodies on my way toward the Arab assassin. Rhiana saw me coming, and all five of my companions took off into the crowd.

I hit Faasid hard as he drew his hand from his jacket, the glint of something steel flashing before my eyes as we tumbled to the ground. I had never been much of a ground fighter and, as a cop, had always taken great care to avoid high school wrestlers. I doubted that this Arab had been a high school student, let alone an all-American high school wrestler, but I didn't waste time trying to tie him up on the ground. Besides, he had a knife—and distance was a potential knife victim's best friend. A gun is the knife victim's big, hairy, ex-convict uncle, but I didn't have one—an ex-convict uncle or a gun.

I rolled away from Faasid and scrambled a few feet before coming around on him again. Astonished shoppers surrounded us at a distance, but Barbier wasn't among them. Faasid came to his feet, this time the knife displayed in front of him, blade pointed up—the "heaven grip," lending itself to short slashing movements. We circled, my eyes darting from the blade to the crowd and back—the Arab's eyes were pinned on my chest, where I assume he intended to bury his knife. In his eyes I saw his failure to kill me in Paris, at the bathhouse, and at the Taj. He was highly motivated to do inexplicably horrible things to me with the blade of his knife. He lunged once, then again, swinging the knife toward my hands. I jumped back, sideways, then back again, sprawling into a vendor's table and knocking over burlap bags of dried peas that burst, sending peas in all directions over the uneven ground. I scrambled forward on the hard peas, thousands of ball bearings under my feet. My feet shot from under me, and I slammed to the ground on my elbow. The shock went all the way to my neck and jaw.

Seeing me stunned, Faasid fell forward, leading with his knife, and struck at my sprawling legs. I felt the hot bite of his blade along my shin and I kicked out wildly at his hip, spinning him away from me. I felt another tug on my pant leg as he whipped his knife sideways and fell backward. Keeping the peas between us, I fought to my feet and retreated, feeling my way backward against the edge of a vendor's table.

My shaking hand ran across a small, round wooden post behind me, but I didn't dare take my eyes off the approaching Arab. Gripping the post with all my remaining strength, I pulled and spun, hoping to bring down the small vendor's structure between me and Faasid and give myself a head start down the alley behind us. The plan worked fabulously except on two counts, the post I'd grabbed was in fact not a support post, but a broom, and the alley behind me, although well suited for a short run, was a dead end. Broom in hand, I turned to see Faasid walking confidently toward me, quaking vendors cowering in his wake.

I pulled the broom in front of me and thrust it forward as menacingly as a man holding an old broom can, but Faasid kept coming, his face a mixture of menace and glee. He slowly turned the knife over in his fist and pointed the blade down—"earth grip," designed for repeated stabbings of an all-but-defeated victim.

On impulse I took the broom handle in both hands and brought it out in front of my face. Faasid's grimacing smile widened to reveal the kind of dental wreckage that could only be caused by a lifetime of hygienic disregard. Hoping the broom handle wasn't made of some kind of notoriously solid Yemeni hardwood, I smashed it across my forehead. Hindsight made it pretty clear that my knee would have been the better choice, but the psychological effect of breaking the wooden stick over my head was priceless.

Splinters of broom handle shot twenty feet across the alley and Faasid stopped, a look of astonishment and confusion playing on his face. I shook away the field of celestial bodies that circled my eyes, and I refocused what was left of my disrupted vision on the Arab threat. Somewhere inside my head a band played the French national anthem, but that would certainly go away with time.

I was stunned, but I had what I needed—a sharp stick. And if I had my way about it, someone was going to get a poke in the eye with it. My new high-tech weapon was about eighteen inches long and was, as indicated by the throbbing of my head, made from some kind of hardwood. I now had a police baton.

Taking the stick in my right hand, I poised it over my left shoulder. Faasid paused, apparently considering the development. Flipping my wrist, I brought the stick down with a hiss and, for the first time, got the Arab on his heels. Pressing my advantage, I swung the stick in a sweeping arc in front of his face.

Faasid's confusion turned to determination, and he thrust the blade out again. I brought the stick down in another blinding flip strike and made contact with the Arab's knife hand. He recoiled like he'd been bitten by a snake, but he didn't drop the weapon.

I lunged again, another strike, then another, herding Faasid toward the main street. More people stopped to watch the fight, and as Faasid noticed the crowd, he became visibly agitated. His knife thrusts became ever more tentative as I lashed out with my stick, hitting his arm and hand each time he offered them. He gave up distance as I kept the stick churning in front of him. He looked at the crowd and the attention we were getting, and then his eyes darted toward the midway just behind him. He gave more ground, and at the intersection he cut his losses and ran.

I ran too—away from Faasid and deeper into Old Sana'a, searching the crowd for familiar faces and checking over my shoulder. Each time my foot hit the ground, a bolt of lightning stabbed up my leg, causing me to stumble—a little memento from Faasid's knife.

By the time my lungs and legs could no longer carry me, I was well into Old Sana'a, far from the main gate, where I hoped Rhiana and the others would be waiting for me. I walked to another section of the midway and found a vendor who agreed to a trade: my Timex digital watch, a twelve-dollar value in any Wal-Mart, for a light purple, knee-length dishdasha robe with gray checks, a shumaq to wrap around my head and face, and a cheap, glass bead–festooned, tourist-quality jambiya dagger; I needed a new look and a more formidable weapon. I handed the curious vendor my watch and limped off, trying awkwardly to wrap the shumaq in place.

I pulled my thobe over my head and replaced it with the new, differently colored dishdasha, hiding the broken stick underneath. For the first time I noticed that blood had soaked through my pants and covered my boot. Every step I took left a bloody mark.

I ripped my old thobe into bandage strips and examined the two lacerations the Arab had been kind enough to leave with me. The bleeding was inconsequential, and there didn't seem to be any serious nerve damage. I felt reasonably sure I'd be okay as long as the wounds didn't turn septic, a valid concern under the circumstances. I made two large triangle bandages from the thobe and folded the rest into pads to tie against the cuts.

I didn't know Sana'a very well, but I knew the general direction of the airport and the Sheraton. I could contact the embassy from either place, but first I wanted to check our rally point at the Old City gates on the off chance that someone would be looking for me. Well-intended plans had a way of crumbling apart under stress, and I wouldn't have blamed Rhiana for making a run for the embassy without me. Obviously things were falling apart in Old Sana'a and with Old Kam.

I pulled a corner of my shumaq over my chin and scouted the neighborhood for the busiest vendor on the block. Busy people, especially ones more concerned about thieves than imposters, were less likely to scrutinize my face and language. I found a likely vendor to ask directions and was waved downhill where I was assured I'd eventually find the main gates.

I walked purposefully but slowly on my bum leg, making a pretense of looking at some of the wares for sale along the street and scrutinizing the people who passed me. Each time I stopped to admire a phony ceramic artifact or test the tensile strength of a bit of fabric, I made the most of my peripheral vision to check the faces of people around me, being cautious not to crane my head in every direction like a lost husband at the mall.

The ubiquitous mud-brick architecture tended to give me the feeling of being in a maze, but I continued down the slight slope until I hit the great outer wall and paralleled it until I saw the throngs of people coming and going from the main gate. There was a domed pavilion nearby, put there undoubtedly for some ancient purpose, that was about to serve the modern purpose of giving me a secluded place to do some surveillance on the main gate and watch for a friendly face. I pulled up the sleeve of my robe and looked at the pale tan line my watch had been tattooing for the past two decades and cursed myself for giving it up. The Old City wasn't the kind of place where you could glance up at the nearest Bank of America scrolling marquee and get the time, temperature, and home loan interest rates. Old-timers in these parts organized their days around their five daily prayers. If you asked the time, you might be told "AlKair," which is sometime between morning and evening prayers. Not very informative if you're trying to meet international spies on a strict deadline.

I needed to ask the time, so I chose an Asian couple who had been bartering over a daff, a cheap copy of an Arabic tambourine, at a rickety wooden table covered by a tattered blue tarp. I spoke in English with a heavy Arabic accent to reinforce my new identity, hoping that they wouldn't notice the subtle English inflections.

"Do you have the time?" I asked.

The woman remained silent, as if afraid to speak in the presence of a native male. The man looked at his watch, and instead of answering, he showed it to me. It was two fifty, ten minutes until I should see at least someone from our crew near the gates. I thanked the couple, giving proper credit to Allah, and kept my face averted.

The Asian man told me I was welcome in the most nasal Bostonian accent I'd ever heard. So much for racial profiling. I almost yelled "Go Patriots!" at him, but I figured that would void the contract on the new me, so I simply nodded and shuffled back to the pavilion where I could hide in the shadows and watch.

Several minutes, and then an hour, came and went without any sign of Rhiana or anyone of our crew. I sat on the ground, alone in the madding crowd of the sauq, wondering if Rhiana would risk her life to come back for me . . . or if it was too late for that.

* * *

Five had o'clock passed and, according to another set of tourists wandering around the sauq, so had six. I'd seen no sign of help.

Sitting in the evening shadow of a nearby alley, I pealed the now blood-saturated strips of fabric off my wounds and examined them for infection. It was good news and bad. My platelets had done their thing, and I was no longer bleeding, but it looked pretty gnarly. At some point the wounds had to be cleansed. Taking off my bandage had been a bad idea all around, because not only did it open the wound and allow new germs in, but it also discouraged me.

Seven o'clock brought me no better news at the city gates, and I decided that I would have to go it alone. I could walk well enough to limp around the Old City, but a sustained walk to the embassy was going to be a challenge on my injured leg. I thought briefly about robbing a vendor for enough paper money to get a taxi, but after looking at some of the toothless old men selling junk to feed their families, I decided they were in a worse way than I was—even though I knew they wasted a lot of their profits buying Qat for their afternoon drug high.

I knew better than to hitchhike outside the city, which was just another way to tell the locals, "Kidnap me, please. I'm a stupid foreigner," but I wasn't sure how hitching a ride in the city would go over—especially if I could, indeed, pass myself off as a native. I'd told Pat English in Timor-Leste I could do it, but where the rubber hit the road, I knew there were nuances and subtleties that would eventually give me away. Yemen wasn't as large and diverse as the United States, and you couldn't just throw on a headdress and get away with anything. So far, vacationers had bought my act, but I wasn't willing to push my luck. Even with the clothes and language skills, I was lost and a long way from home.

Lost. My mother used to tell me if I got lost at the store, I was supposed to stay in one place until she found me. It was an early indoctrination into the rules of "escape and evade." If only my current problem could be solved by just sitting tight in the soup aisle.

I decided to leave the Old City and find a place in the modern district of Sana'a to call the embassy. I lowered my head and left the shadows of the domed pavilion, heading for the gates. There were so many people that I didn't have to worry very much about being spotted, especially in my new dishdasha and shumaq. For that matter, even my rescue party would probably miss me, but there was nothing I could do about that except be sure to see them first.

Keeping at least a part of my shumaq over my chin, I was buffeted by the crowd until I found myself outside the walls, where there was some room to breathe and to see. With vain hope, I looked for a waiting Land Cruiser but was disappointed. I skirted a tall picket fence erected along the city walls so I could avoid the surge of humanity that wanted to see the Old City. Turning toward the main thoroughfare, I prepared myself for the long walk to the nearest phone.

I'd taken only a few steps when I saw René Barbier outside the Old City gates scanning the crowd like a lost tourist—pretty cavalier considering he knew I'd be looking for him looking for me. When he turned in my direction, my pulse thrummed against my eardrums, and my stomach dropped.

I didn't make any sudden movements but turned to flank him so I could keep him in my periphery. I strolled past him, head down and knees trembling under the dishdasha. He paid no attention to me, still probing the streets, then his eyes fixed on something and he jogged toward a city taxi and spoke to the driver, Faasid the rotten Arab killer. Their conversation was animated and involved a lot of arm waving and finger pointing in the direction of the Old City. I left them that way, hoping they'd focus on finding Ol' Kam at the sauq.

I found a free public phone next to a hole-in-the-wall leather goods shop three long city blocks from the Old City and tried to get an operator to connect me with the U.S. embassy. It took several tries, but eventually I got a ring and an answer.

In keeping true to my cover, I told the embassy operator I was an American traveling as part of a research expedition who had been separated from his group and injured. The operator was exceedingly helpful and promised a car and driver within half an hour. She asked how I'd be recognized. Without giving away my description, I told her the name of the shop where I'd be waiting and assured her that I'd be standing directly in front of the main doors. "Have it your way," she said. It was U.S. bureaucracy with Burger King flair.

I felt exposed standing in front of the leather shop. I didn't want to be the guy in the spy movies who stands around at the meeting place like a dork and gets picked off, so I walked a block away and stopped at an outdoor news rack, burying my face in the current issue of *Arabia Felix* magazine.

Just over twenty minutes later, Faasid's taxi pulled up in front of the leather goods shop and Barbier got out, looking directly at the spot where I was supposed to be waiting. While Barbier and Faasid loitered there, an embassy car came, waited for less than five minutes, and left without me. With a shrug and frustrated shake of the head, so did Barbier. I watched as Faasid pulled the taxi carrying Barbier back into traffic. It was apparent that my youth wasted on too many spy movies had saved my life yet again. It was also apparent that Barbier had secured some method for listening to embassy phones.

CHAPTER 20

Hiding behind the tails of my shumaq, I limped away from the magazine stand, leg throbbing, back to the sauq to wait for another even-numbered hour and a miracle. I slumped to the ground like a beggar against one of the three-foot-long stones of the Old City wall, the question of trust foremost on my mind.

Barbier might have simply guessed that after the gunplay at the Sheraton we'd gone to ground in Old Sana'a; proximity and convenience might have told him that. But Barbier hadn't shown up at the leather shop as a matter of deduction, which confirmed in my mind that the embassy was severely compromised. It wasn't even worth trying to guess to what extent. The other thing that had been obvious for about a day now was that I'd been under heavy surveillance ever since Paris. Had I been on my game I might have realized that earlier.

Who to trust was the real question. In the old days, nationality determined allegiance, but that dog hadn't hunted since the end of the cold war, if then. On the modern battlefield, money had replaced patriotism, and Barbier and his goon worked for cash, not principles. I had to grant, however, that Faasid's motivation to kill me had probably moved beyond that by now.

"Don't trust anyone" was a worn-out adage that I couldn't ignore, but I had to trust somebody. I was reasonably sure that Rhiana was on my side, but there very well could be a bad apple or two in our group, and I figured they both ate brie.

Sitting on the ground thinking about it was only serving to make me feel worse, so I hoisted myself to my feet and started walking again. Just as I wondered how close it was to Asr, or evening prayer, I heard the familiar tones of the muezzins amplified from the minarets dotted about the city. In all corners of the Muslim world, billions of ornate prayer rugs were being rolled out, and twice as many knees were descending on them for evening prayer.

Again with the prayer, I thought. This morning my overly religious friends had done it, albeit in a more subtle way than the locals, and then the whole day had turned to mayhem. On the other hand, maybe they were all safe and cozy because they'd prayed, and I was all by myself as a result of my apathy. Like anything religious, it was hard to tell. *God, if you are out there, now would be a good time to kick it in.*

I wasn't an atheist; I believed in God—or something. Maybe I was agnostic; how should I know? Maybe I was a gnostic who was just too lazy to ferret out the secrets of God—therefore I was agnostic by reason of my apathy. I'd always thought of myself as Christian, perhaps because that was consistent with the dominant religious leaning of most of my friends, but in reality, maybe I didn't really know what I was. Perhaps a lazy Christian gone agnostic by virtue of ignorance. The possibilities were dizzying. Under the drone of the chanting muezzins, and without a clear understanding of any deep religious concepts, I let those ideas bob on my brain waves to fend off utter despair as I slowly put one throbbing leg in front of the other, taking measured steps away from the Old City and the possibility of a rescue.

Outside the main gates again, I scanned the crowd in desperation for a familiar face—and then I found one. Leaning against the outer wall barricades looking over the crowd, I saw the sun-toughened scalp of Pierre, the French soldier. He had changed his clothes since I'd last seen him, and he looked relaxed as people from many nations moved past him. I was pretty sure Pierre saw me, but he merely glanced to his left and went on with his patient wait.

I looked in the area he'd glanced at and saw the muscular black biceps of Dandré draped over the open driver's door of a taxi as if waiting for a scheduled fare. Too weary to distrust the Frenchmen, I limped through the crowd toward the taxi. Dandré opened the back door for me. As soon as he hit the driver's seat, the taxi lurched forward into traffic. Within the safety of the taxi, I let go of the intense fatigue that had hold of my body. I didn't speak. I found myself silently thanking God for kicking it in.

"We're all accounted for now," said Dandré.

"At the embassy?"

"Safe house."

"We have a safe house?"

"We have a safe house now."

Dandré didn't say any more, and inside of half an hour we pulled into the parking lot by the safe house—a seedy motel.

Apparently seedy motels all over the world looked about the same, except the Yemenis had the good sense to avoid hot pink and purple doors.

Dandré turned into a parking lot on the back side of the building and pulled up outside a partially open door. He helped me from the backseat and escorted me into a dim room, made darker by means of drawn shades, where a visibly strained group of religious scholars waited for news of their lost sheep.

"Kamir." Rhiana had a horrified look on her face as I limped, more from exhaustion than pain, into the small room. "Kamir, what happened?"

"Barbier? You didn't see him?"

Clyde said, "We saw you throwing Arab tourists all over the midway and got out of there."

The inside of the motel room was just as shabby as the outside. An oblong-shaped section of natural fiber that smelled like it had just been shorn from a musk ox covered a bare double mattress on the floor, and rusty watermarks striped the whitewashed walls like a visual counterpart to the odor. Those amenities and the lingering stench left behind by countless penniless patrons completed the ambiance.

I was well acquainted with motel classifications in Yemen. The no-sheet version was a room with a mattress on the floor and a few filthy blankets. The one-sheet upgrade boasted bed sheets, but they were generally laundered on a pretty conservative schedule—maybe once or twice a month regardless of the guest cycle. Nice. A two-sheeter meant clean sheets and maybe a bathroom with a real toilet. We were very fortunate, though, that our safe house, which probably fit into the one-sheet classification, boasted individual rooms. Anywhere outside of Sana'a and we'd have been sleeping in a cramped dormitory.

Clyde stepped around the mattress on the floor. "You're okay?"

"Yep." I nodded and took a painful step toward a short wicker chair—a major upgrade for any local motel.

"Kam, what happened?" asked Rhiana.

"Have you guys contacted the embassy yet?" I asked.

Rhiana shook her head, clearly still more interested in my physical condition than our current state.

"Don't bother," I said.

Pierre and Dandré exchanged glances, glances I didn't particularly like, and Rhiana just looked bewildered.

I looked at Pierre. "Is it safe to stand outside?"

He shook his head.

"Rhi?" I nodded at the door to the miniscule bathroom, barely large enough to accommodate two people standing up. In fact, it was barely accommodating, period. Indoor plumbing was a recent trend in some quarters of Yemen, and in this motel, a hole in the floor passed for a toilet and a single spigot over a galvanized tin basin did the sink duties. Standing inches from Rhiana in the smelly little room, I told her what had happened in Old Sana'a.

"Barbier and Faasid," I said.

"Faasid?"

"Barbier's goon. I call him 'rotten.' *Faasid.*"

"Are you hurt?"

"I left the Old City and called the embassy for help. Ten minutes later, guess who showed up?"

"Did you tell that to Dandré?" Rhiana leaned against the tin basin.

"No. What makes you think he's not part of the problem?"

"Who did you talk to at the embassy?" Rhiana asked.

"I don't know. The operator lady. She seemed helpful. Didn't ask many questions."

Rhiana's face hardened. "I have to talk to Pierre."

"Pierre? At the moment, I don't trust either of them."

"Don't be absurd," she said. I leaned against the wall to give her room to pass me, but she didn't. She stayed where she was, standing inches from me. "Pierre and Dandré are professionals. They follow orders."

"Oh, that's comforting. Whose orders? Orders from our embassy or orders from the some foreign control center run by the French?"

Rhiana seemed to realize the magnitude of the problem we faced. "I don't know." She dropped her shoulders and let out a breath. "What have I done?"

I took her hands in mine and said softly, "Hey, you're not alone here. You have me." I hadn't been this close to Rhiana for a long time and looking into her eyes, despite the lack of romantic atmosphere, brought with it a warm sensation in my chest. "I can tell how important this mission is to you."

She nodded. "It's my job."

"I mean personally. You have feelings for this man, the hostage."

She didn't deny it, and her eyes moistened. It hurt. Rhiana shook her head; it was resignation, not denial.

"He's someone you've gotten close to?"

"It's not like that, Kam. He's . . ."

Pierre chose that moment to throw open the flimsy door that separated the grimy bathroom from the grubby sleeping room. "Mademoiselle?" Sensing he'd interrupted, he hesitated, looking back and forth between us. Then, carefully, with a voice much softer than his initial demeanor, he said, "When you are finished. I need to speak with you."

Rhiana let go of my hands and brushed her fingers across her face to erase the evidence of tears forming at the corners of her eyes.

"When you're ready," he said before he closed the door.

"We'll talk later," she said to me, summoning up the former stoic look of determination she'd brought into the room, and she followed Pierre out.

I stayed in the bathroom just long enough to appreciate the marvels of modern plumbing and to think about Rhiana, a tough woman hardened and tempered by the job she did. But I'd seen behind the facade and would always know that under it all beat the heart of a human being—an amazing woman—who I'd spent the last two years of my life hurting and who had apparently moved on. Now it was my turn to ask, *What have I done?*

By the time I opened the door to the bathroom, Rhiana and our French escorts were no longer in the room. I was left alone to stare into the vacant faces of four very defeated civilians. I limped out, and Clyde offered me his place on the bed.

"Where are you hurting?"

"My leg," I said.

Clyde pulled up my dishdasha while Madeline, who'd been amazingly quiet, and Father Andrew looked on. Darrin didn't seem to have the stomach for it and knelt on the other side of the mattress with his back to us.

"Is everyone else okay?" I asked. Better late than never.

"Physically, I suppose. How did this happen?" Clyde was unlacing my boot. "This dressing is filthy. Normally, I wouldn't take the bandages off, but . . ."

"They have to be replaced," said Madeline. Her sense of empathy had nudged past her deep suspicions. Every relationship has to start somewhere.

Father Andrew nodded. "Are you cut anywhere else?" He pushed up my sleeves and examined my hands and arms. "Sometimes you don't notice." Father Andrew Marcy: knife-fighting expert.

Clyde gently unrolled the makeshift bandages, revealing two deep and ragged lacerations that already showed light scarlet on the edges. Then he gently extracted a clump of wool-sock fuzzies out of one of the cuts, opening it up and starting a good bleed.

"So, what's your story? While I was harassing tourists, what did you guys do?" I asked.

"What could we do? We lost ourselves in the crowd, and by the time we surfaced again, Pierre and Dandré were waiting for us with new cars."

"We need medical supplies," I said.

Darrin must have been listening because he said, "I had some stuff in the trucks. I don't know where any of that is. I don't even know where my suitcase is." His voice started to crack. "They wouldn't tell us. I don't know . . ." Darrin's voice just trailed off, probably sheepish for putting his own worries before the group's. I understood; he was simply expressing what everyone else was feeling, including me.

"Anyone have a toothbrush?" asked Clyde. "This needs to be scrubbed." He made a big smiley face at me.

I cringed at the thought of sharing someone's gingivitis with my vital blood supply, but no one had a toothpick, much less a toothbrush.

"I'll get some water," said Father Andrew, making his way to the bathroom. He returned leaving a trail of water from his cupped hands and doused my leg with what was left. When it hit my leg I thought for an instant that it wasn't going to hurt. I was wrong. A moment later I threw myself flat on the mattress and took a great handful of dusty musk-ox blanket in each fist.

Clyde used his fingers, the cleanest medical implements available, to scrub the two wounds as best he could. The agitation made the cuts bleed, which presented itself as a minor problem because we still didn't have any clean dressings.

Pierre, followed by Rhiana and Dandré, walked back into the small room. Rhiana reacted to the sight of my leg with a defeated sigh and a sympathetic look.

"Dandré," Pierre said, and Dandré turned about-face and left the room.

Pierre knelt in front of Clyde and examined the wounds. "It is nothing."

Dandré returned with a small green duffel and ushered everyone out of his way. Pierre smiled, which did nothing to reassure me.

Dandré unfolded the duffel to reveal an assortment of shiny medical things I'd never be able to name—but it looked like serious medical equipment. After snapping on a pair of thin rubber gloves, he filled a small hypodermic with clear liquid and jabbed me several times around the wounds. He stained my skin brown with Betadine solution from a small foil packet. I winced and then realized that the solution didn't sting. Dandré chuckled at that. Then, using a small disposable plastic brush, he made sure that I paid the ultimate painful price in exchange for clean wounds. He scrubbed for five minutes— the prescribed amount of torture, he assured me—then dabbed the wounds dry with clean gauze. From inside a sealed foil wrapper he took a sterile plastic minispatula and a tube of cyanoacrylate, otherwise known as superglue, which he spread liberally over the wounds before he pinched them together. After a few seconds he announced, "It is not pretty, but it will heal."

"I'm too old for beauty contests anyway. Beats the knit-one, pearl-two method," I said, refusing a bubble pack of pills he offered me. "I don't need anything for the pain."

Dandré laughed again. "I wouldn't give you anything for the pain even if you asked for it. Those are for the infection. Silly American. Take four now and one every six hours until they're gone if you want to keep it." He threw the pills on the ox blanket.

"Keep what?" asked Darrin, who had been drawn to the medical procedure like a passerby to a car wreck.

"The leg," said Dandré, folding up his kit and zipping it shut before braving the bathroom sink to wash up.

Darrin's face went green, all inquisitiveness extinguished.

Pierre called the group to order, apparently having assumed tactical command from Rhiana. "To use an American saying," he said, trying his hardest to cover his French accent, "We're up a creek without an oar."

"Hey, as long as we still have a paddle," I said. Rhiana and the representative religious community were not amused, and our foreign contingent didn't understand just how funny I was.

"Perhaps," Pierre said, "we've upset the delicate religious balance in this community." Apparently Rhiana and the Frenchmen were playing their cards pretty close to the vest, neither wanting to admit publicly that we were literally under siege with no one to trust. I wondered what other lies we'd be told before Pierre was done talking.

"We'll spend the night here," said Pierre without explanation.

"Why can't we just call the embassy? That's what they're there for," Madeline said. It was an obvious question, but her tone made it sound like an accusation.

"We aren't certain," said Rhiana, maybe thinking that the explanation would come better from a fellow countryman, "that the embassy is completely secure."

"Why can't you just tell us what's going on?" asked Darrin. "We're part of this now."

"If the American government can't protect us, what about the Yemeni police?" asked Father Andrew.

Judging by the look on his face, Pierre was done answering questions from the peanut gallery. The main concern of the moment was to get the group to accept a new line of authority and a new set of priorities. Speaking directly to Clyde, I said, "At this moment, it is very unclear what forces might be attempting to keep us from the embassy and how broad their span of control is. I think it's best to take a defensive stance and follow the tactical lead of our escort." I might make secretary of state yet. I just hoped I'd said what Rhiana wanted.

None of the scholars spoke. They were clearly out of their element. Father Andrew was the first to suggest a pact with the soldiers. "I say we do what they say, guys. We don't know anything about this."

Darrin demurred with a nod and so did Madeline, although she didn't look too happy about it.

"Fantastique," said Pierre, using a word I would have saved for a different occasion.

Posing as a Yemeni, I rented three additional rooms from a clerk who never even looked up at me. The eight of us split up, the women sharing one room and the men splitting up between the other two. This time, I drew Father Andrew. Our soldiers said they didn't need a room.

None of us possessed anything resembling luggage, and so what followed was a very indelicate session of laundry in the rust-laden water of the bathroom faucet. I let Father Andrew go first and made a visit to Rhiana's room, where much the same thing was happening. Madeline was indisposed in the bathroom, which gave me the perfect opportunity to visit with Rhiana.

"They've been calling in situational reports on their sat phone," whispered Rhiana.

"Status reports on a sat phone, huh? Spectacular spook speak, Rhiana. You've been doing the same thing, haven't you? It's a pretty standard procedure. It doesn't explain what happened when I called our embassy."

"Maybe not," said Rhiana. It sounded like an apology. "But I don't think it's helping. After what happened when you called the embassy, I don't trust any of our comms, especially not the United Nations command center in Vienna. I asked Pierre if he'd skip his next status report. He won't budge. We have to figure out a way to

stop the hourly status reports to Vienna without making Pierre suspicious. Once we leave here, I don't want anyone knowing our route to
the embassy."

"You're not admitting that the U.N. and their two French fops
might have something to do with sabotaging this mission, are you?"

"I'm not admitting anything," said Rhiana. "I just think we might
need to consider who has something to gain from sabotaging our
mission. There's one way to find out. It's called following the money."
She tapped the end of my nose with her finger. "Didn't anyone ever
teach you that?"

CHAPTER 21

Madeline opened the bathroom door on Rhiana and me, interrupting our intimate chat; her demeanor clearly spoke to the issue of my being in her motel room. In the interest of decorum, I went back to my room, where Father Andrew was gingerly wringing out a T-shirt.

"At least it's clean," I said to him as he scanned the room for a place to hang it.

Father Andrew was clean too, having dared a spit shower from the raw nib of pipe sticking out of the bathroom wall. He looked fresh, which made me feel all the dirtier. I peeked into the tiny bathroom and examined the mildew-stained floor and rust-striped walls and decided it was cleaner than I was.

I washed up as best I could, trying not to ruin the dressing on my leg, and rinsed out my dishdasha. Father Andrew and I made a field-expedient clothesline and tried our best to dry our clothes in our room.

"Hungry?" asked Father Andrew.

I hadn't thought about food until that moment. "I could use an egg roll and almond chicken from the New Garden Restaurant."

"Brats and kraut from Clause's Bakery for me," said Father Andrew.

"How about a big greasy sausage dog, with onions and relish and a fat yellow stripe of hot mustard on the crest."

"Now you're talking my language," said Father Andrew. "If you like good sausage, you'd like South Bend, Indiana."

"I figured you Catholics would be more into Italian."

"Is the Pope Polish?" He shook his head and smiled. "That line used to work better when he was actually Polish." Father Andrew flopped down on the bed and laced his fingers behind his head. "I'd even settle for a 7-Eleven—a Big Gulp and six-month-old pepperoni stick."

"So would I . . . a 7-Eleven and . . ." I bolted out the motel door half-dressed and in bare feet and tiptoed recklessly to Rhiana's room. Madeline opened the door and looked me up and down; I sensed an untoward remark just about to cross her lips before she announced me to Rhiana.

"Out here," I said to Rhiana.

Rhiana met me on the crumbling sidewalk, and we walked away from the windows to where prying ears wouldn't hear us.

"We'll ruin their phones," I said.

"Whose phones?"

"Pierre's. Dandré's."

"That's going to be difficult. Have you noticed the size of Dandré's biceps?"

"Yes. But even his big guns can't stop this."

"Okay." Rhiana took a step back and smiled. "Just what kind of Lucy Ricardo scheme are you getting us into?"

"Rhiana, I promise, it's more like James Bond. You are going to love this."

"Kam? Is this going to get me fired?"

"Do you want to secure your place in the unwritten history of great CIA gags?"

"No. There is no unwritten history of gags."

"Oh, please. Do you want to be mentioned in every academy class at the Farm in Maryland from now until forever? Do you want to be an international legend before age thirty-five?"

"Kam? No. What have you done?" A hint of Rhiana's former misgiving made its way to the surface through her voice.

"I haven't done anything yet, but I need your phone."

With reluctance written all over her face, she went to her room and brought back her phone. She handed it to me, and I looked at the buttons for a minute then handed it back.

"Make it work," I said.

"And you're going to use your superior understanding of secure satellite communications to disable the French phones? I had no idea you were so handy. I remember when you couldn't work the washer and dryer."

"That was just a ploy so you wouldn't make me do laundry. Just unlock the phone, Rhi."

She extended the thick, black antenna and punched buttons, listening to the receiver intermittently until the satellite phone was doing whatever satellite phones do.

"Dial direct," she said, handing the phone to me.

I did. Information. "Dallas, Texas . . . 7-Eleven, their corporate headquarters . . . Thank you."

"Ordering a Slurpee?" asked Rhiana.

"Big Gulp." I winked and pushed the pound button when the recorded voice asked me if I wanted her to connect.

"Jerry Packard," I said into the transmitting end, and Rhiana could hear only one side of the conversation. "If you could interrupt him and transfer me directly, this is extremely important. Thanks," I said to a receptionist.

"I am so in trouble," said Rhiana, shaking her head.

"Jerry? Kam Daniels . . . Kam . . . Daniels . . . of the Seattle Police Department."

His voice was Ma Bell clear, and I hoped the recollection of our former relationship would return to him. Jerry was one of those "friends" I'd made during an investigation into the inconvenient phone habits of one of his subordinates at corporate 7-Eleven in Dallas, Texas. I'd never met Jerry in person, and he didn't owe me bupkus, but we had spent ten or twelve pleasurable phone hours together during our joint investigation, and I felt I knew him.

"I know, it's been a while—look I don't have much time," I said. "You remember when . . . Yes, exactly. I need a huge favor, actually, not for me but for your country . . . But you have to remember, he was a criminal and you're a patriot. Sorry. Yes, I'll tone down the dramatics . . . but will you do it? Operation Fax Me?" I was pretty clever, coming up with an operation name on the fly like that.

I listened while Jerry listed about six really valid objections to Operation Fax Me.

"If you get fired, I will personally bring the influence of a grateful nation to your defense."

"He's not the only one who's getting fired for this," mumbled Rhiana.

"What number? An international one . . ." I covered the mouth-piece. "Rhiana, Pierre's number?"

She rolled her eyes—apprehension, regret, terror, embarrassment.

"The number?" I asked Rhiana. I relayed it to Jerry as she gave it to me.

"Relax," I told Jerry. "You're more likely to get a medal than get fired . . . No, I'm not drunk."

I nodded to Rhiana. This was going to work.

"I realize that," I said to Jerry over the phone, "but it's kind of like the mandatory seat belt laws. Yes, it's against the law not to wear your seat belt, but there's another law that lets cops break that law. Just think of it that way."

Rhiana looked a little sick, but then again, she was half smiling. I think the seat belt thing won her over, and the visions of hard time in Leavenworth were fading.

"Go ahead and tell your boss. Better yet, put your secretary on, and I'll dictate . . . Okay, administrative assistant. I'll dictate the request to her so she can . . . Okay, *him.* So he can vouch for you. I'll make sure you both get an official letter of commendation from our department."

"You're not a cop anymore." Rhiana punched my shoulder.

I covered the mouthpiece. "I didn't say which department—get out your spy letterhead. You're going to owe this guy a letter. And quit hitting."

"It worked so well against us," I reminded Jerry, "we thought we'd try it on someone else . . . Hey, you may not get a ticker-tape parade, but you're a hero, man."

I smiled a proud yet sophisticated smile at Rhiana. She smirked back.

"It needs to happen by 0500 . . . okay, that's 5 AM. So, that would be . . ."

I shrugged at Rhiana, and she mouthed the word *plus* and held up nine fingers then pointed to a half-bent finger.

I did the math and consulted my knowledge of time zones and couldn't figure out why there was a stray half hour in there. I looked at Rhiana and mouthed a questioning "half" at her. She nodded. "So if you start Operation Fax Me by seven thirty tonight your time . . . Thanks, man." I sighed a big mental sigh. "Hey, Jer? Trust me. What? Oh, well trust me anyway." I punched out, unable to conceal my pride.

"So," Rhiana said, "what national and international laws have we just broken? And how on earth is the 7-Eleven corporation helping us break those laws?"

"Every hour, as each time zone on the planet wakes up, 7-Eleven sends out marketing instructions by fax—what's on promotion in the store today, what's new in the 7-Eleven inventory, what giant, bigger-than-life cardboard posters need to be set up, and so forth—to every one of its stores. As soon as Jerry makes the appropriate adjustments to their faxing system, Pierre's sat phone will receive each and every one of those faxes. Millions of them. Fax tones transmitted directly into his ear. He won't be able to call out or receive calls."

"Millions?" Rhiana cocked her head.

I thought for second. "Almost twenty-eight thousand stores on planet earth."

"You're sure?"

"Of course I'm sure. I wrote the police report."

"You're just full of interesting tidbits, aren't you?"

"Not only will their phones be ringing nonstop, but the faxes that don't get a recognition signal from another fax machine on Pierre's end will continue to call indefinitely. I guarantee Pierre and Dandré won't be calling out for Chinese on their fancy little French phone. At least long enough for us to get everyone to the embassy."

"Do I want to know how you came up with this one?" Rhiana asked.

"The city of Seattle switchboard was down for two days, including the 911 system."

"Why in the world would somebody . . ."

"Brand new employee of 7-Eleven. Freshly graduated from U-Dub with a major in business and an emphasis in not showing up for court. I guess he figured we wouldn't come looking for him in Texas after what he did to our phones, but even Texas wasn't big enough. The guy got six months in a county jail, a ten-thousand-dollar fine, none of it suspended. And he's now a felon for the rest of his life. Dolt."

The mystery of college-punk logic notwithstanding, Rhiana got back to our problems. "Our window of opportunity begins when?"

"Tomorrow morning at 0500 lima. That's spy talk for local time."

Rhiana rolled her eyes. "I'm guessing Pierre will call in his status report just before we leave."

"He'll try," I said.

CHAPTER 22

Morning in Sana'a was a mixture of high desert air and fresh natural breezes being ushered away by the stale smells of the city coming awake. I stood just outside my door to hear the muezzins moaning out morning prayer and listened to the flat tones roll through the cityscape while I took in the last of the fresh air.

Outside our motel room, I spotted Dandré by one of our cars. He had the carpet liner out of the trunk and was balancing an oblong black duffel bag on the edge of the back fender. I walked over to him. His damp T-shirt stuck to his Adonis-like form. He was truly impressive.

"Stolen?" I asked about our new wheels.

"Purchased at a discount," he said. "We don't take stolen cars through checkpoints."

"And yesterday's taxi?"

Dandré grinned. "An even bigger discount. That one won't be going through any checkpoints."

Yemen was famous for its checkpoints. You couldn't travel in the city or on a main highway without passing at least a half dozen of them. It was part of the Yemeni government's attempt to control the free movement of terrorist cells and equipment, mainly weapons, throughout their country. It was a valiant, if only semieffective, attempt, but one that was incumbent on the Yemenis if they wanted Western aid and support. Secondary roads, which in Yemen can be anything from patchy asphalt to a seldom-used goat trail, were similarly beset with checkpoints, staffed mostly by Yemeni patriots unendorsed by the Yemeni government—in other words, tribal thugs. Some people called them terrorists. The more culturally savvy called them warlords. The truth may encompass a little of both, but the rural people of Yemen still recognized ancient tribal boundaries and controlled them by whatever means was at their disposal. A small amount of patronizing and a large amount of *bakshish,* or what in polite company might be called a "gift of funds," went a long way with these people.

I'd heard Western tourists in Sana'a cafés grumble about the rampant bribery among the barbaric tribesmen, characterizing the Yemeni people as uncultured and uncivilized. I wondered what they thought of the politicians, big and small, of their own countries who bartered in money and favors. I preferred the Yemeni way—money over the hood of your car instead of under the table. Yet whatever Dandré was hiding in the trunk of the car was also most certainly a form of barter in rural Yemen. The threat of violence was still valid currency wherever it occurred on the earth.

There was an awkward silence, and then I heard Rhiana's motel door open. I looked down the sidewalk and watched as she stepped from her door and ran her fingers through her hair to perfect that slightly tousled look, apparently immune to bedhead. She saw me and approached on the sidewalk. I met her halfway, and she had news for me.

"I called Roger," she said quietly. "The command center in Vienna can't get through to their people here. They think it's a satellite problem. I told Roger that we were all okay and to pass that along to Vienna. He's going to have plainclothes Marines secure the main roads near the embassy. All we have to do is get close. Apparently Operation Big Gulp did the trick."

"It was Operation Fax Me."

"The incessant ringing should be taking its toll by now. I don't know what to think about Pierre and Dandré," she said.

"Pierre's a weasel. That's my situational report for the day."

Rhiana ignored my professional assessment and walked over to Pierre, who was hovering over a map spread out on the hood of the Audi.

Father Andrew and Madeline were up and about and came out to the sidewalk. Clyde came out of his room, followed by a bleary-eyed Darrin. We had two cars now, a newer Audi sedan and a bright yellow Datsun 510, built sometime in the seventies—when Datsuns were cool. I was pretty sure the cargo hidden under the trunk liner of the

Datsun in a small black duffel bag would get us all arrested and taken to a Yemeni prison if it were discovered at a roadblock. A person can fit some pretty formidable firepower in a small black duffel bag.

I think everyone was breathing a little easier now that we were preparing for our short trip to the embassy. I know I always felt better about things in the morning. No one had tried to kill me yet today, so things were shaping up nicely.

Then I realized that I didn't hear Pierre's phone ringing.

Looking over his shoulder at me, Pierre said, "Would you join us, please." He was standing next to a crestfallen Rhiana.

"Very clever," Pierre said as I approached. "I'd like to acknowledge a nice bit of field craft. Once I find out how you disabled my phone, I'll be using that trick someday." He pulled his sat phone from his pocket. "The ringer turns off, by the way. And," he thumbed buttons on the device, "the calls can be forwarded."

At that moment, Rhiana's phone began to ring. She pressed a couple of buttons and it stopped.

"So, now neither of us has an operable phone." He held out his hand, and Rhiana slapped her phone into his palm. "Get in the cars," he ordered.

The map on the hood wasn't a map of Sana'a; it was a map of the Al Jawf, a district of northern Yemen that bordered on Saudi Arabia—the very essence of desolation. Rhiana saw me eyeing the map, but her demeanor didn't change. Apparently, we weren't going to the embassy.

"You're looking at the wrong map," I said. I tended to get cheeky in these kinds of situations, a habit that normally made things worse.

"Get them in the cars," Pierre told Rhiana.

"Take Kam and me. You don't need them," said Rhiana.

"Travel passes for eight don't go over very well for groups of four at roadblocks, Ms. Monroe."

"You can put them in one of the cars, and we'll go with you. I can explain everything at the roadblocks."

"I'm afraid not. You know very well what would happen at the first stop. Get in the cars."

"You mean we're not going to the embassy?" asked Madeline, picking up on the gist of the conversation.

Rhiana intervened. "Maddy, no."

"Maddy?" I said.

"It's his fault, isn't it? I knew I didn't like him from the very first," said Madeline as she looked at me.

"What do you have against me?" I pointed to Pierre and Dandré, who seemed to be enjoying the show. "What about them?"

"Folks," said Father Andrew. "Let's not take our frustration out on . . ."

"I don't like them either," said Madeline. "The bald one creeps me out."

"Madeline, please." Clyde went to her side and put his arm around her to calm her down.

She threw Clyde's arm off. "No. I don't care. I want to go to the embassy."

"Put her in the car," Pierre said to Dandré as casually as if he was telling the bag boy at the local grocery store where to set the milk.

Dandré took a step toward Madeline, and she shuffled toward the car.

To the rest of us, Pierre said, "There's been a change in travel plans. Your trip to the embassy will be delayed." He didn't elaborate, and our scholarly friends seemed to pick up on the fact that we had little choice in the matter.

Rhiana took her seat in the Audi without a word, so I followed suit, climbing into the Datsun. Clyde followed Madeline into the Audi, leaving Darrin and Father Andrew to ride in the Datsun with me. I chose a backseat behind Dandré, and Father Andrew reluctantly got in the front passenger seat. We were all too stunned to speak as our two-vehicle convoy left the motel parking lot and drove out of the city.

Sana'a, like all the cities in Yemen, just plain ended—without warning. One minute we were boxed in on both sides by mud, brick, and gingerbread buildings, and the next minute we were alone on a strip of uneven pavement that wound around the local scrub and disappeared into the early morning heat vapors. Behind us loomed the city of Sana'a like a bland-colored Oz on the horizon.

Not far from the city we hit our first roadblock, which consisted of two Toyota Land Cruisers and a series of fifty-gallon drums, presumably filled with concrete, blocking one lane of traffic. The attending soldiers were a little rough around the edges. Their uniforms matched in a random sort of way, as did their equipment. A smallish Yemeni officer with dark, wavy hair and an enviable mustache left a conversation with three other soldiers at the hut and sauntered toward the makeshift barricade, looking over our approaching vehicles with a critical eye. From the looks of his frayed leather belt and worn boots, it seemed like weekly paychecks may have been a bit random as well. Those things notwithstanding, Yemen boasted one of the Middle East's preeminent military police forces, and their many roadblocks did a fair job of hindering the free movement of terrorists and criminals within their country. Not a small accomplishment.

Pierre got out of the Audi, armed with our travel documents, and approached the little mustached officer. Dandré got out too and strode to the rear of the Datsun, smiling and pretending to get a good stretch. I knew why he was back there.

Darrin squirmed in his seat and looked around at the soldiers; I knew exactly what was on his mind. He wanted to make a break for it, hoping the soldiers would protect us.

I looked back at Dandré and knew just what our chances would be. I put a calming hand on Darrin's elbow and shook my head. Minutes later, after our passports had been scrutinized, we were waved past the barricades.

Rhiana had done a good job of putting our papers in order and making sure we had all the travel documents we needed to move around Yemen as a group. She'd been able to do the impossible and get passes for us from the office of tourism that allowed us to travel just about anywhere in the country, no small feat in a country where travel is strictly controlled. We managed to pass three more checkpoints without a hitch. I had to applaud Rhiana's efficiency—maybe I'd tell her that when Pierre lined us up for execution out in the desert of Al Jawf.

The Datsun rumbled along the crumbling strip of intermittent concrete and hardpan called the Sana'a-Ma'rib highway, throwing Dandré's elbows up and down as he fought to control the car on the rough surface. We ventured north and then east through a small town called Ar Rawdah, deeper into trouble and further away from help.

The landscape surrounding us was Craters of the Moon meets the stepped mountains and fertile soil of the Andes. The hillsides in places had been terraced to facilitate the local farming that sustained the small villages dotting the olive-drab mountains.

Sana'a sits in the cradle of the Asir Mountain Range that extends well into Saudi Arabia to the north. The roads leading northeast out of Sana'a climbed into the Asir range by virtue of an endless series of switchbacks and cambered corners that threw us against the window posts of the small cars. After cresting several mountain summits, we descended onto a high desert landscape that was markedly paler than the red rock you might find in Arizona, but with a vastness that stretched well into Saudi Arabia and beyond. Along the way, we were treated to the sight of hundreds of Yemeni tribesmen, young and old, buying guns and qat from dirty cinder-block huts that lined the highway. Every man had a rickety assault rifle slung on his shoulder, a curved tribal dagger, and a paper bag of unrefined narcotics in hand. As we drove further east, desolation replaced delinquency, and we saw fewer and fewer signs of life.

"I think we're headed to Ma'rib," I told Father Andrew.

Dandré's head snapped toward me then back to the pothole-stricken road. "No talking," he said. "Just . . ." He shrugged. "Just don't cause trouble."

Ahead of us, the Audi turned onto the highway leading to the great ruins of Barakesh in northern Yemen and eventually pulled to the side of the road, leaving one lane open.

We were allowed out of the cars to stretch—what were we going to do? Run away into the desert? My shin was stiff, but the pain was bearable, and my muscles and joints ached—too little sleep and too much running, fighting, and flying off hotel balconies. Looking around did very little good because other than the tire ruts on the rocky surface of the earth, the landscape was featureless. It was pretty much colorless too, unless you considered anemic brown a color. We were a long way from Seattle, and no one but us knew we were here.

CHAPTER 23

We settled down amid a set of pale rocks where each of us found an uncomfortable place to put a foot up or sit down. Father Andrew, always the gentleman, brushed the dust off a boulder with a flourish of his hands so that Madeline could sit. I looked at my arm, where my watch was conspicuously absent from my wrist, and then gazed up at the sun, which was not yet even at a forty-five-degree angle from the east—midmorning.

Dandré had his foot on the bumper of the Datsun under the slightly ajar trunk, his eyes scanning the desert horizon. Pierre paced in front of the parked cars and pressed a few buttons on Rhiana's phone. He listened and then threw his arms down.

I shrugged at Rhiana, and she responded with a grin. She'd done something to her phone before she handed it to Pierre in Sana'a. It was a small victory. If Dandré noticed Rhiana's reaction, he didn't care, but he did seem a lot nicer yesterday, when he was reupholstering my leg.

It seemed like a long time passed before Pierre stalked back to us, his lips pursed and his face red. He passed by the Audi and threw Rhiana's phone onto the driver's seat. To Dandré he said, "We need to get rid of these people."

"We can't let them drive away by themselves until we've made contact," said Dandré. "Maybe we should tell them."

Pierre gave that a shake of the head. "We continue north and wait. They'll find us." I assumed Pierre wasn't talking about the Red Cross.

There was nothing in the north but a vaguely conceived border with Saudi Arabia and a lot of loose rock. It was a perfect place to lose four scholars, a CIA agent, and an Arab-American ex-cop with language skills.

Rhiana approached Pierre. "These people are not going any farther," she said. "Put them in one of the cars and let them go back to Sana'a. I'll go north with you."

Pierre looked at our little group for a moment, almost as if he were considering Rhiana's offer. "No," was all he said.

"What do you mean, no?" said Madeline. "What's he talking about?" She leaped from her rock, took three long steps toward Pierre, and shoved him in the chest before he realized what she was doing. The result was about what you'd expect when a sociology professor shoves a Special Forces soldier—not much. None of us said anything, too stunned to take it all in. Madeline got a gold star in my book. She would probably get us all killed, but she'd die with a gold star and my respect.

I doubt that Pierre had been shoved like that since third grade, but it didn't seem to upset him much. He simply smiled and nodded to Dandré, who was now holding a Heckler and Koch MP5 submachine gun. The weapon was capable of delivering a lethal string of nine-millimeter parabellum rounds in less time than it takes to scream, "I surrender." I knew, because I'd carried one just like it on the SPD SWAT team. The relatively short barrel sacrificed long-range accuracy in exchange for maneuverability, but Dandré looked to have the finesse required to make good use of the weapon at any distance under several hundred yards.

When Rhiana saw the weapon, she wasn't surprised, but Madeline gasped. Father Andrew, bless his soul, appeared calm, as did Clyde, but Darrin's lip quivered.

Pierre stepped away from Rhiana and addressed the group. "None of you are going to Sana'a. We go north." He turned to Dandré and nodded toward the cars.

Dandré, with sub gun in hand, opened the car doors and waited as our miserable and confused group took their seats. I had only the briefest chance to look at Rhiana for any indication of what was happening, and her stolid look told me nothing. I had suspected our French escorts were trouble, but I hadn't figured on this.

Father Andrew opened the back door of the Datsun, but Dandré grabbed him by the shoulder before he could get in. "No, you drive."

The same scenario was playing out at the Audi, with Pierre pushing Darrin toward the driver's seat.

"Non, non," said Dandré. He stalked toward the Audi and pulled Darrin out of the driver's seat by the shirt and pointed to Madeline.

"Not on your life, French boy," she said, earning herself another gold star. "I can't drive a shift."

Pierre looked confused, and Dandré said, "Darrin is too good a driver." Dandré nodded at Clyde. He slipped into the driver's seat, took the wheel, and drove us north toward millions of square miles of nothing. The Empty Quarter was easily the most dangerous place in Yemen, not only because of the scorching desert days, the frigid desert nights, and the merciless desert sandstorms, but because the people here were as raw and ruthless as the naked, gritty landscape. We had no water, no food, only what gas was left in the tanks, and worse—no idea what kind of nightmare lay ahead for us.

There comes a time in any investigation that you have to ask the dreaded *why?* questions. Ask too early and you confuse yourself with unlikely scenarios and dead ends. Ask too late and you run the risk of not seeing the obvious. I hadn't asked them at all. For all my talk about investigations and following the money, I'd been a tremendous fool. The United Nations takes a sudden and unexpected interest in an unpublicized Yemeni hostage incident. American Special Forces are replaced at the last moment by French soldiers. And the man who is out to kill me is named René and talks like he's coughing up escargot. *Get your head in the game, Daniels.*

I wasn't sure how our embassy communications had been compromised, but I was certain that somebody French was behind it. As for the United Nations, their culpability was probably minimal, but so was their competency, and whether they were institutionally aware of the problem we were having was anyone's guess. And anyway, questions about the United Nations were somewhat moot at the moment—we had more immediate concerns.

We rumbled down the hardpan, occasionally being popped out of our seats by a chunk of indigenous rock in the road while Father Andrew wrestled the steering wheel. I didn't know our final destination, but I did know that unless we did something, our destination would be all too final.

Father Andrew would be missed, but he would leave no grieving children and no waiting bride. I wasn't sure who Madeline would be survived by, but her family and friends would surely mourn her passing. It would be the same with Darrin, and more poignantly with Clyde, whose absence would create an empty spot where a father and husband should be. Last of all, Rhiana would be survived by a father who had been absent for most of her life. She would not be survived by her estranged husband . . . He would share her fate in the Empty Quarter of Yemen.

* * *

We didn't drive much further before we stopped again. This time we were not allowed to get out of the cars. Instructed to do so by Dandré, Father Andrew pulled the Datsun directly behind Clyde in the Audi. Pierre got out of the passenger side of the Audi. "Watch the hillsides," he said to Dandré. I did a little looking around myself. This was most definitely the kind of place bad guys would take a group of victims to do away with them. I doubted very much that the reality of our situation was hitting home with anyone else, except maybe Rhiana. Someone had to do something; I wasn't going to wait until the situation got worse.

Pierre scanned the southern horizon from behind the Datsun, and after a few sweltering minutes, he walked back toward us along the side of the car. When his shadow reached my window, I pulled the latch and thrust the door into him. The top edge of the window frame hit him in the chest, sending him backward holding his sternum.

I leaped from the backseat of the Datsun, ready to take whatever punishment Pierre was about to inflict on me, and charged toward him. I grabbed the top of his head and threw a knee toward his face. The strike missed and glanced off his ear. He made a threatening remark that failed to strike fear into my heart—just how scary can a man sound in French? I couldn't respond in French, but I did manage to insult Pierre's parentage in succinct English.

I glanced into the Datsun to see Father Andrew hanging off of Dandré's shoulders like a necktie. That struggle between holy man and warrior wasn't destined to last long, but snaps to Father Andrew for giving me a few extra seconds to live.

Pierre came to his feet in a defensive stance, shaking off the surprise. French or not, this man was dangerous, and I was little threat to him. Physically outmatched, I turned to flippancy.

"Hey Pierre," I taunted, "what do you call a Frenchman with his arms up?"

Pierre wasn't in the mood for jokes. He lunged forward toward my legs.

"A soldier," I yelled as I jumped backward. I snap-kicked his thigh and he rolled sideways, off balance but unhurt. I fell sideways into him, and he grasped my arm, twisting it behind my back. I pulled up on my arm and broke his grip, but not before he took a handful of my shirt and dragged me to the ground. We both toppled to the sand, and I struggled to stay on my back so I could keep my hands and feet pointed up at him. I got a clean elbow on the side of Pierre's bald head as we went down, but he drove his knee into my chest and ran it up under my chin as he sprawled over me.

I was dazed. Before I could recover, Pierre was on top of me, hands on my throat. I kicked my legs and tried to get on my side, but Pierre worked his knees onto my shoulders. I struggled to free a hand to strike him, but before I could, the hammering sound of gunfire startled both of us.

Dandré stood above us, holding the smoking barrel of his MP5 submachine gun pointed toward the ground in one hand. He backed off a few steps to get everyone within his deadly field of fire. The others were in a small group by the car, Father Andrew nursing a sore face, no doubt a result of his ill-advised fight with Dandré.

"Stay on the ground," Pierre ordered as he pushed himself away from me and got to his knees. "Dandré, keep these people under control."

Madeline was beyond consoling and marched toward Pierre. "What are *you* doing, you little French tart?"

Go girl. It was a three-star day for Madeline, but her bravado was short-lived. Dandré took a menacing step toward her, and she scuttled back to the group.

"This one is inconvenient." Pierre pointed at me. "I don't have time for him." He came closer, and I hoped he was going to stake me out in the sand and give me a sporting chance against the elements, but I didn't think Pierre was a loose-ends kind of guy.

Dandré approached us with his MP5 slung across his chest, the folded stock tucked in the crease of his elbow and his hand around the trigger guard. The shadow of his large, black, muscular frame eclipsed me, and as his body blocked the sun, I could see his wind-reddened eyes staring down at me. Sand stuck in the creases of his brown skin, and a single rivulet of perspiration ran in a crooked line from his temple to his chin. He didn't cock his gun like a bad actor in a B movie. The weapon was already charged, a bullet in the chamber, and he had nothing to do but pull the trigger and end my life.

Madeline would never get over seeing a man die in front of her—even if it was me. If she lived, she'd go on to teach at Boston College, earn academic accolades, and escort her students through graduation, but the spark that was in her was about to go out. It's not easy to see a man killed. Father Andrew would be able to handle it; he'd seen enough of life to understand death. Clyde, likewise, would soon let what he was about to see slip from his consciousness only to be bothered by it in bad dreams. For Darrin, it would never go away. He'd talk about it, reliving it often and burning the image of it into his brain. Eventually he would make friends with those images, but they'd be with him always.

Rhiana? She'd feel responsible for my death, and the guilt would affect every relationship she'd ever have. The selfish part of me didn't care, but I loved her and had to let her move on. I'd had my chance. I hated my last thought to be that Rhiana was somehow better off without me, but I had very little time left to convince myself otherwise. Somewhere, at the end of this odyssey, was the man—the hostage—whom Rhiana had bent and broken every rule to rescue.

I stared at the barrel of the MP5, heart racing, and waited for Dandré to squeeze his trigger finger and end what was left of my life.

CHAPTER 24

It never happened.

"Get up," said Dandré. Then to Pierre, "Unless you make contact before they get here, I don't think it's safe to send them away in a car."

Pierre looked completely exasperated. He dialed Rhiana's phone again, listened, and then shook his head. He turned to Rhiana. "Trigger your extraction. Contact your helicopters."

Rhiana hedged. "But they'll only take me and . . ." She didn't finish her sentence. It wasn't going to serve any good purpose to tell four very scared scholars that we hadn't planned for their rescue, only our own.

"The sooner, the better," said Pierre. "My associates don't seem inclined to answer a call from your phone. My phone is, as you well know, indisposed." He threw her the phone he'd confiscated earlier.

Dandré was no longer pointing his gun at me, so I slowly stood up. Pierre waved me toward the others. Apparently he was done threatening to have me killed and was on to more important things.

"What about killing me?" I asked. My question went unanswered. I turned my attention to Rhiana. "Are you calling the helicopters?" Those two questions encapsulated my two most pressing concerns at the moment.

Rhiana pushed buttons on her phone and then stopped. "If I call for an extraction, there won't be another attempt to rescue the hostage," she said.

I looked at our tired, hungry, and dirty group as they staggered to the doors of the two cars. Rhiana wasn't thinking straight. "These are the people who need rescuing. Look at them. Your hostage is probably dead by now anyway."

Rhiana's head jerked back toward me. "No."

"Rhiana, whoever he is, he's . . . Rhi, are you in love with this guy?"

"Kam, I can't . . ."

Pierre threw his head back impatiently. But, I was on his side, so he let me take the argument from here.

"That's what this has been all about," I said. "Rhiana, you can't risk the lives of innocent people just because . . ." I bit my lip. I couldn't say it. "Just get the helicopters coming, Rhi."

"I'm not going with you."

"Yes, Rhi, you are."

Rhiana was crying now, making no attempt to hold back. It wasn't the stoic case officer that stood before us all; it was a very raw woman pushed to her limit. A very hurt and tender girl. It was a girl I hadn't seen for a long time.

"I'll try to locate a landmark they can key on," I said. There was plenty of terrain but nothing significant to mark our location for the rescue copters. The land rose and fell in terraced sections and several deep ravines, or wadis, ran along the road, cutting it in places where we'd had to ease our small cars over the deep, dry ruts. Not far distant, steeply terraced hills rose to angled peaks and formed a small mountain range, but nothing about the terrain was unique; the landscape looked the same for hundreds of miles.

"They can track the phone by GPS. All I have to do is place the call. I don't even have to say anything." With tears still running down her face, she keyed in the final numbers and waited. It was a relief for all of us, but what prompted Pierre's psychotic bipolar mood swings was still a mystery. He seemed completely reassured that he could take us hostage at force of death one minute and see to our certain rescue the next. No problem.

Dandré had gone to the front of the Audi, where Rhiana was standing. "Can they track the phone if we're moving?" he asked her.

"I don't think so," she said. "I key in the number and the information is logged on an aircraft carrier in the Gulf of Aden. The extraction teams will probably take a couple of hours to get to the location where the call originated."

"Did you already make the connection?" asked Dandré.

"Yes, a few seconds ago. Why?"

Then the rest of us saw them. Swirling along the horizon from the south were four very angry clouds of dust accompanied by the whine of vehicle engines. It wasn't the helicopters—not by a long shot.

Dandré and Pierre looked at each other. Dandré said, "Your friends are here. There's no chance for you now."

Pierre took a deep breath and let it out through clenched teeth. "Not if they begin negotiations the way they usually do," Pierre answered. "They weren't expecting a group this size. Get them out of here."

"Pierre," said Dandré, "Don't do this. There will be another chance. This is too risky."

"Did I miss something?" I asked. I looked at Rhiana for reassurance, but she seemed as baffled as the rest of us.

The sound of the trucks grew louder. We could see the rooftops of the approaching vehicles through a flurry of dust. Two of the four trucks came equipped with heavy firepower mounted on tripods sticking up from their beds, the heads of young Arab gunners bouncing up and down behind them.

Dandré went to the front seat of the Audi, retrieved the .45, and handed it to Pierre.

Pierre accepted the weapon but shook his head. "They won't appreciate that in my waistband." He held the gun out to me, grip first. "I have to go."

Dandré shook his head and gripped Pierre by the shoulders. Then he nodded at his boss. "They await, mon ami."

Before we could ask who "they" were, the big guns opened up on us.

* * *

The ground erupted into streaks of flying rock and sand; scholars and spies went in every direction. Dandré herded Rhiana and the scientists forward to the low side of the terraced berms between us and the deadly machine guns.

The four trucks spread out as best they could considering the uneven terrain, the ones equipped with the .60-caliber machine guns taking the flanks as their drivers positioned themselves. Had the Bakil manning the .60s known their capacity, they'd have made shredded cabbage out of us hundreds of yards ago.

Dandré flung open the trunk of the Datsun and pulled the strap of his black tactical bag over his shoulder. Extending the folding stock on his MP5 and bracing it against his shoulder, he moved to the front of the vehicle and crouched behind the engine block.

I ran to the Audi and skidded to a stop across the rocks. Kneeling behind the hood and using the front wheel for cover, I pressed the release button on my pistol and dropped the magazine into my palm. Seven rounds—stacked. Each was going to be a counter; I couldn't afford to waste one shot. From the Audi I dove toward the ditch beside the road and clawed my way into a depression in the cut bank flanking the highway. I wasn't in a very good offensive position, but there was enough dirt and rock between me and the .60s to prevent me from becoming a colander.

"Slow, aimed fire," yelled Dandré over the cacophony of the salvo of the first .60 caliber to fire. "We need to keep them occupied while Pierre makes his way to the Bakil position."

"What?" I yelled back, but the sound of my voice was covered by rapid bursts of gunfire from the Bakil. Tall spits of dust exploded into the air in a line running past us as the Arab manning one of the .60 cals lost control of the weapon's recoil and his aim climbed upward. Dandré aimed his MP5 toward the gunner at a distance of about two hundred yards and knocked him to his back in the bed of his truck. Then Pierre bolted toward the same ditch I was in and took cover beside me.

"First you want to kill me. Now you want to kill yourself. What kind of French tactic is this? Do you have some kind of deal going with the Bakil?" I asked Pierre over the noise of the guns.

Pierre shook his head. "It is a French problem. It requires a French solution. You and Dandré are free to save your own people if you can. I have someone to find." Pierre watched the Bakil movement on the hill for a moment and then took off up the ravine and out of sight—Q & A was over.

Two hundred yards was well out of my range. Realizing this, Dandré put up a hand to signal me to hold my fire. Great, I had to be the whites-of-their-eyes guy.

Rhiana was behind a long, rocky berm with the rest of our group, where they could stay low and feel reasonably safe from the gunfire. I didn't have the heart to tell them what a .60-caliber round will do to soft ground cover. Why ruin their illusion of safety?

Dandré popped up from the cut bank and fired another short salvo, putting another of the gunners out of commission, at least temporarily. The military called it suppressive fire—rounds fired to keep the heads of the Arabs down, and Dandré was well trained for it. I called it blind panic shooting.

Dandré's work with the MP5 slowed the onslaught of Arab troops, but I knew eventually they'd realize that the two of us were no match for them. I tried to pick out a leader, but they all had their heads down now, and only an occasional rifle round came our way. Neither of the .60-caliber gunners wanted to stand tall in the back of their pickup and let Dandré pick them off. If they had only recognized that they had the advantage . . .

Dandré signaled for me to move toward him as he loosed a three-round salvo toward one of the trucks. "Crazy Frenchman," I said, not loud enough for him to hear. I sprinted up the road, barely out of sight of the Arab gunners, head down and cringing.

"Distance," Dandré said when I got to him. "The Bakil will have the advantage until we're in close."

"They'll have the advantage unless I grow Barrett light .50-caliber machine guns out of my shoulders."

Dandré shrugged. "True." He surveyed the battlefield like a general assessing his position, paying particular attention to the terrain feature running along the Bakil flank. "If you move forward along that wadi, we can at least establish a tactical *L* and give the appearance of superior strength and position." He pointed to the wadi along the road that rose gently toward a high mound of rocks upon which grew a single tall shrub. Dandré's choice of flanking position wasn't bad, but the route to get there lacked a little something. As dry stream beds go, this one was shallow and wide. It was just what I would have wanted one of our enemies to crawl down. It looked like certain death to me.

Dandré looked into the sky. "It will be sundown soon. We hold them off until dark and then escape into the night," he said.

A single round from a rifle sailed over my head like a hypersonic bee passing too close to my ear, and I flinched. Unaffected, Dandré reached into his duffel and withdrew three additional magazines for my pistol and handed them to me, giving me twenty-eight chances to die fighting. "Until dark," he said and nodded the nod of a sergeant sending a brave soldier off to war.

"You've been holding out on me," I said, accepting the magazines and stuffing them in my back pocket. I nodded toward the wadi. "You're insane," I told Dandré.

"You will die a hero," he said. French chivalry in action.

I examined the miniscule dry rivulet that took a crooked path along the side of the Bakil position. If I were able to make the first major bend in the wadi, where it appeared to get deeper, I could maneuver into a good fighting position and maybe even do some damage with the .45, assuming I didn't die trying.

"I'll have to lob the rounds in from that distance," I told Dandré. The .45 is a formidable weapon, and it packs a significant wallop, but the bullets are large and don't travel very far. At a distance, a shooter has to arc rounds onto the target.

"I've seen it done," he said without taking his eyes off the higher ground where the Bakil were digging in.

I took a last look at Rhiana, cowering with the rest of our group. Then into the wadi I slid.

Hugging the near side of the wadi, or in my lingo "the ditch," I made my way on hands and knees in relative safety for the first fifty yards. I could hear sporadic gunfire still being exchanged between Dandré and the Bakil tribesmen, but none was coming my way. I reached an area where the wadi became deeper and dipped well below sight of the Bakil. I ran at a crouch and covered another fifty yards quickly.

As my vantage point changed, I was better able to assess the strength of the Bakil contingent, which would have been formidable if even one of them had Dandré's capabilities. I couldn't see all of the Bakil, but I now estimated fewer than fifteen men, not the invading horde of my imagination. Only two of the men I could see had taken tactical shooting positions at their vehicles. The others stayed well to the rear and yelled at each other. So much for paradisiacal zeal. I guess they were saving martyrdom for bigger foes.

A short burst of gunfire came from Dandré's location, and one of the Arabs crouched behind his pickup, fell sideways, and crawled backward holding his hip. Several Arabs ran to help him, and one Arab ordered someone to take his place, waving his hands wildly. That was my man—the man in charge. He wore olive-drab fatigues and a jungle hat, the military's olive-drab version of Uncle Bob's fishing hat. Very trendy for eastern Yemen.

I wormed my way higher on the crest of the hillside along the wadi and leveled my pistol in the direction of the leader. I estimated my distance to the target at just under one hundred yards; he measured about the height of my thumbnail at arm's length. Knowing that the .45 wouldn't have the gusto to send rounds down range on a flat trajectory, I held my aim well over the target's head and squeezed the trigger. The weapon bucked in my hand, and the sights settled back on target. There was a flicker of dust well in front of the Arab leader, but he didn't appear to notice it. But an Arab rifleman did.

I slid back down the slope just as a hailstorm of bullets ripped the edge of the wadi apart, sending dirt and rocks whipping into my face and down the back of my collar. I moved sideways on my stomach, keeping my head close to the ground and my eyes closed. I had to move and fire again before the Bakil realized that I was alone. I knew Dandré would try to discourage a full-out assault in my direction, but I wanted to create the illusion of superiority along the Bakil flank.

I edged my way along the rim of the wadi and took up a new position where I could see the activity behind the trucks. The leader was urging an Arab onto the tailgate of one of the trucks to man the .60, and another set of Arabs were dragging a body from the bed of the other truck. While I was at the ridgeline, I took another potshot, this time kicking up dust just behind the Arab leader. I let one more round go before retreating into the wadi and moving another twenty yards further toward the Arabs' rear flank.

Another clattering volley tore up the berm in my direction, most of the rounds burying themselves well off to my side. I ran another forty yards at a crouch, placing myself well past the attacking Bakil.

Single rounds lobbed in from the short barrel of a .45 were little more than an irritating distraction for the Bakil, but my contribution to the firefight did serve to split the attention of the Bakil and take some heat off Dandré. Dandré was providing the bulk of the defense and keeping our small band of scholars alive. Even so, it wasn't going to hurt matters if I got in closer to inflict significant damage to the Bakil and reinforce the pretense that we were a formidable force. Had the Bakil known just how ill-equipped we were for such a battle, they'd have overrun us during the first few seconds of the conflict.

There was high ground behind the Bakil positions, but it was probably over three hundred yards back, and there was no cover between where I was and where it was. Beyond where I knelt, my wadi became steadily shallower until it became little more than a rut. I'd gone as far as I could go, and I wasn't going to reach my original objective, the boulder mound on which sat the lone shrub. Now it was just me and my pistol.

I climbed the side of my ditch and emptied the last four rounds in my magazine in the direction of the Bakil leader. Just as I ducked below the edge of the wadi, the air above me broke apart, and the earth exploded into my face.

The deep sting of dust and rock chips locked my eyes shut, and my cheeks and forehead went numb as the particulates pulverized my face. I rolled to the bottom of the wadi, covering my eyes with my hands. I tried to pull them open with my fingers but the muscles of my face just wouldn't allow it. Clawing along the bottom of the wadi and navigating by feel, I groped back the way I'd come. The relentless assault of the .60 ranged along the top of the wadi, cutting through the earth as if it weren't there.

I blinked in an effort to form tears, but the mud and dust in my eyes was too thick. Using my sleeve, I rubbed at my eyes, trying to induce some kind of moistening reaction. All it did was hurt. In the deepest part of the wadi, I curled up and tried to control my breathing.

I thought I was immune to fear—or at least that I'd come to understand how to handle it. I was wrong. Gasping to try to keep up with my oxygen needs, I snagged the collar of my shirt and pulled it over my nose. Recycling the carbon dioxide I was exhaling helped prevent hyperventilation and helped me calm down until my eyes started to blink on their own. I took long, even breaths, fighting the feeling that I was suffocating.

The pounding of the .60 was intermittent now but still kicked up fountains of earth over my head as it raked the edge of the wadi. As my mind started to clear, I groped on the ground for the pistol but couldn't find it. I opened one eye and searched for the weapon, then realized I'd dropped it when the .60 cals forced me to the bottom of the wadi.

Off to the side, I heard the two big guns trading rounds with the popping sound of Dandré's MP5. The Bakil were making a push; I had to get back to the pistol and take the heat off of Dandré. Hoping the gunners were focusing their attention somewhere other than my wadi, I stood and ran up the side of the ditch to retrieve my .45. Debris covered the weapon, which was locked back on an empty chamber, allowing sand and rock into the barrel and magazine well. I ejected the empty magazine and let it fall on the ground as I slid down the side of the wadi and retrieved another magazine to insert into the pistol.

I scrambled back up the side of the wadi and threw my arms over the edge. The sun was well below the western horizon, casting Dandré and the others in shadow. Through blurry eyes I aimed the front sight of the pistol over the head of the closest .60 gunner and squeezed the trigger. The gun didn't fire. Instinctively I slapped the base of the magazine, racked the slide, and squeezed the trigger again. Still nothing.

With my head and shoulders well above the ridge of the wadi, I was an easy target, and the Arab leader saw me and shouted, waving his arms and pointing. Dandré's gun had gone silent, allowing a team of two Arabs to advance toward my wadi, their AK-47s at low ready. It was either slow them down or face them from the bottom of the ditch.

I pulled the loaded magazine from my gun and worked the slide back and forth, letting small flecks of sand fall from the mechanism, then plunged the magazine back into the well. Strings of Arab oaths grew louder as I raised the .45, released the slide, and squeezed the trigger, taking seven well-aimed shots at the exposed men. One of the Bakil went down, grabbing the other for support. I dropped below the edge of the wadi, flipping the empty magazine out of the gun and replacing it with a fresh one. Without much conscious thought, I ran several yards and climbed the side of the ditch again, this time firing three rounds. The injured Arab slid to the ground. One more shot hit the second Arab, who clutched his stomach and fell to his knees.

Dandré's weapon came alive again, and one of the .60 gunners dropped to the bed rail of the truck and then cascaded over the side. Another man hoisted himself into the bed and was cut down by another burst from Dandré. I spent the last three rounds of my magazine adding to the general fire in the direction of the Bakil leader. Then I exchanged the empty magazine for my last full one. Seven more rounds.

Persistence on Dandré's part had made the job of .60 gunner very unpopular for the tribesmen, and the gun battle turned into a standoff. There was some movement around the Bakil vehicles, but for the most part the Arabs had stopped shooting at what they couldn't see in the impending darkness and were determined to wait it out. For our part, I was pleased that Dandré, still hunkered down in the depression of the cut bank along the highway, had conserved his scant supply of ammunition for at least this long.

Silence replaced the peal of machine-gun fire, and everyone seemed to take a few deep breaths.

The gritty sand of the desert under my eyelids still burned as it grated across my eyes. My chest heaved off the stress of the last . . . how long had it been? The sun sat just below the western horizon, and its shadow had eclipsed us. Twilight wouldn't last long in the desert, and it would soon be dark—and cold. I waited until the shadows deepened and risked another trip to the edge of the wadi to look around.

Dandré's gun had gone silent. I looked at my little .45 and then at the Arabs kneeling behind their trucks. Rhiana and the scholars were still clutching the sand behind an earthen terrace. Something told me we were in for a long night.

CHAPTER 25

As twilight faded and blackness enveloped the rocky landscape, the Arabs moved their trucks to fan their headlights in an arc out over the valley, creating a stark light against the deep shadows.

Dandré took a few potshots, but with no effect. The alien-like shadows of the rocks and rivulets in front of the trucks distorted the uneven ground, reaching out dozens of feet in the glare of the headlights. The Bakil leader moved back and forth in the shadows behind the trucks while his men waited for full darkness, when they would undoubtedly attack. When he took off his jungle hat, matted locks of greasy hair dropped around his shoulders. I recognized him immediately—my rotten friend. Faasid. "Die trying," Dandré told me.

I raised the .45 and extended my arm across the top of the berm. I placed the front sight several feet over Faasid's head to allow for distance and started to squeeze the stiff trigger. A shout went up on the far side of the Arab position, and Faasid took off at a run. I held my fire.

Several other Arabs ran behind Faasid, but in the darkness I couldn't make out what was happening. A few moments later, a man I hadn't seen among the Arabs walked to the center of the Bakil position at Faasid's side. It was Pierre, up to his ears in his French solution. That his French problem somehow involved Barbier, I had no doubt. Whatever he was doing had been well planned. Pierre walked among the Bakil like a compatriot. I had to hand it to him—he was bold.

In the sky, there was only a hazy violet band over the western horizon that faded to deep indigo in the east, but the ground was cloaked in shadow. Now that Pierre was with the Bakil, our situation was dire. Once they were aware that only two of us presented a threat and that our ammunition was limited, we were done. The situation was even worse than that. Pierre could tell the Bakil precisely where Rhiana and the scholars were hiding. I couldn't afford to give Pierre time to brief Faasid.

I shot one round toward the dark human shapes behind the Bakil trucks, and I was on my feet running toward them in the open. The Arabs ducked behind their trucks and then peered out to see where the shot came from. I stopped, knelt, and shot another round out of the darkness, the flash signature at the end of my barrel the only thing that would give my position away. I got to my feet and bolted sideways as rounds kicked up flecks of rock where I'd been kneeling. I shot my last five rounds and felt the slide of the pistol lock back on an empty chamber as I ran toward the boulder pile with the shrub on top behind the Bakil position. I dove for the cover of the rocks as one of the .60 cals churned up the ground behind me. The gunner lost me in the darkness and the gunfire ceased, leaving the Yemen countryside in silence.

I climbed the pile of rocks and rested against the tall shrub, out of sight of the Bakil. I heard Faasid's voice, carrying over the rocks, screaming orders at his men, but I couldn't make out any specific commands. But the Arabs now knew they had at least one man behind them, and I hoped Dandré would be smart enough to retreat into the darkness as the Arabs looked for me. That was my plan, anyway, and unless something miraculous happened, I was probably going to die carrying it out.

A faint flutter in the air over the horizon behind the Bakil drew my attention, the beating of rotors cutting the still air. Our Little Birds. I craned my head around but couldn't see the approaching helicopters. It sounded like they were all around us. The Bakil heard it too and were searching the skies, firing their AK-47s blindly into the air. One of the Bakil ran back to his truck and braved a position behind one of the .60 cals. The tremendous hammering of the .60 didn't stop the pounding of the rotors. One of the Little Birds hanging in the air over our heads banked sideways and opened fire on the Bakil position. A string of bright phosphorous trails reached out of the sky and enveloped one of the trucks with a .60 cal in back. The pressure of the concussion nearly split my head. When I was able to look up again, the truck and the big gun were aflame under a column of smoke. The Bakil were no longer paying any attention to me.

I crawled around the trunk of the shrub and peered into the darkness where I'd left Dandré and the others near the highway. In the yellow light of the three remaining truck headlights, I saw Dandré with our group in a fighting retreat, taking measured steps backward as he held the thin folding stock of his MP5 against his shoulder, stopping only long enough to kneel and fire aimed rounds in the direction of the remaining Bakil .60 cal.

With the attention of the Arabs on the aircraft, and Dandré leading the others away, I had to make a run for the extraction point or be left behind. Unnoticed by the Bakil, I tripped and stumbled over the rocks into another shallow wadi leading toward Dandré.

The sound of the battle behind me intensified as another Little Bird crested the horizon, moving low over the Bakil position. As it overcame me, the wash of the rotors threw sand and small rocks into my face, making me lose my footing and sending me sliding and sprawling across the desert floor. In the eyes of the night vision-equipped pilots, I must have looked like a little green jumble of arms and legs rolling across the terrain.

The two helicopters flew down the path of the wadi and banked sideways as their cylindrical, strut-mounted guns sent streaks of phosphorous and lead over the Bakil positions. The Arabs were running in every direction, and the only resistance now was sporadic small-arms fire from around their vehicles.

I churned up dust and rocks getting to my feet and willed my tortured legs to carry me toward the helicopter settling into the sand behind our bullet-riddled Audi. The other helo hovered overhead, the threat of its heavy arms pointed toward the Bakil position. Dandré was at the open side of the machine, yelling in at the copilot so he wouldn't dispose of me as a precaution in the darkness.

I took the last excruciating strides to the open side of the helicopter, fell to my knees, and wrapped my arms around the landing skid support where I heaved for oxygen. A frantic Rhiana met me there and wrapped her arms around me. It would have been a good time to kiss her.

"Get in," I yelled, but I couldn't even hear myself over the throb of the rotors.

Rhiana was fighting tears and made no move to climb into the helicopter.

I leaned in toward her ear. "Please, Rhiana. There's nothing else we can do now."

"Kam. I love you," Rhiana yelled over the swell of the engines.

I thought about the other man, the hostage we'd nearly lost eight lives to rescue. It must have shown on my face.

Rhiana shook her head and put her hand to my ear. "Kam. The hostage is my father."

* * *

Against her will, I hoisted Rhiana up to the open side of the small heli-copter where she was greeted by two ape hooks attached to the boul-dery shoulders of a tough-looking, camo-faced, buzz-shorn, military man. After he flopped Rhiana across the deck, he showed me a perfect set of shimmering white teeth and a smile as wide as Texas. "God bless America," he shouted over the concussive whirl of the rotors.

The small cabin inside the Little Bird was designed for far fewer occupants than we'd brought with us—it was a tangle of arms, legs, and bodies, but each of the various owners slowly got their niche and found something to cling to.

A shadow in the dark sky, the second Little Bird hovered over us at no more than thirty feet, the threat of its vastly superior firepower keeping the Bakil resistance to a minimum. The burly Texan turned his head away just as the loudest whirring noise in the world lit the other helicopter aglow as it sprayed muzzle flash from cylindrical guns mounted on the skids dozens of yards into the near darkness. The noise intensified as the rotating gun gathered speed and spat devasta-tion at the assaulting Arab force. The gun slowed down like a carnival ride, rolling to a stop and leaving us in relative silence.

Unaffected, my Texan rescuer grinned. "Don't worry. We're just shooting up their trucks and stuff. No use startin' a war," he shouted over the whir of the Little Bird's rotors.

I offered him my arm, and he just looked at me.

"You're riding the sled," he screamed.

"What?" I was drowned out by the rotor noise, but the soldier must have been a lip reader.

"No troop platform. Only guns. We were only expecting two people. Just hang on." The Texan slapped the support beam of the landing skid and winked; everything is bigger in Texas.

I wrapped one arm around the support beam and stepped onto the skid, searching for something else to hold onto in the event the pilot got creative with his flying while getting us out of the hot zone. Rhiana sat on the deck, safely inside the aircraft, sandwiched between Father Andrew on the far side and Clyde nearest to me. Madeline was hanging half out on the other side of the aircraft, crying like Nancy Kerrigan and clawing at anything within reach. Darrin, ever the gentleman, slithered over her lap and grasped the skid support and swung himself out to leave her room to get her whole body inside the aircraft. A second later I saw him standing on the skid, a mirror image of myself. If there was ever a no-room-at-the-inn moment, this was it. I didn't know much about aviation, but I was pretty certain this Little Bird wasn't designed to carry this many folks plus a full complement of weaponry and ammunition. Darrin may never get to be a Marine, but he was going to ride like one.

I searched the darkness for Dandré and saw him on the far side of the helicopter, holding his MP5 at hip level and giving the Bakil the good news with the business end through the curtain of blowing sand kicked up by the rotors. After everyone was aboard, he took his place on the skid next to Darrin.

"Secure on the sleds, boys?" asked our Texan host. He nodded over his shoulder at the pilot, who shrugged—not the most confident of gestures.

"In case of a water landing," yelled the Texan, "ain't no flotation devices 'cause there ain't no seat cushions, on account of there ain't no seats." The big Texan guffawed as the idling engine surged and the noise level doubled. The rotor wash about blew me off my skid, so I hugged the upright tighter and wrapped a leg around a skid for good measure.

The little aircraft whined and rattled, the engine trying to push us off the ground. The pilot craned around and shook his head.

The sound of gunfire, exceptionally loud even over the sound of the aircraft, turned into a pelting of the side of the Little Bird. Everyone, including the Texan, winced as the bullets strafed the side of the ship. In response, the Little Bird hovering above us let loose with another incredible display of firepower. The remaining Arab .60 cal was silenced forever. Then the copter tilted forward and edged out in front of us to cover our takeoff.

The pilot, looking out over the battlefield through his night vision goggles, made a comment to his copilot, and the mini-guns wound up again and destroyed whatever threat was out there. The Texan flinched and then turned around with a great big smile. "Oooh, someone out there thought it'd be a good idea to uncrate an RPG—a rocket-propelled grenade. It wasn't," he yelled. "Are you guys sure it was smart to fight all them Arabs with a pistol and an MP5?"

The Texan rocked sideways as our captain thrust the throttles forward and the Bird lifted about six feet off the ground, rolled back and forth, and struggled to break free of the earth.

I peered over the deck at Rhiana, who may have been the only person who didn't want to leave Yemen. In her eyes, I saw her heart breaking. Would I have done anything differently if I'd known all along that the hostage was her father? Where would I start? Not getting jealous for one thing.

Rhiana's struggle between good sense and professionalism and her desperation to get her father back played out on her pained face, and the risks she'd taken made perfect sense. My throat constricted, and my heart started to tear apart.

Our pilot fought with the controls as we slipped sideways and still failed to break free of the ground. He poured more fuel into the engine, and the Bird lifted just higher than a basketball standard, but he sacrificed stability for altitude, and the Bird tipped dangerously as he fought to steady it. There were just too many people aboard.

What happened next defied understanding. Maybe I was thinking—maybe not. Beneath the helicopter was a dark, swirling dust funnel, but none of that seemed to matter. The only thing that did matter was what I'd seen in Rhiana's eyes. Her life would never be the same—maybe if I hadn't destroyed it so thoroughly . . .

Rhiana was still looking at me. With one arm wrapped around the sled support, I gestured with the other. I pointed to my right eye, then to my nose—but I couldn't finish.

It happened quickly. I swung my leg over the support strut and braced my stomach on the landing skid, holding onto the frame of the helicopter with both hands.

Rhiana gasped, then screamed, but it was too late. She struggled to reach for me, but Clyde held her tight. She clawed at his arms, but he wouldn't let go. I let go and fell five . . . ten . . . twelve feet, maybe more, to the hard, uneven ground. Rhiana's heartrending protests faded into the air above me.

Both legs collapsed as I hit the ground, and I fell sideways, jarring my left shoulder and striking my head. I lay still; there was momentary blackness. Something heavy hit me from above, wrenching my body and driving hot lightning down both my legs.

The Little Bird canted to the left and began to rise slowly as it grew quieter and drifted upward, out of sight. The other Little Bird let go with the mini-guns once more, stabbing a brilliant jet of phosphorus into the sand around the cowering Arabs. The surviving Arab rifles were silent as the last Little Bird dropped behind the horizon, hugging the terrain into the night. I was alone in the remnants of the swirling dust left by the helicopter rotors in the darkness of eastern Yemen, the image of Rhiana struggling to free herself from Clyde's grip fading into the foggy recesses of my mind.

CHAPTER 26

"Kam?"

I heard my name being called softly through the blackness. It came from nearby.

"Kam? Are you there? Are you okay?"

I'd lost my orientation; I hoped my mind hadn't gone with it. I rose to my knees, moving my head slowly to locate the Arabs. In the glow of their headlights I could make out several forms congregating on a small rise near the vehicles, angry recriminations barely audible over the moaning wind.

"Kam?"

"Darrin?" I crawled forward and saw his prone shape lying in a shallow ravine only several feet away from me. "Darrin?"

"Uh-huh."

"You okay?" I asked.

"Sort of."

"What happened?"

"I wasn't expecting it to be that far. Can you come over here?"

"Just sit still." The Arabs were doing a lot of shouting into the intense desert darkness. I couldn't make out any real dialogue, but the gist of their concerns centered on the helicopters; they apparently hadn't seen the two bodies that had dropped off during takeoff.

I heard Darrin breathing heavily, like a person who was injured or crying. I shimmied closer to the sound. "Where are you hurt? Can you tell?" If he felt at all like me, it was difficult to identify specific points of injury.

"That was a long fall," he said.

"You didn't happen to grab a duffel bag of gear or anything before you fell?"

"I didn't think we were so far up."

"I'll take that as a negative. How about a gun? You didn't borrow Dandré's gun, did you? Maybe snag a bandoleer of extra magazines as you fell past?"

"That was a long way, Kam. I think I'm hurt."

"Lie still, Darrin. I'm right here. The bad guys are leaving." I reached out into the darkness in the direction of Darrin's voice. I touched his arm, then his heaving chest. "I'm right here, Darrin." I'm not sure which one of us was comforting the other, but eventually Darrin's breathing evened out. We lay for a long time after we heard the truck doors slam and the last Bakil tribesman load up.

And there you had it. I was on my stomach somewhere in eastern nowhere; I had a religious studies graduate student from Brigham Young University lying half alive on the ground with me; a couple of truckloads of Arabs were very upset with me, for no other reason than . . . who knows why; I had an estranged wife who was probably questioning my sanity flying off to safety on a U.S. Army Little Bird; and I had her father to find and rescue. Presumably he was in Yemen—or if not, he was somewhere else. And that was my situational assessment. I decided to dispense with the situational assessments altogether from then on.

"Kam? Where are we?" Darrin asked a little too loudly.

"We're in Yemen, Darrin. Be quiet."

"Kam? I forgot. Why are we in Yemen?"

The Arabs hadn't seen us come off the aircraft. No one was looking for us. Under the circumstances, that would have to be considered our good luck. But that bit of luck seemed to have been nullified by the fact that Darrin's mind was somewhere between Disneyland and never-never land. You can't have everything.

"We're in Yemen to rescue a hostage."

"Oh? Good," said Darrin.

The Bakil trucks that had not been destroyed by Little Bird ordnance rumbled to life, and soon the sound of the last remaining vehicle faded as it struggled along the rough highway. The resulting quiet was disconcerting.

"Kam?" said Darrin.

"Yes?" I was able to speak louder now and may have sounded patronizing. Not that it mattered to Darrin at the moment.

"Why are *we* rescuing a prisoner in Yemen? Do we know how to do that?"

"Really, Darrin, what would you rather be doing?"

Darrin didn't answer, but he rolled over; the fact that he could was a load off my mind.

"Look, Darrin, I kind of figured I'd do this by myself."

As bad as it seemed to have Darrin with me, it was actually very reassuring. Not only did a little company take the sting out of my situation, but Darrin was a lot tougher than he'd probably ever gotten credit for. He didn't fall—he jumped to be with me. I knew it.

"Can you stand up?" I asked. We both made our way haltingly to our feet, unsteady at first while working out some of the stiffness. "You hurt?"

"How are we defining *hurt*?" he asked, giving me a little more reassurance that his senses were returning.

"Are you dead?"

"No."

"Do I have to carry you?"

"I don't think so," said Darrin, twisting his hips and grimacing.

"Then I guess, for our purposes, you're not hurt."

"Perhaps not. How about you?" asked Darrin. "Are you okay?"

"Me? I'm definitely not okay."

We both gave my little remark a polite chuckle and worked out a few more injuries. During the last few days, I'd started stacking injury on injury.

"Seriously?" I asked. "Tell me where you're hurting."

"My legs have felt better, and I think I jarred my wrist. I'm sure I hit my head."

"Ya think?" I said. "I'm a little concerned that I'm two inches shorter than I was a few minutes ago, but I can walk. It might be good for me to move around."

"It's going to get cold," said Darrin.

He was right. The Middle East isn't usually considered the coldest place on the planet, but nights in the high desert could be brutal.

"We'll be okay if we're walking," I said. A little false hope between buddies in a hopeless situation.

At that we started to pick our way through the rocks to the road. When we got there, we had to make our first decision as partners.

"Which way?" I asked. "You'll never pass for a native." Even if he'd had a thobe like mine, Darrin wasn't going to fool anyone into thinking he was Yemeni.

"Where's the hostage?" he asked.

"You're not going for the hostage. Do you want to head back toward Sana'a—more people, maybe more risk, but a better chance of getting some help? Or we can head further east and hope to find an out-of-the-way place to get on a phone and sit tight until help comes for you."

"For me? What about you?"

I didn't answer.

"I'm not going to let you . . ." he started saying.

"We'll talk about it later," I told him.

"I'm staying with you," said Darrin.

This would have been a good time for a lot of protesting on my part, but I didn't have it in me. Darrin wasn't the type to make a decision lightly, and there was little possibility I'd change his mind. The truth was that neither of us stood a chance at finding Jim Monroe, if he was even alive, and neither of us had any business trying. "So how did you fall?" I asked, knowing that he'd jumped.

Darrin didn't answer, which was answer enough. In the investigation business, we called that an omission. If you were a clever report writer and had a good prosecutor, you could get good mileage out of a suspect omission even without a formal admission or detailed confession. Even if you weren't talking to a police investigator, failing to answer a simple, direct question was pretty condemning. I should know; I'd failed to answer the direct and simple questions about my life for over a year now. Just because I'd acted as my own prosecutor, judge, and jury didn't mitigate the truth.

"We have absolutely no chance of success and a very good likelihood of utter disaster," I told Darrin as we stared at the road leading away in two directions.

"Fine," said Darrin.

"That's just my warm and fuzzy way of saying that we'll probably die."

"Fine," he said again.

"And that's a final kind of death—not an end-of-season cliff-hanger. No waking up from a nightmare and being alive again. It's really dead," I told him.

"Okay."

"I mean dead. D-E-D, dead. Dead, dead, dead." I looked at Darrin for a long time, wondering what kind of man was hidden behind the nerdy exterior.

"Maybe it would be an improvement," he said. "Everyone dies, but not everyone lives."

"You didn't just make that up."

"Nope. I can't remember who said it, though."

"Well, he's probably right," I said.

"Or she."

"Oh, brother. Women don't get quoted, they get misquoted. Haven't you ever had a girlfriend?"

"You'd never survive in academia," said Darrin. "Not with those kinds of statements running through your brain."

Academia? I didn't survive in my own marriage.

"We need a car," I said, looking back and forth along the forlorn highway. Neither direction beckoned. There was only rock and coarse sand in both directions. It was fully dark, and the stars, brilliant in the absence of city lights, still didn't do enough to illuminate the rough terrain.

"If we head back toward Sana'a, we'll find a phone by tomorrow, but we'll run into a lot of people sympathetic to the Bakil. I think we're actually closer to Ma'rib. We'll find phones there, too, and we'll run into fewer people."

"People sympathetic to the Bakil?" asked Darrin.

"No, they'll probably *be* Bakil. It's sixes."

"You're very persuasive," said Darrin, kicking a rock over the hardpan. He walked out into the roadway and examined each direction as if the road itself would tell him something. "Let's start walking one way, and if it doesn't feel right, we'll turn around. How about toward Ma'rib?"

"Fine, but I have to warn you that any feelings I ever had are on the ground under that helicopter. They got jarred out of me and scattered over the ground out there," I said.

"You feel plenty, Kam," said Darrin. "Believe me. Or you'd be hanging off a helicopter rushing toward safety making goo-goo eyes at Rhiana."

"What? It was that obvious?"

"All day. Like teenagers at the mall. It was sick," said Darrin.

"If it's any consolation, I *am* married to her," I said.

Darrin looked around while he considered what I'd said. "I kind of figured you knew her. Why the charade? Top-secret stuff?"

"No. It wasn't really a charade. I hadn't seen her for almost a year. I . . ." What *had* I done? I didn't really know how to put it. "We separated, and then I took a job in Timor-Leste . . . without telling her."

"Dili?" Darrin asked. "Or Philly?" He laughed.

"I was suffering from a combination of shock and stupidity when I told you guys that."

"That may be, but I believed you," Darrin said.

"Really?" I asked.

"No. Do I look like an idiot?"

We started limping back along the road to where we'd abandoned the cars, hoping to find at least enough pieces left to make one working specimen. We carried our aching bodies nearly a half a mile, maybe more.

"I think we passed them," said Darrin. "They weren't this far away."

I squinted into the haze of starlight glowing off the rocks and uneven gullies. It all looked so different now. "Maybe. I didn't see anything."

"They can't be this far."

"Let's go a little farther." I looked into the Yemeni sky. Even the stars looked different. After some searching, I found Orion in the south and estimated due east. "We're going the right way. The cars must be close by."

"You don't suppose the Arabs took them?" asked Darrin.

"I guess they could have. Either that or we just missed them." I really could have gone for a four-letter word, but Darrin wasn't the type. Without any more discussion, we both continued walking. "You ever swear?" I asked.

"Try not to."

"But you do?" I said.

"That depends on what you consider swearing," said Darrin.

"I suppose being a Mormon at BYU . . ."

"You'd be surprised. In fact, I frequently am."

"I always imagined Utah as a place where . . ." I didn't know quite how to make my point delicately. "I guess like an Amish farm, without the hats."

"Ever been there?" Darrin asked.

"Sure. I skied there a couple of times. We did the Police and Fire Games there one year."

"And you still think of Utah like that?"

"I guess I just thought they were hiding all the Mormons while all the rowdy civil servants were there," I said.

We slowed for a sharp turn in the road with a slight rise on one side that blocked our view. We didn't want to walk into a hornet's nest. Neither one of us was paying a lot of attention, though.

"They don't hide the Mormons. It's getting harder and harder to spot one these days. The kids on campus . . . holy moly. I sometimes wonder," said Darrin.

"Holy moly?" I laughed. "You must like being a Mormon."

"That's a new way of thinking about it. I guess so. It gives me a sense of purpose."

"Why? Because God loves you?" I knew I sounded critical. I wasn't trying to; the religious talk brought it out in me.

"I find a sense of purpose knowing that I came here for a reason—to prove myself or improve myself. I've never been a fan of a god whose only concern was that his minions return to him. I like to think that He's preparing me for something, just like a father does with a child. I have a purpose."

"How would it be?" I said.

"Huh?"

"Nothing," I said. As we rounded the bend, we got a sweeping view of the landscape, illuminated by starlight, and there were no cars in sight. "We've gone far enough. What now?"

"I don't know. What did you have in mind when you jumped from the helicopter?" he asked.

"What makes you think I jumped?" I avoided a direct answer as long as I could, then said, "I was living a short fantasy called 'Helping Rhiana.' It ends bad."

"Badly."

"Well, it doesn't end goodly, professor."

Darrin said, "Does Ma'rib still feel right?"

"Ma'rib hurts." We both laughed, more from necessity than anything else. "It would be nice if we had a car."

"There must be a reason we don't," said Darrin.

Religious people always said that. I didn't have a response.

"Let's keep moving forward," said Darrin. He led off along the road heading east. "You don't always get what you want, you know."

I might have argued, but without a solid car option, I wasn't going to win.

We'd walked and talked for about two hours before the cold started to suck the energy out of us. We tried to jog, just to keep our heat up, but the physical demands were too much, especially for me. I resorted to storytelling.

"I knew this guy once—or I knew of him. During the selection process for the British Special Air Service—they're the world's preeminent anti-terrorist unit . . ."

"I've heard of them," said Darrin.

"Oh, right. You and the Marines. Anyway, this guy jogged twenty-some-odd miles over the Brecon Beacons in Wales. Rough, steep, jagged terrain. In order to complete the selection process, he had to meet a truck at a certain coordinate without getting caught by the SAS instructors who were chasing him." I struggled over a small furrow of sand, realizing how difficult it was getting to pick my feet up.

"Does this story have a happy ending?" asked Darrin.

"When he saw the truck parked in a low valley waiting for him, he knew he was home free. So he swaggers toward the truck and lets go of the adrenaline that had gotten him through the day."

"So he made it?"

"But it's not over. When you're on the verge of being accepted into that kind of select company, they don't want to know if you can make it or not. They want to know if you can really make it. They want to know if you can ramp it up again and keep going, even after you think the drama is all over."

"He didn't make it, then?" asked Darrin.

"Just before this guy reaches the truck, the driver leans out the window and tells him that if he wants to be in the SAS, he's going to have to hike ten more miles through the rugged terrain and that the instructors who are searching for him are getting closer. Then the truck disappears into the Brecon Beacons again."

Darrin was silent as we exerted ourselves to make it up a small rise and back down again. I stumbled and staggered until I could no longer summon the strength to lift my feet over the rocks on the road that grabbed at the tread of my boots. Falling sideways, I veered off the road and fell in a defeated slump in the dry, prickly ground shrubs. Darrin wavered over me until he could no longer hold himself upright and collapsed ungraciously in the brambles by my side.

"So?" said Darrin. "Did he?"

"Did he what?"

"That guy. Did he make it?"

"As it turns out, that experience was nothing compared to what he'd experience as a member of the SAS years later. He's now the most decorated member of the service. Yes," I said, looking into the weary gleam in Darrin's eyes, "he sucked it up and started marching. He made it."

"Then I suppose there's hope for us," he said.

"I suppose."

Darrin pulled his arms up into his sleeves and shivered.

I gazed up at the stars painted across a crystal sky that promised no hope of a warm night. "I suppose."

CHAPTER 27

The hands of Darrin's wristwatch told the tale of his fall from the helicopter, smashed as they were at 9:16 PM. If I ever had the chance to write my memoirs, at least I could state with some authority that my life had changed forever at precisely 2116 hours. What day it was was anyone's guess. My watch, which told the date and day of the week in Indiglo brilliance, was probably working just swell—on the arm of a Yemeni vendor eating hummus on flatbread somewhere in a safe, warm home in Sana'a.

Darrin stared at the remains of his watch. There was no telling how much of the night had passed since we started walking east toward Ma'rib.

I said, "What do you figure?"

"After midnight. I used to be able to tell."

"By the stars?" I asked.

"No, my watch," said Darrin.

There was no telling how long we sat by the roadside with stupid grins on our faces. We finally saw evidence of life when a faint pinprick of light crossed a hillside miles ahead of us in the direction of Ma'rib.

"Must be on the road," I said. "It wouldn't be such a bad idea to make ourselves scarce." Another light flashed along the road, then another. At least three vehicles approached in a caravan, the noise of each carrying across the barren landscape.

Darrin stood and walked a few steps up the road. "Up here."

I watched as the lights traversed the winding road ahead. They were at least a couple of miles from us when I joined Darrin, who'd found a small depression well away from the road on the high side where we wouldn't be seen, but we would still be able to hear the engines pulsing as the trucks passed us.

A few moments later, we heard the rumble of the vehicles as they neared us. Every time the sound seemed almost on top of us, one of us would peek over the rocky landscape and decide the headlights were yet a long ways off, rounding another bend in the road.

"They're trucks," Darrin said. "How far are we from Ma'rib?"

"Not too far. I think Ma'rib is at the top of a high ridge."

"What do you suppose they're doing?" Darrin asked about the trucks.

"It's kind of late for a joyride. They're probably looking for us. Can you tell what kind of trucks?"

"Does it matter?" Darrin made another foray over the lip of the depression and came back shaking his head. "They sound like diesel."

"Then they're probably large and hold a lot of people."

As the rumble of the trucks got closer, Darrin and I squeezed closer to the ground. Darrin's breathing quickened, and I noticed some deepening respirations in myself. I guess neither of us liked our chances if we got caught. I risked one more look as the trucks moved past us. There were two pickup trucks of unknown make and a one-ton with a canvas canopy. There was no telling how many men rode in them.

"Do you think they know we're here?" Darrin asked after the trucks passed and the sound of their engines softened to a dull buzz.

"Good question. The firefight probably stirred up the local militias. Maybe they'll just think it was a minor warlord skirmish and leave the whole thing alone. Or maybe the Bakil are looking for the two idiots who fell off the helicopter."

"'Idiots' pretty much says it," said Darrin.

"Good point." I pushed myself to my hands and knees, fighting against the stiffness that had settled in my joints while my body was still.

"Do you still wish we were in a car?" asked Darrin. "We'd have a tough time hiding a car from whoever was in those trucks."

Whatever inference he wanted me to draw, I wasn't sure. Maybe I was, but I didn't want to go there.

He said, "Sometimes God gives you what you need, not what you want."

"Right now, we need to keep walking," I said.

The downtime had allowed my joints to inflame, and I could barely lift myself to my feet. The cuts on my leg, compliments of Faasid, had worked their way open, and jagged flaps of skin rubbed against my filthy thobe. I didn't have any more handy superglue. Darrin was struggling too, stumbling onto his hands but unable to get upright. It was far too cold to wait out the night; movement was our only option to stay warm.

Though the enfeebled form of his previous self, Darrin eventually made it to his feet and started to take tentative steps toward the road. The uneven ground gave him trouble. I wasn't much more stable as I navigated the ragged stones down to the road, and we quickly ended up arm in arm. I wasn't sure who was helping whom.

"I still want a car," I said.

We made slow but appreciable progress the rest of the night and into the early morning hours. The cold intensified before twilight approached.

Darrin stumbled repeatedly, and I worried that hypothermia was affecting him. Or maybe it was me.

"Do you need to stop?" I asked.

"Nope."

"Pretty stout dude for a college professor," I said.

"I'm not a professor yet. I am a scoutmaster, though."

"Boy Scouts?" I said. "You don't seem the type." I regretted the statement as the last syllable rolled off my tongue.

"I know. That's kind of what the Marines said. But they were kinder. They said I looked more like a Boy Scout than a Marine." Darrin tripped, nearly falling but for my grip on his shoulder. "I teach scouting skills with one eye on the kids and one eye on the Boy Scout manual."

"I was never much into that kind of thing. Why do you do it?" Although I was only mildly interested, I thought maybe Darrin would do better if I kept him talking. It wasn't a bad thing for me either. "Were you big into Boy Scouts as a kid?"

"No," he said. "I would have been, but my parents were more into violin lessons and science club. But even for all that, I made Eagle when I was fourteen. It was in one ear and out the other. I did it because it was expected. I don't regret it."

"So why the scoutmaster gig? Giving back?"

"It was a calling. In our church, people are called to perform certain duties. You do them until you are released."

"Sounds like a prison sentence," I said.

"It is what it is. You do what you do. By the time I'm any good at scoutmaster, they'll find something else for me to do."

"Sounds inefficient," I said.

"What's the point of sitting around doing what you're good at?" asked Darrin.

"Um, I don't know, because you're good at it?"

"Yeah, but you don't progress," said Darrin. "Maybe you should be my assistant scoutmaster. Our trek through Yemen will be a very inspirational story someday."

"Very tempting," I said. "If we live to see sunset tomorrow, I'll get back to you."

I helped Darrin along, sometimes vice versa, and I heard his breath coming in shorter and shorter gasps. I wasn't sure exactly what that meant, but I didn't think it was a good thing. "Stop for a breather?" I asked him.

"No." Darrin just kept putting one foot in front of the other.

We moved ever onward, each helping the other, until the predawn cold had sapped both our energy and resolve. I thought Darrin would collapse, but he kept on walking, small step after small step. I was afraid if Darrin did have to stop, we'd both succumb to the cold and be ravished by scorpions before anyone ever found our bodies. I shuddered. I was tired, too. In fact, I secretly hoped Darrin would beg to stop. I didn't want to be the one who caused our imminent demise, but I was game to let Darrin cause it. But he just kept walking. And then he started to mumble. I thought at first he was delirious, but I spoke to him occasionally, and he seemed all there. I listened to his mumbling and decided, after a while, that he was singing.

"What's the song?" I asked.

"A hymn," he said.

"Appropriate."

"'The song of the righteous,'" Darrin quoted, "'is a prayer unto me.'"

"Do you have one for the unwashed heathen?"

"Funny. Some of this sentimental religious stuff seemed a little trite a month ago when all I had to worry about was grades and girls."

"Girls?" I asked.

"Okay, just grades."

"I'm a little closer to God right now myself," I said. "Imminent death does that for me."

"That's ironic. Maybe your song is more authentic than mine right now."

"Maybe someday you'll write about this conversation in one of your professional journals. Maybe the way a person lives their religion has less to do with geography and demographics than you suspect," I said.

"'It shall be answered with a blessing upon their heads,'" said Darrin, continuing to quote.

"That'd be handy," I said.

Darrin stopped to shake some of the stiffness from his legs. "We need water."

"That'd be handy too."

The grade of the winding road had increased and required more physical strength to climb. Darrin was really breathing hard and was exerting himself far beyond what I thought his capacity would allow. I was in no better shape, wheezing and coughing as we ascended the hill. Even the slight change in altitude affected the temperature, giving us even more reason to keep moving and press on.

"So, what's the song?"

"Uh, 'Lead, Kindly . . .' something. I can't remember," he said.

"Try."

Darrin licked his chaffed lips. "'Lead, Kindly . . .'" He paused, thinking. ". . . 'Light,'" he finally blurted. His memory apparently needed a few moments to kick in. "'Amid th'encircling gloom,'" he sang through a parched throat. "'Lead thou me on.'"

We used precious moisture by talking, but it seemed the lesser of two evils. We would either dehydrate and die or drift off into frozen oblivion and die. I guess if we had to go, Darrin would go out singing. "'Help of the helpless . . .'" he croaked. Then he said, "No, I think that's a different song."

"But apt."

"'Keep thou my feet; I do not ask to see.'"

"It wouldn't hurt my feelings to see," I said.

"'The distant scene—one step enough for me.'"

I answered, as if in refrain, "I don't know any hymns."

Darrin hummed for a few minutes, then he sang like a strangled sailor, "'Pride ruled my will. Remember not past years.'" He hummed for a minute and then sang again. "'O'er moor and fen, o'er crag and torrent, till the night is gone.'" His voice grew stronger. "'And with the morn those angel faces smile, which I have loved long since, and lost awhile.'"

Darrin's hoarse verses died in the gathering blackness of the hour just before dawn.

I said, "Did you think you were going to die with me in Yemen when you jumped from the helicopter?"

"I guess I've always had this romantic notion that I would be willing to leave the ninety and nine, all safe and sound, and go after the one," said Darrin, looking into the darkness.

"Well, you're living that fantasy now, aren't you?" I looked at the starlight gleaming off Darrin's scared little eyes. I'd just learned a new definition for courage from a pinheaded Mormon college boy.

"I must be here for a reason. I won't die until that reason comes to fruitation," he said.

"Fruitation? Don't you mean *fruition,* professor?" Darrin's mind was slowly going, but we both laughed anyway. I had to applaud his optimism. Besides, *fruitation* seemed like an altogether more descriptive word. "Why don't you sing us up a car? We could really use one."

"'You can't always get what you want . . .'" Darrin croaked and gasped the old Stones lyric.

"'But you can try sometimes,'" I added, definitely not singing.

Darrin picked up the rest of the chorus, "'And you just might find, you get what you need.'" He said, "I love it when you can go to the Stones for doctrine."

"I thought this whole 'want' and 'need' thing was religion, not sixties rock-and-roll wisdom."

Darrin shrugged. "At this point, I'll take wisdom wherever I can get it."

"We really need a car, Darrin," I said. His lips were worse than I'd ever seen anyone's, and he quit walking and was dragging his feet where the terrain would allow it. There wasn't much left in the man. There wasn't much left in me, either.

The predawn chill turned into a morning cool, the direct sunlight driving some of the stiffness out of my body but exacerbating the dryness of my tongue and throat. Daylight brought with it the hope of warmth and the dread of discovery. What we hadn't been able to see last night was the size of the hill we were climbing. The road wound around the face of a steeply terraced cliff somewhere in the area of a thousand feet high, maybe twice that. Several more miles to the east sat modern-day Ma'rib behind the decayed remains of the ancient city and stories-high sandstone buildings jutting up from the desolate landscape. I'd visited once, and the memory was vague.

Looking back into the valley from where we'd come, I saw the place we'd hidden from the trucks. We'd only managed to travel a couple of miles; Ma'Rib would have to wait until nightfall, assuming we made it that long in the heat of day. There were already wide cracks in Darrin's lips, and what little perspiration he was producing ran into them.

"You, my friend, could use some lip balm."

"Nope," he said. "I have some." He stuck his dry, swollen tongue out and ran it roughly over his lips, breaking open a crack that bled down his chin. "Nature's Chapstick."

I couldn't tell if Darrin just had a weird sense of humor or if one or the other of us was losing his frail grip on reality. We needed help.

"Do you see that?" asked Darrin, holding tightly to my shoulder and squinting off into the barren yonder.

I looked around. "No."

"Right there."

I followed his finger to the smooth, unnatural outline of something just off the roadway. It looked like . . . a car.

CHAPTER 28

"Is it?" I asked, stumbling over the rocky ground behind Darrin. I strained to see the object. For a minute I thought we were sharing a hallucination, but after some effort it began to take shape.

"It is . . ." Darrin was mesmerized, leaning toward the apparition as he tripped forward. As we got closer, we could both see it was an abandoned hulk.

"A car?" I said, "It used to be a car. It looks like the kind of thing I used to find half-buried on Grandma's farm."

"Hey, you got the car you wished for," said Darrin. "You've been whining about it all night."

"Funny. I was thinking of something a little more operable."

"You only said you wanted a car," said Darrin.

"I get it. This is like one of those leprechaun wishes where you get exactly what you asked for, and the little green guy sits back and cackles his head off."

"No. That would be funny, though. I suppose, in this case, God does have a sense of humor . . . or irony. But you get what you need, right?" Darrin said, stepping around the car and staring as if he wanted to buy it.

"Or *He's* messing with us," I said, leaning against the crushed iron remnants.

Darrin, even in his diminished capacity, dove in and started rummaging.

"Anything we can use?" I asked. "Steak sandwich in the glove box? Bottle of Gatorade?"

"Help me with this." Darrin, leaning into the backseat, tugged on a corner of the headliner.

I went to other side, reached into the broken-out window, and helped separate the liner from the roof frame. "Blanket?"

"Could be. Let's use the carpet for that. I have plans for this liner."

We stretched the vinyl headliner until it tore away from the roof of the car. Darrin threw it aside and went to work on the carpet. Without a sharp implement, though, he wasn't getting very far.

I untied the P38 can opener from my bootlaces and tore the black tape from around it. Darrin watched as I ripped and cut the rest of the floor covering out of the old car. He was wrapping pieces of it around his shoulders when I finished. "What else?" I asked.

"Hubcap."

I pulled one of the rusty caps off the driver's side wheel and threw it on the headliner. "Anything else, MacGyver?"

He nodded. "Can we get this bumper thing off?"

The car was old and foreign. The bumpers, once chrome, were now rusted and loose. I jumped on one and got it to move, but I couldn't get the piece to fall off. It didn't take long to break it free after Darrin added his five-foot-nine, buck-twenty-soaking-wet frame to the battle. The bumper crashed to the ground with a squeal and snap, and once it was off, Darrin dragged it over to his pile of plunder.

"Rocks, about the size of a loaf of bread."

"You need some?" I asked.

"About eight of them. Then, one perfect-sized . . ." Darrin groped in the yellow dirt for his perfect-sized something while I gathered bread-loaf-sized rocks to satisfy his apparent dementia.

I threw my rocks on our pile of treasures ripped from the car and found myself sitting in a fatigued lump next to it before Darrin had located his necessary something, which turned out to be a rock.

"Now we dig a hole," Darrin announced.

"For what?" The extracurricular activity wasn't doing anything for me.

"You want to drink, don't you? Let's dig the hole away from the road, where it won't be seen, and where we won't be seen tending it."

"You want me to tend a hole in the ground?" I kicked over one of the large rocks I'd collected, and it rolled into Darrin's foot.

"Hand me the bumper," he said. Darrin was going to die if he exerted himself.

"Where do you want me to dig?" I asked. I picked up the bumper, examined both ends, and then rammed the most shovel-like end into the ground. It hit the rocky soil and penetrated about as far as if I'd beaten my head against the ground—the comparison wasn't lost on me.

"I think we can get water out of the ground with this stuff," said Darrin. "We need a hole, maybe two or three feet deep and a few feet in diameter."

Balancing on the fine line between trusting and patronizing, I gave the ground a scrape and drove the bumper in again, this time churning up an infinitesimal amount of rock and dirt, which I whipped away at the end of my makeshift shovel.

"Another three million of those and we'll have a gopher hole."

"Let me . . ." Darrin tried to take the bumper.

"I got it." The slight irritation led to better determination—either that or anger fueled the digging fire. Once I got beneath the surface rocks, the digging went a little faster and Darrin's hole was prepared as requested, but at a considerable cost in effort and body fluid.

Darrin dropped the hubcap in the hole and threw out the old vinyl headliner like he was throwing a tablecloth over the hole. He placed rocks the size of bread loaves on the edges of the headliner until it was suspended over the hole, held in place by the weight of the rocks. Making sure the headliner was droopy, he tossed his special-sized rock, about the size of a baseball, on the middle of the headliner.

"There you go. Water."

"Good. After you turn that hubcap into water, will you turn my hair into an ever-renewable source of gold thread?"

"It's a solar still. According to the former scoutmaster, it'll suck a quart of water from the ground overnight. We might even get a little water in there by afternoon. Looks like a car was the perfect wish."

"I was looking for a car to get us out of this mess."

Darrin mocked me in a whiny voice. "I was looking for a car. I didn't get the one I wanted." He shook his head and slid behind the black plastic steering wheel on the foam rubber and steel springs of the front seat. The sun was well into the sky, and Darrin threw an odd-shaped section of upholstery over his face for shade.

"Sorry, man," I said.

Darrin smiled. "Don't be. We have a hot day ahead of us."

And Darrin's words didn't even begin to describe the day we had. Never could I have imagined that sitting and doing nothing could be so physically and mentally devastating. The shade of the car was made unbearable because the heat of the metal around us turned the interior into a slow oven. Direct sunlight was even worse, so when we ventured out to crawl under the shade of a low-growing shrub, we covered up in the disintegrating carpet. Although neither of us had a working watch, Darrin marked the movement of the shadow cast by the car simply to give us some hope that tomorrow was still coming—Shakespeare could learn a thing or two about its petty pace. Darrin said something about it and then had to explain the whole Shakespeare reference to me.

"You're smarter than you look, Darrin. Actually, you look pretty smart."

"There aren't many choices for guys like me," said Darrin. "You're either smart, or you don't have anything going for you. I learned that pretty early in life."

I wasn't sure what to say. "That's not . . . I wasn't . . ."

"Oh, please. I'm only on this trip because Brother Holmes took pity on me. I don't get out much."

"Oh, I can't imagine anyone taking pity on you," I said. "Clyde . . . I don't have to call him Brother, do I?"

"No."

"Clyde told me that you were a whiz kid. They can barely keep you under intellectual control." He hadn't, but we were going to die soon anyway, and I figured that a little white lie as salve for a guy's feelings was acceptable. Besides, Darrin probably was that smart.

"Grades aren't the issue. I'm not . . . social," said Darrin.

"No girlfriend?" I asked.

"It's not that. I mean, I don't have one, but that's not the problem. I've never been much of a people person."

This level of male interaction was a little foreign to me, so I didn't know what to say. "You just need to let people get to know you."

"Maybe through my research?" Darrin didn't sound very confident.

"Or . . . not." I said, then regretted it. "A lot of people will get to know you through your research, Darrin. But you're a lot more than that. It wasn't Darrin 'the religionist' who jumped off that helicopter just to keep me company. There's someone of real substance inside there." I pointed to Darrin's chest.

He looked down and didn't answer.

We both spent the next several hours in quiet retrospection. By the time the sun was overhead, I could tell that Darrin was in big trouble physically. I tried to get him to run his leathery tongue over the salt from his own body, but whatever perspiration he was still producing was immediately taken by the cruel forces of evaporation. I said as much, and Darrin told me that our doom and our salvation depended on those cruel forces of evaporation. "Those cruel forces," he said, "are pulling moisture from the ground under our solar still and making dew drops form on the headliner. The force of gravity is taking those drops down into our hubcap. We live and die by those forces."

"Okay. I'll quit arguing, Professor MacGyver," I said.

"Can I ask you a question?" said Darrin. "What's between you and Rhiana? You said you guys aren't together anymore?"

What *was* between us? There was so much behind that question. I didn't say anything for a long time. I didn't know what to say. I'd given her every reason to hate me—but the last thing I'd heard her say was that she loved me.

"You don't have to tell me," said Darrin. For a few moments, neither of us said anything.

"I killed a family," I blurted out. I'd never said it that way before, but that was the phrase that haunted my waking dreams. I'd killed a family.

Darrin waited for the other shoe to drop.

"I was a cop," I told him. "One night I saw a drunk stumbling through the parking lot of a bar. He had his keys in his hand, so I drove into the lot and had a talk with him. I wanted to prevent a crime; you have to understand that. I wanted to do the right thing."

"Yeah," Darrin said, as if that was obvious.

He didn't really understand, but I went on anyway. "He told me he wasn't really going to drive, but what else are you going to say to a cop? I knew he was going to drive."

"Probably," said Darrin.

"A couple of his friends came out after him, and one was the designated driver, who assured me he'd get his drunken friend home safely. A crime prevented. A job well done."

Darrin probably noted the venom in my voice. "It sounds like you did your job."

"Five hours later, I responded to an MVA on a cloverleaf of Interstate 5."

"MVA?" said Darrin.

"Motor vehicle accident. Both parents and two of the three children were killed. The drunk wasn't even hurt. I should have let him get in his car and start driving. Then I could have popped him for driving under the influence."

"Did he get arrested?" asked Darrin.

"Yeah. He got four years for manslaughter; he'll be out in two and a half."

"At least he got put in jail."

"The little boy, the one who survived—his sentence is for life," I said.

Darrin didn't say anything.

"I was no good at work after that," I told Darrin. "Rhiana and I were never able to talk about it. I left her. I quit my job and moved to the other side of the world. When we met in Paris, I didn't know she was going to be there. I was . . ."

"You looked a little off balance," said Darrin. "But back to that other thing. It doesn't sound like it was your fault."

"That's what everybody says. I think I kind of gave up after it happened. On my job, on my marriage. That's when I decided to run away."

"I remember when I was in Primary. My teacher gave us a lesson on putting on the whole armor of God."

"What's Primary—like church?" I asked.

"Close enough. Anyway, she went through all the things that protect us from evil: the breastplate, the helmet, the shield, the sword, and all that. Metaphorical, of course."

"Of course."

"Then she said something that really stuck with me. She told us that there wasn't much on that list to protect us from the back."

Darrin didn't elaborate, maybe hoping that I had a clue what he was talking about. I didn't.

After a few silent moments, he explained it to me. "So, you have to keep moving forward. If you turn your back, you have no protection."

That I did understand. Only too well. "Interesting," I said. Even if I'd been inclined to talk about it with Darrin, I wouldn't have known what to say. Besides, it was too late. I'd turned my back a long time ago.

Darrin probably sensed that I was uncomfortable, and the conversation ended there.

Several cars made the trek down the grade near where we were hidden. Only one gave me the feeling that something official was going on. It was an older-model Range Rover with searchlights mounted on the front doorframe. Whether its occupants were looking for us or not was impossible to tell, but I was sure we were doing the right thing by lying low, even though when I looked at Darrin's parched skin and pinched face, I considered surrendering.

By late afternoon, Darrin said his science project was probably done, even though it worked much better at night. "Tap the headliner to get the water to run down into the hubcap," he told me. I did so and was surprised to see how much water was clinging to the rubberized material. I licked the moisture from the headliner, everything that wouldn't drain into the hubcap. My parched gums absorbed it, leaving me very little to swallow. The small hubcap was nearly half full of dirty, brackish water, pulled right from the soil, just as Darrin had promised.

"The fruits of your labor," I said, presenting him with the hubcap.

"You first," said Darrin, always the hero.

"I already drank my share."

Darrin peered into the half-full hubcap and then at me.

I leaned closer to Darrin and held the hubcap to his lips. He drank slowly, savoring small sips. I dipped my finger in the water—uncouth, I know—and massaged his lips with dabs of moisture. It didn't really help to soften the cracks, but it made me feel better about looking at his face. It looked like road rash and was starting to peel. The mirrors in the car were long gone, and I was glad not to have to see myself.

The water was gone too soon.

"Do we drag this stuff with us?" I asked about the materials we'd used to make the solar still.

Darrin's eyes were glazed over, and he didn't answer. It was still hot, even as the sun descended, so I draped the thin carpet over him to shade his head and pulled him to his feet. He was unsteady and minimally coherent. Sundown looked to be only a short time away, and I wanted to be sorted out before dark. The afternoon traffic going in the direction of Ma'rib had all but gone, and we could probably make some distance up the cliff in the twilight.

"Darrin?" I said. "I'm glad we weren't driving a car. The Bakil would have had us before we even got started. I'd probably be separated from my head by now."

I looked into his eyes and saw just the glimmer of coherence. "'Lead, kindly light,'" he murmured.

* * *

A grueling night spent on the hilly desert, traveling in less than fifty-yard intervals between rest stops, left both Darrin and me physically incapacitated and morally dejected. In the predawn haze I saw the steep grade give way to a gradual slope just ahead of us, so I left Darrin in a cleft in the hillside and ventured up for a look on my own. I settled on a rock just near the top to rest and catch my breath. Over the drone of my labored breathing, I heard what sounded like bells. Tinkling metal? An angel getting its wings?

Clinging to the ground so I didn't silhouette myself against the sky behind me, I groped upward and pushed my head up between two large boulders that would help disguise the shape of my noggin if someone happened to be looking in my direction. I heard the ringing louder now, and I was sure I'd see signs of life at the top of the grade.

The night hadn't been overly kind to Darrin, and he wasn't going to last very long without some serious help. He'd been nonresponsive for a good part of the night and was in worse condition than yesterday. Any plan we had to find a phone and some help was over.

A new plan was necessary—cross our fingers and find the nearest help available. The new plan was in full swing when the yelling started.

CHAPTER 29

"*Ab, Ab.*" The young boy yelled as he ran out of sight on the cliff's edge several hundred feet to my right and disappeared over the short horizon. "Father, Father."

I scrambled for the top of the ridge and ran into a confused herd of goats outfitted with bells. The goats scattered in a harmony of Christmas sounds, drawing attention in my direction. Startled by my appearance on the ridge, the boy stopped to see what kind of lunatic was stalking his goats. Another man spun around to see what the commotion was about.

A large, multicolored Bedouin tent made of colorful wool had been erected not far from the edge of the cliff. Another head popped out to look at me from behind the brightly striped material. The head was attached to the body of an ancient man who stepped from the tent holding a Russian-made assault rifle. I was pretty sure the gig was up as subsonic rifle rounds from the AK-47 flew in my direction. The goats were further perturbed, and I just stood there, grimacing with my eyes squeezed shut. A bullet was preferable to death by dehydration and exhaustion.

I adjusted my filthy Arab attire and opened my eyes. I wasn't dead. Confronting Arabs in the desert often meant enduring the endearing ritual of having rounds fired over your head. It was tradition in these parts. I opened both hands so they could see I wasn't armed and then bent over for a handful of sand. I thrust the sand in the air and let it drift off in the slight wind—a signal of peace I'd learned in my youth but had never had to bet my life on. Throwing sand was a social sign that had developed between neighboring

Bedouins in the Empty Quarter. In the West, we are greeted with a disingenuous "How are you," and in the East, it's rifle fire and tossed sand. I'm not sure which one makes less sense.

"Walid ana ismee." My name is Walid. I used the first name that came to mind. "Good morning."

The two men and the boy, maybe about twelve years old, stood in shocked and apprehensive silence. The oldest man, who looked anywhere from fifty-nine to ninety-nine years old, wore a dirty white robe, his head wrapped in a generous gutrah that spilled onto his shoulders and over his back. He'd probably never shaved his glistening chrome beard. His wizened, brown eyes sparkled over the iron sights of his rifle.

A middle-aged man, maybe even as young as me, with tight black curls shorn close to his head and a clean-shaven face, stood beside the old man. In contrast, he wore jeans and a T-shirt with the BBC emblem on it. The black-haired boy wore a purple oxford shirt and a futa revealing his dusty ankles and sandals. He carried a stout stick for working with his goats. Oddly, only the boy wore the traditional jambiyah dagger that virtually every male of age in the rural areas carried all the time as a sign of maturity and manhood. I guess the old man figured the rifle was enough.

Apparently noticing my condition, the men's looks turned from surprise to compassion.

"Maa'." I recognized the word for water spoken by the eldest Arab.

Without the normal juvenile griping and delaying, the boy ran off, presumably to get me water. To say I was grateful would have been an understatement, but I was concerned that Darrin, just over the cliff, needed cool, clear *maa'* worse than I.

The boy took a swollen bladder from the back of a goat bearing a small wooden pack saddle and offered it to me. He nodded, as if giving me permission to drink. I didn't hesitate.

The liquid, although warm, tasted as good as spring water. I let the fluid run over my lips and felt bad for Darrin.

"I have a partner," I told my hosts. "Over the edge." I gestured to the cliff, and the boy ran over. He soon confirmed my statement with the excited waving of his arms.

Pretty soon, all three Arabs were watching as I pulled Darrin up the hill. As we got near the top, several brown arms reached out to help us both. The color of Darrin's skin didn't seemed to matter to these men. Yet, anyway.

Darrin took in water at a slow but healthy pace. We both knew that recovery from dehydration wasn't accomplished with a few swigs of water and a rugged forearm across the mouth. That worked for cowboys in the movies—not for real men in Yemen.

The Arab men went to work on Darrin without a word. The boy untied a small bundle of wool and sticks from the pack saddle of one of his goats and spread it out on the ground. From it he erected a lean to as expertly as if he'd invented tents. Darrin's troop of Boy Scouts would have ripped their tent-setting-up merit badges right off their sashes and given them to the boy. The men laid Darrin in the shade of the small tent and bent over him to listen. Through his split and bleeding lips, Darrin was singing one of his hymns. The eldest man, his long beard moving like a living extension of his chin, stared up at me.

"*Risaala,*" he said

The younger man put his ear closer to Darrin's mouth, nodded, and then repeated what the elder Arab had said. "*Risaala.*"

He then clasped his hands and bowed his head in prayer. Although Yemen was a country of frequent prayer, this wasn't a prostrated, repetitive Muslim litany but a heartfelt appeal to God. This was a Nasrani prayer, a Christian prayer.

After the younger man raised his head, the old man looked at me. "I am Ali Selah. You are welcome at my camp."

The younger man, about my own age, put his hand on the old man's shoulder. "This is my father-in-law. I am Safwan Al-Saghier, and this," he gestured to the obedient young boy, "is my son, al-aHad." The boy nodded and smiled at us. *Al-aHad* was the word for Sunday.

"This is Darrin, my employer," I said. "He's a scientist. I was hired as his driver."

Safwan and Ali spoke softly to each other, and then Safwan said to me in perfectly enunciated English, "My father-in-law compliments you on your Arabic, Walid."

Clever. His suspicion that I wasn't an Arab was carefully disguised within a genuine compliment. It wasn't always a good idea to be American in the Middle East, so I summoned my best Suqutri and answered, "Please, tell your father-in-law that I am from the Isle of Socotra, and I am grateful for the compliment regarding my speech."

Ali looked at Safwan and shook his head.

Safwan shot his hand out to me, and we shook. "I attended the University of Nebraska for my PhD," he said. "Before that, I lived in London."

I looked at the old man, whose smile grew behind the beard, and I knew I wasn't going to buffalo him. "I'm from Seattle."

"Please, don't be afraid," Safwan said.

"You're a Christian?" I asked. It wasn't unusual to be a Christian living in Yemen; in the years after the Soviets gave up control of the country, an infinitesimally small percentage of the locals had abandoned Islam. But it wasn't the norm in rural areas, and some of the other Arab folks didn't accept the infidel religion easily, especially in the eastern parts.

"Yes, I am," said Safwan.

"And a Cornhusker?" I said.

"I was there for six years. After that, I did a postdoctorate in Phoenix."

"What did you study?" asked Darrin, trying to sit up. Nothing like the mention of academia to bring a half-dead man back to life; it worked the other way around for me.

Ali, the grandpa, shook his head and pushed Darrin back down. He told Safwan in Arabic that if the foolish Westerner threw up, he'd lose more liquids and die. I trusted that of all the people in the world, Ali of the Empty Quarter of Yemen knew something about dehydration.

"Lie down, Darrin," I said.

"I'm a conservationist," said Safwan to me. "I studied environmental science with an emphasis in soils. If we can learn to use our water more efficiently out here, as has been done in the arid parts of your country, we'd all eat like princes."

"Like Americans," said the boy, al-aHad.

"My father-in-law is a goatherd." Safwan turned to his father-in-law. "He already lives like a prince, don't you, Father?"

Ali shrugged.

"I lived in America too," said al-aHad in unaccented English.

We talked for a while, me telling them about my Yemeni mother and my frequent visits to southern Yemen and Socotra, and Safwan telling me about his travels in the U.S. Al-aHad was sure to tell me that he knew how to play both American football and baseball. I was impressed. The subject of what I was doing wandering the desert with a Mormon boy from Utah was graciously avoided. But it was also inevitable.

"Darrin," I said, "is a graduate student in religious studies at BYU. He's an innocent bystander."

"And you're not?" asked Safwan.

I looked into the deep pools of wisdom behind Ali's eyes. "I'm a government operative from the United States. My colleagues escaped by helicopter, and we were left behind."

"The shooting?" asked Ali. "The Bakil tribesmen; they've been talking about it. You're not safe wandering in the desert."

"I take it you're not with the Bakil," I said.

Safwan and Ali exchanged glances. Ali let Safwan answer. "You are in Bakil territory."

"But you don't fear them because of your . . ." I made praying hands.

Safwan said, "No."

Ali, though proud, looked away.

"Even though you're Nasrani?"

Safwan looked at al-aHad. "We don't bother them, and they don't bother us."

I looked around the barren campsite, taking in the simplicity of life for a goat herder in the desert. The goats roamed freely on the rock and sand, obedient to the voice and long stick of the goatherd, in this case the boy al-aHab. A dark smear in the sand indicated a recent campfire, and the multicolored tent looked large enough to accommodate more than the three of them.

"You need a phone," Safwan said, obviously trying to distract me.

"Do you have one?" Maybe the "Can you hear me now?" guy from Verizon had been there.

"Ma'rib," he said.

I glanced again at the tent and thought I saw some movement at the entrance.

"I can get you to Ma'rib," Safwan said. "It's not far from here, and there are phones. The Bakil don't own Ma'rib, just the surrounding countryside."

I nodded. "Is it just the three of you?"

Safwan didn't say anything, but he glanced at both al-aHad and Ali. Another movement at the entrance to the tent caught my eye. A woman parted the tent's long entrance flap with a gentle hand. This time her face was not covered and her straight black hair framed the same set of luminescent green eyes that I'd seen in both Paris and Sana'a just before being attacked. It was the same girl, I was sure.

CHAPTER 30

"You," I said, coming to my feet and facing the girl at the tent door.

Safwan and Ali both looked toward her.

"Adara," said Ali rather loudly. He looked back and forth between the girl and me. I think what he wanted to say was something more along the lines of an order to get herself back in the tent, but what came out was, "Come. Meet our guests. Americans."

She lowered her eyes and obediently brushed past the tent flap and into the open. She wore Western denim pants and a light bronze blouse edged with lace. Her head was covered in a light azure silk scarf. She took short steps to Ali's side and took his hand.

"Adara, this man is . . ." He looked at me.

"Kamir Daniels."

"Kamir." Ali presented his daughter with a wave of his hand. "Adara."

Adara nodded her head, chancing just one glance at me.

"We've met. Sort of," I said.

Both Ali and Adara looked confused. Safwan said, "You've met my sister-in-law?"

"Paris," I nodded at Adara, but she didn't acknowledge the meeting. "And Sana'a. You were there, both times."

She turned toward her father and gently shook her head.

"You saved my life. You were there." I looked at Safwan. "She was there. At the nightclub." I stepped toward Adara, and she retreated further behind her father. "It was you. The Arab. Remember? You told me to be careful. Then just a few days ago in Sana'a. You knew my name. You saved my life." Ali looked down at his daughter, then to his son-in-law, Safwan.

"She told me to find you. And to give you a message—*Risaala*."

Safwan put up a hand to stop me and stepped closer.

"I saw her in Paris," I said.

Safwan took my arm and pulled me away. Ali comforted his daughter, who was starting to tremble.

"But Safwan . . ." He tugged at my thobe, so I shut up and went with him. Ali and Adara retreated into the tent.

"Safwan," I said, "I saw her. She saved my life. And I heard her voice. And those eyes. You don't mistake those eyes. It was her."

Safwan stopped and simply nodded, staring at me. Al-aHad was ghostlike by his father's side, not wanting to miss anything. Safwan told al-aHad gently, "Tend to your business." The boy reluctantly shuffled off toward Darrin. "More water," said Safwan over his shoulder to the boy. Al-aHad drenched a towel with water and dabbed Darrin's face. Once Safwan was sure al-aHab was distracted by his task, we stepped away to speak privately.

"Please don't be offended by my sister-in-law," he said.

"I'm not offended. I'm confused. I know what I saw. I know what she told me."

"Kamir," said Safwan, taking time to consider his words carefully. "My sister-in-law doesn't speak. And she never leaves her father's side."

"She was in Paris. I'd be dead if she hadn't warned me." I explained Adara's role in saving my skin, both in Paris and in Sana'a. "She knew I was in trouble." Even before I finished, I realized how improbable my story was. Safwan listened patiently, like a big brother indulging a kid. I thought he was going to tell me that I was delirious, but he didn't. Instead, a tear began to form in the corner of his eye.

"Almira," he said, choking on the name.

"What?"

"The young woman. What did she say?" asked Safwan. He wiped the moisture from his cheeks.

"She told me to tell you that she was okay. Who is she?" I asked.

Safwan blinked back more tears. "Anything else?"

I thought back to my encounters with the mysterious Arab woman. "I don't know. I don't remember. I don't think she ever had a chance to tell me the message." Then it hit me. The risaala—the message. Safwan and Ali had been waiting for it; they said as much when they heard Darrin singing.

Safwan looked disappointed, or perhaps resigned. He looked to see if al-aHad was still tending to Darrin, then turned his suddenly worn face to me. "Almira was Adara's sister. My wife. Almira was brutalized by Bakil tribesmen when Adara was a young woman. Adara watched and has not spoken since."

I was stunned and took a deep breath. "I'm sorry," I said.

Safwan looked again in the direction of the tent and leaned closer. "My father-in-law, Ali, was a lieutenant of the Bakil," he said. "One of the most feared men. When the Bakil found out that we had a copy of the Bible and that we . . . The attack was his punishment for embracing the infidel religion." Safwan summoned the courage to keep speaking. "Almira died several days after. Al-ahad was a child."

"You think it was Almira?" I asked. "The woman who warned me? But she's dead."

Safwan ignored me. "After what happened to my wife, al-Ahad and I traveled to the United States for my education. My father has been shepherding goats in the area ever since—waiting for the risaala. Hoping."

"I'm sorry," I said, just as lame as before. "What message?"

"My father-in-law was intrigued by Western Christianity. It was his Bible the Bakil found. After the death of his daughter, Ali was no longer able to accept the doctrines of the book, nor of Islam for that matter." Safwan thought for a moment, his eyes still moist. "Almira died before she had a chance to study the new religion and decide for herself. We have been told by the Christians that it is too late for her. This saddens my father-in-law. I think in his heart he wishes to embrace the Christian religion. Also, there is the . . ." Safwan looked closely into my eyes, probing. Whatever he saw made him go on. "The prophecy." He shook his head. "The dream. Call it what you want. For years, Ali prayed to understand the Christian doctrine, but the sects confused us. There were Anglicans here, many sects of Evangelicals too. The Russian Orthodox Church had a following after the communists left. Of course, the Catholic presence has been here for a very long time. They all traveled in the area, careful not to prose-lyte officially, but doing it informally anyway."

I nodded at Safwan. I'd been around enough to know that there was a Christian presence in Yemen, if not a very large one. It was probably very weak in this region, but in Aden and Sana'a, Christian sects survived, relatively speaking, mostly because of the Westerners in residence. "And the prophecy?" I asked.

"Ali was told not to align with any of them, but that a message would someday come—from his family in the great beyond . . . through strangers."

"But you don't think . . ."

"A white man near to death, singing hymns to God, and an Arab imposter who is not wholly Arab. The prophecy describes you and your partner."

I got the willies immediately. "Now you're freakin' me out."

"Too improbable?" Safwan said. "I said the same thing until today. Ali had the dream many years ago. He'd given up on it."

I thought about each time I saw the girl. What had she said? Tell them . . . something, but what? *Tell them he's* . . . but she never finished. "Safwan, when I saw her, there was so much happening. People were trying to kill me. She was warning me. She didn't have time to give me the message."

Safwan looked hurt, empty. He walked back to Darrin and knelt beside him. Darrin was awake but didn't say anything as al-aHad wiped his face with a wet rag.

I was way out of my depth and unsure what to say. Somehow, the doctrine of "You can't always get what you want" wasn't going to cut it here. "She was beautiful," I said to Safwan.

It wasn't what he wanted to hear, but his countenance lightened as he nodded. "The most beautiful woman in Yemen." Through quiet laughter he said, "You would have liked Almira. Just before she died, she joked that she would send a message back to us." Safwan smiled and shook his head. "That's why I wondered . . ." The smile faded from Safwan's face. "But she had never had the chance to believe. She died ignorant. Maybe there is no message. Just an old man's fantasy."

I thought about the conversation I'd had with Clyde on the plane to Yemen. Safwan didn't know the same loving God he knew. "Maybe you should talk to Darrin," I said. "He's a religion expert."

Darrin looked panicked.

"Come on, you can maroon yourself in Yemen in the middle of a Bakil firefight, but you can't tell this guy about your church? Oh brother. Al-aHad, where do you get the water?" I asked.

"Ghayls," said al-aHad, like I was too stupid to live.

Safwan said, *"Ghayls.* Subterranean channels. You must have passed several dozen access holes on your way here. They are marked with three rocks and usually have a rope and can nearby. There's plenty of water out here if you know where to look."

Safwan wasn't smug in a pejorative way, but smug is smug. I looked around and saw nothing but rocks and sand.

"Only an outsider would show up here parched like you two," said Safwan. "How do you think Ali knew you were not a local guide for hire?"

"Show me," I said to al-aHad. We rounded up his select goats, the ones equipped with wooden packs and draped with water bladders, and walked off into the desert in search of a ghayl.

About a half an hour later, we came back with a goatload of plump water bladders, and this time I poured the water on my face. No one cared that I was wasting it—except maybe al-aHad, who had to fetch more if we ran out.

Propped up on his elbow, Darrin was sipping on and off from a small bladder while giving a sermon to Safwan and Ali. They both listened and didn't even acknowledge al-aHad and me as we lifted the heavy water sacks off the goats' backs. He wasn't wearing a white shirt and tie, but he was doing his thing. Good for Darrin.

Al-aHad and I had better things to do, so after the water was stowed and the goat packs stacked by the tent, we walked about a hundred yards away and played catch with a ball made from some kind of animal bladder. Al-aHad was simply happy to find someone not afraid to use their hands to play catch. That can be a problem in soccer countries.

After the worst of the afternoon sun had given way to the promise of a cool evening, a convoy of trucks passed on the highway within a half mile of our encampment. Ali motioned for me to get under the lean-to with Darrin, then slipped into the tent, only to return with his rifle. Safwan and al-aHad busied themselves with the goats, unnecessarily herding them into a tighter group. The trucks didn't even slow for the Selah family goat settlement but hurried on to the hairpin grade that would take them west toward Sana'a—or the highway to Barakesh where Dandré and I had so narrowly cheated death at the hands of the Bakil.

"So, what's with the Bakil?" I asked. "What's their deal? Run around and terrorize the neighborhood? What's in it for them?" I knew the answer, or thought I did, but I wanted to make a disparaging remark about the Bakil, simply to put into words what Ali and Safwan would not.

"What else? Money," said Safwan.

"Taxes?" I asked.

"You mean extortion? No. They are capitalists," Safwan said. "Before our civil war, they favored the Soviets. Tomorrow, who knows?"

"And today?"

Safwan didn't speak. Ali cleared his throat. "It's bad business."

I looked back and forth between the old man and his son-in-law. "I'd like to know."

"In Barakesh," said the old man. "They hire Socotrans. Many Socotrans."

"Socotrans?" Rhiana had said that the men who kidnapped Monroe spoke the Socotran dialect.

Safwan nodded. "Telling us that you were Socotran was not a good idea."

"I'm one of the good Socotrans. What would they be doing out by Barakesh?" I asked. "What's out there?"

"Nothing. Ruins," said Safwan. "Gateway to the north and beyond that Saudi Arabia. Nothingness."

"Children," said Ali. "They are taken from their homes and sold into Saudi Arabia and then the world. Children are worth a great deal of money."

"I have to go there," I said. "Can you get me to Barakesh?"

Darrin stirred and rolled over to hide his face from the bright light, then pushed himself up to his knees. He was unsteady, even on his knees, and Safwan urged him to lie back down.

"Maybe in a day or two. He's not ready," said Ali.

I looked at Darrin, who stared at me in disbelief. "Remember what you taught me about turning my back?" I told him.

He nodded, confusion in his bloodshot eyes.

"I got your point," I said. "I have to face this." I stood up and turned to face Ali. "Darrin's not coming."

CHAPTER 31

Despite his reluctance and Darrin's protests, Safwan borrowed a vehicle from a colleague in Ma'rib, a VW microbus that had been yellow years earlier. He drove me along the well-worn ruts to within several miles of the ruins at Barakesh. We left in the night while Darrin slept in the tent under the watchful care of the silent Adara.

Safwan's maps, although designed with water conservation issues in mind, provided me with a bird's-eye view of the Barakesh ruins, which I studied by the dim dash lights of the rattling vehicle. He argued when I left the map in the car, but I didn't want anything on my person that would lead the Bakil to Safwan, Ali, or anyone in the family. They'd had enough trouble with the Bakil, and a water map too obviously belonged to Safwan Al-Saghier, the local water conservationist. The only article I now had that belonged to Safwan was a sixteen-ounce bladder canteen that he said was common enough to be ignored in the event I was caught and questioned.

In the predawn darkness, I walked the last two miles toward the ruins of Barakesh, stopping occasionally to study the terrain ahead of me and to make sure I didn't walk into a wandering night patrol or a Bakil encampment. The terrain was a mixture of rough soil and rocks, fatiguing to walk on.

The Barakesh ruins themselves were an imposing sight. Anciently a principal city on the caravan trade route, Barakesh had been built within a fortified wall of crumbling calcite stones that rose up from the desert floor like the walls of a gigantic football stadium, miles in circumference.

Although foreboding, the sight of the Barakesh walls was welcome. Unfortunately it meant that the hard part of the trip was just beginning.

It would be first light soon, and the barren area around Barakesh would be watched by Bakil guards. From here on out, I would be traveling on my belly.

Most people think of crawling as an activity that takes place on hands and knees—but that's not the way it is for a soldier. The low crawl is perhaps the most grueling torture imposed on an infantry soldier. It involves literally dragging the entire body, from the sides of the face to the sides of the heels, along the ground at a pace no faster than the speed of slug travel.

The rule of thumb when low-crawling is that you cannot move any faster than anything else in your environment. That would have allowed me to move a few inches at a time—just the distance that the tall grass swayed in the breeze—if there had been any tall grass. Unfortunately, the rocks and dirt clods didn't move in the wind, which very dramatically affected my speed.

I hauled myself along the ground with my elbows for most of the morning, letting the sharp rocks and hard dirt roll beneath my body and taking the hottest hours of the day to rest and drink by pouring water sideways into my mouth from a prone position. Safwan, the expert on water in the area, told me that I should avoid drinking the local water unless I didn't mind a raging case of dysentery. The nearby Wadi al Jawf occasionally had water running in it, but it came with the same disclaimer.

It would have been a lot smarter to travel at night, but I was impatient and wanted to be inside the walls today in case Rhiana's father was alive somewhere in the ruins, so I kept pace with the rocks, sliding inch by inch on my belly. No form of tactical travel was more physically demanding, and my muscles trembled and burned.

I made the walled ruins by late afternoon and hid in the rubble outside. My thobe reeked of stale sweat and clung to my body. I brushed away a few of the small rocks under me and stretched out on the eremic landscape as the sun traveled further west in the sky. I saw no sign of Bakil tribesmen, but I knew they were there somewhere. I had every reason to believe that Jim Monroe had been there too, investigating the child slave trade—prompting his urgent message to Rhiana—but I had little hope that he was still alive.

The wall surrounding the ruins was far higher than I had first thought. I guessed fifty feet in places with at least one crumbled opening where a set of tire tracks led inside. The cut stones, although eroding in places, were well constructed and smooth. Groping my way over the toppled rocks, I explored closer to the well-traveled opening to find that it was guarded by two natives, no doubt Socotrans for hire. I retreated back to my little hollow and looked again at the imposing and impenetrable wall, miles in circumference. A wall this massive had to have a number of gates, but whether they were all guarded or not was anyone's guess. I suppose, under the circumstances, it wasn't up to me to guess. If I wanted in, I had to find out.

I hugged the wall as I made my way around the structure, moving away from what I considered the main access where the guards were stationed. In places I was forced to scramble over boulders, which left me exposed and in plain sight if anyone was watching, but I tried to move tactically in places where I could stay concealed when there were such places.

It must have been over two hundred yards to the next breach in the wall, and this one was guarded by a tribesman with a large curved knife and a rickety AK-47 rifle with a severely damaged wooden stock. He wore a long, loose robe like most of the Bedus and Bakil in this area, and he sat casually on a stone. He wore headphones under his shumaq, covering his head in several wraps. The way his head rocked back and forth suggested music. The speed at which he undulated made it undoubtedly rock and roll. He was just a kid.

I looked up at the wall, dizzy with the exertion, and contemplated a free climb. There were cracks between the shaped stones, but I could just see myself clinging to the wall halfway up while Arabs with barely functioning rifles took potshots at me and laughed. I'd already been hurled into space twice this vacation, and once more wasn't necessary. I didn't relish the thought of another fight with an Arab, but this guard looked less formidable.

I had several options. There was the old bum-a-smoke-off-ya—karate-chop-across-the-neck—sleep-for-hours technique. Sadly, that technique only worked on TV and occasionally in the movies. The reality was that I would probably have to kill this young man.

I retreated several dozen yards and found a place behind a large stone in a sliver of shade to think about the inevitability of this man's death. I wondered if he'd forgive me in the afterlife. I wondered if once he found out that herding kidnapped children across the Saudi Arabian border to be sold into an unthinkable future was wrong, he'd understand my need to kill him. Ironic that I was wondering about an afterlife I wasn't even sure I believed in.

I had no way to see inside the city wall, and I didn't know if the guard had a vehicle or a radio. Of course, he could have a two-way radio under his robe and a Ferrari around the next corner. The odds were against the Ferrari but not the radio.

I considered luring the guard outside the wall by pretending to be hurt, then taking him down out in the open. That was no good. It would give him a chance to report something by radio if he had one. I had to act fast and dominate. Fast meant close, and I couldn't get any closer than about twenty yards before he'd see me. Dominating meant presenting a bigger threat to him than he could to me—and he had a rifle. I didn't even have my pointy stick anymore. The solution was somewhere between quick and lucky. Resigned to enter Barakesh whatever the cost, I chose the bum-a-cigarette-off-ya ruse.

I walked beside the high wall and into the open, where I caught the guard's attention and nodded to him. Feigning that I had every reason to approach from out of nowhere, I made the international sign for cigarette and looked hopeful. The guard looked confused and peered around to see if anyone else was with me, and then he reached beneath his robe. He didn't level the rifle at me, leaving it slung with the barrel up over his shoulder.

The guard's hand came out empty, and he shook his head, still looking around to see if I was alone. I closed on him and got a pretty good view of the rubble inside the walls. There was no one else there—and no Ferrari.

Climbing over the broken stones at the breach in the wall, I gestured with my head as if to a partner outside the walls. The guard stepped closer to me, looking outside the walls for a second man. His fatal mistake. By the time he figured out I was alone, I was too close.

I grabbed the pistol grip of his rifle just behind the trigger assembly and tore the weapon from his shoulder. The leather shoulder strap fell to his elbow, and he struggled to pull the rifle back. Dropping to my knees, I fought the barrel toward his head and told him in precise Arabic, heavy with Suqutri dialect, not to make me pull the trigger. With his hands wrapped around the forestock, he pushed the barrel away from his face.

I couldn't afford to shoot him and put the whole place on high alert, but that was up to him. He yanked on the strap, still around his elbow, and pulled us both off balance. We fell, the rifle beneath us, and he reached for his dagger.

I grasped the handle of the dagger, still in its sheath, and clamped down to prevent him from drawing it. The young Arab guard slapped his sweaty hand over mine and pried at my fingers. We were locked in a battle for weapons, each with one hand on the rifle and one on the knife. The first one to lose control of either would lose the fight.

I drew my knee up and tried to kick him, but I was too close. The Arab rolled on top of me and swung a wild elbow at my face, narrowly missing. I thrust my hips up and knocked him off of me and almost lost my grip on the dagger.

I was losing my grip on his rifle, my fingers slowly breaking free under pressure from the guard's hand. He jerked away from me, still trying to unsheathe the knife. Then I saw my chance.

The rifle sling was attached to the stock with a standard military quick-release swivel. I let go of the rifle grip and reached for the release swivel. I fumbled with the mechanism as the Arab guard tried to worm his finger onto the trigger. The sling release came free. Letting go of the knife hilt, I shoved the Arab off me and pulled the rifle away from him, the sling whipping freely around his elbow and hitting him on the chin. Lying on my back, I brought the rifle into position and aimed it at his chest. He pulled his dagger from its sheath and made ready to lunge. Standoff.

But now I had a rifle, and he didn't.

Chest heaving from the exertion, he stood, close enough that I could see the small nicks on the blade of his dagger. If he threw himself at me, I wasn't sure I could get a round off in time. I'd been trained that inside of twenty-one feet, a knife holder can easily cut a man armed with a gun, and he was well within that do-or-die lunge area. Then I noticed he was shaking.

CHAPTER 32

The young Arab guard stood with his knife poised in a trembling hand. For him death meant paradise and lots of promises. To me it meant the great unknown. I wasn't afraid, not exactly, but despite having told myself over and over during the last two years that I'd be better off dead, I wasn't ready to die.

With the rifle pointed at the Arab's chest, I fought to my feet using one hand to push myself up and the other to hold the firearm steady and on target. The Arab backed away a few steps, still holding the knife in front of him. It was clear that he wasn't an accomplished knife fighter, or I'd have been cut by then.

I stepped to a more level spot of ground, further from the Arab, and started to breathe again. As my tactical position improved, the will to fight drained out of the Arab. His knife hand slowly dropped, and his resign to send me to infidel hell wavered. Tears welled up in his eyes and ran down his cheeks. I'd won the fight, but I'd lost my advantage—I couldn't kill this kid. I would have to take him prisoner. Just what I needed—a sobbing hostage.

"Stinking Arab. You're crying?" I muttered instinctively in English.

The Arab dropped the dagger, and his eyes widened. *"Amreekeyy?"*

"Socotran," I said.

Now he smiled. "American," he said. He was nodding as if we had a secret between us.

He put his hands in the air in a gesture of surrender, but the smile seemed destined to remain.

"Socotran, you idiot," I said in Arabic. "Now, step away from that knife and get on your knees."

The Arab did as he was told. I wasn't a very good secret agent. Not only had I blown my thin cover, but I was unable to bring myself to dispatch this guy and get on with the mission.

I picked up the dagger and thrust it in my belt. Approaching my prisoner from behind, I gave him a standard pat down for other weapons. He didn't have any, but I took his belt and sheath, which seemed to really displease him. Disarming an Arab man in that way was pretty emasculating. The tears started to form again.

"American," he said, this time with some pleading evident in his voice.

"Yes, yes, American," I told him. "I'm not going to kill you." I wasn't sure about that yet, or maybe I was, but it wasn't going to help to start him crying again. "This doesn't happen in spy movies," I mumbled in English.

"Spy." He caught that word. His English must have been pretty good, which wasn't unusual in western Yemen but less so in the east.

"No, movies. Movies. James Bond. Harry Palmer."

"Movies?" Maybe he was mimicking me more than understanding.

"Nothing. Shut up." I still had the rifle pointed at him, and he understood that well enough.

I was inside the walls now, for what it was worth, but the whole thing was a letdown. Inside stood hundreds of acres of jumbled, partially fallen buildings. The streets led off in all angles and were strewn with rocks and stones so thick that we were going to have to crawl over them to get anywhere. That was a special challenge while leading a prisoner—as if I needed a special challenge at this point.

"Ism," I said, asking him for a name.

He looked around. "Barakesh," he said.

"No, you dolt." I pointed to him. *"Ism."*

"Mohammed."

"My name is . . ." I thought about that for a minute. I could reveal my real name, Arabic as it was, and it would be giving away nothing. I could use Walid, which hadn't worked so well with Ali and Safwan. Or I could tell him . . . "My name is Simon. You get that? Simon says. You ever play that? If you don't do what Simon says, he shoots you in the belly." I repeated myself in Arabic, and Mohammed got the message if not the reference.

We moved around the rubble in the interior of the city with Mohammed picking his way around the ruined structures and me following as best I could with the rifle. I told him very quietly where to step, and he did his best, following my instructions to the letter. Every once in a while he'd want to confirm that I was American, and I'd reassure him that I was a famous singer from Nashville, here to retrieve the lost Beatles recordings. This intrigued Mohammed because he knew of the Beatles.

"Prisoners?" I asked him.

Mohammed nodded and pointed to himself, very certain of what role he played in this charade.

"No, American prisoners," I said.

He nodded and gestured in a direction toward the main entrance.

"Children?" I asked.

Mohammed put his head down. Guilt is guilt in any language. He made a small nod and gestured in the same direction.

"How many?"

Mohammed had a sudden case of "language barrier-itis."

"How many," I repeated, not louder but accompanied by a gun barrel in his face.

"Twenty? Thirty?" Mohammed spoke English very well. He shook his head.

"What?" I said.

Now his shoulders were involved, and his whole body swept back and forth. He had that pouting look on his face again. I suppose I'd be a little stressed too.

"What?" I asked. "You don't like selling children?"

"I don't like it." He pointed to himself. "Slave."

It hadn't occurred to me, but I realized that it made sense that the Bakil would keep some of the older boys and train them to menial tasks like guarding some back-alley breach in the wall. Some of the men shooting at Dandré and me from the pickups may have been children kidnapped long ago. What a tangled mess.

"So, why are you a part of this? You know where these kids come from?"

He didn't say anything.

"Mohammed? Answer me!" I would have shaken him by his lapels except that his thobe had no lapels. Besides, I was busy pointing a firearm at him.

Mohammed shrugged. "I want to leave." He sobbed once, then his manhood got the better of him, and he did a little sniveling and was over it.

This wasn't how I'd had this operation planned. This wasn't what I'd wanted, and I was certain it wasn't what Mohammed wanted—to be walked around at the point of his own rifle. But maybe it was what we both needed. If I ever saw Darrin again, I was going to punch him in the nose for introducing me to the need/want concept. It really made a mess of my tight, little self-absorbed life.

"How do we do this?" I asked Mohammed.

He just looked at me and shrugged. "Find the lost Beatles . . ."

"No." I cut him off. "I want the American hostage and the children."

"And Mohammed?" He slapped his chest. "You'll rescue Mohammed, too."

Now I wanted to cry. Maybe it was Mohammed and maybe it was because of the mess I was in. I hemmed and hawed as long as I could, then looked into Mohammed's glistening brown eyes. "Maybe. Okay? Maybe you, too."

Mohammed's face lightened, and he smiled through his tears. "Thank you, Simon."

"How old are you?" I asked.

"Sixteen," he said.

I was seized at the throat, and my whole chest tightened up. I might have killed a sixteen-year-old kid.

"I know the building where they are kept," said Mohammed. "Come with me."

I followed Mohammed as we wound through the ruins. I was still at port arms with the rifle across my chest and ready to put it to use, but I wasn't so focused on my prisoner. Did I trust him? Not hardly.

Mohammed kept turning his head around and giving me what had now turned into a toothy smile—and I use the term *toothy* with some discretion because dentistry in eastern Yemen is hit and miss.

If my internal compass was correct, we were near the southern entrance to the Barakesh wall, where I'd seen evidence of vehicles coming and going and where I knew two guards had been posted.

Mohammed slowed down, and I followed suit. We eventually found ourselves taking a knee beside an intact wall to listen to muted voices over the soft sound of Arab music. The language of the speakers was French. I edged closer to the corner and got a look. I wasn't surprised. I could only see part of him, but I recognized Barbier's houndstooth cap. I couldn't see the man he was talking to, but I had a pretty good idea who it was.

The static-laden sound of music was replaced mid-song by the muezzin call broadcast via several portable radios surrounding a cleared compound. Already on his knees, Mohammed scooted back and started to assume the prayer position.

I slid the cold flash suppressor at the end of the barrel of the AK-47 onto Mohammed's neck and felt him stiffen. "The next person who stops in the middle of everything to pray gets shot."

Mohammed looked a little hurt.

I said, "We'll visit with our God later. Right now I need to know how many men are here."

Mohammed rose to an upright kneeling position, no doubt wondering where our bonding experience had gone south. "Ten men, sometimes twenty or thirty. They travel to and from Barakesh."

"Right now. Guess."

"Maybe fifteen. Possibly more," he said. Great, he could say anything he wanted. I think he was a little upset about the gun on the neck thing, and he had good reason to be a little on edge.

"Where are the prisoners?"

Mohammed crawled forward and peered around the corner of the rubble. He leaned back and said, "There. That building," and pointed to a pretty well-preserved structure across a narrow compound. "In the basement."

The building was three stories high and appeared to have narrow air vents at ground level indicating a basement or crawl space. I sat back on my heels for a moment trying to decide what to do. After dismissing a half a dozen or so really bad ideas, I concluded that I really didn't have many options. Go forward.

I waited out the evening prayer and let the French voices fade away as the two men speaking in the compound left the area. Mohammed told me that the prisoners, children and adults alike, were rarely heavily guarded within Barakesh because the outer walls were watched, somewhat sporadically, and escape meant a physical feat of trekking through the desert, impossible given the condition of the prisoners. It functioned like Alcatraz—dare to escape, but you still have to swim the bay.

Mohammed didn't know the prisoners' names, but he was certain that there had been an American with the children.

"Had been?" I asked him.

"The American escaped," he said.

CHAPTER 33

"He's probably dead," said Mohammed. He pointed in the direction of the outer wall and the desert.

"How did he get out?"

"The American escaped during the battle two days ago. Many of our men left Barakesh to fight the invading forces to our west, and he was unguarded. He's probably dead now."

"Wait. West of here? What kind of battle, Mohammed?"

"*Dakhm.*" Massive. He drew his arms outstretched to indicate that this was no ordinary battle. "All our forces. The American was gone when the survivors of the battle returned to the ruins. Our scouts have been searching for the American's body for two days. *Dakhm,*" he said again, emphasizing the scale of the battle.

I hardly thought Dandré and I constituted an invading army, but these kinds of events had a way of getting exaggerated in the retellings. It didn't surprise me that Monroe had waited for his opportunity and had tried to walk out rather than die a hostage to a two-bit local tribe. Although I hadn't known about Jim Monroe's secret life as a government informant, the more I thought about it, the more I realized I should have guessed.

It did occur to me that I should have asked Mohammed about this at the breach in the wall, long before I found myself inside the Bakil compound, but what was done was done. I had virtually no plan for rescuing anyone—even if I had found Monroe here—and I had no plan for my own escape from this place. I probably wasn't going to leave alive. I did know one thing, though. I wasn't going to stand by while children were sold into a life of perverse servitude. The last time I'd shortcut my responsibilities, I'd ruined lives, including a good portion of my own.

Mohammed and I retreated back to his post, and I found a secluded place to wait out the day. I put Mohammed on his honor not to narc me off to his boss. By evening he'd been replaced by an older and tougher-looking man. Mohammed and I had arranged to meet just after last light near where we'd heard the French voices. To his credit and my amazement, Mohammed showed up, and he was alone.

"Mohammed, your earphones." I reached for his neck, and he recoiled. "Easy, man. I just need the earphones."

"Easy, man." Mohammed copied what I said, hungry for American idiom, and pulled the device over his head.

Thus I found myself, on Mohammed's advice that I wouldn't be noticed, boogieing across an open area with top-forty hits blasting in my ears. No one could tell that the headphones weren't plugged into anything. I was completely focused on getting to the building where Mohammed said Yemeni children were being held.

I had a better view of the Bakil operation as I walked across what might have been the town square or an open-air sauq thousands of years ago. Inside the main gates of the ancient city sat two troop trucks that had front ends like huge VW bugs. The trucks were old and well used, but I assumed they were fully functional. There was also a Land Rover off to the side. For those too important to travel by truck, I presumed. Several of the buildings in this area were still standing and had recently been reinforced with new, yellow lumber. It looked like the place could accommodate far more men than Mohammed said were here.

Behind the trucks stood the door to the dank building where the children were supposedly housed. There were lights in the building, temporary bare bulbs strung in through a window from a generator that could be heard humming softly in the distance.

Once inside the door I was assaulted with the stench of body odor, curry, stale tobacco, and rotting flesh—very unpleasant, but a sure indicator that people inhabited the building.

Two men slumped on boxes with their backs against the wall saw me walk inside. Bobbing my head to the rhythm on my headphones,

I kept my eyes down and my face averted. I got no more than half-interested stares from the guards. That's a pretty typical reaction from disorganized troops, but I could feel my pulse in the veins on the top of my head, and I started to suck for enough air to support my slow-functioning noodle.

"Who are you?" one of them called from the other room. "What are you doing?" He spoke traditional Arabic, but I recognized the Socotran accent.

In the Suqutri dialect, I answered. "Checking on the children."

Neither acknowledged me for a long moment. Thinking it might strike them as unusual for someone else to be checking on the children, I added, "On the electricity down there."

They answered with a grunt, and one of them said something about not being bitten by the little insects. I think he was joking about the children. They both laughed. I kept walking.

Dim shadows and gloomy passageways led off the main hallway. I went straight for the back of the building, where Mohammed told me to look for a stairway leading to the basement cut from the hard-packed sand and bedrock. The simplicity of the building made it easy to find, as did the series of wires that led to a lightbulb illuminating the stairs. Mohammed was right about the security. The problem wasn't breaking in—it was getting back out to freedom.

As I moved out of sight of the loafing Arab men, I shrugged Mohammed's rifle sling off my shoulder and drew the weapon snug up against my cheek. Looking over the iron sights, I descended the stairs to the lower level.

The foul odors became more pronounced, hanging in the stale air. There were no windows in the hallway, but a vertical duct had been cut through the center of the building to allow fresh air to reach the people inhabiting the lower levels—low-tech air-conditioning. I stopped briefly at the rough-hewn vent, several feet in circumference, to inhale some cool fresh air, but the stench was so pronounced that my eyes watered. I jerked my head away from the hole and moved on. Who crawled in there and died?

As my pupils adjusted to the faint light of the single bulb hanging from the ceiling of the basement, I saw the outlines of six irregular openings leading off the main hallway at intervals. Taking short, measured steps, I stalked forward, peering over the rifle sights. I stopped just short of the first set of rooms, one on either side of the hallway. I glanced back at the stairwell and then at the duct opening. There wasn't much chance of escape from down here if I awakened a sleeping giant.

I turned my back to the room on the right and took slow, sideways steps around the opening on the left, ready to engage any threat in my field of fire. With each step I saw more of the interior of the empty room.

I used the same techniques to clear rooms down the hallway. One after the other the rooms were empty, and I was convinced I was in the wrong place by the time I got to the last set of rooms. I turned the corner of the fifth room, rifle up, and looked down the sight into the curious, gleaming eyes of children. Soundlessly, they sat staring at the armed intruder in their midst. There were nearly two dozen children in the room, most very young, dressed in filthy, tattered clothes and bearing the gaunt faces of starvation. They didn't react to my presence as I turned and left the room.

The sixth room was packed with web strapping, thick tape, ropes, and a few metal shackles—a tack room for human chattel. The crumbling stone walls were splattered with dark stains. I shuddered.

After I was satisfied that only children occupied the basement level, I went back into the children's room. Four older children congregated against the back wall, three boys and a girl. I knelt in front of one of the smaller children and cupped his gaunt face in my hand. The older girl marched fearlessly to the center of the room and spit on me. I didn't like getting spit on, but I liked her style.

Raising an accusing finger, I pointed at her and grimaced. A school teacher once told me that when working with children, you never smile until after Christmas break. Armed with that as the foundation for my child management philosophy, I told the girl I was here to help and that they should keep their mouths shut and do exactly as I told them.

I faced the girl, who was still giving me a surly look, and pointed to myself. "Kam-Dan." She repeated the strange name several times.

I pointed to her and pronounced her title. "Captain."

She nodded and turned to her roommates, raising one finger. "Captain." It was obviously a word she'd heard before, and she liked it.

"Captain," I said, "you are in charge of these kids. Everyone does as I say, or we will not escape." My captain seemed to catch on and even got excited. She apparently thought I was going to be able to pull off a rescue. The situation presented a small logistical problem for me. Gee, when I jumped off the helicopter, things seemed so simple.

"I'm looking for a male prisoner. A Western man." I wasn't looking for Roy Rogers, but the word *American* had certain undertones that I didn't want to bring up.

My captain shook her head and looked at the others, who were shrugging and looking around at each other.

"I need to know," I said. "I don't leave without him."

One of the older boys looked sheepishly at the others and stepped forward. His shirt was missing its buttons, revealing his bare chest, and his futa skirt was too big around his waist and hung well below his knees. He held it on with one hand. "He's gone."

"When?" I asked.

He looked to his friends for help. "Two days?" he said.

"Escaped," I asked, "or taken away?"

"Very sick. Very weak," said the boy.

Another said, "Maybe he was taken away."

"No," said my captain. "He escaped." She turned to me. "He escaped and he sent you?"

"I'm here because of him, yes." Misleading, but technically accurate.

I didn't think for a moment that my father-in-law had walked into the desert after weeks of captivity, malnourishment, and who knows what kind of abuse. Jim Monroe was either dead or hiding. If he were still alive, he wasn't far away. He wouldn't have left the children.

I did most of my work with the intemperate girl, my captain, even though culture dictated that I deal with one of the boys. In this case, though, the boys seemed to realize they were in the presence of a natural leader and gave deference to her. This might be the only time in her life that this girl would be shown the respect she deserved.

My captain told me that children had been showing up here in groups of two or three for about a month now. Anyone causing trouble had been taken away. She didn't know what happened to them. None of the children knew exactly what was going to happen to them ultimately, but the older ones had a vague idea that they were to be sold. They'd been told by several of their captors what to expect. I asked if they knew Mohammed, and they all nodded. Upon further investigation, though, they each seemed to know a different Mohammed, none of which was my new friend waiting for me outside the building.

I made a more thorough search of the basement, this time with the gun slung over my shoulder, but Monroe wasn't hiding in the shadows of any of the six rooms. That meant he was either somewhere in the Barakesh ruins or worse, somewhere in the desert—or . . .

I'd been trained that a good search includes any place a person could possibly hide—like an air duct. It had been dug only a few feet deeper than the floor and it didn't take me long to see what, or rather who, was at the bottom.

CHAPTER 34

It was too dark to see clearly, but the body was that of a man. I bent into the duct and touched the man's neck. The hole smelled of human waste and body odor. I gagged once and drew myself out, fearing that my dry heaves would bring the guards to the dungeon. I took deep breaths of the stale air of the basement, and when I braved the hole again, I saw a straggly beard and two dull eyes staring back at me.

I hadn't prepared a rescuer's speech, so I said, "You want out of that hole?"

There was no response.

"Can you talk?"

Nothing. The man's head dropped back almost into his lap, but he groped upward with his arms.

"I'll take that as a yes?" I said. I didn't think I had the strength to pull this man out of the duct, but I reached for his arms. They were frail.

Though raspy, his voice was unmistakable. "A rescue party?"

"Yes, Jim," I said. *Party of one.*

I pulled him by his sinewy armpits and eventually flopped him out of the air duct and onto the floor.

"Put me back in the hole, Kamir," he said, but he didn't make any move to crawl back in.

"Don't you think I'm in enough trouble from your daughter already?" I helped the old man to his feet, and we stumbled toward the room with the children in it.

"I have some issues with you," he said. "You ran away and abandoned my daughter."

"You're a hostage hiding in a hole in the wildest part of Yemen. Do you want to escape or not?"

"I already escaped."

I stopped walking and for the briefest of moments thought about putting him back.

He said, "Okay, you can help me this time, but I still have issues with you." Monroe was getting his voice back.

I had twenty-some-odd kids under the command of a spitting teenage girl and a crotchety Father-in-Law Time draped over my shoulder. He wanted to be rescued but not by me. Great. I wondered how many husbands could claim this level of complexity in their relationship with their in-laws.

I lowered Monroe to the floor against the wall in the children's room. The children hovered close and uttered thanks to Allah at the reappearance of the adult hostage who had been held with them. Apparently they didn't know Monroe the way I did.

"What's the plan?" he asked after he was settled on the floor. He was in for a little letdown.

I looked at my captain and said in English, "You want to tell him?"

She had no idea what I was talking about.

"Tell me what?" asked Monroe. "Who's out there? Marines? Army Rangers? The Delta Force D-Boys?"

"It's more of an international coalition," I said, wondering if the other half of my coalition was still outside waiting for me or if he'd reported me to his superiors.

Monroe said, "I don't care if it's a battalion from the Women's Auxiliary Air Force—you're burning daylight. What's the plan?"

"How often do they check on you down here?"

"They don't check on me at all. I escaped. As for the children, the Arabs are down here a couple times a day to slop 'em. Other than that, they don't care. They took out of here the other day in a hissy fit. That's when I escaped."

"You were hiding fifty feet from where they kept you."

"Right." He kind of glossed over the fact that you couldn't really count that as an escape. "Other than that, they don't come down here. It smells. Now, what's your communications situation? I have some information I need to pass along."

I know I wasn't doing myself any favors by lying to Monroe, but I just didn't have it in me to tell him that his rescue party was me and one of the bad boys I met outside this afternoon. "Uh, the radios are . . . down."

"Okay, comms are down. What about timings? When do we leave?"

"I don't have a watch," I said.

"You . . . you have no watch?"

"No. I also don't have a Marine, an Army Ranger, or anyone from Delta Force with me." I shuffled my feet. "And, no WAAFs either. But you should be thankful I'm here."

Monroe pulled his back a little more upright and worked his legs out straight from the wall. "Really? And why is that, Officer Daniels?"

CHAPTER 35

I could have yelled and screamed at Monroe, telling him that I'd jumped off a helicopter into the middle of a Bakil firefight to rescue him, but I really wanted that information to come from his darling daughter after he'd had a chance to demean me in front of every person who would listen to him. Suddenly, I developed real motivation to get Monroe out of here. I wanted him to eat crow. "You need to learn that you don't always get what you want. It's me and Mohammed. That's what you got. Deal with it. Now pony up some ideas to get a mob of starving children and a grumpy, ungrateful old man out of here."

My captain shoved my shoulder and put her finger to her lips. "Shh, Kam-Dan. Shh." Pretty bold for a woman destined to be a second-class citizen for the rest of her life—I wondered if she was related to Rhiana. That single thought brought me back. If I wanted another chance with Rhiana, I had to get out alive.

"Who is Mohammed?" asked Monroe.

"At the moment, he's my only friend, and he's sixteen years old. Now, how do we get out of here and get away? Do the trucks work?"

"That was my problem," Monroe said. "Away to where? I was waiting for them to haul the kids out of here. I figured I could sneak off after they'd done their business. But then what? Into the desert in my condition? That's its own death sentence. The trucks run, but I haven't been up to stealing one." He looked at the four older kids. "I was just going to wait for them to take the kids away and work things out after that." Monroe swallowed hard. "I mean, what's one guy going to do for these kids?"

Tell me about it. "Do you know when they planned on taking the kids out of here?"

"No idea," said Monroe.

I asked my captain the same question in Arabic, and she shook her head.

Monroe said, "They don't do much by way of guarding us during the day. At night I think they have an upstairs guard schedule. If an escape by stealth were possible, I would have been out of here my first day." Monroe blinked a few times and shook his head. He looked faint. He took a few deep breaths and rubbed his face. Apparently it was strenuous to hate me. I wanted to tell him it was harder work being his son-in-law.

I heard voices upstairs and a fair amount of scuffling footsteps. It wasn't long before the noises got louder and we knew we were about to have visitors in the basement. With help from the children, I hauled Monroe into a shadowed corner of the room and told the little kids to stand in front of us. The result looked a little like a third-grade class picture, but the two Bakil wouldn't see us unless they really looked.

The two Arab men made their way down the stairs and did a cursory walkthrough, deeply involved in a discussion about the best places to buy qat. They barely looked into the children's room and wouldn't have noticed if Monroe and I had been tap dancing.

I started to breathe a little easier as the two men started back toward the stairs, and then all was chaos. My captain, bless her heart, could stand no more. She walked into the hallway and yelled at the guards, telling them off in unladylike terms and bragging about the Americans who were about to rescue her. *Fantastique,* as Pierre might say.

I ran into the hallway, rifle tucked into my shoulder, and ordered the two men to the ground. Luckily, they were laughing at the girl and were caught unaware by a rifle-wielding American.

I ordered them to place their rifles on the ground and get on their knees. Then I ordered my captain to bind them. She went to the chattel room and brought back the necessary material and got to work.

"This is only good until someone comes to relieve them," I told Monroe.

"We can go for one of the vehicles and take off. Maybe outrun them," he said.

It was a pretty good idea from a desperate point of view, but I couldn't leave the children, and neither could Monroe. I knew his daughter, and I knew him—indefatigable. He didn't hide in an air duct to avoid helping these kids. The Jim Monroe I knew would have happily died in the desert to help those kids rather than let them remain captives of the Bakil slave traders. I'm sure we both realized that saving this handful of kids from a life of indescribably perverse servitude wasn't even the proverbial drop in the bucket, but we had to live with ourselves. That meant not taking the easy way out. The kids were coming with us.

I told my captain to get the kids ready to sneak upstairs. She nodded and went to work, explaining to the little ones that they couldn't make a peep.

"You and I will go up and disable all but one truck," I said to Monroe.

He nodded, but as soon as we got to the steps, we had problems. Monroe had been starved and beaten, then had spent days cramped in a hole. His legs wouldn't carry him up the steep stairs.

Plan B—I'll do it myself. "You stay down here. Give me a few minutes, and then have the kids help you up the stairs and outside."

Monroe was a proud, ornery man, but he knew when to shut up and do as he was told. I made my way up the stairs to the front entrance of the building and hoped I'd find my partner still waiting in the dark. He was.

There was no one else in sight, so I waved Mohammed over and gave him his rifle. "Cover me," I said. "When I finish with the trucks, I'll wave to you. You get the children."

Mohammed nodded and retreated into the shadows with the weapon.

The trucks were parked in the open area about a hundred feet from the front of the building. I walked as casually as I could to them and ducked behind the fender of the first one.

I wriggled under the truck and started pulling any wire or hose that would come loose from the engine compartment. What I couldn't pull loose, I bent, including the fan blades. One truck down.

The Range Rover proved more of a challenge. I wasn't able to reach much of the important stuff from underneath, and most of the hoses were on too tight for me to force off. The driver's door was open, so I reached under the dash and ripped every wire I could touch. With luck, they'd have more than trouble with the dome light when the fun started.

I waved into the darkness and watched as Mohammed's shadowy figure emerged from the shadows and slipped into the building. Moments later, I heard the noise of the children as they marched out the door where Mohammed pointed them toward the correct truck. The older kids were doing everything they could to keep the children quiet, but there's only so much a seven-year-old understands. Monroe, helped by one of the older boys, was last out the door of the building.

The string of children drew out longer than I'd expected and wound halfway across the open area as the older kids struggled to keep them together. There was still no one about, and I guessed it might be as late as midnight, but I didn't know.

As he limped up to the cab of the truck, Monroe was mumbling. "You didn't have a plan, did you? I knew you didn't have a plan. What happened to you? You used to be a real man. If you think she's gonna take you back just because you came for me, you're delusional."

I helped him inside and shoved him to the passenger side of the wide bench seat. "Yeah, yeah, delusional. For once in my life can't you give me a break? I'm sorry. I'm sorry to you. I'm sorry to Rhiana. And I'm sorry to myself. Do you have any idea what it was like at that accident? Do you? Do you know what it was like to be responsible for the destruction of a whole family?"

Monroe's eyes drifted to the floorboard. "You didn't kill them, Kam. The drunk driver did. But I do know what it's like to ruin a family," he said, still staring down. "I destroyed mine when I put the needs of my nation above the needs of my little girl. I never looked back, and I never stopped running away." He looked up into my eyes, really seeing me for the first time since we'd met. "Are you ready to stop running, son?"

Maybe it was me seeing him for the first time, too. "All I want," I said, "is another chance with Rhiana."

"Get me out of here alive. I'll see what I can do." He looked up at me and smiled.

I may have even smiled back.

I went around to the back of the truck and looked inside. The kids were doing their best to keep things quiet as Mohammed stood guard by the tailgate.

"Mohammed, you drive."

He looked at me. "Easy, man." It lost something contextual in the translation, but he sounded 1970s cool.

"You do know how to drive?" I asked.

My captain, roughly the same age as Mohammed, sat at the rear of the cargo area, watching us through the opening in the canvas covering. Mohammed's eyes went from me to her and back. He didn't know how to drive, but he couldn't bring himself to admit it in front of the girl.

"I'll drive," I said. What a time to be nursing the pride of a sixteen-year-old lovelorn Arab. I told Mohammed to go sit in the cab while I checked with my captain.

I had to roll my eyes. My captain noticed. *He likes you,* I mouthed, pointing in Mohammed's direction. She smiled. She had everything under control.

I took a last look around the deserted compound and walked to the cab of the truck. I hoisted myself in and sat behind the huge steering wheel. The gearshift lever had a big round button on it, indicating that the vehicle had a two-speed axle. I didn't know how to use it, but I figured that if I could get the thing rolling, I could do the old, grind-'em-till-ya-find-'em gear thing.

I flipped the dashboard switch to heat the glow plugs of the diesel engine and watched as the indicator light turned quickly from red to green. As I leaned forward to push the rubber starter button, I felt a hand touch me on my left shoulder.

"What are you doing?" a voice asked in Suqutri.

I turned and looked into the sleepy eyes of an Arab guard staring into the cab.

"Following orders," I said. "Back to your quarters. There's been a change of plan."

"You can't leave," said the man.

Mohammed was silent, staring forward and shaking slightly. Monroe covered his face with his arm, and I held my breath. I reached down toward the start button and slowly depressed the clutch.

The guard paced to the back of the truck and swung open the canvas flap, exposing the dirty faces of the children. "Here," the Arab said, "you have to latch the tailgate or the cargo will fall out." He secured the tailgate with a linchpin hanging from the bed of the truck by a thin chain and then struck the fender twice. "Precious cargo." He laughed.

I pushed the starter button and heard the diesel clamor to life and felt the rattle of the cab. When I slipped the truck in gear and let out the clutch, the truck lurched forward and the engine roared, sending a plume of black smoke into the air. I heard voices behind us as the wheels rolled forward. Men were streaming out of ruined buildings, hastily organizing themselves and pushing fresh magazines into their rifles. Welcome to the rodeo.

In my long, side mirror, I saw René Barbier walking out the door of a building with his shirt in his hand. He looked around his compound at the confusion of running men, none sure exactly what to do, and threw his shirt on the ground in anger.

Barbier stomped over to his Range Rover and flung open the door. I'd left the wires from under the dash hanging out under the steering wheel. He slammed the side of the Rover with his fists.

Faasid appeared from the same doorway where Barbier had come from. He was spinning, trying to take it all in. Pierre followed close behind, completely dressed in green fatigues and wearing his silly French beanie. Did the man never sleep?

I stomped on the accelerator several times, but the behemoth merely slogged along. In the mirror, I watched Barbier wave his arms at Faasid and pull open the rear gate of the Range Rover. He slid a long wooden box partially out the back and motioned for Faasid to open it. Barbier didn't seem to be in much of a hurry. That worried me.

I depressed the clutch again and pulled the truck into the next gear, hearing only the metal grating sound of the transmission. The truck slowed to a slow roll, and the racing engine told me the transmission was in neutral.

CHAPTER 36

As Faasid lifted the lid on the wooden box, I worked the gear shifter forward and back, but I couldn't engage the transmission.

"I can't get it in gear," I yelled, more out of frustration than to tell Monroe something he didn't already know. I leaned on the shift lever and the transmission reluctantly popped into the next gear, lugging onward and slowly building speed back up.

Arabs were running up to the back of the truck to jump aboard, but the children were giving them the good news with their fists and feet, and several Arabs fell behind the slow-rolling truck. The fallen Arabs ran back for their troop truck—the one they'd never get started.

I checked my mirror and watched Faasid draw a sleek metal tube from the box. A Russian RPG. We weren't going to survive.

I'd never used a Russian RPG and didn't even know what the Russian name for it was. Regardless of the name, it was one of the most destructive weapons in the third-world arsenal, capable of accurately delivering high explosives on targets at a considerable distance. Americans sometime called the device a Rocket-Propelled Grenade launcher, although the initials stood for something completely different in Russian. It didn't matter—we couldn't outrun it in any language.

Faasid worked at loading the weapon while Barbier yelled at him. But even if we passed outside the ruins onto the road before he got it ready, Faasid would simply walk to the main gates of the ruins, shoulder the weapon, and incinerate us all with one touch of the trigger.

"Take the wheel," I told Mohammed. He looked at me with the same reluctant panic as before, but he reached over and held onto the steering wheel. I stomped on the gas a couple of times until Mohammed got the idea and took over the accelerator with his left foot.

Monroe watched in horror as I opened the driver's side door and leaped out. I heard my collarbone snap as I rolled over the rocky terrain outside the main wall. The truck bounced past me, and the last thing I saw were the faces of hopeful children staring over the tailgate at me through a cloud of dust.

CHAPTER 37

The truck lumbered on, the engine racing in a low gear, but it wasn't going to outrun the RPG. I scrambled behind a pillar at the main entrance, cradling my left arm.

Faasid appeared with the RPG on his shoulder, ready to fire. He was completely fixated on the truck and went to one knee to brace himself for a shot. As he aimed the weapon, I bolted from behind the pillar and threw myself at him, flattening him on the road with my good shoulder and sending the RPG tube rolling across the ground. We both dove for it at the same time.

Faasid pulled the forward end of the RPG up and fought for control of the trigger assembly as I pushed the dangerous end of the weapon toward the ground. Barbier stepped through the entrance, livid that Faasid hadn't shot the truck yet. Then realizing why, he ran toward us. I wasn't going to be able to fight them both, and the truck was nowhere near out of range yet.

I let Faasid draw the weapon up and, summoning all my remaining strength, I drove the back end of the weapon into the ground and used the tube as a lever to pull Faasid off balance and force the dangerous end of the RPG back toward the ruins, letting Faasid maintain his hold on the trigger. I kicked his hand and the RPG erupted in white-hot smoke, sending thousand-degree gasses out the back end of the weapon into Faasid's chest. He was someone else's problem now.

A line of smoke trailed the rocketing explosive into the ruins, striking the remaining truckful of Bakil guards and erupting in a fire-ball that ascended into a mass of black smoke and billowed into the vastness of the Empty Quarter. The heat seared my face, and the concussion rocked me onto my broken shoulder in the dirt. Barbier hid his face in his hands and recoiled from the concussion against the main wall of the ruins.

When I opened my eyes, Barbier was standing over me, his face and bare chest pocked and bloodied by shrapnel from the blast. He held a pistol in his hand and pointed it at my head. "You've cost me a lot of money, Daniels. A lot of money."

"If I remember right from our last conversation, you told me the money was for Bakil schools and hospitals. And by the way, I was holding a soup spoon to your throat, not a knife."

"I should have killed you in Paris," said Barbier.

"Faasid tried. Remember?"

"All you've done is delay the inevitable." With his thumb, Barbier disengaged the safety on the side of the pistol.

"If the inevitable involves a lot of brimstone and hot weather, I'll meet you there," I said.

"If you hadn't been such a thorn in my side, I'd thank you for doing my dirty work for me." He waved a hand at the charred troop truck, still flaming in spots, and the bodies of his soldiers, including Faasid's limp body, burned by the explosive gasses of the RPG. "No witnesses." He walked to the center of the road, still pointing the pistol at my head, and looked at the cloud of dust made by the truck full of children rumbling down the road in the distance. "You may have saved those children, but they can be replaced."

Barbier lifted the toe of his boot and nudged my shoulder. "Something doesn't look right there. You should get that checked." Then he reared his leg back and kicked me hard. It was the Fourth of July in my head.

Barbier's mouth turned up in a grin as he stepped back and straightened his arm, preparing to pull the trigger of his pistol. I saw the barrel waver as his grip tightened around the trigger. I didn't care. I was through running, and I was through being scared.

"Would it be too much to ask for you to surrender?" I asked. Famous last words.

I saw the flash of a muzzle and heard the concussion of the shot, but I didn't feel anything. Barbier's body slumped to the ground beside me.

"You didn't think I was going to let him kill you, silly American?" It was Pierre, clinging to the Barakesh wall with a pistol of his own in his hand. He was bleeding from the neck and stumbled forward and fell onto the road beside me.

"The famous French solution, I presume."

"Well said. I've been working René Barbier for seven years—a good part of my career went into this trip to Yemen." He held up his smoking pistol. "I've wanted an excuse to do that for a long time."

"You've been after Barbier this whole time?" I said.

"And trying to stop the sale of children along the border. Barbier developed a network of well-placed accomplices all over the Middle East. He even had someone in the embassy in Sana'a. Why do you think Dandré and I wanted to have a duplicate communications system at a secure command post in Vienna?"

I shook my head. "Are you suggesting that I should have trusted you?"

"I didn't trust you either," said Pierre. "I guess we're even." He let go of his pistol and let it drop to the ground. Neither one of us had a use for it now. He said, "I had enough on Barbier to bury him in a French dungeon for the rest of his life. In some ways, it would have been more fun to see him squirm at trial."

I looked at Barbier's lifeless body, then at Pierre. We both smiled. "It would have been too good for him," I said. "So the act? Taking us hostage?"

"I needed your travel permits—they weren't much good without all of you to make it look legitimate."

"You used us."

"And you used the religious scholars. It's the way the game is played." Pierre rolled onto his back and coughed again. I heard the rattle of fluid in his lungs.

"And Dandré knew?"

"Of course." Pierre smiled.

"Where is he now?" I asked.

"Somewhere on the Saudi–Yemen border. Instead of kids, those maggots at the exchange point are going to purchase a truckful of men just like Dandré. Frankly, I don't think they'll like what they get."

My heart warmed at the thought.

Pierre coughed so hard he started to choke. I tried to sit up and help him, but I wasn't able. Gently, I turned my head to see if there were any other survivors, but they were all gone. Barakesh was empty, but for the two of us.

Pierre's breathing was shallow. It was impossible to tell where he was losing the most blood; he was covered in it. I don't suppose I looked much better.

I placed my good hand on his neck to try and stem the flow of blood, but it was hopeless.

"Non, mon ami. We are both soldiers. Allow me an honorable soldier's death. René Barbier will sell no more children—my work is complete."

I almost said that there would be others to take Barbier's place, but Pierre didn't need to hear that. I turned my head away from the sun and blinked back a tear. "Hey, Pierre," I said. "Sorry about the French jokes." Of course, he didn't answer.

Eventually—I don't know when—the sun faded behind the horizon, and I drifted into the blackness. Maybe it was a gift from an all-knowing God, but for whatever reason, I was allowed a few moments of reflection. I'd made mistakes, some small and some big. A couple had been very big. I think Rhiana knew in the end that I loved her. Monroe would remind her for me.

I thought about Darrin, the would-be Marine. I felt sorry—not for him, but for all the people who would never take the time to get to know him. He was ten times the man I was.

What about Megawati and the others? I wondered if they still played sockball, even without me. Maybe they'd dedicate a game to me. Hans Bafus could officiate.

And what of Safwan and his family? No God would simply abandon them. And the girl—the Arab girl who'd saved me from Faasid on two different continents. She asked me to tell her family that he is . . . No. Of course. That *He* is.

The fabled lights of the afterworld began to materialize somewhere in the ether around me. I saw them, and although I could no longer move my body, the beams of light became brighter and brighter. As they closed in on me, I felt a vibration. Angel wings? Then it stopped, and I heard hymns. Singing angels? "Be still my soul: the Lord is on thy side . . ." Male voices . . . a single male voice. The lights were still bright, and I felt someone touch my neck . . . Why would God check my pulse?

"Kam?" said a comforting, familiar voice.

"Yes," I answered.

"You alive?"

"Nope."

"I brought you the car you wanted," said the voice. The singing had stopped.

I opened my eyes and saw Darrin staring in to my face.

"Darrin? What the devil are you doing here?"

"Safwan told me where you'd gone. Don't worry—he drove."

"Hello there," said Safwan, standing over us. "You're a mess."

"Safwan," I said, trying to sit up. "The message from your wife. I remember."

Darrin pushed me back down, and Safwan knelt beside us. "The risaala?"

"Yes, yes. She wanted you to know for sure. She said, *He* is. Tell them *He* is."

Safwan thought for a moment. "Thank you," he said. Tears formed in his eyes and slid down his cheeks.

I looked up at Darrin. "Thanks, Marine, for not leaving me behind."

"Semper Fi," said Darrin.

"Did Rhiana . . . Did they make it out?"

"She's on the aircraft carrier . . . waiting for you to come home."

"Ooh-rah."

ABOUT THE AUTHOR

Willard Boyd Gardner, "Bill," writes from his experience as a police detective and SWAT team member in the state of Washington. He attributes his hair-raising stories to the heroic actions of his fellow officers—the hair-brained stories, well, he can't imagine how he came up with those. Retired from police work, Bill and his family of girls now live in peaceful Midway, Utah, where he writes and eats dark chocolate—not necessarily in that order.